THE HEART OF THE HILLS

The
Heart of the Hills

JOHN FOX Jr.

Foreword by Darlene Wilson

THE UNIVERSITY PRESS OF KENTUCKY

Scholarly publisher for the Commonwealth,
serving Bellarmine College, Berea College, Centre
College of Kentucky, Eastern Kentucky University,
The Filson Club, Georgetown College, Kentucky
Historical Society, Kentucky State University,
Morehead State University, Murray State University,
Northern Kentucky University, Transylvania University,
University of Kentucky, University of Louisville,
and Western Kentucky University.

Editorial and Sales Offices: The University Press of Kentucky
663 South Limestone Street, Lexington, Kentucky 40508-4008

00 99 98 97 96   5 4 3 2 1

Library of Congress Cataloging-in-Publication Data

Fox, John, 1863-1919.
    The heart of the hills / John Fox, Jr. : foreword by Darlene
Wilson.
        p.   cm.
    Includes bibliographical references.
    ISBN 0-8131-1981-2 (alk. paper). —ISBN 0-8131-0882-9 (alk.
paper)
    I. Title.
PS1702.H38   1996
813'.4—dc20   96-29474

IN

GRATEFUL MEMORY OF

MY FATHER

WHO LOVED THE GREAT MOTHER, HER FORMS,

HER MOODS, HER WAYS.

TO THE END SHE LEFT HIM THE JOY OF YOUTH

IN THE COMING OF SPRING

June 28, 1912

FOREWORD

BOTH admirers and critics of Kentucky-born novelist John Fox Jr. (1862-1919) will welcome this publication. They may initially be surprised, for *The Heart of the Hills* (1912) is rarely cited as one of his significant works. Indeed, treatments of Fox's career have tended to shrink in recent years to three volumes: the 1901 collection of allegedly nonfiction essays, *Blue Grass and Rhododendron,* and two short novels, *The Little Shepherd of Kingdom Come* (1903) and *The Trail of the Lonesome Pine* (1907).

Still, one can mention John Fox in and beyond Kentucky, receive a blank look, and yet arouse recognition by adding either "Kingdom Come" or "Lonesome Pine." While fewer admit to having actually read a work by Fox, many older Americans and film buffs of all ages recall young Henry Fonda as the unkempt mountain lad competing for June Tolliver against suave outsider Jack Hale (Fred MacMurray) in the 1936 film *The Trail of the Lonesome Pine.* Despite the eastern woodlands setting for Fox's novel, the movie was shot in Big Bear, California, ninety miles from Los Angeles in the San Bernardino mountains, but few moviegoers noticed the topographic absurdities or the radical changes to Fox's story.

In 1936, when the film was released, Fox's surviving siblings expressed outrage on behalf of their late brother. Publicity releases and movie posters were especially offensive: in Sylvia Sydney's "pert portrayal of June Tolliver turned hellcat," she "dared to love in a hell of hate!"[1] Determined to protect their famous brother's literary reputation, his sisters Minerva and Elizabeth and brother Rector recalled how "dear Johnny" struggled during the last decade of his life to protect his intellectual property in *Trail, Little Shepherd,* and *Heart of the Hills.* In their view, the latter novel was not a failure but instead was subsumed by headlines about John's divorce and legal battles with film producers over copyright. *The Heart of the Hills* is perhaps best described as an "eclipsed" novel.

It is unfortunate that the novel has remained in obscurity, given the high expectations of its author and his father. With this novel they sought to make amends for the actions of coalfield operatives and publicists of mountaineer "difference." Here are the distinct threads of a textual "apology," painful admissions of personal culpability by Fox Junior and Fox Senior, who had begun to comprehend the powerful politics of class and cultural representation. Acute financial need in the 1890s had led Fox Junior to the lecture circuit with a set of anecdotes and monologues about the people of the Cumberlands, collected as *Blue Grass and Rhododendron* in 1901. Though he tried to break away from the mountain genre, claiming he was a southern writer, he again mined the motif for *Little Shepherd* and *Lonesome Pine.*

In 1910, suffering further financial and personal problems, Fox returned to the mountaineer motif for *The Heart of the Hills.* But here he suggests that men of the southern mountains had been not only maligned and mistreated but also betrayed, along with other southern white males, by members of their respective classes.

Held in contempt by northerners and southerners alike since their "flaccid, flabby" pose of neutrality during the Civil War (Fox's terms), Kentucky's men saw their manhood newly threatened by internal corruption, inter- and intra-class tensions, and economic treachery. Fox's last mountain novel expresses these personal and public anxieties as Fox revises his long history with the mountaineer motif.

My reading of the literature of John Fox Jr. differs from most interpretations in that I treat him and his fascinating family as historical figures and assess them alongside Fox's literary output. Together the family and the books provide an insightful conduit into the passions and prejudices of southern whites at the end of the nineteenth century. Reading New York City newspapers and tabloids from this period alongside the Fox family's papers in Special Collections at the University of Kentucky provides clues to Fox's anxieties and his father's intensely held views. Such readings expose the personal, professional, and political strings tugging at *The Heart of the Hills*.

On April 8, 1910, Virginia lawyer/author Thomas Nelson Page delivered the keynote address for the annual gathering of the National Society of the Daughters of the American Revolution. Having read his old friend John Fox Jr.'s essays in *Blue Grass and Rhododendron* and the novel Teddy Roosevelt called "Lonesome Pine," Page felt qualified to speak about the "Mountaineer of the South." He implored the elite membership "to use your many affiliations" to reallocate some of the "vast resources of your class" to help educate Appalachian natives. To explicate their neediness, he put forward a pet theory he had first heard from Fox's father:

> Where the outer world has reached [the southern mountaineers], it has mainly been to trade upon their ignorance and rob them of what should have been their wealth. There are lands which were bought of them for a few dollars an acre, which are bonded now for as many thousands, and the justification for such legalized robbery at the hands of predatory wealth is that which is as old as Cyrus—that it was of more use to the taker than to the lawful holder. It is small wonder that they are suspicious as to the advances of civilization where the advance couriers are the land agent and the coal prospector—little wonder that, when evictors come under color of ancient patents to drive them from the lands which their fathers have held for generations, they should break out in feuds and violence.[2]

In many ways, Page himself was an "advance courier" of civilization. By 1910, Page was a trusted confidant of Woodrow Wilson, the emerging Democratic candidate for president, and would soon be named Wilson's ambassador to Rome. A practicing attorney with extensive land experience, Page had also inherited mining rights to mineral deposits in the Virginia and West Virginia mountains. Nevertheless, he sent a copy to Fox Junior, who shared his track record as an "advance courier" but believed himself to be a victim of predatory wealth. Fox responded immediately with delight over Page's treatment of his father's regular sermons on the topic, writing that "I couldn't have made an appeal like that."[3] But Fox was about to do just that, in the form of a novel.

The sentiments regarding predatory wealth and thievery run amok in the Kentucky and Virginia mountains appear around 1900 in contexts connected to John Fox Sr., a farmer, schoolteacher, surveyor, and lay botanist. While acting as "overseer" for his son James and other absentee investors in the coalfields of Wise County, Virginia, Fox Senior maintained faithful diaries, meticulous business ledgers, and extensive correspondence. He was troubled that several of his own sons (especially the eldest, James, who recruited his half-brothers John Junior, Oliver, and Horace) had been intimately involved in that thievery, and he found little comfort in their rationalizations that "better men of higher class were equally greedy."[4]

In 1910 Fox Senior was eighty years old and, to his regret, still living in Big Stone Gap, Virginia. This never-to-boom town was created in the 1880s by outside speculators and their resident agents at the edge of enormous bituminous coal reserves in eastern Kentucky and the southwestern corner of Virginia. The large family of a wife and ten children had officially relocated there in 1890 from Paris, Kentucky, at son James's request for assistance in monitoring his new acquisitions of land and mineral options. Two decades later, Fox Senior considered the venture to have been financially and socially disastrous for the entire family. Despite his advanced age, he had only recently quit trying to fulfill his wife's dream of moving back to Kentucky.

Since 1895, his fourth son's literary career—or, more accurately, the reputation earned by John Junior's most popular work and his publicity tours—had embarrassed the old man. Native mountaineers, especially younger ones, threatened to tar and feather young Fox for his misrepresentations of their lifestyle, moral sensibilities, and communities. Suspicious of financial speculation and get-rich-quick schemes, some mountain residents tried to remain aloof to the new social and economic order. Most, however, quickly comprehended the scope of fraudulent land and mineral rights acquisition conducted by such men as James Fox and his colleagues and competitors. John Junior had briefly acted as a land agent for his brother, but his primary role in the emerging rail and coal industries was that of publicist or promoter. From 1885 until late 1893, he haunted the financial centers of northern U.S. cities, penning quick sketches for the commercial press and "hustling" his brother's paper assets, mainly options on lands adjacent to critical transportation corridors in eastern Kentucky, eastern Tennessee, and the southwestern corner of Virginia.[5] By the time the dust cleared after the financial collapse of 1893, John Junior had reinvented himself as a traveling storyteller and lecturer and had left the region, he thought for good.

By 1910, those mountain natives remaining in eastern Kentucky and southwest Virginia perceived the degree of duplicity with which James Fox and other coalfield operatives had secured effective legislative constraints against local opposition, even taxation, in the state capitals at Frankfort, Nashville, and Richmond.[6] There would be no more promises of economic boom for the Cumberland mountain folk; too many had been dispossessed of their ancestral holdings in distant courtrooms. Acting for two decades as *chargé d'affaires* for his sons James and John Junior, who preferred to live in New York City, Fox Senior had personally listened to the complaints of local farmers along the Powell River with whom he traded for supplies. Some were amateur naturalists who shared, and patiently instructed, his passionate appreciation for mountain ecology, especially its unique flora. He feared that their feelings of hostility and resentment toward his sons and other "advance couriers" of industrialization were justified.[7]

More important, especially for students of environmental history and geography, Fox Senior vowed to identify and preserve every vanishing species of the lush environment that suffered so from corporate exploitation after 1890. Terrified of both fire and flood, he and his neighbors watched in impotent dread as deforestation moved in lockstep with railroad expansion, leaving oddly scalped hillsides around Powell Valley and the Gap. Eroding soil and debris cluttered the creeks and river beds. Every summer and fall, long weeks would pass during which Big Stone Gap residents could not detect the sun through hazy barriers of smoke as fires alternately raged or smoldered in the timber industry's wastage of less marketable trees and uprooted undergrowth. He knew from his reading that the situation was the same in Kentucky, North Carolina, and Tennessee. Alert to ecosystem interdependency, he feared for the Kentucky and Cumberland rivers as well as his own water supply, the once teeming Powell River that now ran dark and thin, reeking with upstream coal mine discharges and the daily deposits of the town's sewer lines and garbage. In John Senior's sensibilities, an ecological tragedy had occurred, and he, as an individual, could do little to stop its spread across the landscape as railroads and timber cutters aimed for remoter regions.[8]

The year 1910 also proved to be a difficult one for John Junior. He was in the midst of the most contentious stage of his brief marriage to comic opera star Fritzi Scheff, a flamboyant Austrian divorcée with legitimate high opera credentials and demonstrable press appeal. Her performance schedule and the raucous lifestyle of traveling theater professionals demanded much of Fox, both financially and physically. Reportedly he still looked boyish, but privately he admitted to feeling all the strains of his forty-eight years. His health was precarious: his eyesight and teeth were failing, he believed, from prolonged episodes of extreme poverty and poor nutrition in childhood. He had suffered from prostate trouble since age twenty-one. His closest encounters with Fritzi had been "unsatisfactory," he wrote to his brother, adding that this was "not surprising given my trouble." He had learned that Fritzi shared tales of their marital woes and his lack of ardor with theater friends and tabloid journalists who followed her well attended shows around the country.[9]

Refusing an invitation from Page to visit his Maine estate for the summer of 1910, John Junior complained, "as always, cash is scarce," despite his phenomenal book sales earlier in the decade.[10] He needed cash not only to meet his personal expenses but also to help support his father's household and to pay off the family's debts from 1893, when the Big Stone Gap boom had fizzled and the Bluegrass Kentucky-born entrepreneurs began fighting in court for the scraps.[11] After the collapse, neither James nor John Junior ever really resided at the Gap again, and Fox Senior was left to deal with his sons' creditors and frustrated townspeople. Some portion of earnings from John Junior's lectures and book sales were faithfully applied to the accumulated debts after 1395, but as late as 1910 John Senior often ended the month with less than a dollar in hand. He farmed on James's land, trading surpluses in hogs, corn, wheat, hay, and vegetables within the wider regional market. James's tenants around the Gap were not allowed to plant personal gardens or hunt game on surrounding acreage, thus ensuring a local market for Fox Senior and other farmers nearby.

Although hindsight shows that in 1910 he stood just beyond the peak of his literary career, John Junior faced new challenges caused by technological innovations. Nickelodeons and the new two-reelers pulled increasingly larger audiences away from traditional entertainment. Many authors and publishers worried, but Fox's style of light romantic fiction appealed to moviemakers, and several offered him royalties for use of his more popular titles. Other silent movie producers, however, were stealing his plots and titles without respect to his property rights. Fox was not the only author affected by such theft, for the New York press reported widespread litigation and copyright disputes among prominent authors, publishing houses, and the emerging film industry. By the end of 1910, twenty-six silent films had been released that featured pieces of Fox's plot lines, characters, or titles. He was determined that future usurpers of his stories would pay up or be challenged in court.[12]

Looking to combine his still considerable audience of women and adolescent boys with the explosive public interest in film, Fox decided that he needed a new bestseller to coincide with the opening of his dream venture, a new stage and screen version of *The Trail of the Lonesome Pine* over which he retained firm script control. For the winter of 1910-11, he "retired to the mountains" to toss off a quick manuscript at Big Stone Gap, where he would be "free of the distractions of pleasant company."[13] Approaching the mountains by train from the north, he traveled under an assumed name within the Cumberland railroad district. There is evidence that his family was instructed to keep his presence in the Gap secret for two reasons: that mountain natives would not bombard him with "their petty criticisms" and that tabloid journalists would not find him "to answer Fritzi's most recent insult."[14]

For extended periods through that winter and into the next year, John Junior remained close to the Gap. Sleeping during the day, he walked for exercise before dawn after a night shift of writing and reading long passages aloud to his insomniac father. The manuscript began to reflect Fox Senior's concerns and anecdotes, even his personality. John Junior regularly depended upon others for mountain experiences from which to draw inspiration. His own contact with mountain people was limited at first by his own choice, for he had despised mountain life as "common-place" from his first summer there in 1882 and preferred New York City when he could afford to live there. But he especially avoided the mountains after 1895, when students from Berea College heard his "lecture of the southern mountaineer" and promised that Fox would henceforth "be an unwelcome visitor" among mountain neighborhoods.[15] For nearly twenty years, he did not care to travel in eastern Kentucky or some corners of Virginia. Having marginalized himself from his subject culture, Fox turned to his father for advice and eagerly absorbed his impressions and apprehensions.[16]

By mid-summer 1911 John Junior felt socially and physically stifled. He attempted to reconcile with Fritzi, meeting her tour in Philadelphia and again in Washington, D.C. According to his father's letters to James, he "came back very much upset" and seemed depressed, for "he worries himself a great deal about Fritzi."[17] Twice he went to Lexington and Frankfort to do research. Visiting Kentucky's state university, he was invited by Professor White to take "his place on the rostrum." As the University's school newspaper reported,

> Mr. Fox was quite fatigued from lack of sleep, and accordingly did not feel able to make more than a brief talk but his few remarks were very gratifying to all those interested in the State University. For among other things, he said that he was following the course of his hero and that he had come to his entrance to the State University, "where," said Mr. Fox, "I hope his actions will be entirely proper." This statement was greeted with loud applause, as was Mr. Fox's appearance on the rostrum.
>
> The Junior and Senior classes gave "nine 'rahs" for Fox.[18]

Shortly after this trip Fox learned of another problem. The new production of *The Trail of the Lonesome*

Pine had fizzled in its first stage outing at Philadelphia. The director had not remained faithful to the script Fox had approved, and Charlotte Walker, the actress playing June Tolliver, was "sooting her face" and "blackening her teeth" in order "to inspire pathos."[19] Such creative differences gave him the excuse he needed to leave the Gap, for attorneys, financial backers, and theater agents now required his presence in New York. With the nearly completed manuscript in hand, he left Virginia, promising his father to "remain true to the themes we discussed" while polishing the novel and to "return at the first sign" that his father's health might be growing worse. Fox Junior was to dedicate the book to his father; subsequent diary entries show that Fox Senior was pleased with the dedication and offered his "sincere hope that it will be well-read and received."[20]

Succumbing to a lifetime of hard work, the elder Fox wore down in the summer of 1912, shortly after the first installment of the manuscript appeared in *Scribner's* monthly magazine. He died before the novel was released as a separate volume in 1913 and before leading tabloids boasted headlines of his son's messy divorce. Reviews of the new novel were eclipsed by published reports from divorce court and civil court, where Fritzi had filed for financial relief from Fox Junior. Whereas her audiences soared and roared their approval of her boldness, Fox's clucked disapprovingly at such antics. At the same time, he began a protracted and fruitless legal battle to stop the Broadway Picture Company from releasing its rendition of *The Trail of the Lonesome Pine*.

The title *The Heart of the Hills* was not Fox's first

choice. In a pocket-sized notebook devoted to this novel, he had tried out several possible titles: "Sons of the Hills," "Sires of the Hills," "The Mountains Gave Birth," "Where the Mountains Meet," "The Meeting of the Mountains," and his personal underscored favorite, "The Spread of Greed." Under the heading "Statement of Conditions in Mountains," he wrote, "foreigners buy up lands for a song. Depopulating the hills. family goes Bluegrass as tobacco tenants. Ravage of woodlands. Prescient shadow to tobacco troubles." The plot of *Heart of the Hills* does follow this skeletal outline closely, and Fox never strays far from the theme of spreading greed. The finished text and characterizations also suggest Page's speech to the DAR. As the native guide for the "advance couriers, the land agent and coal prospector," Fox offers Arch Hawn, who attempts to bridge the two Kentucky worlds separated by the Knobs and profit from land options leveraged from his relatives and neighbors at such low prices as to make absentee buyers sing. The buyer of these options is a Bluegrass lawyer, Colonel Pennington, whose lapses in moral integrity can be traced to an entirely honorable cause: like John Fox Senior, he has no head for business. One wealthy predator is shadowy Morton Sanders, who buys up both mountain coal deposits and prime Bluegrass farms, strips the land of trees, and relocates displaced mountaineers into tenant cabins and fields to tend his tobacco. The only honorable coal prospector is a poor science teacher, a geologist or "jologist" who, more than any other character, reflects the scholarly interests and class consciousness of Fox Senior.

The plot offers recognizable characters and situations from Kentucky history. The "university president" suggests the University of Kentucky's early administrator James Patterson; the dead autocrat is, of course, gubernatorial candidate William Goebel, assassinated following the contested state elections of 1899.[21] Other characters are more likely to be composites that rely upon the experiences of others living in the mountains. When Fox's mountain boy-hero Jason Hawn paraphrases the geologist in a brilliant ecological critique of Kentucky mineral extraction, timbering, and agriculture, he echoes Fox Senior. These criticisms—and the colorful concept of "spitting out" one's birthright in tobacco juice—are themes Fox Senior heard from local farmers.

Also, John Junior has the rare opportunity to draw from personal experience. In the early pages Arch Hawn contemplates his standard sales pitch: "The mountain people could do nothing with the mineral wealth of their hills; the coal was of no value to them where it was; they could not dig it, they had no market for it, and they could never get it into the markets of the outside world." John Junior had used the same arguments in 1887 in Harlan County, Kentucky, when he tried to buy mineral options from native land dwellers, following a script prepared by his brother James. The clinching argument was that native mining entrepreneurs would find it "impossible to get their coal onto the new [rail]roads," which were controlled by the same moneyed interests that John Junior and James represented.[22]

The Heart of the Hills thus is imbued with a confessional spirit that offers amends for misdeeds by some

and miscalculations by many. But the overriding theme
is "manhood," a complex category for John Junior in-
volving both public and private arenas of conflict. Kentucky men were faring badly in the business world, publishing, and movies. Polite society seemed to laugh at
Kentuckians, not unlike the way Fritzi scoffed at Fox's
pretensions to popularity and manliness. The 1900 as-
sassination of Goebel on the lawn of the state capitol in
Frankfort undermined the fiction that political feuding
with gunplay was a mountain-only phenomenon and further indicted Kentucky as a laughingstock for national
media.

For several years before his death, these same concerns troubled Fox Senior. Having fathered ten children
by two Kentucky women, the elder Fox was nearing the
end of his life and wondering why only one of them by
then had produced a grandchild. Where was the manhood that would lead Kentucky in the new century, he
wondered. Toward the end of the novel, readers will find
Colonel Pendleton trying to find answers to the same
question.[23]

Appalachian scholars have long argued that John Fox
Jr. was a major mythmaker who reinforced the idea of
an Appalachian "other" and encouraged several waves
of social reformers to descend upon the mountains with
schemes for cultural uplift and nationalistic
mainstreaming.[24] I have argued that his life and literary output help to contextualize a critical juncture in
American journalism and literature at the beginning of
the twentieth century. This period's rising literacy rates

and improvements in transportation and communication nurtured a lively publishing market for novelists, journalists, and storytellers. The local color genre with which Fox's work is closely identified had faded but not yet given way to stark realism and muckraking. As a "white-winged" missionary in the cause of Anglo-American culture, Fox offered to interpret alien cultures for reading audiences and left a critical lens into this fusion of travel writing, industrial public relations, and yellow journalism. Thus, his career best illustrates "the felicitous convergence of mythmaking and capital accumulation."[25]

Close examination of Fox's personal and literary career challenges our collective understanding of Appalachian history as to the patterns of fraudulent land- and mineral-acquisition by venture capitalists. Non-natives in particular justified their colonization of the region by appealing to dominant ideologies of labor, gender, race, and, underlying all else, class superiority. Fox's politicized subtexts and discourses reveal gendered, racialized, and class-drenched conflicts between—as well as within the ranks of—the colonized and their colonizers.

This old but new Fox novel offers multiple themes for exploration. When *Heart of the Hills* first appeared, for instance, America's favorite sweetheart, actress Mary Pickford, found inspiration in the character Mavis to fashion a feminist film challenge to male domination.[26] New readers may be challenged as well to contemplate recent Kentucky history through Fox's scenario: Will Jason rescue his and Kentucky's manhood from national ridicule? What attitudes must Jason acquire for the new industrial order to accept and endorse his political progression? Will men like Jason succeed in halting the insidious spread of greed, or will it continue, stilling the heart of Kentucky's hills?

—DARLENE WILSON

Notes

1. For movie memorabilia and clippings, see family scrapbooks in Fox family papers, 1852-1962 (bulk dates 1852-1920). 64M122, 5.4 cubic feet, archived in the Division of Special Collections and Archives, Margaret I. King Library, University of Kentucky, Lexington. Hereinafter referred to as "Fox-UK."

2. Reprinted in Harriett Holman, *John Fox and Tom Page As They Were* (Miami, Fla.: Field Research Projects, n.d.); copy in John Cook Wylie Library, Clinch Valley College, Wise, Virginia.

3. Fox to Page, from Big Stone Gap, Virginia, November 3, 1910.

4. See diaries of John W. Fox Sr., 1899-1909, especially. Quote is from letter from James to his father, August 6, 1903, in correspondence files. All in Fox-UK.

5. See Letter from John Junior to James, January 3, 1887:

My dear Jim: Hoop-la! . . . with Comstock the other day . . . you ought to have seen the glint come into his eyes as I talked. When I came in, he nodded from his desk carelessly when I left he raised from his chair and bowed. Hoop-la! How I do enjoy it. Ah, the magic of dollars when thousands are mentioned. I enjoy the power, the privilege of talking of thousands. My chest expands, I can feel the pupils of my eyes expand (I can *see* my victim's expand)—My voice becomes full, resonant, superior. I confer. I offer privileges with graceful carelessness. In all honesty, I can look back and see that if I had trained to do this work, I couldn't have selected a better plan than I have followed unintentionally [with James's recruitment]. All this philosophical and professional (from a fiction stand-point) interest in this is about to keep me from mentioning that Comstock gave me a nice letter to his bankers and broker who received me very nicely and made an appointment with me tomorrow morning to discuss the investments. . . . I shall beard [Thompson] tomorrow afternoon [and] I shall get a whack, I think, at V.K. Stevenson, the real estate magnate.

See also letter from John Junior to James, September 3, 1887: "It takes monumental cheek to s— up and talk to a man about investing $10,000 when you have but $10 in your pocket. It makes me feel like a fraud." See also letter from John Junior to James, December [?] 1884, regarding the "feuding" assignment for *Commercial Advertiser*; and John Junior to James, September 3, 1887: "I saw the managing editor of the Commercial Advertiser and he wants me to write a series of sketches on the mountains, the 'boom', the people, life, manners, etc. & also an article on 'moonshining.' I hate very much to use material that I might incorporate in stories for newspaper sketches but *I'll have to do it for the money.* Now can you give me a little information about moonshining, its present status, any newspaper articles you may have on the subject, etc. Take $1/2$ hour sometime and write me your own experiences." Emphasis added. All in correspondence files, Fox-UK.

6. See, e.g., *The Mountaineers; or, Bottled Sunshine for Blue Mondays*, published in 1902 in Nashville, Tennessee. The author is "Jean Yelsew," a pen name that inverted the real middle name of the author, J. Wesley Smith, D.D., a Methodist circuit rider based in upper East Tennessee.

7. See diaries, especially 1895, when it became clear to all participants that the long-awaited "boom" would not occur, in Fox-UK.

8. John Fox Senior was an avid "nature observer" who recorded various environmental data for his own pleasure and for comparative analysis. He was especially interested in the differences between naturally-occurring species of flora in the highlands and the flora in flatter Clark County, Kentucky, where he grew up. His diaries and

FOREWORD

personal correspondence provide rich details for students of environmental history and ecological theory. Corroborating reports of fre-
quent fires and poor visibility can be found in several local newspapers in Kentucky and southwest Virginia; for Fox's backyard, see the
Big Stone Gap Post; its complete microfilm collection is housed at
Clinch Valley College, Wise, Virginia. Fox expected his sons, relatives, and other correspondents to send him any newspaper or journal they acquired from any source. This way, despite being perenni-
ally short of funds for personal subscriptions, he received regular
reading materials from multiple sites—New York City, Washington,
D.C., California, Texas, and several Kentucky towns and cities. When
John Junior was at Harvard 1880-1883, he and his father often exchanged well read newspapers and clippings by mail.

9. See letter from John to James, December 1909, in Fox-UK.

10. See letter from John to Page, April 1910, reprinted in Holman,
n.d.; photocopy in Fox-UK.

11. Among them were Joshua Bullitt, R. Tate Irvine, R.C. Ballard-
Thruston, and Henry Clay McDowell as well as six Fox brothers:
James, John, Horace, Oliver, Richard, and Rector. See Index of Wise
County (Virginia) Court docket, 1893-1905.

12. See correspondence files for 1908-1912 and scrapbooks for cop-
ies of John Junior's correspondence about the silent-film industry.
Also see the *New York Times* and *Sun*, especially the Theater sections for the same years.

13. Fox Junior to Page, cited in Holman, n.d.

14. See, in Fox-UK correspondence files, series of September 1910
letters from John Junior to his father, James, his mother, and his
sister Minnie, who was then traveling as Fritzi's chaperone.

15. See Fox family scrapbook for 1895 clipping from Cincinnati
newspaper reporting that Berea students were angry over Fox's reading and refused to share the stage with him for a program of readings and music arranged by Berea College president William Frost.

16. To account for John Junior's activities during this period, I
relied most heavily on John Senior's diaries and correspondence with
James in New York City.

17. See several letters from John Senior to James, July 1911, in
Fox-UK. Also see diaries of John Senior for 1910 and 1911.

18. Copy in family scrapbook, Fox-UK.

19. See letters from John Junior to James and to brother Rector in 1911 correspondence file, Fox-UK.

20. See diary entries by Fox Senior for October-December 1911.

21. Though some claimed later that he was already dead, Goebels was administered the oath of office so that his lieutenant governor, J.C.W. Beckham, could then be sworn in as governor. A mountaineer named Caleb Powers was arrested with others, but after four trials Powers's conviction was overturned by a pardon from the next Republican governor, Augustus E. Willson (1907-11). Fox's reference to two mountain men involved in a shootout may be based on the 1900 Colson-Scott shootout in the lobby of the Capitol Hotel at Frankfort when Col. David Colson of Middlesboro was badly wounded and Ethelbert Scott was killed; four innocent bystanders were also killed and two wounded.

22. Letter from John Junior to James, en route to England, May 1887; John Junior reports on a failed sales pitch to Mr. Phipps in Harlan County: "He [says] a railroad will run through the back of his land (21,700 acres) and for only 2000 acres he has already been offered $10 per acre. He says that the residents are getting too shrewd for options. . . . [O]nly by a ruse, can anyone obtain them for six months even—that is, by pretending to want that time to look up titles." John Junior also reported that Phipps laughed about the number of "capitalists trooping into the mountains . . . [such] that lands are hopping up $5 per acre a day" and informed Fox that he was "trying to get at Jay Gould." James's response could not be postponed until he returned home; he cabled Johnny with a set of terse responses. See correspondence file for 1887 in Fox-UK.

23. See Fox Senior's diaries for 1908-1910.

24. See Don Askins, "John Fox, Jr.: A Re-Appraisal; or With Friends Like That, Who Needs Enemies?" in Helen Lewis, et al., eds., *Colonialism in Modern America: The Appalachian Case* (Boone, N.C.: Appalachian Consortium Press, 1978); Henry D. Shapiro, *Appalachia on Our Mind: The Southern Mountains and Mountaineers in the American Consciousness, 1870-1920* (Chapel Hill: University of North Carolina Press, 1978); Ronald D. Eller, *Miners, Millhands, and Mountaineers: Industrialization of the Appalachian South, 1880-1930* (Knoxville: University of Tennessee Press, 1982); David Whisnant,

FOREWORD

All That Is Native and Fine (Chapel Hill: University of North Carolina Press, 1983); and Allen Batteau, *The Invention of Appalachia* (Tucson: University of Arizona Press, 1990). Other discerning scholars interested in Fox include Rodger Cunningham, "Signs of Civilization: *The Trail of the Lonesome Pine* as Colonial Narrative" in *Journal of Appalachian Studies Association*, Vol. 2, 1990; and Dwight Billings and Kathleen Blee, "'Where the Sun Set Crimson and the Moon Rose Red': Writing Appalachia and the Kentucky Mountain Feuds," forthcoming. In another reading, Fox's work is offered as an example of gendered discourse fraught with the "romance of reunion" and characteristic of postbellum relations between North and South, as deftly argued by Nina Silber in *The Romance of Reunion: Northerners and the South, 1865-1900* (Chapel Hill: University of North Carolina Press, 1993). Silber's pick from Fox's shelf is *The Little Shepherd of Kingdom Come,* in which a mountain boy first learns to control his manhood in the company of well-bourboned Bluegrass gentlemen. When the battle over secession leaves Kentuckians divided over slavery, the boy-cum-man finds he can abide by his higher boyhood loyalties to the Founding Fathers and still keep intact his faith in white supremacy.

Recently, Fox's themes have been appropriated without critical analysis into the play *The Kentucky Cycle* by Robert Shenkkan (recipient of the 1992 Pulitzer Prize for drama); and Gary Dean Best, *Witch Hunt in Wise County: The Persecution of Edith Maxwell* (Westport, Conn.: Praeger, 1994). Their citation here should not be taken as an endorsement.

25. See Wilson, "The Felicitous Convergence of Mythmaking and Capital Accumulation: John Fox Jr. and the Formation of An(Other) Almost-White American Under-Class," in *Journal of Appalachian Studies* 1, no.1 (Fall 1995): 5-45: "Influenced by self-identification with a Boston-to-Bluegrass corporate and social 'aristocracy,' [Fox] helped to create and/or perpetuate myths of Appalachian 'otherness' for two purposes clearly identified in his texts and journals—1) to achieve corporate and class hegemony by marginalizing indigenous peoples and existing sociocultural structures, and 2) to undermine local resistance via an acknowledged policy of forced depopulation." The term "white-winged" is borrowed from Albion Tourgee's brilliant expose of the Ku Klux Klan's rise in the South, *The Invisible*

FOREWORD

Empire (1880; reprint, Baton Rouge: Louisiana State University Press, 1989), 18: "What is known as the 'Southern Question' is not by any means a settled or even a quiet one in these days. Despite the failure of Reconstruction, the . . . resumption of 'the white man's government,' and the return of white-winged peace, . . . there is evidently still some disturbing influence at work."

26. See J.W. Williamson, Southern Mountaineer Filmography: "1919 HEART O' THE HILLS / FIRST NATIONAL Directed by SIDNEY FRANKLIN Starring: MARY PICKFORD, HAROLD GOODWIN, SAM DEGRASSE, FRED W HUNTLY; Comments: Tale of a Ky mtn girl who saves her mother's land from land sharks and becomes a night rider to avenge her father's death. In it, Mary Pickford was supposed to be breaking new ground (she'd long been America's cuddly little girl) playing the wild girl of the hills ('I can lick any boy in town'). Based on a John Fox story." Filmography in Williamson, *Hillbillyland: What the Movies Did to the Mountains and What the Mountains Did to the Movies* (Chapel Hill: University of North Carolina Press, 1995).

THE
HEART OF THE HILLS

I

TWIN spirals of blue smoke rose on either
side of the spur, crept tendril-like up two
dark ravines, and clearing the feathery green crests
of the trees, drifted lazily on upward until, high
above, they melted shyly together and into the
haze that veiled the drowsy face of the mountain.
Each rose from a little log cabin clinging to the
side of a little hollow at the head of a little creek.
About each cabin was a rickety fence, a patch of
garden, and a little cleared hill-side, rocky, full of
stumps, and crazily traced with thin green spears
of corn. On one hill-side a man was at work with
a hoe, and on the other, over the spur, a boy—
both barefooted, and both in patched jean trousers upheld by a single suspender that made a wet
line over a sweaty cotton shirt: the man, tall,
lean, swarthy, grim; the boy grim and dark, too,
and with a face that was prematurely aged. At
the man's cabin a little girl in purple homespun
was hurrying in and out the back door clearing

up after the noonday meal; at the boy's, a comely
woman with masses of black hair sat in the porch
with her hands folded, and lifting her eyes now
and then to the top of the spur. Of a sudden the
man impatiently threw down his hoe, but through
the battered straw hat that bobbed up and down
on the boy's head, one lock tossed on like a jet-
black plume until he reached the end of his straggling row of corn. There he straightened up and
brushed his earth-stained fingers across a dull-
red splotch on one cheek of his sullen set face.
His heavy lashes lifted and he looked long at the
woman on the porch—looked without anger now
and with a new decision in his steady eyes. He was
getting a little too big to be struck by a woman,
even if she were his own mother, and nothing like
that must happen again.

A woodpecker was impudently tapping the top
of a dead burnt tree near by, and the boy started
to reach for a stone, but turned instead and went
doggedly to work on the next row, which took
him to the lower corner of the garden fence, where
the ground was black and rich. There, as he
sank his hoe with the last stroke around the last
hill of corn, a fat fishing-worm wriggled under his
very eyes, and the growing man lapsed swiftly
into the boy again. He gave another quick dig,
the earth gave up two more squirming treasures,
and with a joyful gasp he stood straight again—
his eyes roving as though to search all creation

2

for help against the temptation that now was his. His mother had her face uplifted toward the top of the spur; and following her gaze, he saw a tall mountaineer slouching down the path. Quickly he crouched behind the fence, and the aged look came back into his face. He did not approve of that man coming over there so often, kinsman though he was, and through the palings he saw his mother's face drop quickly and her hands moving uneasily in her lap. And when the mountaineer sat down on the porch and took off his hat to wipe his forehead, he noticed that his mother had on a newly bought store dress, and that the man's hair was wet with something more than water. The thick locks had been combed and were glistening with oil, and the boy knew these facts for signs of courtship; and though he was contemptuous, they furnished the excuse he sought and made escape easy. Noiselessly he wielded his hoe for a few moments, scooped up a handful of soft dirt, meshed the worms in it, and slipped the squirming mass into his pocket. Then he crept stooping along the fence to the rear of the house, squeezed himself between two broken palings, and sneaked on tiptoe to the back porch. Gingerly he detached a cane fishing-pole from a bunch that stood upright in a corner and was tiptoeing away, when with another thought he stopped, turned back, and took down from the wall a bow and arrow with a steel head around which was wound a long

3

hempen string. Cautiously then he crept back along the fence, slipped behind the barn into the undergrowth and up a dark little ravine toward the green top of the spur. Up there he turned from the path through the thick bushes into an open space, walled by laurel-bushes, hooted three times surprisingly like an owl, and lay contentedly down on a bed of moss. Soon his ear caught the sound of light footsteps coming up the spur on the other side, the bushes parted in a moment more, and a little figure in purple homespun slipped through them, and with a flushed, panting face and dancing eyes stood beside him.

The boy nodded his head sidewise toward his own home, and the girl silently nodded hers up and down in answer. Her eyes caught sight of the bow and arrow on the ground beside him and lighted eagerly, for she knew then that the fishing-pole was for her. Without a word they slipped through the bushes and down the steep side of the spur to a little branch which ran down into a creek that wound a tortuous way into the Cumberland.

II

ON the other side, too, a similar branch ran
down into another creek which looped around
the long slanting side of the spur and emptied,
too, into the Cumberland. At the mouth of each
creek the river made a great bend, and in the
sweep of each were rich bottom lands. A century before, a Hawn had settled in one bottom,
the lower one, and a Honeycutt in the other. As
each family multiplied, more land was cleared
up each creek by sons and grandsons until in each
cove a clan was formed. No one knew when and
for what reason an individual Hawn and a Honeycutt had first clashed, but the clash was of course
inevitable. Equally inevitable was it, too, that
the two clans should take the quarrel up, and for
half a century the two families had, with inter-
mittent times of truce, been traditional enemies.
The boy's father, Jason Hawn, had married a
Honeycutt in a time of peace, and, when the war
opened again, was regarded as a deserter, and had
been forced to move over the spur to the Honeycutt side. The girl's father, Steve Hawn, a ne'er-
do-well and the son of a ne'er-do-well, had for his
inheritance wild lands, steep, supposedly worth-
less, and near the head of the Honeycutt cove.

Little Jason's father, when he quarrelled with his kin, could afford to buy only cheap land on the Honeycutt side, and thus the homes of the two were close to the high heart of the mountain, and separated only by the bristling crest of the spur. In time the boy's father was slain from ambush, and it was a Hawn, the Honeycutts claimed, who had made him pay the death price of treachery to his own kin. But when peace came, this fact did not save the lad from taunt and suspicion from the children of the Honeycutt tribe, and being a favorite with his Grandfather Hawn down on the river, and harshly treated by his Honeycutt mother, his life on the other side in the other cove was a hard one; so his heart had gone back to his own people and, having no companions, he had made a playmate of his little cousin, Mavis, over the spur. In time her mother had died, and in time her father, Steve, had begun slouching over the spur to court the widow—his cousin's widow, Martha Hawn. Straightway the fact had caused no little gossip up and down both creeks, good-natured gossip at first, but, now that the relations between the two clans were once more strained, there was open censure, and on that day when all the men of both factions had gone to the county-seat, the boy knew that Steve Hawn had stayed at home for no other reason than to make his visit that day secret; and the lad's brain, as he strode ahead of his silent little companion, was busy with the significance of what was sure to come.

At the mouth of the branch, the two came upon a road that also ran down to the river, but they kept on close to the bank of the stream which widened as they travelled—the boy striding ahead without looking back, the girl following like a shadow. Still again they crossed the road, where it ran over the foot of the spur and turned down into a deep bowl filled to the brim with bush and tree, and there, where a wide pool lay asleep in thick shadow, the lad pulled forth the ball of earth and worms from his pocket, dropped them with the fishing-pole to the ground, and turned ungallantly to his bow and arrow. By the time he had strung it, and had tied one end of the string to the shaft of the arrow and the other about his wrist, the girl had unwound the coarse fishing-line, had baited her own hook, and, squatted on her heels, was watching her cork with eager eyes; but when the primitive little hunter crept to the lower end of the pool, and was peering with Indian caution into the depths, her eyes turned to him.

"Watch out thar!" he called, sharply.

Her cork bobbed, sank, and when, with closed eyes, she jerked with all her might, a big shining chub rose from the water and landed on the bank beside her. She gave a subdued squeal of joy, but the boy's face was calm as a star. Minnows like that were all right for a girl to catch and even

7

for him to eat, but he was after game for a man. A moment later he heard another jerk and another fish was flopping on the bank, and this time she made no sound, but only flashed her triumphant eyes upon him. At the third fish, she turned her eyes for approval—and got none; and at the fourth, she did not look up at all, for he was walking toward her.

"You air skeerin' the big uns," he said shortly, and as he passed he pulled his Barlow knife from his pocket and dropped it at her feet. She rose obediently, and with no sign of protest began gathering an apronful of twigs and piling them for a fire. Then she began scraping one of the fish, and when it was cleaned she lighted the fire. The blaze crackled merrily, the blue smoke rose like some joyous spirit loosed for upward flight, and by the time the fourth fish was cleaned, a little bed of winking coals was ready and soon a gentle sizzling assailed the boy's ears, and a scent made his nostrils quiver and set his stomach a-hungering. But still he gave no sign of interest —even when the little girl spoke at last:

"Dinner's ready."

He did not look around, for he had crouched, his body taut from head to foot, and he might have been turned suddenly to stone for all the sign of life he gave, and the little girl too was just as motionless. Then she saw the little statue come slowly back to quivering life. She saw the bow bend, the shaft of the arrow drawing close to the boy's paling cheek, there was a rushing hiss through the air, a burning hiss in the water, a mighty bass leaped from the convulsed surface and shot to the depths again, leaving the headless arrow afloat. The boy gave one sharp cry and lapsed into his stolid calm again.

The little girl said nothing, for there is no balm for the tragedy of the big fish that gets away. Slowly he untied the string from his reddened wrist and pulled the arrow in. Slowly he turned and gazed indifferently at the four crisp fish on four dry twigs with four pieces of corn pone lying on the grass near them, and the little girl squatting meekly and waiting, as the woman should for her working lord. With his Barlow knife he slowly speared a corn pone, picking up a fish with the other hand, and still she waited until he spoke.

"Take out, Mavie," he said with great gravity and condescension, and then his knife with a generous mouthful on its point stopped in the air, his startled eyes widened, and the little girl shrank cowering behind him. A heavy footfall had crunched on the quiet air, the bushes had parted, and a huge mountaineer towered above them with a Winchester over his shoulder and a kindly smile under his heavy beard. The boy was startled— not frightened.

"Hello, Babe!" he said coolly. "Whut devil-mint you up to now?"

9

The giant smiled uneasily:

"I'm keepin' out o' the sun an' a-takin' keer o' my health," he said, and his eyes dropped hungrily to the corn pone and fried fish, but the boy shook his head sturdily.

"You can't git nothin' to eat from me, Babe Honeycutt."

"Now, looky hyeh, Jason——"

"Not a durn bite," said the boy firmly, "even if you air my mammy's brother. I'm a Hawn now, I want ye to know, an' I ain't goin' to have my folks say I was feedin' an' harborin' a Honeycutt—'specially *you*."

It would have been humorous to either Hawn or Honeycutt to hear the big man plead, but not to the girl, though he was an enemy, and had but recently wounded a cousin of hers, and was hiding from her own people, for her warm little heart was touched, and big Babe saw it and left his mournful eyes on hers.

"An' I'm a-goin' to tell whar I've seed ye," went on the boy savagely, but the girl grabbed up two fish and a corn pone and thrust them out to the huge hairy hand eagerly stretched out.

"Now, git away," she said breathlessly, "git away—quick!"

"Mavis!" yelled the boy.

"Shet up!" she cried, and the lips of the routed boy fell apart in sheer amazement, for never before had she made the slightest question of his tyrannical authority, and then her eyes blazed at the big Honeycutt and she stamped her foot.

"I'd give 'em to the meanest *dog* in these mountains."

The big man turned to the boy.

"Is he dead yit?"

"No, he ain't dead yit," said the boy roughly.

"Son," said the mountaineer quietly, "you tell whutever you please about me."

The curiously gentle smile had never left the bearded lips, but in his voice a slight proud change was perceptible.

"An' you can take back yo' corn pone, honey."

Then dropping the food in his hand back to the ground, he noiselessly melted into the bushes again.

At once the boy went to work on his neglected corn-bread and fish, but the girl left hers untouched where they lay. He ate silently, staring at the water below him, nor did the little girl turn her eyes his way, for in the last few minutes some subtle change in their relations had taken place, and both were equally surprised and mystified. Finally, the lad ventured a sidewise glance at her beneath the brim of his hat and met a shy, appealing glance once more. At once he felt aggrieved and resentful and turned sullen.

"He throwed it back in yo' face," he said. "You oughtn't to 'a' done it."

Little Mavis made no answer.

"You're nothin' but a gal, an' nobody'll hold nothin' agin you, but with my mammy a Honeycutt an' me a-livin' on the Honeycutt side, you mought 'a' got me into trouble with my own folks." The girl knew how Jason had been teased and taunted and his life made miserable up and down the Honeycutt creek, and her brown face grew wistful and her chin quivered.

"I jes' couldn't he'p it, Jason," she said weakly, and the little man threw up his hands with a gesture that spoke his hopelessness over her sex in general, and at the same time an ungracious acceptance of the terrible calamity she had perhaps left dangling over his head. He clicked the blade of his Barlow knife and rose.

"We better be movin' now," he said, with a resumption of his old authority, and pulling in the line and winding it about the cane pole, he handed it to her and started back up the spur with Mavis trailing after, his obedient shadow once more.

On top of the spur Jason halted. A warm blue haze transfused with the slanting sunlight overlay the flanks of the mountains which, fold after fold, rippled up and down the winding river and above the green crests billowed on and on into the unknown. Nothing more could happen to them if they went home two hours later than would surely happen if they went home now, the boy thought, and he did not want to go home now. For a moment he stood irresolute, and then, far down the river, he saw two figures on horse-back come into sight from a strip of woods, move slowly around a curve of the road, and disappear into the woods again.

One rode sidewise, both looked absurdly small, and even that far away the boy knew them for strangers. He did not call Mavis's attention to them—he had no need—for when he turned, her face showed that she too had seen them, and she was already moving forward to go with him down the spur. Once or twice, as they went down, each glimpsed the coming "furriners" dimly through the trees; they hurried that they might not miss the passing, and on a high bank above the river road they stopped, standing side by side, the eyes of both fixed on the arched opening of the trees through which the strangers must first come into sight. A ringing laugh from the green depths heralded their coming, and then in the archway were framed a boy and a girl and two ponies—all from another world. The two watchers stared silently—the boy noting that the other boy wore a cap and long stockings, the girl that a strange hat hung down the back of the other girl's head —stared with widening eyes at a sight that was never for them before. And then the strangers saw them—the boy with his bow and arrow, the girl with a fishing-pole—and simultaneously pulled their ponies in before the halting gaze that was levelled at them from the grassy bank. Then they all looked at one another until boy's eyes rested on boy's eyes for question and answer, and the stranger lad's face flashed with quick humor.

"Were you looking for us?" he asked, for just so it seemed to him, and the little mountaineer nodded.

"Yes," he said gravely.

The stranger boy laughed.

"What can we do for you?"

Now, little Jason had answered honestly and literally, and he saw now that he was being trifled with.

"A feller what wears gal's stockings can't do nothin' fer me," he said coolly.

Instantly the other lad made as though he would jump from his pony, but a cry of protest stopped him, and for a moment he glared his hot resentment of the insult; then he dug his heels into his pony's sides.

"Come on, Marjorie," he said, and with dignity the two little "furriners" rode on, never looking back even when they passed over the hill.

"He didn't mean nothin'," said Mavis, "an' you oughtn't——"

Jason turned on her in a fury.

"I seed you a-lookin' at him!"

"'Tain't so! I seed you a-lookin' at *her!*" she retorted, but her eyes fell before his accusing

14

gaze, and she began worming a bare toe into the sand.

"Air ye goin' home now?" she asked, presently.

"No," he said shortly, "I'm a-goin' atter him. You go on home."

The boy started up the hill, and in a moment the girl was trotting after him. He turned when he heard the patter of her feet.

"Huh!" he grunted contemptuously, and kept on. At the top of the hill he saw several men on horseback in the bend of the road below, and he turned into the bushes.

"They mought tell on us," explained Jason, and hiding bow and arrow and fishing-pole, they slipped along the flank of the spur until they stood on a point that commanded the broad river-bottom at the mouth of the creek.

By the roadside down there, was the ancestral home of the Hawns with an orchard about it, a big garden, a stable huge for that part of the world, and a meat-house where for three-quarters of a century there had always been things "hung up." The old log house in which Jason and Mavis's great-great-grandfather had spent his pioneer days had been weather-boarded and was invisible somewhere in the big frame house that, trimmed with green and porticoed with startling colors, glared white in the afternoon sun. They could see the two ponies hitched at the front gate. Two horsemen were hurrying along the river road

beneath them, and Jason recognized one as his
uncle, Arch Hawn, who lived in the county-seat,
who bought "wild" lands and was always bringing in "furriners," to whom he sold them again.
The man with him was a stranger, and Jason understood better now what was going on. Arch
Hawn was responsible for the presence of the man
and of the girl and that boy in the "gal's stockings," and all of them would probably spend the
night at his grandfather's house. A farm-hand
was leading the ponies to the barn now, and Jason
and Mavis saw Arch and the man with him throw
themselves hurriedly from their horses, for the
sun had disappeared in a black cloud and a mist
of heavy rain was sweeping up the river. It was
coming fast, and the boy sprang through the
bushes and, followed by Mavis, flew down the
road. The storm caught them, and in a few moments the stranger boy and girl looking through
the front door at the sweeping gusts, saw two
drenched and bedraggled figures slip shyly through
the front gate and around the corner to the back
of the house.

III

THE two little strangers sat in cane-bottomed chairs before the open door, still looking about them with curious eyes at the strings of things hanging from the smoke-browned rafters —beans, red pepper-pods, and twists of home-grown tobacco, the girl's eyes taking in the old spinning-wheel in the corner, the piles of brilliantly figured quilts between the foot-boards of the two beds ranged along one side of the room, and the boy's, catching eagerly the butt of a big revolver projecting from the mantel-piece, a Winchester standing in one corner, a long, old-fashioned squirrel rifle athwart a pair of buck antlers over the front door, and a bunch of cane fishing-poles aslant the wall of the back porch. Presently a slim, drenched figure slipped quietly in, then another, and Mavis stood on one side of the fire-place and little Jason on the other. The two girls exchanged a swift glance and Mavis's eyes fell; abashed, she knotted her hands shyly behind her and with the hollow of one bare foot rubbed the slender arch of the other. The stranger boy looked up at Jason with a pleasant glance of recognition, got for his courtesy a sullen glare that travelled from his broad white collar down to his stockinged legs, and his face flushed; he would have trouble with that mountain boy. Before the fire old Jason Hawn stood, and through a smoke cloud from his corn-cob pipe looked kindly at his two little guests.

"So that's yo' boy an' gal?"

"That's my son Gray," said Colonel Pendleton.

"And that's my cousin Marjorie," said the lad, and Mavis looked quickly to little Jason for recognition of this similar relationship and got no answering glance, for little did he care at that moment of hostility how those two were akin.

"She's my cousin, too," laughed the colonel, "but she always calls me uncle."

Old Jason turned to him.

"Well, we're a purty rough people down here, but you're welcome to all we got."

"I've found that out," laughed Colonel Pendleton pleasantly, "everywhere."

"I wish you both could stay a long time with us," said the old man to the little strangers. "Jason here would take Gray fishin' an' huntin', an' Mavis would git on my old mare an' you two could jus' go flyin' up an' down the road. You could have a mighty good time if hit wasn't too rough fer ye."

"Oh, no," said the boy politely, and the girl said:

"I'd just love to."

The Blue-grass man's attention was caught by the names.

"Jason," he repeated; "why, Jason was a mighty hunter, and Mavis—that means 'the song-thrush.' How in the world did they get those names?"

"Well, my granddaddy was a powerful b'ar-hunter in his day," said the old man, "an' I heerd as how a school-teacher nicknamed him Jason, an' that name come down to me an' him. I've heerd o' Mavis as long as I can rickellect. Hit was my grandmammy's name."

Colonel Pendleton looked at the sturdy mountain lad, his compact figure, square shoulders, well-set head with its shock of hair and bold, steady eyes, and at the slim, wild little creature shrinking against the mantel-piece, and then he turned to his own son Gray and his little cousin Marjorie. Four better types of the Blue-grass and of the mountains it would be hard to find. For a moment he saw them in his mind's eye transposed in dress and environment, and he was surprised at the little change that eye could see, and when he thought of the four living together in these wilds, or at home in the Blue-grass, his wonder at what the result might be almost startled him. The mountain lad had shown no surprise at the talk about him and his cousin, but when the stranger man caught his eye, little Jason's lips opened.

"I knowed all about that," he said **abruptly**.

"About what?"

"Why, that mighty hunter—and Mavis."

"Why, who told you?"

"The jologist."

"The what?"   Old Jason laughed.

"He means ge-ol-o-gist," said the old man, who had no little trouble with the right word himself. "A feller come in here three year ago with a hammer an' went to peckin' aroun' in the rocks here, an' that boy was with him all the time. Thar don't seem to be much the feller didn't tell Jason an' nothin' that Jason don't seem to remember. He's al'ays a-puzzlin' me by comin' out with somethin' or other that rock-pecker tol' him an'—" he stopped, for the boy was shaking his head from side to side.

"Don't you say nothin' agin him, now," he said, and old Jason laughed.

"He's a powerful hand to take up fer his friends, Jason is."

"He was a friend o' all us mountain folks," said the boy stoutly, and then he looked Colonel Pendleton in the face—fearlessly, but with no impertinence.

"He said as how you folks from the big settlemints was a-comin' down here to buy up our wild lands fer nothin' because we all was a lot o' fools an' didn't know how much they was worth, an' that ever'body'd have to move out o' here an' you'd get rich diggin' our coal an' cuttin' our timber an' raisin' hell ginerally."

He did not notice Marjorie's flush, but went on fierily: "He said that our trees caught the rain an' our gullies gethered it together an' troughed it down the mountains an' made the river which would water all yo' lands. That you was a lot o' damn fools cuttin' down yo' trees an' a-plantin' terbaccer an' a-spittin' out yo' birthright in terbaccer-juice, an' that by an' by you'd come up here an' cut down our trees so that there wouldn't be nothin' left to ketch the rain when it fell, so that yo' rivers would git to be cricks an' yo' cricks branches an' yo' land would die o' thirst an' the same thing 'ud happen here. Co'se we'd all be gone when all this tuk place, but he said as how I'd live to see the day when you furriners would be damaged by wash-outs down thar in the settlements an' would be a-pilin' up stacks an' stacks o' gold out o' the lands you robbed me an' my kinfolks out of."

"Shet up," said Arch Hawn sharply, and the boy wheeled on him.

"Yes, an' you air a-helpin' the furriners to rob yo' own kin; you air a-doin' hit yo'self."

"Jason!"

The old man spoke sternly and the boy stopped, flushed and angry, and a moment later slipped from the room.

"Well!" said the colonel, and he laughed good-

21

humoredly to relieve the strain that his host
might feel on his account; but he was amazed
just the same—the bud of a socialist blooming in
those wilds! Arch Hawn's shrewd face looked a
little concerned, for he saw that the old man's
rebuke had been for the discourtesy to strangers,
and from the sudden frown that ridged the old
man's brow, that the boy's words had gone deep
enough to stir distrust, and this was a poor start
in the fulfilment of the purpose he had in view.
He would have liked to give the boy a cuff on the
ear. As for Mavis, she was almost frightened by
the outburst of her playmate, and Marjorie was
horrified by his profanity; but the dawning of
something in Gray's brain worried him, and presently he, too, rose and went to the back porch.
The rain had stopped, the wet earth was fragrant
with freshened odors, wood-thrushes were singing,
and the upper air was drenched with liquid gold
that was darkening fast. The boy Jason was
seated on the yard fence with his chin in his hands,
his back to the house, and his face toward home.
He heard the stranger's step, turned his head, and
mistaking a puzzled sympathy for a challenge,
dropped to the ground and came toward him,
gathering fury as he came. Like lightning the
Blue-grass lad's face changed, whitening a little as
he sprang forward to meet him, but Jason, mo-
tioning with his thumb, swerved behind the chimney, where the stranger swiftly threw off his coat,

the mountain boy spat on his hands, and like two diminutive demons they went at each other fiercely and silently. A few minutes later the two little girls rounding the chimney corner saw them—Gray on top and Jason writhing and biting under him like a tortured snake. A moment more Mavis's strong little hand had the stranger boy by his thick hair and Mavis, feeling her own arm clutched by the stranger-girl, let go and turned on her like a fury. There was a piercing scream from Marjorie, hurried footsteps answered on the porch, and old Jason and the colonel looked with bewildered eyes on the little Blue-grass girl amazed, indignant, white with horror; Mavis shrinking away from her as though she were the one who had been threatened with a blow; the stranger lad with a bitten thumb clinched in the hollow of one hand, his face already reddening with contrition and shame; and savage little Jason biting a bloody lip and with the lust of battle still shaking him from head to foot.

"Jason," said the old man sternly, "whut's the matter out hyeh?"

Marjorie pointed one finger at Mavis, started to speak, and stopped. Jason's eyes fell.

"Nothin'," he said sullenly, and Colonel Pendleton looked to his son with astonished inquiry, and the lad's fine face turned bewildered and foolish.

"I don't know, sir," he said at last.

23

"Don't know?" echoed the colonel. "Well——"

The old man broke in:

"Jason, if you have lost yo' manners an' don't know how to behave when thar's strangers around, I reckon you'd better go on home."

The boy did not lift his eyes.

"I was a-goin' home anyhow," he said, still sullen, and he turned.

"Oh, no!" said the colonel quickly; "this won't do. Come now—you two boys shake hands."

At once the stranger lad walked forward to his enemy, and confused Jason gave him a limp hand. The old man laughed. "Come on in, Jason— you an' Mavis—an' stay to supper."

The boy shook his head.

"I got to be gittin' back home," he said, and without a word more he turned again. Marjorie looked toward the little girl, but she, too, was starting.

"I better be gittin' back too," she said shyly, and off she ran. Old Jason laughed again.

"Jes' like two young roosters out thar in my barnyard," and he turned with the colonel toward the house. But Marjorie and her cousin stood in the porch and watched the two little mountaineers until, without once looking back, they passed over the sunlit hill.

IV

ON they trudged, the boy plodding sturdily ahead, the little girl slipping mountain-fashion behind. Not once did she come abreast with him, and not one word did either say, but the mind and heart of both were busy. All the way the frown overcasting the boy's face stayed like a shadow, for he had left trouble at home, he had met trouble, and to trouble he was going back. The old was definite enough and he knew how to handle it, but the new bothered him sorely. That stranger boy was a fighter, and Jason's honest soul told him that if interference had not come he would have been whipped, and his pride was still smarting with every step. The new boy had not tried to bite, or gouge, or to hit him when he was on top—facts that puzzled the mountain boy; he hadn't whimpered and he hadn't blabbed—not even the insult Jason had hurled with eye and tongue at his girl-clad legs. He had said that he didn't know what they were fighting about, and just why they were Jason himself couldn't quite make out now; but he knew that even now, in spite of the hand-shaking truce, he would at the snap of a finger go at the stranger again. And little Mavis knew now that it was not fear that made the stranger girl scream—and she, too, was puzzled. She even felt that the scorn in Marjorie's face was not personal, but she had shrunk from it as from the sudden lash of a whip. The stranger girl, too, had not blabbed but had even seemed to smile her forgiveness when Mavis turned, with no good-by, to follow Jason. Hand in hand the two little mountaineers had crossed the threshold of a new world that day. Together they were going back into their own, but the clutch of the new was tight on both, and while neither could have explained, there was the same thought in each mind, the same nameless dissatisfaction in each heart, and both were in the throes of the same new birth.

The sun was sinking when they started up the spur, and unconsciously Jason hurried his steps and the girl followed hard. The twin spirals of smoke were visible now, and where the path forked the boy stopped and turned, jerking his thumb toward her cabin and his.

"Ef anything happens"—he paused, and the girl nodded her understanding—"you an' me air goin' to stay hyeh in the mountains an' git married."

"Yes, Jasie," she said.

His tone was matter-of-fact and so was hers, nor did she show any surprise at the suddenness of what he said, and Jason, not looking at her, failed to see a faint flush come to her cheek. He turned to go, but she stood still, looking down into the gloomy, darkening ravine below her. A bear's tracks had been found in that ravine only the day before. "Air ye afeerd?" he asked tolerantly, and she nodded mutely.

"I'll take ye down," he said with sudden gentleness.

The tall mountaineer was standing on the porch of the cabin, and with assurance and dignity Jason strode ahead with a protecting air to the gate.

"Whar you two been?" he called sharply.

"I went fishin'," said the boy unperturbed, "an' tuk Mavis with me."

"You air gittin' a leetle too peart, boy. I don't want that gal a-runnin' around in the woods all day."

Jason met his angry eyes with a new spirit.

"I reckon you hain't been hyeh long."

The shot went home and the mountaineer glared helpless for an answer.

"Come on in hyeh an' git supper," he called harshly to the girl, and as the boy went back up the spur, he could hear the scolding going on below, with no answer from Mavis, and he made up his mind to put an end to that some day himself. He knew what was waiting for him on the other side of the spur, and when he reached the top, he sat down for a moment on a long-fallen, moss-grown log. Above him beetled the top of his world. His great blue misty hills washed their

turbulent waves to the yellow shore of the dropping sun. Those waves of forests primeval were
his, and the green spray of them was tossed into
cloudland to catch the blessed rain. In every
little fold of them drops were trickling down now
to water the earth and give back the sea its own.
The dreamy-eyed man of science had told him
that. And it was unchanged, all unchanged since
wild beasts were the only tenants, since wild Indians slipped through the wilderness aisles, since
the half-wild white man, hot on the chase, planted
his feet in the footsteps of both and inexorably
pushed them on. The boy's first Kentucky ancestor had been one of those who had stopped in
the hills. His rifle had fed him and his family;
his axe had put a roof over their heads, and the
loom and spinning-wheel had clothed their bodies.
Day by day they had fought back the wilderness,
had husbanded the soil, and as far as his eagle
eye could reach, that first Hawn had claimed
mountain, river, and tree for his own, and there
was none to dispute the claim for the passing of
half a century. Now those who had passed on
were coming back again—the first trespasser long,
long ago with a yellow document that he called
a "blanket-patent" and which was all but the
bringer's funeral shroud, for the old hunter started
at once for his gun and the stranger with his patent took to flight. Years later a band of young
men with chain and compass had appeared in the

hills and disappeared as suddenly, and later still another band, running a line for a railroad up the river, found old Jason at the foot of a certain oak with his rifle in the hollow of his arm and marking a dead-line which none dared to cross.

Later still, when he understood, the old man let them pass, but so far nobody had surveyed his land, and now, instead of trying to take, they were trying to purchase. From all points of the compass the "furriners" were coming now, the rock-pecker's prophecy was falling true, and at that moment the boy's hot words were having an effect on every soul who had heard them. Old Jason's suspicions were alive again; he was short of speech when his nephew, Arch Hawn, brought up the sale of his lands, and Arch warned the colonel to drop the subject for the night. The colonel's mind had gone back to a beautiful woodland at home that he thought of clearing off for tobacco—he would put that desecration off a while. The stranger boy, too, was wondering vaguely at the fierce arraignment he had heard; the stranger girl was curiously haunted by memories of the queer little mountaineer, while Mavis now had a new awe of her cousin that was but another rod with which he could go on ruling her.

Jason's mother was standing in the door when he walked through the yard gate. She went back into the cabin when she saw him coming, and met him at the door with a switch in her hand. Very coolly the lad caught it from her, broke it in two, threw it away, and picking up a piggin went out without a word to milk, leaving her aghast and outdone. When he came back, he asked like a man if supper was ready, and as to a man she answered. For an hour he pottered around the barn, and for a long while he sat on the porch under the stars. And, as always at that hour, the same scene obsessed his memory, when the last glance of his father's eye and the last words of his father's tongue went not to his wife, but to the white-faced little son across the foot of the death-bed:

"You'll git him fer me—some day."

"I'll git him, pap."

Those were the words that passed, and in them was neither the asking nor the giving of a promise, but a simple statement and a simple acceptance of a simple trust, and the father passed with a grim smile of content. Like every Hawn the boy believed that a Honeycutt was the assassin, and in the solemn little fellow one purpose hitherto had been supreme—to discover the man and avenge the deed; and though, young as he was, he was yet too cunning to let the fact be known, there was no male of the name old enough to pull the trigger, not even his mother's brother, Babe, who did not fall under the ban of the boy's deathless hate and suspicion. And always his mother, though herself a Honeycutt, had steadily fed his purpose, but for a long while now she had kept disloyally still, and the boy had bitterly learned the reason.

It was bedtime now, and little Jason rose and went within. As he climbed the steps leading to his loft, he spoke at last, nodding his head toward the cabin over the spur:

"I reckon I know whut you two air up to, and, furdermore, you air aimin' to sell this land. I can't keep you from doin' it, I reckon, but I do ax you not to sell without lettin' me know. I know somep'n' 'bout it that nobody else knows. An' if you don't tell me——" he shook his head slowly, and the mother looked at her boy as though she were dazed by some spell.

"I'll tell ye, Jasie," she said.

V

DOWN the river road loped Arch Hawn the next morning, his square chin low with thought, his shrewd eyes almost closed, and his straight lips closed hard on the cane stem of an unlighted pipe. Of all the Hawns he had been born the poorest in goods and chattels and the richest in shrewd resource, restless energy, and keen foresight. He had gone to the settlements when he was a lad, he had always been coming and going ever since, and the word was that he had been to far-away cities in the outer world that were as unfamiliar to his fellows and kindred as the Holy Land. He had worked as teamster and had bought and sold anything to anybody right and left. Resolutely he had kept himself from all part in the feud—his kinship with the Hawns protecting him on one side and the many trades with old Aaron Honeycutt in cattle and lands saving him from trouble on the other. He carried no tales from one faction to the other, condemned neither one nor the other, and made the same comment to both—that it was foolish to fight when there was so much else so much more profitable to do. Once an armed band of mounted Honeycutts had met him in the road and demanded news of a similar band of Hawns up a creek. "Did you ever hear o' my tellin' the Hawns anything about you Honeycutts?" he asked quietly, and old Aaron had to shake his head.

"Well, if I tol' you anything about them to-day, don't you know I'd be tellin' them something about you to-morrow?"

Old Aaron scratched his head.

"By Gawd, boys—that's so. Let him pass!"

Thus it was that only Arch Hawn could have brought about an agreement that was the ninth wonder of the mountain world, and was no less than a temporary truce in the feud between old Aaron Honeycutt and old Jason Hawn until the land deal in which both leaders shared a heavy interest could come to a consummation. Arch had interested Colonel Pendleton in his "wild lands" at a horse sale in the Blue-grass. The mountaineer's shrewd knowledge of horses had caught the attention of the colonel, his drawling speech, odd phrasing, and quaint humor had amused the Blue-grass man, and his exposition of the wealth of the hills and the vast holdings that he had in the hollow of his hand, through options far and wide, had done the rest—for the matter was timely to the colonel's needs and to his accidental hour of opportunity. Only a short while before old Morton Sanders, an Eastern capitalist of Kentucky birth, had been making inquiry

33

of him that the mountaineer's talk answered precisely, and soon the colonel found himself an intermediary between buried coal and open millions, and such a quick unlooked-for chance of exchange made Arch Hawn's brain reel. Only a few days before the colonel started for the mountains, Babe Honeycutt had broken the truce by shooting Shade Hawn, but as Shade was going to get well, Arch's oily tongue had licked the wound to the pride of every Honeycutt except Shade, and he calculated that the latter would be so long in bed that his interference would never count. But things were going wrong. Arch had had a hard time with old Jason the night before. Again he had to go over the same weary argument that he had so often travelled before: the mountain people could do nothing with the mineral wealth of their hills; the coal was of no value to them where it was; they could not dig it, they had no market for it; and they could never get it into the markets of the outside world. It was the boy's talk that had halted the old man, and to Arch's amazement the colonel's sense of fairness seemed to have been touched and his enthusiasm seemed to have waned a little. That morning, too, Arch had heard that Shade Hawn was getting well a little too fast, and he was on his way to see about it. Shade was getting well fast, and with troubled eyes Arch saw him sitting up in a chair and cleaning his Winchester.

"What's yo' hurry?"

"I ain't never agreed to no truce," said Shade truculently.

"Don't you think you might save a little time —waitin' fer Babe to git tame? He's hidin' out. You can't find him now."

"I can look fer him."

"Shade!"—wily Arch purposely spoke loud enough for Shade's wife to hear, and he saw her thin, worn, shrewish face turn eagerly—"I'll give ye just fifty dollars to stay here in the house an' git well fer two more weeks. You know why, an' you know hit's wuth it to me. What you say?"

Shade rubbed his stubbled chin ruminatively and his wife Mandy broke in sharply:

"Take it, you fool!"

Apparently Shade paid no heed to the advice nor the epithet, which was not meant to be offensive, but he knew that Mandy wanted a cow of just that price and a cow she would have; while he needed cartridges and other little "fixin's," and he owed for moonshine up a certain creek, and wanted more just then and badly. But mental calculation was laborious and he made a plunge:

"Not a cent less'n seventy-five, an' I ain't goin' to argue with ye."

Arch scowled.

"Split the difference!" he commanded.

"All right."

A few minutes later Arch was loping back up the river road. Within an hour he had won old Jason to a non-committal silence and straightway volunteered to show the colonel the outcroppings of his coal. And old Jason mounted his sorrel mare and rode with the party up the creek.

It was Sunday and a holiday for little Jason from toil in the rocky corn-field. He was stirring busily before the break of dawn. While the light was still gray, he had milked, cut wood for his mother, and eaten his breakfast of greasy bacon and corn-bread. On that day it had been his habit for months to disappear early, come back for his dinner, slip quietly away again and return worn out and tired at milking-time. Invariably for a long time his mother had asked:

"Whut you been a-doin', Jason?" And invariably his answer was:

"Nothin' much."

But, by and by, as the long dark mountaineer, Steve Hawn, got in the daily habit of swinging over the ridge, she was glad to be free from the boy's sullen watchfulness, and particularly that morning she was glad to see him start as usual up the path his own feet had worn through the steep field of corn, and disappear in the edge of the woods. She would have a long day for courtship and for talk of plans which she was keeping secret from little Jason. She was a Honeycutt and she had married one Hawn, and there had been much trouble. Now she was going to marry another of the tribe, there would be more trouble, and Steve Hawn over the ridge meant to evade it by straightway putting forth from those hills. Hurriedly she washed the dishes, tidied up her poor shack of a home, and within an hour she was seated in the porch, in her best dress, with her knitting in her lap and, even that early, lifting expectant and shining eyes now and then to the tree-crowned crest of the ridge.

Up little Jason went through breaking mist and flashing dew. A wood-thrush sang, and he knew the song came from the bird of which little Mavis was the human counterpart. Woodpeckers were hammering and, when a crested cock of the woods took billowy flight across a blue ravine, he knew him for a big cousin of the little red-heads, just as Mavis was a little cousin of his. Once he had known birds only by sight, but now he knew every calling, twittering, winging soul of them by name. Once he used to draw bead on one and all heartlessly and indiscriminately with his old rifle, but now only the whistle of a bob-white, the darting of a hawk, or the whir of a pheasant's wings made him whirl the old weapon from his shoulder. He knew flower, plant, bush, and weed, the bark and leaf of every tree, and even in winter he could pick them out in the gray etch-

ing of a mountain-side—dog-wood, red-bud, "sar-
vice" berry, hickory, and walnut, the oaks—white,
black, and chestnut—the majestic poplar, prized
by the outer world, and the black-gum that defied
the lightning. All this the dreamy stranger had
taught him, and much more. And nobody, native born to those hills, except his uncle Arch,
knew as much about their hidden treasures as
little Jason. He had trailed after the man of science along the benches of the mountains where
coal beds lie. With him he had sought the roots
of upturned trees and the beds of little creeks
and the gray faces of "rock-houses" for signs of
the black diamonds. He had learned to watch
the beds of little creeks for the shining tell-tale
black bits, and even the tiny mouths of crawfish
holes, on the lips of which they sometimes lay.
And the biggest treasure in the hills little Jason had
found himself; for only on the last day before the
rock-pecker had gone away, the two had found
signs of another vein, and the geologist had given
his own pick to the boy and told him to dig, while
he was gone, for himself. And Jason had dug.
He was slipping now up the tiny branch, and
where the stream trickled down the face of a
water-worn perpendicular rock the boy stopped,
leaned his rifle against a tree, and stepped aside
into the bushes. A moment later he reappeared
with a small pick in his hand, climbed up over a
mound of loose rocks and loose earth, ten feet

around the rock, and entered the narrow mouth
of a deep, freshly dug ditch. Ten feet farther
on he was halted by a tall black column solidly
wedged in the narrow passage, at the base of
which was a bench of yellow dirt extending not
more than two feet from the foot of the column
and above the floor of the ditch. There had been
mighty operations going on in that secret passage; the toil for one boy and one tool had been
prodigious and his work was not yet quite done.
Lifting the pick above his head, the boy sank it
into that yellow pedestal with savage energy,
raking the loose earth behind him with hands and
feet. The sunlight caught the top of the black
column above his head and dropped shining inch
by inch, but on he worked tirelessly. The yellow
bench disappeared and the heap of dirt behind
him was piled high as his head, but the black
column bored on downward as though bound for
the very bowels of the earth, and only when the
bench vanished to the level of the ditch's floor
did the lad send his pick deep into a new layer
and lean back to rest even for a moment. A few
deep breaths, the brushing of one forearm and
then the other across his forehead and cheeks,
and again he grasped the tool. This time it came
out hard, bringing out with its point particles of
grayish-black earth, and the boy gave a low, shrill
yell. It was a bed of clay that he had struck—
the bed on which, as the geologist had told him,
the massive layers of coal had slept so long. In

a few minutes he had skimmed a yellow inch or two more to the dingy floor of the clay bed, and had driven his pick under the very edge of the black bulk towering above him.

His work was done, and no buccaneer ever gloated more over hidden treasure than Jason over the prize discovered by him and known of nobody else in the world. He raised his head and looked up the shimmering black face of his find. He took up his pick again and notched foot-holes in each side of the yellow ditch. He marked his own height on the face of the column, and, climbing up along it, measured his full length again, and yet with outstretched arm he could barely touch the top of the vein with the tips of his fingers. No vein half that thick had the rock-pecker with all his searching found, and the lad gave a long, low whistle of happy amazement. A moment later he dropped his pick, climbed over the pile of new dirt, emerged at the mouth of the passage, and sat down as if on guard in the grateful coolness of the little ravine. Drawing one long breath, he looked proudly back once more and began shaking his head wisely. They couldn't fool him. He knew what that mighty vein of coal was worth. Other people—fools—might sell their land for a dollar or two an acre, even old Jason, his grandfather, but not the Jason Hawn who had dug that black giant out of the side of the mountain.

"Go away, boy," the rock-pecker had said.

"Get an education. Leave this farm alone—it won't run away. By the time you are twenty-one, an acre of it will be worth as much as all of it is now."

No, they couldn't fool him. He would keep his find a secret from every soul on earth—even from his grandfather and Mavis, both of whom he had already been tempted to tell. He rose to his feet with the resolution and crouched suddenly, listening hard. Something was coming swiftly toward him through the undergrowth on the other side of the creek, and he reached stealthily for his rifle, sank behind the bowlder with his thumb on the hammer just as the bushes parted on the opposite cliff, and Mavis stood above him, peering for him and calling his name in an excited whisper. He rose glowering and angry.

"Whut you doin' up here?" he asked roughly, and the girl shrank, and her message stopped at her lips.

"They're comin' up here," she faltered.

The boy's eyes accused her mercilessly and he seemed not to hear her.

"You've been spyin'!"

The dignity of his manhood was outraged, and humbly and helplessly she nodded in utter abasement, faltering again:

"They're comin' up here!"

"Who's comin' up here?"

"Them strangers an' grandpap an' Uncle Arch —an' another rock-pecker."

"Did you tell 'em?"

The girl crossed her heart and body swiftly.

"I hain't told a soul," she gasped. "I come up to tell *you*."

"When they comin'?"

The sound of voices below answered for her. The boy wheeled, alert as a wild-cat, the girl slid noiselessly down the cliff and crept noiselessly after him down the bed of the creek, until they could both peer through the bushes down on the next bend of the stream below. There they were—all of them, and down there they had halted.

"Ain't no use goin' up any furder," said the voice of Arch Hawn; "I've looked all up this crick an' thar ain't nary a blessed sign o' coal."

"All right," said the colonel, who was puffing with the climb. "That suits me—I've had enough."

At Jason's side, Mavis echoed his own swift breath of relief, but as the party turned, the rock-pecker stooped and rose with a black lump in his hand.

"Hello!" he said, "where did this come from?"

The boy's heart began to throb, for once he had started to carry that very lump to his grandfather, had changed his mind, and thoughtlessly dropped it there. The geologist was looking at it closely and then began to weigh it with his hand.

"This is pretty good-looking coal," he said, and he laughed. "I guess we'd better go up a little farther—this didn't come out all by itself."

42

The boy dug Mavis sharply in the shoulder.

"Git back into the bushes—quick!" he whispered.

The girl shrank away and the boy dropped down into the bed of the creek and slipped down to where the stream poured between two bowlders over which ascent was slippery and difficult. And when the party turned up the bend of the creek, Arch Hawn saw the boy, tense and erect, on the wet black summit of one bowlder, with his old rifle in the hollow of his arm.

"Why, hello, Jason!" he cried, with a start of surprise; "found anything to shoot?"

"Not yit!" said Jason shortly.

The geologist stepped around Arch and started to climb toward the foot of the bowlder.

"You stop thar!"

The ring of the boy's fiery command stopped the man as though a rattlesnake had given the order at his very feet, and he looked up bewildered; but the boy had not moved.

"Whut you mean, boy?" shouted Arch. "We're lookin' for a vein o' coal."

"Well, you hain't a-goin' to find hit up this way."

"Whut you want to keep us from goin' up here fer?" asked the uncle with sarcastic suspicion. "Got a still up here?"

"That's my business," said little Jason.

"Well," shouted Arch angrily again, "this ain't

43

yo' land an' I've got a option on it an' hit's my business to go up here, an' I'm goin'!"

As he pushed ahead of the geologist the boy flashed his old rifle to his shoulder.

"I'll let ye come just two steps more," he said quietly, and old Jason Hawn began to grin and stepped aside as though to get out of range.

"Hol' on thar, Arch," he said; "he'll shoot, shore!" And Arch held on, bursting with rage and glaring up at the boy.

"I've a notion to git me a switch an' whoop the life out o' you." The boy laughed derisively.

"My whoopin' days air over." The amazed and amused geologist put his hand on Arch's shoulder.

"Never mind," he said, and with a significant wink he pulled a barometer out of his pocket and carefully noted the altitude.

"We'll manage it later."

The party turned, old Jason still smiling grimly, the colonel chuckling, the geologist busy with speculation, and Arch sore and angry, but wondering what on earth it was that the boy had found up that ravine. Presently with the geologist he dropped behind the other two and the latter's frowning brow cleared into a smile at his lips. He stopped, looking still at the black lump and weighing it once more in his hand.

"I think I know this coal," he said in a low voice, "and if I'm right you've got the best and

44

thickest vein of coking coal in these mountains. It's the Culloden seam. Nobody ever has found it on this side of the mountain, and it is supposed to have petered out on the way through. That boy has found the Culloden seam. The altitude is right, the coal looks and weighs like it, and we can find it somewhere else under that bench along the mountain. So you better let the boy alone."

Little Jason stood motionless looking after them. Little Mavis crept from her hiding-place. Her face showed no pride in Jason's triumph and few traces of excitement, for she was already schooled to the quiet acquiescence of mountain women in the rough deeds of the men. She had seen Jason going up that ravine, she could simply not help going herself to learn why, she was mystified by what he had done up there, but she had kept his secret faithfully. Now she was beginning to understand that the matter was serious, and for that reason the boy's charge of spying lay heavier on her mind. So she came slowly and shyly and stood behind him, her eyes dark with penitence.

The boy heard her, but he did not turn around.

"You better go home, Mavie," he said, and at his very tone her face flashed with joy. "They mought come back agin. I'm goin' to stay up here till dark. They can't see nothin' then."

There was not a word of rebuke for her; it was his secret and hers now, and pride and gratitude filled her heart and her eyes.

"All right, Jasie," she said obediently, and down the bowlder she stepped lightly, and slipping down the bed of the creek, disappeared. And not once did she look around.

The shadows lengthened, the ravines filled with misty blue, the steep westward spur threw its bulky shadow on the sunlit flank of the opposite hill, and the lonely spirit of night came with the gloom that gathered fast about him in the defile where he lay. A slow wind was blowing up from the river toward him, and on it came faintly the long mellow blast of a horn. It was no hunter's call, and he sprang to his feet. Again the winding came and his tense muscles relaxed—nor was it a warning that "revenues" were coming—and he sank back to his lonely useless vigil again. The sun dipped, the sky darkened, the black wings of the night rushed upward and downward and from all around the horizon, but only when they were locked above him did he slip like a creature of the gloom down the bed of the stream.

VI

THE cabin was unlighted when Jason came in sight of it and apprehension straightway seized him; so that he broke into a run, but stopped at the gate and crept slowly to the porch and almost on tiptoe opened the door. The fire was low, but the look of things was unchanged, and on the kitchen table he saw his cold supper laid for him. His mother had maybe gone over the ridge for some reason to stay all night, so he gobbled his food hastily and, still uneasy, put forth for Mavis's cabin over the hill. That cabin, too, was dark and deserted, and he knew now what had happened—that blast of the horn was a summons to a dance somewhere, and his mother and Steve had answered and taken Mavis with them; so the boy sat down on the porch, alone with the night and the big still dark shapes around him. It would not be very pleasant for him to follow them—people would tease him and ask him troublesome questions. But where was the dance, and had they gone to it after all? He rose and went swiftly down the creek. At the mouth of it a light shone through the darkness, and from it a quavering hymn trembled on the still air. A moment later Jason stood on the threshold of an open door and an old couple at the fireplace lifted welcoming eyes.

"Uncle Lige, do you know whar my mammy is?"

The old man's eyes took on a troubled look, but the old woman answered readily:

"Why, I seed her an' Steve Hawn an' Mavis a-goin' down the crick jest afore dark, an' yo' mammy said as how they was aimin' to go to yo' grandpap's."

It was his grandfather's horn, then, Jason had heard. The lad turned to go, and the old circuit rider rose to his full height.

"Come in, boy. Yo' grandpap had better be a-thinkin' about spreadin' the wings of his immortal sperit, stid o' shakin' them feet o' clay o' his'n an' a-settin' a bad example to the young an' errin'!"

"Hush up!" said the old woman. "The Bible don't say nothin' agin a boy lookin' fer his mammy, no matter whar she is."

She spoke sharply, for Steve Hawn had called her husband out to the gate, where the two had talked in whispers, and the old man had refused flatly to tell her what the talk was about. But Jason had turned without a word and was gone. Out in the darkness of the road he stood for a moment undecided whether or not he should go back to his lonely home, and some vague foreboding started him swiftly on down the creek. On top of a little hill he could see the light in his

48

grandfather's house, and that far away he could
hear the rollicking tune of "Sourwood Mountain."
The sounds of dancing feet soon came to his ears,
and from those sounds he could tell the figures
of the dance just as he could tell the gait of an
unseen horse thumping a hard dirt road. He
leaned over the yard fence—looking, listening,
thinking. Through the window he could see the
fiddler with his fiddle pressed almost against his
heart, his eyes closed, his horny fingers thumping the strings like trip-hammers, and his melan-
choly calls ringing high above the din of shuffling feet. His grandfather was standing before
the fireplace, his grizzled hair tousled and his face
red with something more than the spirits of the
dance. The colonel was doing the "grand right
and left," and his mother was the colonel's partner—the colonel as gallant as though he were
leading mazes with a queen and his mother sim-
pering and blushing like a girl. In one corner
sat Steve Hawn, scowling like a storm-cloud, and
on one bed sat Marjorie and the boy Gray watching the couple and apparently shrieking with
laughter; and Jason wondered what they could
be laughing about. Little Mavis was not in sight.
When the dance closed he could see the colonel
go over to the little strangers and, seizing each by
the hand, try to pull them from the bed into the
middle of the floor. Finally they came, and the
boy, looking through the window, and Mavis,

who suddenly appeared in the door leading to the porch, saw a strange sight. Gray took Marjorie's right hand with his left and put his right arm around her waist and then to the stirring strains of "Soapsuds Over the Fence" they whirled about the room as lightly as two feathers in an eddy of air. It was a two-step and the first round dance ever seen in these hills, and the mountaineers took it silently, grimly, and with little sign of favor or disapproval, except from old Jason, who, looking around for Mavis, caught sight of little Jason's wondering face over her shoulder, for the boy had left the blurred window-pane and hurried around to the back door for a better view. With a whoop the old man reached for the little girl, and gathered in the boy with his other hand.

"Hyeh!" he cried, "you two just git out thar an' shake a foot!"

Little Mavis hung back, but the boy bounded into the middle of the floor and started into a furious jig, his legs as loose from the hip as a jumping-jack and the soles and heels of his rough brogans thumping out every note of the music with astonishing precision and rapidity. He hardly noticed Mavis at first, and then he began to dance toward her, his eyes flashing and fixed on hers and his black locks tumbling about his forehead as though in an electric storm. The master was calling and the maid answered—shyly at first, coquettishly by and by, and then, for-

getting self and onlookers, with a fiery abandon
that transformed her. Alternately he advanced
and she retreated, and when, with a scornful toss
of that night-black head, the boy jigged away,
she would relent and lure him back, only to send
him on his way again. Sometimes they were
back to back and the colonel saw that always
then the girl was first to turn, but if the lad
turned first, the girl whirled as though she were
answering the dominant spirit of his eyes even
through the back of her head, and, looking over
to the bed, he saw his own little kinswoman
answering that same masterful spirit in a way
that seemed hardly less hypnotic. Even Gray's
clear eyes, fixed at first on the little mountain
girl, had turned to Jason, but they were undaunted
and smiling, and when Jason, seeing Steve's face
at the window and his mother edging out through
the front door, seemed to hesitate in his dance,
and Mavis, thinking he was about to stop, turned
panting away from him, Gray sprang from the
bed like a challenging young buck and lit facing
the mountain boy and in the midst of a double-
shuffle that the amazed colonel had never seen
outdone by any darkey on his farm.

"Jenny with a ruff-duff a-kickin' up the dust,"
clicked his feet.

> "Juba this and Juba that!
> Juba killed a yaller cat!
> Juba! Juba!"

"Whoop!" yelled old Jason, bending his huge
body and patting his leg and knee to the beat of
one big cowhide boot and urging them on in a
frenzy of delight:

"Come on, Jason! Git atter him, stranger!
Whoop her up thar with that fiddle—Heh—ee—
dum dee—eede-eedle—dedee-dee!"

Then there was dancing. The fiddler woke like
a battery newly charged, every face lighted with
freshened interest, and only the colonel and Marjorie showed surprise and mystification. The
double-shuffle was hardly included in the curricu-
lum of the colonel's training school for a gentleman, and where, when, and how the boy had
learned such Ethiopian skill, neither he nor Marjorie knew. But he had it and they enjoyed it
to the full. Gray's face wore a merry smile, and
Jason, though he was breathing hard and his
black hair was plastered to his wet forehead,
faced his new competitor with rallying feet but
a sullen face. "The Forked Deer," "Big Sewell
Mountain," and "Cattle Licking Salt" for Jason,
and the back-step, double-shuffle, and "Jim
Crow" for Gray; both improvising their own
steps when the fiddler raised his voice in "Comin'
up, Sandy," "Chicken in the Dough-Tray," and
"Sparrows on the Ash-Bank"; and thus they
went through all the steps known to the negro or
the mountaineer, until the colonel saw that game
little Jason, though winded, would go on till he

dropped, and gave Gray a sign that the boy's generous soul caught like a flash; for, as though worn out himself, he threw up his hands with a laugh and left the floor to Jason. Just then there was the crack of a Winchester from the darkness outside. Simultaneously, as far as the ear could detect, there was a sharp rap on a window-pane, as a bullet sped cleanly through, and in front of the fire old Jason's mighty head sagged suddenly and he crumbled into a heap on the floor. Arch Hawn had carried his business deal through. The truce was over and the feud was on again.

VII

KNOWING but little of his brother in the
hills, the man from the lowland Blue-grass
was puzzled and amazed that all feeling he could
observe was directed solely at the deed itself and
not at the way it was done. No indignation was
expressed at what was to him the contemptible
cowardice involved—indeed little was said at all,
but the colonel could feel the air tense and lowering with a silent deadly spirit of revenge, and
he would have been more puzzled had he known
the indifference on the part of the Hawns as
to whether the act of revenge should take precisely the same form of ambush. For had the
mountain code of ethics been explained to him
—that what was fair for one was fair for the
other; that the brave man could not fight the
coward who shot from the brush and must, there-
fore, adopt the coward's methods; that thus the
method of ambush had been sanctioned by long
custom—he still could never have understood how
a big, burly, kind-hearted man like Jason Hawn
could have been brought even to tolerance of ambush by environment, public sentiment, private
policy, custom, or any other influence that moulds
the character of men.

Old Jason would easily get well—the colonel himself was surgeon enough to know that—and he himself dressed and bandaged the ragged wound that the big bullet had made through one of the old man's mighty shoulders. At his elbow all the time, helping, stood little Jason, and not once did the boy speak, nor did the line of his clenched lips alter, nor did the deadly look in his smouldering eyes change. One by one the guests left, the colonel sent Marjorie and Gray to bed, grandmother Hawn sent Mavis, and when all was done and the old man was breathing heavily on a bed in the corner and grandmother Hawn was seated by the fire with a handkerchief to her lips, the colonel heard the back door open and little Jason, too, was gone—gone on business of his own. He had seen Steve Hawn's face at the window, his mother had slipped out on the porch while he was dancing, and neither had appeared again. So little Jason went swiftly through the dark, over the ridge and up the big creek to the old circuit rider's house, where the stream forked. All the way he had seen the tracks of a horse which he knew to be Steve's, for the right forefoot, he knew, had cast a shoe only the day before.

At the forks the tracks turned up the branch that led to Steve's cabin and not up toward his mother's house. If Steve had his mother behind him, he had taken her to his own home; that, in

Mavis's absence, was not right, and, burning with sudden rage, the boy hurried up the branch. The cabin was dark and at the gate he gave a shrill, imperative "Hello!"

In a few minutes the door opened and the tousled head of his cousin was thrust forth.

"Is my mammy hyeh?" he called hotly.

"Yep," drawled Steve.

"Well, tell her I'm hyeh to take her home!" There was no sound from within.

"Well, she ain't goin' home," Steve drawled.

The boy went sick and speechless with fury, but before he could get his breath Steve drawled again:

"She's goin' to live here now—we got married to-night." The boy dropped helplessly against the gate at these astounding words and his silence stirred Steve to kindness.

"Now, don't take it so hard, Jason. Come on in, boy, an' stay all night."

Still the lad was silent and another face appeared at the door.

"Come on in, Jasie."

It was his mother's voice and the tone was pleading, but the boy, with no answer, turned, and they heard his stumbling steps as he made his way along the fence and started over the spur. Behind him his mother began to sob and with rough kindness Steve soothed her and closed the door.

Slowly little Jason climbed the spur and dropped on the old log on which he had so often sat—fighting out the trouble which he had so long feared must come. The moon and the stars in her wake were sinking and the night was very still. His reason told him his mother was her own mistress, and had the right to marry when she pleased and whom she pleased, but she was a Honeycutt, again she had married a Hawn, and the feud was starting again. Steve Hawn would be under suspicion as his own father had been, Steve would probably have to live on the Honeycutt side of the ridge, and Jason's own earlier days of shame he must go through again. That was his first thought, but his second was a quick oath to himself that he would not go through them again. He was big enough to handle a Winchester now, and he would leave his mother and he would fight openly with the Hawns. And then as he went slowly down the spur he began to wonder with fresh suspicion what his mother and Steve might now do, what influence Steve might have over her, and if he might not now encourage her to sell her land. And, if that happened, what would become of him? The old hound in the porch heard him coming and began to bay at him fiercely, but when he opened the gate the dog bounded to him whining with joy and trying to lick his hands. He dropped on the porch and the loneliness of it all clutched his heart so that he had to gulp back a sob in his throat and blink his eyes to keep back the tears. But it was not until he went inside finally and threw himself with his clothes on across his mother's empty bed that he lost all control and sobbed himself to sleep. When he awoke it was not only broad daylight, but the sun was an hour high and streaming through the mud-chinked crevices of the cabin. In his whole life he had never slept so long after daybreak and he sprang up in bed with bewildered eyes, trying to make out where he was and why he was there. The realization struck him with fresh pain, and when he slowly climbed out of the bed the old hound was whining at the door. When he opened it the fresh wind striking his warm body aroused him sharply. He wondered why his mother had not already been over for her things. The chickens were clustered expectantly at the corner of the house, the calf was bawling at the corner of the fence, and the old cow was waiting patiently at the gate. He turned quickly to the kitchen and to a breakfast on the scraps of his last night's supper. He did not know how to make coffee, and for the first time in his life he went without it. Within an hour the cow was milked and fed, bread crumbs were scattered to the chickens, and alone in the lonely cabin he faced the new conditions of his life. He started toward the gate, not knowing where he should go. He drifted aimlessly down the creek and he began to wonder about Mavis, whether she had got home and now knew what had happened and what she thought about it all, and about his grandfather and who it was that had shot him. There were many things that he wanted to know, and his steps quickened with a definite purpose. At the mouth of the creek he hailed the old circuit rider's house, and the old man and his wife both appeared in the doorway.

"I reckon you couldn't help doin' it?"

"No," said the old man. "Thar wasn't no reason fer me to deny 'em."

He looked confused and the old woman gulped, for both were wondering how much the lad knew.

"How's grandpap?"

"Right porely I heerd," said the old woman. "The doctor's thar, an' he said that if the bullet had 'a' gone a leetle furder down hit would 'a' killed him."

"Whar's Mavis?"

Again the two old people looked confused, for it was plain that Jason did not know all that had happened.

"I hain't seed her, but somebody said she went by hyeh on her way home about an hour ago. I was thinkin' about goin' up thar right now."

The boy's eyes were shifting now from one to the other and he broke in abruptly:

"Whut's the matter?"

The old man's lips tightened.

"Jason, she's up thar alone. Yo' mammy an' Steve have run away."

The lad looked at the old man with unblinking eyes.

"Don't ye understand, boy?" repeated the old man kindly. "They've run away!"

Jason turned his head quickly and started for the gate.

"Now, don't, Jason," called the old woman in a broken voice. "Don't take on that way. I want ye both to come an' live with us," she pleaded. "Come on back now."

The little fellow neither made answer nor looked back, and the old people watched him turn up the creek, trudging toward Mavis's home.

The boy's tears once more started when he caught sight of Steve Hawn's cabin, but he forced them back. A helpless little figure was sitting in the open doorway with head buried in her arms. She did not hear him coming even when he was quite near, for the lad stepped softly and gently put one hand on her shoulder. She looked up with a frightened start, and at sight of his face she quit her sobbing and with one hand over her quivering mouth turned her head away.

"Come on, Mavie," he said quietly.

Again she looked up, wonderingly this time, and seeing some steady purpose in his eyes rose without a question.

With no word he turned and she followed him

60

back down the creek. And the old couple, sitting in the porch, saw them coming, the boy striding resolutely ahead, the little girl behind, and the faces of both deadly serious—the one with purpose and the other with blind trust. They did not call to the boy, for they saw him swerve across the road toward the gate. He did not lift his head until he reached the gate, and he did not wait for Mavis. He had no need, for she had hurried to his side when he halted at the steps of the porch.

"Uncle Lige," he said, "me an' Mavis hyeh want to git married."

Not the faintest surprise showed in Mavis's face, little as she knew what his purpose was, for what the master did was right; but the old woman and the old man were stunned into silence and neither could smile.

"Have you got yo' license?" the old man asked gravely.

"Whut's a license?"

"You got to git a license from the county clerk afore you can git married, an' hit costs two dollars."

The boy flinched, but only for a moment.

"I kin borrer the money," he said stoutly.

"But you can't git a license—you ain't a man."

"I ain't!" cried the boy hotly; "I *got* to be!"

"Come in hyeh, Jason," said the old man, for it was time to leave off evasion, and he led the lad into the house while Mavis, with the old woman's arm around her, waited in the porch. Jason came out baffled and pale.

"Hit ain't no use, Mavis," he said; "the law's agin us an' we got to wait. They've run away an' they've both sold out an' yo' daddy left word that he was goin' to send fer ye whenever he got wharever he was goin'."

Jason waited and he did not have to wait long.

"I hain't goin' to leave ye," she flashed.

"Hit ain't no use, Mavis," he said; "the law's agin us an' we got to wait"

VIII

S T. HILDA sat on the vine-covered porch of
her little log cabin, high on the hill-side,
with a look of peace in her big dreaming eyes.
From the frame house a few rods below her, mountain children—boys and girls—were darting in and
out, busy as bees, and, unlike the dumb, pathetic
little people out in the hills, alert, keen-eyed,
cheerful, and happy. Under the log foot-bridge
the shining creek ran down past the mountain
village below, where the cupola of the court-
house rose above the hot dirt streets, the ramshackle hotel, and the dingy stores and frame
dwellings of the town. Across the bridge her eyes
rested on another neat, well-built log cabin with
a grass plot around it, and, running alongside and
covered with honeysuckle—a pergola! That was
her hospital down there—empty, thank God.
With a little turn of her strong white chin, her
eyes rested on the charred foundation of her
school-house, to which some mean hand had applied the torch a month ago, and were lifted
up to the mountain-side, where mountain men
were chopping down trees and mountain oxen
yanking them down the steep slopes to the bank

63

of the creek, and then the peace of them went deeper still, for they could look back on her work and find it good. Nun-like in renunciation, she had given up her beloved Blue-grass land, she had left home and kindred, and she had settled, two days' journey from a railroad, in the hills. She had gone back to the physical life of the pioneers, she had encountered the customs and sentiments of mediæval days, and no abbess of those days, carrying light into dark places, needed more courage and devotion to meet the hardships, sacrifice, and prejudice that she had overcome. She brought in the first wagon-load of window-panes for darkened homes before she even tapped on the window of a darkened mind; but when she did, no plants ever turned more eagerly toward the light than did the youthful souls of those Kentucky hills. She started with five pupils in a log cabin. She built a homely frame house with five rooms, only to find more candidates clamoring at her door. She taught the girls to cook, sew, wash and iron, clean house, and make baskets, and the boys to use tools, to farm, make garden, and take care of animals; and she taught them all to keep clean. Out in the hills she found good old names, English and Scotch-Irish. She found men who "made their mark" boasting of grandfathers who were "scholards." In one household she came upon a time-worn set of the "British Poets" up to the

64

nineteenth century, and such was the sturdy character of the hillsmen that she tossed the theory aside that they were the descendants of the riff-raff of the Old World, tossed it as a miserable slander and looked upon them as the same blood as the people of the Blue-grass, the valleys, and the plains beyond. On the westward march they had simply dropped behind, and their isolation had left them in a long sleep that had given them a long rest, but had done them no real harm. Always in their eyes, however, she was a woman, and no woman was "fitten" to teach school. She was more—a "fotched-on" woman, a distrusted "furriner," and she was carrying on a "slavery school." Sometimes she despaired of ever winning their unreserved confidence, but out of the very depth of that despair to which the firebrand of some miscreant had plunged her, rose her star of hope, for then the Indian-like stoicism of her neighbors melted and she learned the place in their hearts that was really hers. Other neighborhoods asked for her to come to them, but her own would not let her go. Straightway there was nothing to eat, smoke, chew, nor wear that grew or was made in those hills that did not pour toward her. Land was given her, even money was contributed for rebuilding, and when money was not possible, this man and that gave his axe, his horse, his wagon, and his services as a laborer for thirty and sixty days. So that those axes gleaming in the sun on the hillside, those straining muscles, and those sweating brows meant a labor of love going on for her. No wonder the peace of her eyes was deep.

And yet St. Hilda, as one forsaken lover in the Blue-grass had christened her, opened the little roll-book in her lap and sighed deeply, for in there on her waiting-list were the names of a hundred children for whom, with all the rebuilding, she would have no place. Only the day before, a mountaineer had brought in nine boys and girls, his stepdaughter's and his own, and she had sadly turned them away. Still they were coming in name and in person, on horseback, in wagon and afoot, and among them was Jason Hawn, who was starting toward her that morning from far away over the hills.

Over there the twin spirals of smoke no longer rose on either side of the ridge and drifted upward, for both cabins were closed. Jason's sale was just over—the sale of one cow, two pigs, a dozen chickens, one stove, and a few pots and pans— the neighbors were gone, and Jason sat alone on the porch with more money in his pocket than he had ever seen at one time in his life. His bow and arrow were in one hand, his father's rifle was over his shoulder, and his old nag was hitched to the fence. The time had come. He had taken a farewell look at the black column of coal he had unearthed for others, the circuit rider would tend

his little field of corn on shares, Mavis would live
with the circuit rider's wife, and his grandfather
had sternly forbidden the boy to take any hand
in the feud. The geologist had told him to go
away and get an education, his Uncle Arch had
offered to pay his way if he would go to the Blue-
grass to school—an offer that the boy curtly declined—and now he was starting to the settlement school of which he had heard so much, in
the county-seat of an adjoining county. For,
even though run by women, it must be better than
nothing, better than being beholden to his Uncle
Arch, better than a place where people and country were strange. So, Jason mounted his horse,
rode down to the forks of the creek and drew up
at the circuit rider's house, where Mavis and the
old woman came out to the gate to say good-by.
The boy had not thought much about the little
girl and the loneliness of her life after he was
gone, for he was the man, he was the one to go
forth and do; and it was for Mavis to wait for
him to come back. But when he handed her
the bow and arrow and told her they were hers,
the sight of her face worried him deeply.

"I'm a-goin' over thar an' if I like it an' thar's
a place fer you, I'll send the nag back fer you, too."

He spoke with manly condescension only to
comfort her, but the eager gladness that leaped
pitifully from her eyes so melted him that he
added impulsively:

"S'pose you git up behind me an' go with me right now."

"Mavis ain't goin' now," said the old woman sharply. "You go on whar you're goin' an' come back fer her."

"All right," said Jason, greatly relieved. "Take keer o' yourselves."

With a kick he started the old nag and again pulled in.

"An' if you leave afore I git back, Mavis, I'm a-goin' to come atter you, no matter whar you air—some day."

"Good-by," faltered the little girl, and she watched him ride down the creek and disappear, and her tears came only when she felt the old woman's arms around her.

"Don't you mind, honey."

Over ridge and mountain and up and down the rocky beds of streams jogged Jason's old nag for two days until she carried him to the top of the wooded ridge whence he looked down on the little mountain town and the queer buildings of the settlement school. Half an hour later St. Hilda saw him cross the creek below the bridge, ride up to the foot-path gate, hitch his old mare, and come straight to her where she sat—in a sturdy way that fixed her interest instantly and keenly.

"I've come over hyeh to stay with ye," he said simply.

St. Hilda hesitated and distress kept her silent.

"My name's Jason Hawn. I come from t'other side o' the mountain an' I hain't got no home."

"I'm sorry, little man," she said gently, "but we have no place for you."

The boy's eyes darted to one side and the other.

"Shucks! I can sleep out thar in that wood-shed. I hain't axin' no favors. I got a leetle money an' I can work like a man."

Now, while St. Hilda's face was strong, her heart was divinely weak and Jason saw it. Un-hesitatingly he climbed the steps, handed his rifle to her, sat down, and at once began taking stock of everything about him—the boy swinging an axe at the wood-pile, the boy feeding the hogs and chickens; another starting off on an old horse with a bag of corn for the mill, another ploughing the hill-side. Others were digging ditches, working in a garden, mending a fence, and making cinder paths. But in all this his interest was plainly casual until his eyes caught sight of a pile of lumber at the door of the work-shop below, and through the windows the occa-sional gleam of some shining tool. Instantly one eager finger shot out.

"I want to go down thar."

Good-humoredly St. Hilda took him, and when Jason looked upon boys of his own age chipping, hewing, planing lumber, and making furniture, so busy that they scarcely gave him a glance, St. Hilda saw his eyes light and his fingers twitch.

"Gee!" he whispered with a catch of his breath, "this is the place fer me."

But when they went back and Jason put his head into the big house, St. Hilda saw his face darken, for in there boys were washing dishes and scrubbing floors.

"Does all the boys have to do that?" he asked with great disgust.

"Oh, yes," she said.

Jason turned abruptly away from the door, and when he passed a window of the cottage on the way back to her cabin and saw two boys within making up beds, he gave a grunt of scorn and derision and he did not follow her up the steps.

"Gimme back my gun," he said.

"Why, what's the matter, Jason?"

"This is a gals' school—hit hain't no place fer me."

It was no use for her to tell him that soldiers made their own beds and washed their own dishes, for his short answer was:

"Mebbe they had to, 'cause thar wasn't no women folks around, but he didn't," and his face was so hopelessly set and stubborn that she handed him the old gun without another word. For a moment he hesitated, lifting his solemn eyes to hers. "I want you to know I'm much obleeged," he said. Then he turned away, and St. Hilda

saw him mount his old nag, climb the ridge opposite without looking back, and pass over the summit.

Old Jason Hawn was sitting up in a chair when
two days later disgusted little Jason rode up to
his gate.

"They wanted me to do a gal's work over thar,"
he explained shortly, and the old man nodded
grimly with sympathy and understanding.

"I was lookin' fer ye to come back."

Old Aaron Honeycutt had been winged through
the shoulder while the lad was away and the feud
score had been exactly evened by the ambushing
of another of the tribe. On this argument Arch
Hawn was urging a resumption of the truce, but
both clans were armed and watchful and everybody was looking for a general clash on the next
county-court day. The boy soon rose restlessly.

"Whar you goin'?"

"I'm a-goin' to look atter my corn."

At the forks of the creek the old circuit rider
hailed Jason gladly, and he, too, nodded with
approval when he heard the reason the boy had
come back.

"I'll make ye a present o' the work I've done
in yo' corn—bein' as I must 'a' worked might'
nigh an hour up thar yestiddy an' got plumb
tuckered out. I come might' nigh fallin' out,
hit was so steep, an' if I had, I reckon I'd 'a'
broke my neck."

The old woman appeared on the porch and she, too, hailed the boy with a bantering tone and a quizzical smile.

"One o' them fotched-on women whoop ye fer missin' yo' a-b-abs?" she asked. Jason scowled.

"Whar's Mavis?" The old woman laughed teasingly.

"Why, hain't ye heerd the news? How long d'ye reckon a purty gal like Mavis was a-goin' to wait fer you? 'Member that good-lookin' little furrin feller who was down here from the settlemints? Well, he come back an' tuk her away."

Jason knew the old woman was teasing him, and instead of being angry, as she expected, he looked so worried and distressed that she was sorry, and her rasping old voice became gentle with affection.

"Mavis's gone to the settlemints, honey. Her daddy sent fer her an' I made her go. She's whar she belongs—up thar with him an' yo' mammy. Go put yo' hoss in the stable an' come an' live right here with us."

Jason shook his head and without answer turned his horse down the creek again. A little way down he saw three Honeycutts coming, all armed, and he knew that to avoid passing his grandfather's house they were going to cross the ridge and strike the head of their own creek. One of them was a boy—"little Aaron"—less than two years older than himself, and little Aaron not only had

72

a pistol buckled around him, but carried a Winchester across his saddle-bow. The two men grinned and nodded good-naturedly to him, but the boy Aaron pulled his horse across the road and stopped Jason, who had stood many a taunt from him.

"Which side air you on *now?*" asked Aaron contemptuously.

"You git out o' my road!"

"Hit's my road now," said Aaron, tapping his Winchester, "an' I've got a great notion o' makin' you git offen that ole bag o' bones an' dance fer me." One of the Honeycutts turned in his saddle.

"Come on," he shouted angrily, "an' let that boy alone."

"All right," he shouted back, and then to his white, quivering, helpless quarry:

"I'll let ye off this time, but next time——"

"I'll be ready fer ye," broke in Jason.

The lad's mind was made up now. He put the old nag in a lope down the rocky creek. He did not even go to his grandfather's for dinner, but turned at the river in a gallop for town. The rock-pecker, and even Mavis, were gone from his mind, and the money in his pocket was going, not for love or learning, but for pistol and cartridge now.

IX

SEPTEMBER in the Blue-grass. The earth
cooling from the summer's heat, the nights
vigorous and chill, the fields greening with a second spring. Skies long, low, hazy, and gently
arched over rolling field and meadow and woodland. The trees gray with the dust that had
sifted all summer long from the limestone turnpikes. The streams shrunken to rivulets that
trickled through crevices between broad flat stones
and oozed through beds of water-cress and crow-
foot, horse-mint and pickerel-weed, the wells low,
cisterns empty, and recourse for water to barrels
and the sunken ponds. The farmers cutting corn,
still green, for stock, and ploughing ragweed
strongholds for the sowing of wheat. The hemp
an Indian village of gray wigwams. And a time
of weeds—indeed the heyday of weeds of every
kind, and the harvest time for the king weed of
them all. Everywhere his yellow robes were hanging to poles and drying in the warm sun. Everywhere led the conquering war trail of the unkingly
usurper, everywhere in his wake was devastation.
The iron-weed had given up his purple crown,
and yellow wheat, silver-gray oats, and rippling
barley had fled at the sight of his banner to the

74

open sunny spaces as though to make their last stand an indignant appeal that all might see. Even the proud woodlands looked ragged and drooping, for here and there the ruthless marauder had flanked one and driven a battalion into its very heart, and here and there charred stumps told plainly how he had overrun, destroyed, and ravished the virgin soil beneath. A fuzzy little parasite was throttling the life of the Kentuckians' hemp. A bewhiskered moralist in a far northern State would one day try to drive the kings of his racing-stable to the plough. A meddling band of fanatical teetotalers would overthrow his merry monarch, King Barleycorn, and the harassed son of the Blue-grass, whether he would or not, must turn to the new pretender who was in the Kentuckians' midst, uninvited and self-throned.

And with King Tobacco were coming his own human vassals that were to prove a new social discord in the land—up from the river-bottoms of the Ohio and down from the foot-hills of the Cumberland—to plant, worm, tend, and fit those yellow robes to be stuffed into the mouth of the world and spat back again into the helpless face of the earth. And these vassals were supplanting native humanity as the plant was supplanting the native products of the soil. And with them and the new king were due in time a train of evils to that native humanity, creating disaffection, dividing households against themselves, and threatening with ruin the lordly social structure itself.

But, for all this, the land that early September morning was a land of peace and plenty, and in field, meadow, and woodland the most foreign note of the landscape was a spot of crimson in the crotch of a high staked and ridered fence on the summit of a little hill, and that spot was a little girl. She had on an old-fashioned poke-bonnet of deep pink, her red dress was of old-fashioned homespun, her stockings were of yarn, and her rough shoes should have been on the feet of a boy. Had the vanished forests and cane-brakes of the eighteenth century covered the land, had the wild beasts and wild men come back to roam them, had the little girl's home been a stockade on the edge of the wilderness, she would have fitted perfectly to the time and the scene, as a little daughter of Daniel Boone. As it was, she felt no less foreign than she looked, for the strangeness of the land and of the people still possessed her so that her native shyness had sunk to depths that were painful. She had a new ordeal before her now, for in her sinewy little hands were a paper bag, a first reader, and a spelling-book, and she was on her way to school. Beneath her the white turnpike wound around the hill and down into a little hollow, and on the crest of the next low hill was a little frame house with a belfry on top. Even while she sat there with parted lips, her face in a tense dream and her eyes dark with dread and indecision, the bell from the little school-house clanged through the still air with a sudden, sharp summons that was so peremptory and personal that she was almost startled from her perch. Not daring to loiter any longer, she leaped lightly to the ground and started in breathless haste up and over the hill. As she went down it, she could see horses hitched to the fence around the yard and school-children crowding upon the porch and filing into the door. The last one had gone in before she reached the school-house gate, and she stopped with a thumping heart that quite failed her then and there, for she retreated backward through the gate, to be sure that no one saw her, crept along the stone wall, turned into a lane, and climbed a worm fence into the woods behind the school-house. There she sat down on a log, miserably alone, and over the sunny strange slopes of this new world, on over the foothills, her mind flashed to the big far-away mountains and, dropping her face into her hands, she began to sob out her loneliness and sorrow. The cry did her good, and by and by she lifted her head, rubbed her reddened eyes with the back of one hand, half rose to go to the school-house, and sank helplessly down on the thick grass by the side of the log. The sun beat warmly and soothingly down on her. The grass and even the log against her shoulders were warm and comforting, and the hum of insects about her was so drowsy that she yawned and settled deeper into the grass, and presently she passed into sleep and dreams of Jason. Jason was in the feud. She could see him crouched in some bushes and peering through them on the lookout evidently for some Honeycutt; and slipping up the other side of the hill was a Honeycutt looking for Jason. Somehow she knew it was the Honeycutt who had slain the boy's father, and she saw the man creep through the brush and worm his way on his belly to a stump above where Jason sat. She saw him thrust his Winchester through the leaves, she tried to shriek a warning to Jason, and she awoke so weak with terror that she could hardly scramble to her feet. Just then the air was rent with shrill cries, she saw school-boys piling over a fence and rushing toward her hiding-place, and, her wits yet ungathered, she turned and fled in terror down the hill, nor did she stop until the cries behind her grew faint; and then she was much ashamed of herself. Nobody was in pursuit of her—it was the dream that had frightened her. She could almost step on the head of her own shadow now, and that fact and a pang of hunger told her it was noon. It was noon recess back at the school and those school-boys were on their way to a playground. She had left her lunch at the log where she slept, and so she made her way back to it, just in time to see two boys pounce on the little paper bag lying in the grass. There was no shyness about her then—that bag was hers —and she flashed forward.

"Gimme that poke!"

The wrestling stopped and, startled by the cry and the apparition, the two boys fell apart.

"What?" said the one with the bag in his hand, while the other stared at Mavis with puzzled amazement.

"Gimme that poke!" blazed the girl, and the boy laughed, for the word has almost passed from the vocabulary of the Blue-grass. He held it high.

"Jump for it!" he teased.

"I hain't goin' to jump fer it—hit's mine."

Her hands clenched and she started slowly toward him.

"Give her the bag," said the other boy so imperatively that the little girl stopped with a quick and trustful shift of her own burden to him.

"She's got to jump for it!"

The other boy smiled, and it strangely seemed to Mavis that she had seen that smile before.

"Oh, I reckon not," he said quietly, and in a trice the two boys in a close, fierce grapple were rocking before her and the boy with the bag went to the earth first.

"Gouge him!" shrieked the mountain girl, and she rushed to them while they were struggling, snatched the bag from the loosened fingers, and,

seeing the other boys on a run for the scene, fled
for the lane. From the other side of the fence
she saw the two lads rise, one still smiling, the
other crying with anger; the school-bell clanged
and she was again alone. Hurriedly she ate the
bacon and corn-bread in the bag and then she
made her way back along the lane, by the stone
wall, through the school-house gate, and gathering her courage with one deep breath, she climbed
the steps resolutely and stood before the open
door.

The teacher, a tall man in a long black frock-
coat, had his back to her, the room was crowded,
and she saw no vacant seat. Every pair of eyes
within was raised to her, and instantly she caught
another surprised and puzzled stare from the
boy who had taken her part a little while before. The teacher, seeing the attention of his
pupils fixed somewhere behind him, turned to
see the quaint figure, dismayed and helpless, in
the doorway, and he went quickly toward her.

"This way," he said kindly, and pointing to a
seat, he turned again to his pupils.

Still they stared toward the new-comer, and he
turned again. The little girl's flushed face was
still hidden by her bonnet, but before he reached
her to tell her quietly she must take it off, she had
seen that all the heads about her were bare and
was pulling it off herself—disclosing a riotous mass
of black hair, combed straight back from her fore-

head and gathered into a Psyche knot at the back of her head. Slowly the flush passed, but not for some time did she lift the extraordinary lashes that veiled her eyes to take a furtive glance about her. But, as the pupils bent more to their books, she grew bolder and looked about oftener and keenly, and she saw with her own eyes and in every pair of eyes whose glance she met, how different she was from all the other girls. For it was a look of wonder and amusement that she encountered each time, and sometimes two girls would whisper behind their hands and laugh, or one would nudge her desk-mate to look around at the stranger, so that the flush came back to Mavis's face and stayed there. The tall teacher saw, too, and understood, and, to draw no more attention to her than was necessary, he did not go near her until little recess. As he expected, she did not move from her seat when the other pupils trooped out, and when the room was empty he beckoned her to come to his desk, and in a moment, with her two books clasped in her hands, she stood shyly before him, meeting his kind gray searching eyes with unwavering directness.

"You were rather late coming to school."

"I was afeerd." The teacher smiled, for her eyes were fearless.

"What is your name?"

"Mavis Hawn."

Her voice was slow, low, and rich, and in some

wonder he half unconsciously repeated the unusual name.

"Where do you live?"

"Down the road a piece—'bout a whoop an' a holler."

"What? Oh, I see."

He smiled, for she meant to measure distance by sound, and she had used merely a variation of the "far cry" of Elizabethan days.

"Your father works in tobacco?" She nodded.

"You come from near the Ohio River?"

She looked puzzled.

"I come from the mountains."

"Oh!"

He understood now her dress and speech, and he was not surprised at the answer to his next question.

"I hain't nuver been to school. Pap couldn't spare me."

"Can you read and write?"

"No," she said, but she flushed, and he knew straightway the sensitiveness and pride with which he would have to deal.

"Well," he said kindly, "we will begin now."

And he took the alphabet and told her the names of several letters and had her try to make them with a lead pencil, which she did with such uncanny seriousness and quickness that the pity of it, that in his own State such intelligence should be going to such broadcast waste for the want of such elemental opportunities, struck him deeply. The general movement to save that waste was only just beginning, and in that movement he meant to play his part. He was glad now to have under his own supervision one of those mountaineers of whom, but for one summer, he had known so little and heard so much—chiefly to their discredit—and he determined then and there to do all he could for her. So he took her back to her seat with a copy-book and pencil and told her to go on with her work, and that he would go to see her father and mother as soon as possible.

"I hain't got no mammy—hit's a step-mammy," she said, and she spoke of the woman as of a horse or a cow, and again he smiled. Then as he turned away he repeated her name to himself and with a sudden wonder turned quickly back.

"I used to know some Hawns down in your mountains. A little fellow named Jason Hawn used to go around with me all the time."

Her eyes filled and then flashed happily.

"Why, mebbe you air the rock-pecker?"

"The what?"

"The jologist. Jason's my cousin. I wasn't thar that summer. Jason's always talkin' 'bout you."

"Well, well—I guess I am. That is curious."

"Jason's mammy was a Honeycutt an' she married my daddy an' they run away," she went on eagerly, "an' I had to foller 'em."

"Where's Jason?" Again her eyes filled.

"I don't know."

John Burnham put his hand on her head gently and turned to his desk. He rang the bell and when the pupils trooped back she was hard at work, and she felt proud when she observed several girls looking back to see what she was doing, and again she was mystified that each face showed the same expression of wonder and of something else that curiously displeased her, and she wondered afresh why it was that everything in that strange land held always something that she could never understand. But a disdainful whisper came back to her that explained it all.

"Why, that new girl is only learning her a-b-c's," said a girl, and her desk-mate turned to her with a quick rebuke.

"Don't—she'll hear you."

Mavis caught the latter's eyes that instant, and with a warm glow at her heart looked her gratitude, and then she almost cried her surprise aloud—it was the stranger-girl who had been in the mountains—Marjorie. The girl looked back in a puzzled way, and a moment later Mavis saw her turn to look again. This time the mountain girl answered with a shy smile, and Marjorie knew her, nodded in a gay, friendly way, and bent her head to her book.

Presently she ran her eyes down the benches where the boys sat, and there was Gray waiting apparently for her to look around, for he too nodded gayly to her, as though he had known her from the start. The teacher saw the exchange of little civilities and he was much puzzled, especially when, the moment school was over, he saw the lad hurry to catch Marjorie, and the two then turn together toward the little stranger. Both thrust out their hands, and the little mountain girl, so unaccustomed to polite formalities, was quite helpless with embarrassment, so the teacher went over to help her out and Gray explained:

"Marjorie and I stayed with her grandfather, and didn't we have a good time, Marjorie?"

Marjorie nodded with some hesitation, and Gray went on:

"How—how is he now?"

"Grandpap's right peart now."

"And how's your cousin—Jason?"

The question sent such a sudden wave of homesickness through Mavis that her answer was choked, and Marjorie understood and put her arm around Mavis's shoulder.

"You must be lonely up here. Where do you live?" And when she tried to explain Gray broke in.

"Why, you must be one of our ten—you must live on our farm. Isn't that funny?"

"And I live further down the road across the pike," said Marjorie.

"In that great big house in the woods?"

"Yes," nodded Marjorie, "and you must come to see me."

85

Mavis's eyes had the light of gladness in them now, and through them looked a grateful heart. Outside, Gray got Marjorie's pony for her, the two mounted, rode out the gate and went down the pike at a gallop, and Marjorie whirled in her saddle to wave her bonnet back at the little mountaineer. The teacher, who stood near watching them, turned to go back and close up the schoolhouse.

"I'm coming to see your father, and we'll get some books, and you are going to study so hard that you won't have time to get homesick any more," he said kindly, and Mavis started down the road, climbed the staked and ridered fence, and made her way across the fields. She had been lonely, and now homesickness came back to her worse than ever. She wondered about Jason—where he was and what he was doing and whether she would ever see him again. The memory of her parting with him came back to her—how he looked as she saw him for the last time sitting on his old nag, sturdy and apparently unmoved, and riding out of her sight in just that way; and she heard again his last words as though they were sounding then in her ears:

"I'm a-goin' to come an' git you—some day."

Since that day she had heard of him but once, and that was lately, when Arch Hawn had come to see her father and the two had talked a long time. They were all well, Arch said, down in the mountains. Jason had come back from the

86

settlement school. Little Aaron Honeycutt had
bantered him in the road and Jason had gone
wild. He had galloped down to town, bought a
Colt's forty-five and a pint of whiskey, had ridden
right up to old Aaron Honeycutt's gate, shot off
his pistol, and dared little Aaron to come out and
fight. Little Aaron wanted to go, but old Aaron
held him back, and Jason sat on his nag at the
gate and "cussed out" the whole tribe, and swore
"he'd kill every dad-blasted one of 'em if only
to git the feller who shot his daddy." Old Aaron
had behaved mighty well, and he and old Jason
had sent each other word that they would keep
both the boys out of the trouble. Then Arch
had brought about another truce and little Jason
had worked his crop and was making a man of
himself. It was Archer Hawn who had insisted
that Mavis herself should go to school and had
agreed to pay all her expenses, but in spite of her
joy at that, she was heart-broken when he was
gone, and when she caught her step-mother weeping in the kitchen a vague sympathy had drawn
them for the first time a little nearer together.

From the top of the little hill her new home
was visible across a creek and by the edge of a
lane. As she crossed a foot-bridge and made her
way noiselessly along the dirt road she heard
voices around a curve of the lane and she came
upon a group of men leaning against a fence.
In the midst of them was her father, and they

were arguing with him earnestly and he was shaking his head.

"Them toll-gates hain't a-hurtin' me none," she heard him drawl. "I don't understand this business, an' I hain't goin' to git mixed up in hit."

Then he saw her coming and he stopped, and the others looked at her uneasily, she thought, as if wondering what she might have heard.

"Go on home, Mavis," he said shortly, and as she passed on no one spoke until she was out of hearing. Some mischief was afoot, but she was not worried, nor was her interest aroused at all.

A moment later she could see her step-mother seated on her porch and idling in the warm sun. The new home was a little frame house, neat and well built. There was a good fence around the yard and the garden, and behind the garden was an orchard of peach-trees and apple-trees. The house was guttered and behind the kitchen was a tiny grape-arbor, a hen-house, and a cistern—all strange appurtenances to Mavis. The two spoke only with a meeting of the eyes, and while the woman looked her curiosity she asked no questions, and Mavis volunteered no information.

"Did you see Steve a-talkin' to some fellers down the road?"

Mavis nodded.

"Did ye hear whut they was talkin' about?"

"Somethin' about the toll-gates."

A long silence followed.

"The teacher said he was comin' over to see you and pap."

"Whut fer?"

"I dunno."

After another silence Mavis went on:

"The teacher is that rock-pecker Jason was always a-talkin' 'bout."

The woman's interest was aroused now, for she wondered if he were coming over to ask her any troublesome questions.

"Well, ain't that queer!"

"An' that boy an' gal who was a-stayin' with grandpap was thar at school too, an' she axed me to come over an' see her."

This the step-mother was not surprised to hear, for she knew on whose farm they were living and why they were there, and she had her own reasons for keeping the facts from Mavis.

"Well, you oughter go."

"I am a-goin'."

Mavis missed the mountains miserably when she went to bed that night—missed the gloom and lift of them through her window, and the rolling sweep of the land under the moon looked desolate and lonely and more than ever strange. A loping horse passed on the turnpike, and she could hear it coming on the hard road far away and going far away; then a buggy and then a

clattering group of horsemen, and indeed everything heralded its approach at a great distance.
She missed the stillness of the hills, for on the
night air were the barking of dogs, whinny of
horses, lowing of cattle, the song of a night-
prowling negro, and now and then the screech of
a peacock. She missed Jason wretchedly, too,
for there had been so much talk of him during the
day, and she went to sleep with her lashes wet
with tears. Some time during the night she was
awakened by pistol-shots, and her dream of Jason
made her think that she was at home again. But
no mountains met her startled eyes through the
window. Instead a red glare hung above the
woods, there was the clatter of hoofs on the pike,
and flames shot above the tops of the trees. Nor
could it be a forest fire such as was common at
home, for the woods were not thick enough. This
land, it seemed, had troubles of its own, as did
her mountains, but at least folks did not burn
folks' houses in the hills.

X

ON the top of a bushy foot-hill the old nag stopped, lifted her head, and threw her ears forward as though to gaze, like any traveller to a strange land, upon the rolling expanse beneath, and the lad on her back voiced her surprise and his own with a long, low whistle of amazement. He folded his hands on the pommel of his saddle and the two searched the plains below long and hard, for neither knew so much level land was spread out anywhere on the face of the earth. The lad had a huge pistol buckled around him; he looked half dead with sleeplessness and the old nag was weary and sore, for Jason was in flight from trouble back in those hills. He had kept his promise to his grandfather that summer, as little Aaron Honeycutt had kept his. Neither had taken part in the feud, and even after the truce came, each had kept out of the other's way. When Jason's corn was gathered there was nothing for him to do and the lad had grown restless. While roaming the woods one day, a pheasant had hurtled over his head. He had followed it, sighted it, and was sinking down behind a bowlder to get a rest for his pistol when the voices of two Honeycutts who had met in the road just under him stopped his finger on the trigger.

"That boy's a-goin' to bust loose some day," said one voice. "I've heerd him a-shootin' at a tree every day for a month up thar above his corn-field."

"Oh, no, he ain't," said the other. "He's just gittin' ready fer the man who shot his daddy."

"Well, who the hell *was* the feller?"

The other man laughed, lowered his voice, and the heart of the listening lad thumped painfully against the bowlder under him.

"Well, I hain't nuver told hit afore, but I seed with my own eyes a feller sneakin' outen the bushes ten minutes atter the shot was fired, an' hit was Babe Honeycutt."

A low whistle followed and the two rode on. The pheasant squatted to his limb undisturbed, and the lad lay gripping the bowlder with both hands. He rose presently, his face sick but resolute, slipped down into the road, and, swaying his head with rage, started up the hill toward the Honeycutt cove. On top of the hill the road made a sharp curve and around that curve, as fate would have it, slouched the giant figure of his mother's brother. Babe shouted pleasantly, stopped in sheer amazement when he saw Jason whip his revolver from his holster, and, with no movement to draw his own, leaped for the bushes. Coolly the lad levelled, and when his pistol spoke,

92

Babe's mighty arms flew above his head and the boy heard his heavy body crash down into the undergrowth. In the terrible stillness that followed the boy stood shaking in his tracks—stood until he heard the clatter of horses' hoofs in the creek-bed far below. The two Honeycutts had heard the shot, they were coming back to see what the matter was, and Jason sped as if winged back down the creek. He had broken the truce, his grandfather would be in a rage, the Honeycutts would be after him, and those hills were no place for him. So all that day and through all that night he fled for the big settlements of the Blue-grass and but half consciously toward his mother and Mavis Hawn. The fact that Babe was his mother's brother weighed on his mind but little, for the webs of kinship get strangely tangled in a mountain feud and his mother could not and would not blame him. Nor was there remorse or even regret in his heart, but rather the peace of an oath fulfilled—a duty done.

The sun was just coming up over the great black bulks which had given the boy forth that morning to a new world. Back there its mighty rays were shattered against them, and routed by their shadows had fought helplessly on against the gloom of deep ravines—those fortresses of perpetual night—but, once they cleared the emi-nence where Jason sat, the golden arrows took level flight, it seemed, for the very end of the

world. This was the land of the Blue-grass—the
home of the rock-pecker, home of the men who
had robbed him of his land, the refuge to his
Cousin Steve, his mother, and little Mavis, and
now their home. He could see no end of the land,
for on and on it rolled, and on and on as far as it
rolled were the low woodlands, the fields of cut
corn—more corn than he knew the whole world
held—and pastures and sheep and cattle and
horses, and houses and white fences and big white
barns. Little Jason gazed but he could not get his
fill. Perhaps the old nag, too, knew those distant
fields for corn, for with a whisk of her stubby tail
she started of her own accord before the lad could
dig his bare heels into her bony sides, and went
slowly down. The log cabins had disappeared
one by one, and most of the houses he now saw
were framed. One, however, a relic of pioneer
times, was of stone, and at that the boy looked
curiously. Several were of red brick and one
had a massive portico with great towering columns, and at that he looked more curiously still.
Darkies were at work in the fields. He had seen
only two or three in his life, he did not know
there were so many in the world as he saw that
morning, and now his skin ruffled with some antag-
onism ages deep. Everybody he met in the road
or passed working in the fields gave him a nod
and looked curiously at his big pistol, but nobody
asked him his name or where he was going or

94

what his business was; at that he wondered, for
everybody in the mountains asked those questions of the stranger, and he had all the lies he
meant to tell, ready for any emergency to cover
his tracks from any possible pursuers. By and
by he came to a road that stunned him. It was
level and smooth and made, as he saw, of rocks
pounded fine, and the old nag lifted her feet and
put them down gingerly. And this road never
stopped, and there was no more dirt road at all.
By and by he noticed running parallel with the
turnpike two shining lines of iron, and his curiosity
so got the better of him that he finally got off his
old nag and climbed the fence to get a better
look at them. They were about four feet apart,
fastened to thick pieces of timber, and they, too,
like everything else, ran on and on, and he
mounted and rode along them much puzzled.
Presently far ahead of him there was a sudden,
unearthly shriek, the rumbling sound of a coming
storm, rolling black smoke beyond the crest of a
little hill, and a swift huge mass swept into sight
and, with another fearful blast, bore straight at
him. The old nag snorted with terror, and in
terror dashed up the hill, while the boy lay back
and pulled helplessly on the reins. When he got
her halted the thing had disappeared, and both
boy and beast turned heads toward the still terrible sounds of its going. It was the first time
either had ever seen a railroad train, and the lad,

with a sickly smile that even he had shared the old nag's terror, got her back into the road. At the gate sat a farmer in his wagon and he was smiling.

"Did she come purty near throwin' you?"

"Huh!" grunted Jason contemptuously. "Whut was that?"

The farmer looked incredulous, but the lad was serious.

"That was a railroad train."

"Danged if I didn't think hit was a saw-mill comin' atter me."

The farmer laughed and looked as though he were going to ask questions, but he clucked to his horses and drove on, and Jason then and there swore a mighty oath to himself never again to be surprised by anything else he might see in this new land. All that day he rode slowly, giving his old nag two hours' rest at noon, and long before sundown he pulled up before a house in a cross-roads settlement, for the mountaineer does not travel much after nightfall.

"I want to git to stay all night," he said.

The man smiled and understood, for no mountaineer's door is ever closed to the passing stranger and he cannot understand that any door can be closed to him. Jason told the truth that night, for he had to ask questions himself—he was on his way to see his mother and his step-father and his cousin, who had moved down from the mountains, and to his great satisfaction he learned that it was a ride of but three hours more to Colonel Pendleton's.

When his host showed him to his room, the boy examined his pistol with such care while he was unbuckling it, that, looking up, he found a half-smile, half-frown, and no little suspicion, in his host's face; but he made no explanation, and he slept that night with one ear open, for he was not sure yet that no Honeycutt might be following him.

Toward morning he sprang from bed wide-awake, alert, caught up his pistol and crept to the window. Two horsemen were at the gate. The door opened below him, his host went out, and the three talked in whispers for a while. Then the horsemen rode away, his host came back into the house, and all was still again. For half an hour the boy waited, his every nerve alive with suspicion. Then he quietly dressed, left half a dollar on the washstand, crept stealthily down the stairs and out to the stable, and was soon pushing his old nag at a weary gallop through the dark.

XI

THE last sunset had been clear and Jack Frost had got busy. All the preceding day the clouds had hung low and kept the air chill so that the night was good for that arch-imp of Satan who has got himself enshrined in the hearts of little children. At dawn Jason saw the robe of pure white which the little magician had spun and drawn close to the breast of the earth. The first light turned it silver and showed it decked with flowers and jewels, that the old mother might mistake it, perhaps, for a wedding-gown instead of a winding-sheet; but the sun, knowing better, lifted, let loose his tiny warriors, and from pure love of beauty smote it with one stroke gold, and the battle ended with the blades of grass and the leaves in their scarlet finery sparkling with the joy of another day's deliverance and the fields grown gray and aged in a single night. Before the fight was quite over that morning, saddle-horses were stepping from big white barns in the land Jason was entering, and being led to old-fashioned stiles; buggies, phaetons, and rock-aways were emerging from turnpike gates; and rabbit-hunters moved, shouting, laughing, run-

ning races, singing, past fields sober with autumn,
woods dingy with oaks and streaked with the fire
of sumac and maple. On each side of the road
new hemp lay in shining swaths, while bales of
last year's crop were on the way to market along
the roads. The farmers were turning over the
soil for the autumn sowing of wheat, corn-shuck-
ing was over, and ragged darkies were straggling
from the fields back to town. From every point
the hunters came, turning in where a big square
brick house with a Grecian portico stood far back
in a wooded yard, with a fish-pond on one side
and a great smooth lawn on the other. On the
steps between the columns stood Colonel Pendleton and Gray and Marjorie welcoming the guests;
the men, sturdy country youths, good types of
the beef-eating young English squire—sunburnt
fellows with big frames, open faces, fearless eyes,
and a manner that was easy, cordial, kindly, independent; the girls midway between the types of
brunette and blonde, with a leaning toward the
latter type, with hair that had caught the light
of the sun, radiant with freshness and good health
and strength; round of figure, clear of eye and
skin, spirited, soft of voice, and slow of speech.
Soon a cavalcade moved through a side-gate of
the yard, through a Blue-grass woodland, and into
a sweep of stubble and ragweed; and far up the
road on top of a little hill the mountain boy
stopped his old mare and watched a strange sight

in a strange land—a hunt without dog, stick, or gun. A high ringing voice reached his ears clearly, even that far away:

"Form a line!"

And the wondering lad saw man and woman aligning themselves like cavalry fifteen feet apart and moving across the field—the men in leggings or high boots, riding with the heel low and the toes turned according to temperament; the girls with a cap, a derby, or a beaver with a white veil, and the lad's eye caught one of them quickly, for a red tam-o'-shanter had slipped from her shining hair and a broad white girth ran around both her saddle and her horse. There was one man on a sorrel mule and he was the host at the big house, for Colonel Pendleton had surrendered every horse he had to a guest. Suddenly there came a yell—the rebel yell—and a horse leaped forward. Other horses leaped too, everybody yelled in answer, and the cavalcade swept forward. There was a massing of horses, the white girth flashing in the midst of the mêlée, a great crash and much turning, twisting, and sawing of bits, and then all dashed the other way, the white girth in the lead, and the boy's lips fell apart in wonder. A black thoroughbred was making a wide sweep, an iron-gray was cutting in behind, and all were sweeping toward him. Far ahead of them he saw a frightened rabbit streaking through the weeds. As it passed him the lad gave a yell, dug his heels into the old mare, and himself swept down the pike, drawing his revolver and firing as he rode. Five times the pistol spoke to the wondering hunters in pursuit, at the fifth the rabbit tumbled heels over head and a little later the hunters pulled their horses in around a boy holding a rabbit high in one hand, a pistol in the other, and his eager face flushed with pride in his marksmanship and the comradeship of the hunt. But the flush died into quick paleness, so hostile were the faces, so hostile were the voices that assailed him, and he dropped the rabbit quickly and began shoving fresh cartridges into the chambers of his gun.

"What do you mean, boy," shouted an angry voice, "shooting that rabbit?"

The boy looked dazed.

"Why, wasn't you atter him?"

He looked around and in a moment he knew several of them, but nobody, it was plain, remembered him.

The girl with the white girth was Marjorie, the boy on the black thoroughbred was Gray, and coming in an awkward gallop on the sorrel mule was Colonel Pendleton. None of these people could mean to do him harm, so Jason dropped his pistol in his holster and, with a curious dignity for so ragged an atom, turned in silence away, and only the girl with the white girth noticed the quiver of his lips and the angry starting of tears.

As he started to mount the old mare, the excited yells coming from the fields were too much
for him, and he climbed back on the fence to
watch. The hunters had parted in twain, the
black thoroughbred leading one wing, the iron-
gray the other—both after a scurrying rabbit.
Close behind the black horse was the white girth
and close behind was a pony in full run. Under
the brow of the hill they swept and parallel with
the fence, and as they went by the boy strained
eager widening eyes, for on the pony was his
cousin Mavis Hawn, bending over her saddle and
yelling like mad. This way and that poor Mollie
swerved, but every way her big startled eyes
turned, that way she saw a huge beast and a yelling demon bearing down on her. Again the
horses crashed, the pony in the very midst. Gray
threw himself from his saddle and was after her
on foot. Two others swung from their saddles,
Mollie made several helpless hops, and the three
scrambled for her. The riders in front cried for
those behind to hold their horses back, but they
crowded on and Jason rose upright on the fence
to see who should be trampled down. Poor Mollie was quite hemmed in now, there was no way
of escape, and instinctively she shrank frightened
to the earth. That was the crucial instant, and
down went Gray on top of her as though she were
a foot-ball, and the quarry was his. Jason saw
him give her one blow behind her long ears and

then, holding a little puff of down aloft, look about him, past Marjorie to Mavis. A moment later he saw that rabbit's tail pinned to Mavis's cap, and a sudden rage of jealousy nearly shook him from the fence. He was too far away to see Marjorie's smile, but he did see her eyes rove about the field and apparently catch sight of him, and as the rest turned to the hunt she rode straight for him, for she remembered the distress of his face and he looked lonely.

"Little boy," she called, and the boy stared with amazement and rage, but the joke was too much for him and he laughed scornfully.

"Little gal," he mimicked, "air you a-talkin' to me?"

The girl gasped, reddened, lifted her chin haughtily, and raised her riding-whip to whirl away from the rude little stranger, but his steady eyes held hers until a flash of recognition came —and she smiled.

"Well, I never—Uncle Bob!" she cried excitedly and imperiously, and as the colonel lumbered toward her on his sorrel mount, she called with sparkling eyes, "don't you know him?"

The puzzled face of the colonel broke into a hearty smile.

"Well, bless my soul, it's Jason. You've come up to see your folks?"

And then he explained what Marjorie meant to explain.

"We're not hunting with guns—we just chase 'em. Hang your artillery on a fence-rail, bring your horse through that gate, and join us."

He turned and Marjorie, with him, called back over her shoulder: "Hurry up now, Jason."

Little Jason sat still, but he saw Marjorie ride straight for the pony, he heard her cry to Mavis, saw her wave one hand toward him, and then Mavis rode for him at a gallop, waving her whip to him as she came. The boy gave no answering signal, but sat still, hard-eyed, cool. Before she was within twenty yards of him he had taken in every detail of the changes in her and the level look of his eyes stopped her happy cry, and made her grow quite pale with the old terror of giving him offence. Her hair looked different, her clothes were different, she wore gloves, and she had a stick in one hand with a head like a cane and a loop of leather at the other end. For these drawbacks, the old light in her eyes and face quite failed to make up, for while Jason looked, Mavis was looking, too, and the boy saw her eyes travelling him down from head to foot: somehow he was reminded of the way Marjorie had looked at him back in the mountains and somehow he felt that the change that he resented in Mavis went deeper than her clothes. The morbidly sensitive spirit of the mountaineer in him was hurt, the chasm yawned instead of closing, and all he said shortly was:

"Whar'd you git them new-fangled things?"

"Marjorie give 'em to me. She said fer you to bring yo' hoss in—hit's more fun than I ever knowed in my life up here."

"Hit is?" he half-sneered. "Well, you git back to yo' high-falutin' friends an' tell 'em I don't hunt nothin' that-a-way."

"I'll stop right now an' go home with ye. I guess you've come to see yo' mammy."

"Well, I hain't ridin' aroun' just fer my health exactly."

He had suddenly risen on the fence as the cries in the field swelled in a chorus. Mavis saw how strong the temptation within him was, and so, when he repeated for her to "go on back," the old habit of obedience turned her, but she knew he would soon follow.

The field was going mad now, horses were dashing and crashing together, the men were swinging to the ground and were pushed and trampled in a wild clutch for Mollie's long ears, and Jason could see that the contest between them was who should get the most game. The big mule was threshing the weeds like a tornado, and crossing the field at a heavy gallop he stopped suddenly at a ditch, the girth broke, and the colonel went over the long ears. There was a shriek of laughter, in which Jason from his perch joined, as with a bray of freedom the mule made for home. Apparently that field was hunted out now, and when the hunters crossed another pike and went into another field too far away for the boy to see the fun, he mounted his old mare and rode slowly after them. A little later Mavis heard a familiar yell, and Jason flew by her with his pistol flopping on his hip, his hat in his hand, and his face frenzied and gone wild. The thoroughbred passed him like a swallow, but the rabbit twisted back on his trail and Mavis saw Marjorie leap lightly from her saddle, Jason flung himself from his, and then both were hidden by the crush of horses around them, while from the midst rose sharp cries of warning and fear.

She saw Gray's face white with terror, and then she saw Marjorie picking herself up from the ground and Jason swaying dizzily on his feet with a rabbit in his hand.

"'Tain't nothin'," he said stoutly, and he grinned his admiration openly for Marjorie, who looked such anxiety for him. "You ain't afeerd o' nothin', air ye, an' I reckon this rabbit tail is a-goin' to you," and he handed it to her and turned to his horse. The boy had jerked Marjorie from under the thoroughbred's hoofs and then gone on recklessly after the rabbit, getting a glancing blow from one of those hoofs himself.

Marjorie smiled.

"Thank you, little—man," and Jason grinned again, but his head was dizzy and he did not ride after the crowd.

"I'm afeerd fer this ole nag," he lied to Colonel
Pendleton, for he was faint at the stomach and the
world had begun to turn around. Then he made
one clutch for the old nag's mane, missed it, and
rolled senseless to the ground.

Not long afterward he opened his eyes to find
his head in the colonel's lap, Marjorie bathing
his forehead with a wet handkerchief, and Gray
near by, still a little pale from remorse for his
carelessness and Marjorie's narrow escape, and
Mavis the most unconcerned of all—and he was
much ashamed. Rudely he brushed Marjorie's
consoling hand away and wriggled away from the
colonel to his knees.

"Shucks!" he said, with great disgust.

The shadows were stretching fast, it was too
late to try another field, so back they started
through the radiant air, laughing, talking, bantering, living over the incidents of the day, the
men with one leg swung for rest over the pommel of their saddles, the girls with habits disor-
dered and torn, hair down, and all tired, but all
flushed, clear-eyed, happy. The leaves—russet,
gold and crimson—were dropping to the autumn-
greening earth, the sunlight was as yellow as the
wings of a butterfly, and on the horizon was a
faint haze that shadowed the coming Indian summer. But still it was warm enough for a great
spread on the lawn, and what a feast for moun-

tain eyes—chicken, turkey, cold ham, pickles, croquettes, creams, jellies, beaten biscuits. And what happy laughter and thoughtful courtesy and mellow kindness—particularly to the little mountain pair, for in the mountains they had given the Pendletons the best they had and now the best was theirs. Inside fires were being lighted in the big fireplaces, and quiet, solid, old-fashioned English comfort everywhere the blaze brought out.

Already two darky fiddlers were waiting on the back porch for a dram, and when the darkness settled the fiddles were talking old tunes and nimble feet were busy. Little Jason did his wonderful dancing and Gray did his; and round about, the window-seats and the tall columns of the porch heard again from lovers what they had been listening to for so long. At midnight the hunters rode forth again in pairs into the crisp, brilliant air and under the kindly moon, Mavis jogging along beside Jason on Marjorie's pony, for Marjorie would not have it otherwise. No wonder that Mavis loved the land.

"I jerked the gal outen the way," explained Jason, "'cause she was a gal an' had no business messin' with men folks."

"Of co'se," Mavis agreed, for she was just as contemptuous as he over the fuss that had been made of the incident.

"But she ain't afeerd o' nothin'."

This was a little too much.

"I ain't nuther."

"Co'se you ain't."

There was no credit for Mavis—her courage was a matter of course; but with the stranger-girl, a "furriner"—that was different. There was silence for a while.

"Wasn't it lots o' fun, Jasie?"

"Shore!" was the absent-minded answer, for Jason was looking at the strangeness of the night. It was curious not to see the big bulks of the mountains and to see so many stars. In the mountains he had to look straight up to see stars at all and now they hung almost to the level of his eyes.

"How's the folks?" asked Mavis.

"Stirrin'. Air ye goin' to school up here?"

"Yes, an' who you reckon the school-teacher is?"

Jason shook his head.

"The jologist."

"Well, by Heck."

"An' he's always axin' me about you an' if you air goin' to school."

For a while more they rode in silence.

"I went to that new furrin school down in the mountains," yawned the boy, "fer 'bout two hours. They're gittin' too high-falutin' to suit me. They tried to git me to wear gal's stockin's like they do up here an' I jes' laughed at 'em. Then they tried to git me to make up beds an' I

tol' 'em I wasn't goin' to wear gal's clothes ner
do a gal's work, an' so I run away."

He did not tell his reason for leaving the mountains altogether, for Mavis, too, was a girl, and
he did not confide in women—not yet.

But the girl was woman enough to remember
that the last time she had seen him he had said
that he was going to come for her some day.
There was no sign of that resolution, however,
in either his manner or his words now, and for
some reason she was rather glad.

"Every boy wears clothes like that up here.
They calls 'em knickerbockers."

"Huh!" grunted Jason. "Hit sounds like 'em."

"Air ye still shootin' at that ole tree?"

"Yep, an' I kin hit the belly-band two shots
out o' three."

Mavis raised her dark eyes with a look of apprehension, for she knew what that meant; when
he could hit it three times running he was going
after the man who had killed his father. But
she asked no more questions, for while the boy
could not forbear to boast about his marksmanship, further information was beyond her sphere
and she knew it.

When they came to the lane leading to her
home, Jason turned down it of his own accord.

"How'd you know whar we live?"

"I was here this mornin' an' I seed my mammy.
Yo' daddy wasn't thar."

Mavis smiled silently to herself; he had found

out thus where she was and he had followed her. At the little stable Jason unsaddled the horses and turned both out in the yard while Mavis went within, and Steve Hawn appeared at the door in his underclothes when Jason stepped upon the porch.

"Hello, Jason!"

"Hello, Steve!" answered the boy, but they did not shake hands, not because of the hard feeling between them, but because it was not mountain custom.

"Come on in an' lay down."

Mavis had gone upstairs, but she could hear the voices below her. If Mavis had been hesitant about asking questions, as had been the boy's mother as well, Steve was not.

"Whut'd you come up here fer?"

"Same reason as you once left the mountains —I got inter trouble."

Steve was startled and he frowned, but the boy gazed coolly back into his angry eyes.

"Whut kind o' trouble?"

"Same as you—I shot a feller," said the boy imperturbably.

Little Mavis heard a groan from her stepmother, an angry oath from her father, and a curious pang of horror pierced her.

Silence followed below and the girl lay awake and trembling in her bed.

"Who was it?" Steve asked at last.

"That's my business," said little Jason. The silence was broken no more, and Mavis lay with new thoughts and feelings racking her brain and her heart. Once she had driven to town with Marjorie and Gray, and a man had come to the carriage and cheerily shaken hands with them both. After he was gone Gray looked very grave and Marjorie was half unconsciously wiping her right hand with her handkerchief.

"He killed a man," was Marjorie's horrified whisper of explanation, and now if they should hear what she had heard they would feel the same way toward her own cousin, Jason Hawn. She had never had such a feeling in the mountains, but she had it now, and she wondered whether she could ever be quite the same toward Jason again.

XII

CHRISTMAS was approaching and no greater wonder had ever dawned on the lives of Mavis and Jason than the way these people in the settlements made ready for it. In the mountains many had never heard of Christmas and few of Christmas stockings, Santa Claus, and catching Christmas gifts—not even the Hawns. But Mavis and Jason had known of Christmas, had celebrated it after the mountain way, and knew, moreover, what the Blue-grass children did not know, of old Christmas as well, which came just twelve days after the new. At midnight of old Christmas, so the old folks in the mountains said, the elders bloomed and the beasts of the field and the cattle in the barn kneeled lowing and moaning, and once the two children had slipped out of their grandfather's house to the barn and waited to watch the cattle and to listen to them, but they suffered from the cold, and when they told what they had done next morning, their grandfather said they had not waited long enough, for it happened just at midnight; so when Mavis and Jason told Marjorie and Gray of old Christmas they all agreed they would wait up this time till midnight sure.

As for new Christmas in the hills, the women paid little attention to it, and to the men it meant "a jug of liquor, a pistol in each hand, and a galloping nag." Always, indeed, it meant drinking, and target-shooting to see "who should drink and who should smell," for the man who made a bad shot got nothing but a smell from the jug until he had redeemed himself. So, Steve Hawn and Jason got ready in their own way and Mavis and Martha Hawn accepted their rude preparations as a matter of course.

At four o'clock in the afternoon before Christmas Eve darkies began springing around the corners of the twin houses, and from closets and from behind doors, upon the white folks and shouting "Christmas gift," for to the one who said the greeting first the gift came, and it is safe to say that no darky in the Blue-grass was caught that day. And the Pendleton clan made ready to make merry. Kinspeople gathered at the old general's ancient home and at the twin houses on either side of the road. Stockings were hung up and eager-eyed children went to restless dreams of their holiday king. Steve Hawn, too, had made ready with boxes of cartridges and two jugs of red liquor, and he and Jason did not wait for the morrow to make merry. And Uncle Arch Hawn happened to come in that night, but he was chary of the cup, and he frowned with displeasure at Jason, who was taking his dram with

Steve like a man, and he showed displeasure before he rode away that night by planting a thorn
in the very heart of Jason's sensitive soul. When
he had climbed on his horse he turned to Jason.

"Jason," he drawled, "you can come back
home now when you git good an' ready. Thar
ain't no trouble down thar just now, an' Babe
Honeycutt ain't lookin' fer you."

Jason gasped. He had not dared to ask a single question about the one thing that had been
torturing his curiosity and his soul, and Arch was
bringing it out before them all as though it were
the most casual and unimportant matter in the
world. Steve and his wife looked amazed and
Mavis's heart quickened.

"Babe ain't lookin' fer ye," Arch drawled on,
"he's laughin' at ye. I reckon you thought you'd
killed him, but he stumbled over a root an' fell
down just as you shot. He says you missed him
a mile. He says you couldn't hit a barn in plain
daylight." And he started away.

A furious oath broke from Jason's gaping
mouth, Steve laughed, and if the boy's pistol had
been in his hand, he might in his rage have shown
Arch as he rode away what his marksmanship
could be even in the dark, but even with his uncle's
laugh, too, coming back to him he had to turn
quickly into the house and let his wrath bite
silently inward.

But Mavis's eyes were like moist stars.

"Oh, Jasie, I'm so glad," she said, but he only stared and turned roughly on toward the jug in the corner.

Before day next morning the children in the big houses were making the walls ring with laughter and shouts of joy. Rockets whizzed against the dawn, fire-crackers popped unceasingly, and now and then a loaded anvil boomed through the crackling air, but there was no happy awakening for little Jason. All night his pride had smarted like a hornet sting, his sleep was restless and bitter with dreams of revenge, and the hot current in his veins surged back and forth in the old channel of hate for the slayer of his father. Next morning his blood-shot eyes opened fierce and sullen and he started the day with a visit to the whiskey jug: then he filled his belt and pockets with cartridges.

Early in the afternoon Marjorie and Gray drove over with Christmas greetings and little presents. Mavis went out to meet them, and when Jason half-staggered out to the gate, the visitors called to him merrily and became instantly grave and still. Mavis flushed, Marjorie paled with horror and disgust, Gray flamed with wonder and contempt and quickly whipped up his horse—the mountain boy was drunk.

Jason stared after them, knowing something had suddenly gone wrong, and while he said nothing, his face got all the angrier, he rushed in for

116

his belt and pistol, and shaking his head from side
to side, swaggered out to the stable and began
saddling his old mare. Mavis stood in the doorway frightened and ashamed, the boy's mother
pleaded with him to come into the house and lie
down, but without a word to either he mounted
with difficulty and rode down the road. Steve
Hawn, who had been silently watching him,
laughed.

"Let him alone—he ain't goin' to do nothin'."

Down the road the boy rode with more drunken
swagger than his years in the wake of Marjorie
and Gray—unconsciously in the wake of anything
that was even critical, much less hostile, and in
front of Gray's house he pulled up and gazed long
at the pillars and the broad open door, but not a
soul was in sight and he paced slowly on. A few
hundred yards down the turnpike he pulled up
again and long and critically surveyed a woodland. His eye caught one lone tree in the centre
of an amphitheatrical hollow just visible over
the slope of a hill. The look of the tree interested him, for its growth was strange, and he
opened the gate and rode across the thick turf
toward it. The bark was smooth, the tree was
the size of a man's body, and he dismounted, nodding his head up and down with much satisfaction. Standing close to the tree, he pulled out
his knife, cut out a square of the bark as high
as the first button of his coat and moving around

the trunk cut out several more squares at the same level.

"I reckon," he muttered, "that's whar his heart is yit, if *I* ain't growed too much."

Then he led the old mare to higher ground, came back, levelled his pistol, and moving in a circle around the tree, pulled the trigger opposite each square, and with every shot he grunted:

"Can't hit a barn, can't I, by Heck!"

In each square a bullet went home. Then he reloaded and walked rapidly around the tree, still firing.

"An' I reckon that's a-makin' some nail-holes fer his galluses!"

And reloading again he ran around the tree, firing.

"An' mebbe I couldn't still git him if I was hikin' fer the corner of a house an' was in a *leetle* grain of a hurry to git out o' *his* range."

Examining results at a close range, the boy was quite satisfied—hardly a shot had struck without a band three inches in width around the tree. There was one further test that he had not yet made; but he felt sober now and he drew a bottle from his hip-pocket and pulled at it hard and long. The old nag grazing above him had paid no more attention to the fusillade than to the buzzing of flies. He mounted her, and Gray, riding at a gallop to make out what the unearthly racket going on in the hollow was, saw the boy going at full speed in a circle about the tree, firing and yelling,. and as Gray himself in a moment more would be in range, he shouted a warning. Jason stopped and waited with belligerent eyes as Gray rode toward him.

"I say, Jason," Gray smiled, "I'm afraid my father wouldn't like that—you've pretty near killed that tree."

Jason stared, amazed.

"Fust time I ever heerd of anybody not wantin' a feller to shoot at a tree."

Gray saw that he was in earnest and he kept on, smiling.

"Well, we haven't got as many trees here as you have down in the mountains, and up here they're more valuable."

The last words were unfortunate.

"Looks like you keer a heep fer yo' trees," sneered the mountain boy with a wave of his pistol toward a demolished woodland; "an' if our trees air so wuthless, whut do you furriners come down thar and rob us of 'em fer?"

The sneer, the tone, and the bitter emphasis on the one ugly word turned Gray's face quite red.

"You mustn't say anything like that to me," was his answer, and the self-control in his voice but helped make the mountain boy lose his at once and completely. He rode straight for Gray and pulled in, waving his pistol crazily before the latter's face, and Gray could actually hear the grinding of his teeth.

"Go git yo' gun! Git yo' gun!"

Gray turned very pale, but he showed no fear.

"I don't know what's the matter with you," he said steadily, "but you must be drunk."

"Go git yo' gun!" was the furious answer. "Go git yo' gun!"

"Boys don't fight with guns in this country, but——"

"You're a d—d coward," yelled Jason.

Gray's fist shot through the mist of rage that suddenly blinded him, catching Jason on the point of the chin, and as the mountain boy spun half around in his saddle, Gray caught the pistol in both hands and in the struggle both rolled, still clutching the weapon, to the ground, Gray saying with quiet fury:

"Drop that pistol and I'll lick hell out of you!"

There was no answer but the twist of Jason's wrist, and the bullet went harmlessly upward. Before he could pull the trigger again, the sinewy fingers of a man's hand closed over the weapon and pushed it flat with the earth, and Jason's upturned eyes looked into the grave face of the school-master. That face was stern and shamed Jason instantly. The two boys rose to their feet, and the mountain boy turned away from the school-master and saw Marjorie standing ten yards away white and terror-stricken, and her eyes when he met them blazed at him with a light that no human eye had ever turned on him before. The boy knew anger, rage, hate, revenge, but contempt was new to him, and his soul was filled with sudden shame that was no less strange, but the spirit in him was undaunted, and like a challenged young buck his head went up as he turned again to face his accuser.

"Were you going to shoot an unarmed boy?" asked John Burnham gravely.

"He hit me."

"You called him a coward."

"He hit me."

"He offered to fight you fist and skull."

"He had the same chance to git the gun that I had."

"He wasn't trying to get it in order to shoot you."

Jason made no answer and the school-master repeated:

"He offered to fight you fist and skull."

"I was too mad—but I'll fight him now."

"Boys don't fight in the presence of young ladies."

Gray spoke up and in his tone was the contempt that was in Marjorie's eyes, and it made the mountain boy writhe.

"I wouldn't soil my hands on you—now."

The school-master rebuked Gray with a gesture, but Jason was confused and sick now and he held out his hand for his pistol.

"I better be goin' now—this ain't no place fer me."

The school-master gravely handed the weapon to him.

"I'm coming over to have a talk with you, Jason," he said.

The boy made no answer. He climbed on his horse slowly. His face was very pale, and once only he swept the group with eyes that were badgered but no longer angry, and as they rested on Marjorie, there was a pitiful, lonely something in them that instantly melted her and almost started her tears. Then he rode silently and slowly away.

XIII

SLOWLY the lad rode westward, for the reason that he was not yet quite ready to pass between those two big-pillared houses again, and because just then whatever his way—no matter. His anger was all gone now and his brain was clear, but he was bewildered. Throughout the day he had done nothing that he thought was wrong, and yet throughout the day he had done nothing that seemed to be right. This land was not for him—he did not understand the ways of it and the people, and they did not understand him. Even the rock-pecker had gone back on him, and though that hurt him deeply, the lad loyally knew that the school-master must have his own good reasons. The memory of Marjorie's look still hurt, and somehow he felt that even Mavis was vaguely on their side against him, and of a sudden the pang of loneliness that Marjorie saw in his eyes so pierced him that he pulled his old nag in and stood motionless in the middle of the road. The sky was overcast and the air was bitter and chill; through the gray curtain that hung to the rim of the earth, the low sun swung like a cooling ball of fire and under it the gray fields stretched with such desolation for him that he dared ride no farther into them. And then, as the lad looked across the level stillness that encircled him, the mountains loomed suddenly from it—big, still, peaceful, beckoning—and made him faint with homesickness. Those mountains were behind him—his mountains and his home that was his no longer—but, after all, any home back there was his, and that thought so filled his heart with a rush of gladness that with one long breath of exultation he turned in his saddle to face those distant unseen hills, and the old mare, following the movement of his body, turned too, as though she, too, suddenly wanted to go home. The chill air actually seemed to grow warmer as he trotted back, the fields looked less desolate, and then across them he saw flashing toward him the hostile fire of a scarlet tam-o'-shanter. He was nearing the yard gate of the big house on the right, and from the other big house on the left the spot of shaking crimson was galloping toward the turnpike. He could wait until Marjorie crossed the road ahead of him, or he could gallop ahead and pass before she could reach the gate, but his sullen pride forbade either course, and so he rode straight on, and his dogged eyes met hers as she swung the gate to and turned her pony across the road. Marjorie flushed, her lips half parted to speak, and Jason sullenly drew in, but as she said nothing, he clucked and dug his heels viciously into the old mare's sides.

Then the little girl raised one hand to check him and spoke hurriedly:

"Jason, we've been talking about you, and my Uncle Bob says you kept me from getting killed."

Jason stared.

"And the school-teacher says we don't understand you—you people down in the mountains—and that we mustn't blame you for—" she paused in helpless embarrassment, for still the mountain boy stared.

"You know," she went on finally, "boys here don't do things that you boys do down there——"

She stopped again, the tears started suddenly in her earnest eyes, and a miracle happened to little Jason. Something quite new surged within him, his own eyes swam suddenly, and he cleared his throat huskily.

"I hain't a-goin' to bother you folks no more," he said, and he tried to be surly, but couldn't. "I'm a-goin' away." The little girl's tears ceased.

"I'm sorry," she said. "I wish you'd stay here and go to school. The school-teacher said he wanted you to do that, and he says such nice things about you, and so does my Uncle Bob, and Gray is sorry, and he says he is coming over to see you to-morrow."

"I'm a-goin' home," repeated Jason stubbornly.

"Home?" repeated the girl, and her tone did what her look had done a moment before, for she knew he had no home, and again the lad was filled with a throbbing uneasiness. Her eyes dropped to her pony's mane, and in a moment more she looked up with shy earnestness.

"Will you do something for me?"

Again Jason started and of its own accord his tongue spoke words that to his own ears were very strange.

"Thar hain't nothin' I won't do fer ye," he said, and his sturdy sincerity curiously disturbed Marjorie in turn, so that her flush came back, and she went on with slow hesitation and with her eyes again fixed on her pony's neck.

"I want you to promise me not—not to shoot anybody—unless you *have* to in self-defence— and never to take another drink until—until you see me again."

She could not have bewildered the boy more had she asked him never to go barefoot again, but his eyes were solemn when she looked up and solemnly he nodded assent.

"I give ye my hand."

The words were not literal, but merely the way the mountaineer phrases the giving of a promise, but the little girl took them literally and she rode up to him with slim fingers outstretched and a warm friendly smile on her little red mouth. Awkwardly the lad thrust out his dirty, strong little hand.

"Good-by, Jason," she said.

"Good-by—" he faltered, and, still smiling, she finished the words for him.

"Marjorie," she said, and unsmilingly he repeated:

"Marjorie."

While she passed through the gate he sat still and watched her, and he kept on watching her as she galloped toward home, twisting in his saddle to follow her course around the winding road. He saw a negro boy come out to the stile to take her pony, and there Marjorie, dismounting, saw in turn the lad still motionless where she had left him, and looking after her. She waved her whip to him, went on toward the house, and when she reached the top of the steps, she turned and waved to him again, but he made no answering gesture, and only when the front door closed behind her, did the boy waken from his trance and jog slowly up the road. Only the rim of the red fire-ball was arched over the horizon behind him now. Winter dusk was engulfing the fields and through it belated crows were scurrying silently for protecting woods. For a little while Jason rode with his hands folded manwise on the pommel of his saddle and with manlike emotions in his heart, for, while the mountains still beckoned, this land had somehow grown more friendly and there was a curious something after all that he would leave behind. What it was he hardly knew; but a pair of blue eyes, misty with mys-

terious tears, had sown memories in his confused
brain that he would not soon lose. He did not
forget the contempt that had blazed from those
eyes, but he wondered now at the reason for that
contempt. Was there something that ruled this
land—something better than the code that ruled
his hills? He had remembered every word the
geologist had ever said, for he loved the man,
but it had remained for a strange girl—a girl—
to revive them, to give them actual life and plant
within him a sudden resolve to learn for himself
what it all meant, and to practise it, if he found
it good. A cold wind sprang up now and cutting
through his thin ʻclothes drove him in a lope toward his mother's home.

Apparently Mavis was watching for him through
the window of the cottage, for she ran out on the
porch to meet him, but something in the boy's
manner checked her, and she neither spoke nor
asked a question while the boy took off his saddle and tossed it on the steps. Nor did Jason
give her but one glance, for the eagerness of her
face and the trust and tenderness in her eyes
were an unconscious reproach and made him feel
guilty and faithless, so that he changed his mind
about turning the old mare out in the yard and
led her to the stable, merely to get away from
the little girl.

Mavis was in the kitchen when he entered the
house, and while they all were eating supper, the

lad could feel his little cousin's eyes on him all the time—watching and wondering and troubled and hurt. And when the four were seated about the fire, he did not look at her when he announced that he was going back home, but he saw her body start and shrink. His step-father yawned and said nothing, and his mother looked on into the fire.

"When you goin', Jasie?" she asked at last.

"Daylight," he answered shortly.

There was a long silence.

"Whut you goin' to do down thar?"

The lad lifted his head fiercely and looked from the woman to the man and back again.

"I'm a-goin' to git that land back," he snapped; and as there was no question, no comment, he settled back brooding in his chair.

"Hit wasn't right—hit *couldn't* 'a' been right," he muttered, and then as though he were answering his mother's unspoken question:

"I don't know *how* I'm goin' to git it back, but if it wasn't right, thar *must* be some way, an' I'm a-goin' to find out if hit takes me all my life."

His mother was still silent, though she had lifted a corner of her apron to her eyes, and the lad rose and without a word of good-night climbed the stairs to go to bed. Then the mother spoke to her husband angrily.

"You oughtn't to let the boy put all the blame on me, Steve—you made me sell that land."

Steve's answer was another yawn, and he rose
to get ready for bed, and Mavis, too, turned indignant eyes on him, for she had heard enough
from the two to know that her step-mother spoke
the truth. Her father opened the door and she
heard the creak of his heavy footsteps across the
freezing porch. Her step-mother went into the
kitchen and Mavis climbed the stairs softly and
opened Jason's door.

"Jasie!" she called.

"Whut you want?"

"Jasie, take me back home with ye, won't you?"

A rough denial was on his lips, but her voice
broke into a little sob and the boy lay for a moment without answering.

"Whut on earth would you do down thar,
Mavis?"

And then he remembered how he had told her
that he would come for her some day, and he
remembered the Hawn boast that a Hawn's word
was as good as his bond and he added kindly:
"Wait till mornin', Mavis. I'll take ye if ye
want to go."

The door closed instantly and she was gone.
When the lad came down before day next morning Mavis had finished tying a few things in a
bundle and was pushing it out of sight under a
bed, and Jason knew what that meant.

"You hain't told 'em?"

Mavis shook her head.

"Mebbe yo' pap won't let ye."

"He ain't hyeh," said the little girl.

"Whar is he?"

"I don't know."

"Mavis," said the boy seriously, "I'm a boy an' hit don't make no difference whar I go, but you're a gal an' hit looks like you ought to stay with yo' daddy."

The girl shook her head stubbornly, but he paid no attention.

"I tell ye, I'm a-goin' back to that new-fangled school when I git to grandpap's, an' whut'll you do?"

"I'll go with ye."

"I've thought o' that," said the boy patiently, "but they mought not have room fer neither one of us—an' I can take keer o' myself anywhar."

"Yes," said the little girl proudly, "an' I'll trust ye to take keer o' me—anywhar."

The boy looked at her long and hard, but there was no feminine cunning in her eyes—nothing but simple trust—and his silence was a despairing assent. From the kitchen his mother called them to breakfast.

"Whar's Steve?" asked the boy.

The mother gave the same answer as had Mavis, but she looked anxious and worried.

"Mavis is a-goin' back to the mountains with me," said the boy, and the girl looked up in defiant expectation, but the mother did not even look around from the stove.

131

"Mebbe yo' pap won't let ye," she said quietly.

"How's he goin' to help hisself," asked the girl, "when he ain't hyeh?"

"He'll blame me fer it, but I ain't a-blamin' you."

The words surprised and puzzled both and touched both with sympathy and a little shame. The mother looked at her son, opened her lips again, but closed them with a glance at Mavis that made her go out and leave them alone.

"Jasie," she said then, "I reckon when Babe was a-playin' 'possum in the bushes that day, he could 'a' shot ye when you run down the hill."

She took his silence for assent and went on:

"That shows he don't hold no grudge agin you fer shootin' at him."

Still Jason was silent, and a line of stern justice straightened the woman's lips.

"I hain't got no right to say a word, just because Babe air my own brother. Mebbe Babe knows who the man was, but I don't believe Babe done it. Hit hain't enough that he was jes' *seed* a-comin' outen the bushes, an' afore you go a-layin' fer Babe, all I axe ye is to make *plumb dead shore.*"

It was a strange new note to come from his mother's voice, and it kept the boy still silent from helplessness and shame. She had spoken calmly, but now there was a little break in her voice.

"I want ye to go back, an' I'd go blind fer the rest o' my days if that land was yours an' was a-waitin' down thar fer ye."

From the next room came the sound of Mavis's restless feet, and the boy rose.

"I hain't a-goin' to lay fer Babe, mammy," he said huskily; "I hain't a-goin' to lay fer nobody —now. An' don't you worry no more about that land."

Half an hour later, just when day was breaking, Mavis sat behind Jason with her bundle in her lap, and the mother looked up at them.

"I wish I was a-goin' with ye," she said.

And when they had passed out of sight down the lane, she turned back into the house—weeping.

XIV

LITTLE Mavis did not reach the hills. At sunrise a few miles down the road, the two met Steve Hawn on a borrowed horse, his pistol buckled around him and his face pale and sleepless.

"Whar you two goin'?" he asked roughly.

"Home," was Jason's short answer, and he felt Mavis's arm about his waist begin to tremble.

"Git off, Mavis, an' git up hyeh behind me. Yo' home's with me."

Jason valiantly reached for his gun, but Mavis caught his hand and, holding it, slipped to the ground.

"Don't, Jasie—I'll come, pap, I'll come." Whereat Steve laughed and Jason, raging, saw her ride away behind her step-father, clutching him about the waist with one arm and with the other bent over her eyes to shield her tears.

A few miles farther, Jason came on the smoking, charred remains of a toll-gate, and he paused a moment wondering if Steve might not have had a hand in that, and rode on toward the hills. Two hours later the school-master's horse shied from those black ruins, and John Burnham kept

on toward school with a troubled face. To him
the ruins meant the first touch of the writhing
tentacles of the modern trust and the Blue-grass
Kentuckian's characteristic way of throwing them
off, for turnpikes of white limestone, like the one
he travelled, thread the Blue-grass country like
strands of a spider's web. The spinning of them
started away back in the beginning of the last
century. That far back, the strand he followed
pierced the heart of the region from its chief
town to the Ohio and was graded for steam-
wagons that were expected to roll out from the
land of dreams. Every few miles on each of
these roads sat a little house, its porch touching
the very edge of the turnpike, and there a long
pole, heavily weighted at one end and pulled
down and tied fast to the porch, blocked the way.
Every traveller, except he was on foot, every
drover of cattle, sheep, hogs, or mules, must pay
his toll before the pole was lifted and he could
go on his way. And Burnham could remember
the big fat man who once a month, in a broad,
low buggy, drawn by two swift black horses,
would travel hither and thither, stopping at each
little house to gather in the deposits of small coins.
As time went on, this man and a few friends began to gather in as well certain bits of scattered
paper that put the turnpike webs like reins into
a few pairs of hands, with the natural, inevitable
result: fewer men had personal need of good roads,

the man who parted with his bit of paper lost his power of protest, and while the traveller paid the small toll, the path that he travelled got steadily worse.   A mild effort to arouse a sentiment for county control was made, and this failing, the Kentuckian had straightway gone for firebrand and gun.   The dormant spirit of Ku-Klux awakened, the night-rider was born again, and one by one the toll-gates were going up in flame and settling back in ashes to the mother earth.   The school-master smiled when he thought of the result of one investigation in the county by law.   A sturdy farmer was haled before the grand jury.

"Do you know the perpetrators of the unlawful burning of the toll-gate on the Cave Hill Pike?" asked the august body.   The farmer ran his fearless eyes down the twelve of his peers and slowly walked the length of them, pointing his finger at this juror and that.

"Yes, I do," he said quietly, "and so do you —and you and *you*. Your son was in it—and yours—and mine; and you were in it yourself. Now, what are you going to do about it?"   And, unrebuked and unrestrained, he turned and walked out of the room, leaving the august body, startled, grimly smiling and reduced to a helpless pulp of inactivity.

That morning Mavis was late to school, and the school-master and Gray and Marjorie all saw that she had been weeping. Only Marjorie suspected the cause, but at little recess John Burnham went to her to ask where Jason was, and Gray was behind him with the same question on his lips. And when Mavis burst into tears, Marjorie answered for her and sat down beside her and put her arms around the mountain girl. After school she even took Mavis home behind her, and Gray rode along with them on his pony. Steve Hawn was sitting on his little porch smoking when they rode up, and he came down and hospitably asked them to "light and hitch their beastes," and the black-haired step-mother called from the doorway for them to "come in an' rest a spell." Gray and Marjorie concealed with some difficulty their amusement at such queer phrases of welcome, and a wonder at the democratic ease of the two and their utter unconsciousness of any social difference between the lords and ladies of the Blue-grass and poor people from the mountains, for the other tobacco tenants were not like these. And there was no surprise on the part of the man, the woman, or the little girl when a sudden warm impulse to relieve loneliness led Marjorie to ask Mavis to go to her own home and stay all night with her.

"Course," said the woman.

"Go right along, Mavis," said the man, and Marjorie turned to Gray.

"You can carry her things," she said, and she

turned to Mavis and met puzzled, unabashed eyes.

"Whut things?" asked little Mavis, whereat Marjorie blushed, looked quickly to Gray, whose face was courteously unsmiling, and started her pony abruptly.

It was a wonderful night for the mountaineer girl in the big-pillared house on the hill. When they got home, Marjorie drove her in a little pony-cart over the big farm, while Gray trotted alongside—through pastures filled with cattle so fat they could hardly walk, past big barns bursting with hay and tobacco and stables full of slender, beautiful horses. Even the pigs had little red houses of refuge from the weather and flocks of sheep dotted the hill-side like unmelted patches of snow. The mountain girl's eyes grew big with wonder when she entered the great hall with its lofty ceiling, its winding stairway, and its polished floor, so slippery that she came near falling down, and they stayed big when she saw the rows of books, the pictures on the walls, the padded couches and chairs, the noiseless carpets, the polished andirons that gleamed like gold before the blazing fires, and when she glimpsed through an open door the long dining-table with its glistening glass and silver. When she mounted that winding stairway and entered Marjorie's room she was stricken dumb by its pink curtains, pink wall-paper, and gleaming brass bedstead with pink coverlid and pink pillow-facings. And she

nearly gasped when Marjorie led her on into another room of blue.

"This is your room," she said smiling, "right
next to mine. I'll be back in a minute."

Mavis stood a moment in the middle of the
room when she was alone, hardly daring to sit
down. A coal fire crackled behind a wire screen
—coal from her mountains. A door opened into
a queer little room, glistening white, and she
peeped, wondering, within.

"There's the bath-room," Marjorie had said.
She had not known what was meant, and she did
not now, looking at the long white tub and the
white tiling floor and walls until she saw the
multitudinous towels, and she marvelled at the
new mystery. She went back and walked to the
window and looked out on the endless rolling
winter fields over which she had driven that afternoon—all, Gray had told her, to be Marjorie's
some day, just as all across the turnpike, Marjorie
had told her, was some day to be Gray's. She
thought of herself and of Jason, and her tears
started, not for herself, but for him. Then she
heard Marjorie coming in and she brushed her
eyes swiftly.

"Whar can I git some water to wash?" she asked.

Marjorie laughed delightedly and led her back
to that wonderful little white room, turned a
gleaming silver star, and the water spurted joyously into the bowl.

"Well, I do declare!"

Soon they went down to supper, and Mavis put out a shy hand to Marjorie's mother, a kind-eyed, smiling woman in black. And Gray, too, was there, watching the little mountain girl and smiling encouragement whenever he met her eyes. And Mavis passed muster well, for the mountaineer's sensitiveness makes him wary of his manners when he is among strange people, and he will go hungry rather than be guilty unknowingly of a possible breach. Marjorie's mother was much interested and pleased with Mavis, and she made up her mind at once to discuss with her daughter how they could best help along the little stranger. After supper Marjorie played on the piano, and she and Gray sang duets, but the music was foreign to Mavis, and she did not like it very much. When the two went upstairs, there was a dainty long garment spread on Mavis's bed, which Mavis fingered carefully with much interest and much curiosity until she recalled suddenly what Marjorie had said about Gray carrying her "things." This was one of these things, and Mavis put it on wondering what the other things might be. Then she saw that a silver-backed comb and brush had appeared on the bureau along with a tiny pair of scissors and a little ivory stick, the use of which she could not make out at all. But she asked no questions, and when Marjorie came in with a new toothbrush and a

little tin box and put them in the bath-room,
Mavis still showed no surprise, but ran her eyes
down the nightgown with its dainty ribbons.

"Ain't it purty?" she said, and her voice and
her eyes spoke all her thanks with such sincerity
and pathos that Marjorie was touched. Then
they sat down in front of the fire—a pair of slim
brown feet that had been bruised by many a
stone and pierced by many a thorn stretched out
to a warm blaze side by side with a pair of white
slim ones that had been tenderly guarded against
both since the first day they had touched the
earth, and a golden head that had never been
without the caress of a tender hand and a tousled
dark one that had been bared to sun and wind
and storm—close together for a long time. Unconsciously Marjorie had Mavis tell her much
about Jason, just as Mavis without knowing it
had Marjorie tell her much about Gray. Mavis
got the first good-night kiss of her life that night,
and she went to bed thinking of the Blue-grass
boy's watchful eyes, little courtesies, and his sympathetic smile, just as Gray, riding home, was
thinking of the dark, shy little mountain girl with
a warm glow of protection about his heart, and
Marjorie fell asleep dreaming of the mountain
boy who, under her promise, had gone back home-
less to his hills. In them perhaps it was the call
of the woods and wilds that had led their pioneer
forefathers long, long ago into woods and wilds,

or perhaps, after all, it was only the little blind god shooting arrows at them in the dark.

At least with little Jason one arrow had gone home. At the forks of the road beyond the county-seat he turned not toward his grandfather's, but up the spur and over the mountain. And St. Hilda, sitting on her porch, saw him coming again. His face looked beaten but determined, and he strode toward her as straight and sturdy as ever.

"I've come back to stay with ye," he said.

Again she started to make denial, but he shook his head. "'Tain't no use—I'm a-goin' to stay this time," he said, and he walked up the steps, pulling two or three dirty bills from his pocket with one hand and unbuckling his pistol belt with the other.

"Me an' my nag'll work fer ye an' I'll wear gal's stockin's an' a poke-bonnet an' do a gal's work, if you'll jus' l'arn me whut I want to know."

XV

THE funeral of old Hiram Sudduth, Marjorie's grandfather on her mother's side, was
over. The old man had been laid to rest, by the
side of his father and his pioneer grandfather, in
the cedar-filled burying-ground on the broad farm
that had belonged in turn to the three in an adjoining county that was the last stronghold of
conservatism in the Blue-grass world, and John
Burnham, the school-master, who had spent the
night with an old friend after the funeral, was
driving home. Not that there had not been many
changes in that stronghold, too, but they were
fewer than elsewhere and unmodern, and whatever profit was possible through these changes
was reaped by men of the land like old Hiram
and not by strangers. For the war there, as elsewhere, had done its deadly work. With the negro
quarters empty, the elders were too old to change
their ways, the young would not accept the new
and hard conditions, and as mortgages slowly ate
up farm after farm, quiet, thrifty, hard-working
old Hiram would gradually take them in, deplet-
ing the old Stonewall neighborhood of its families
one by one, and sending them West, never to
come back. The old man, John Burnham knew,

had bitterly opposed the marriage of his daughter
with a "spendthrift Pendleton," and he wondered
if now the old man's will would show that he had
carried that opposition to the grave. It was more
than likely, for Marjorie's father had gone his
careless, generous, magnificent way in spite of the
curb that the inherited thrift and inherited passion for land in his Sudduth wife had put upon
him. Old Hiram knew, moreover, the parental
purpose where Gray and Marjorie were concerned,
and it was not likely that he would thwart one
generation and tempt the succeeding one to go
on in its reckless way. Right now Burnham
knew that trouble was imminent for Gray's
father, and he began to wonder what for him and
his kind the end would be, for no change that
came or was coming to his beloved land ever escaped his watchful eye. From the crest of the
Cumberland to the yellow flood of the Ohio he
knew that land, and he loved every acre of it,
whether blue-grass, bear-grass, peavine, or pennyroyal, and he knew its history from Daniel Boone
to the little Boones who still trapped skunk, mink,
and muskrat, and shot squirrels in the hills with
the same old-fashioned rifle, and he loved its
people—his people—whether they wore silk and
slippers, homespun and brogans, patent leathers
and broadcloth, or cowhide boots and jeans.
And now serious troubles were threatening them.
A new man with a new political method had en-

tered the arena and had boldly offered an election
bill which, if passed and enforced, would create
a State-wide revolution, for it would rob the people of local self-government and centralize power
in the hands of a triumvirate that would be the
creature of his government and, under the control
of no court or jury, the supreme master of the
State and absolute master of the people. And
Burnham knew that, in such a crisis, ties of blood,
kinship, friendship, religion, business, would count
no more in the Blue-grass than they did during
the Civil War, and that now, as then, father and
son, brother and brother, neighbor and neighbor,
would each think and act for himself, though the
house divided against itself should fall to rise no
more. Nor was that all. In the farmer's fight
against the staggering crop of mortgages that had
slowly sprung up from the long-ago sowing of
the dragon's teeth Burnham saw with a heavy
heart the telling signs of the land's slow descent
from the strength of hemp to the weakness of
tobacco—the ravage of the woodlands, the incoming of the tenant from the river-valley counties, the scars on the beautiful face of the land,
the scars on the body social of the region—and
now he knew another deadlier crisis, both social
and economic, must some day come.

In the toll-gate war, long over, the law had
been merely a little too awkward and slow.
County sentiment had been a little lazy, but it

had got active in a hurry, and several gentlemen, among them Gray's father, had ridden into town and deposited bits of gilt-scrolled paper to be appraised and taken over by the county, and the whole problem had been quickly solved, but the school-master, looking back, could not help wondering what lawless seeds the firebrand had then sowed in the hearts of the people and what weeds might not spring from those seeds even now; for the trust element of the toll-gate troubles had been accidental, unintentional, even unconscious, unrecognized; and now the real spirit of a real trust from the outside world was making itself felt. Courteous emissaries were smilingly fixing their own price on the Kentuckian's own tobacco and assuring him that he not only could not get a higher price elsewhere, but that if he declined he would be offered less next time, which he would have to accept or he could not sell at all. And the incredulous, fiery, independent Kentuckian found his crop mysteriously shadowed on its way to the big town markets, marked with an invisible "noli me tangere" except at the price that he was offered at home. And so he had to sell it in a rage at just that price, and he went home puzzled and fighting-mad. If, then, the Blue-grass people had handled with the firebrand corporate aggrandizement of toll-gate owners who were neighbors and friends, how would they treat meddlesome interference from strangers? Already one

courteous emissary in one county had fled the
people's wrath on a swift thoroughbred, and Burnham smiled sadly to himself and shook his head.

Rounding a hill a few minutes later, the school-
master saw far ahead the ancestral home of the
Pendletons, where the stern old head of the house,
but lately passed in his ninetieth year, had wielded
patriarchal power. The old general had entered
the Mexican War a lieutenant and come out a
colonel, and from the Civil War he had emerged
a major-general. He had two sons—twins—and
for the twin brothers he had built twin houses on
either side of the turnpike and had given each
five hundred acres of land. And these houses
had literally grown from the soil, for the soil had
given every stick of timber in them and every
brick and stone. The twin brothers had married
sisters, and thus as the results of those unions
Gray's father and Marjorie's father were double
cousins, and like twin brothers had been reared,
and the school-master marvelled afresh when he
thought of the cleavage made in that one family
by the terrible Civil War. For the old general
carried but one of his twin sons into the Con-
federacy with him—the other went with the Union
—and his grandsons, the double cousins, who were
just entering college, went not only against each
other, but each against his own father, and there
was the extraordinary fact of three generations
serving in the same war, cousin against cousin,

brother against brother, and father against son. The twin brothers each gave up his life for his cause. After the war the cousins lived on like brothers, married late, and, naturally, each was called uncle by the other's only child. In time the two took their fathers' places in the heart of the old general, and in the twin houses on the hills. Gray's father had married an aristocrat, who survived the birth of Gray only a few years, and Marjorie's father died of an old wound but a year or two after she was born. And so the balked affection of the old man dropped down through three generations to centre on Marjorie, and his passionate family pride to concentrate on Gray.

Now the old Roman was gone, and John Burnham looked with sad eyes at the last stronghold of him and his kind—the rambling old house stuccoed with aged brown and covered with ancient vines, knotted and gnarled like an old man's hand; the walls three feet thick and built as for a fort, as was doubtless the intent in pioneer days; the big yard of unmown blue-grass and filled with cedars and forest trees; the numerous servants' quarters, the spacious hen-house, the stables with gables and long sloping roofs and the arched gateway to them for the thoroughbreds, under which no hybrid mule or lowly work-horse was ever allowed to pass; the spring-house with its dripping green walls, the long-silent blacksmith-shop;

the still windmill; and over all the atmosphere of
careless, magnificent luxury and slow decay; the
stucco peeled off in great patches, the stable roofs
sagging, the windmill wheelless, the fences following the line of a drunken man's walk, the trees
storm-torn, and the mournful cedars harping with
every passing wind a requiem for the glory that
was gone. As he looked, the memory of the old
man's funeral came to Burnham: the white old
face in the coffin—haughty, noble, proud, and the
spirit of it unconquered even by death; the long
procession of carriages, the slow way to the cemetery, the stops on that way, the creaking of
wheels and harness, and the awe of it all to the
boy, Gray, who rode with him. Then the hos-
pitable doors of the princely old house were closed
and the princely life that had made merry for so
long within its walls came sharply to an end, and
it stood now, desolate, gloomy, haunted, the last
link between the life that was gone and the life
that was now breaking just ahead. A mile on,
the twin-pillared houses of brick jutted from a
long swelling knoll on each side of the road. In
each the same spirit had lived and was yet alive.

In Gray's home it had gone on unchecked
toward the same tragedy, but in Marjorie's the
thrifty, quiet force of her mother's hand had been
in power, and in the little girl the same force was
plain. Her father was a Pendleton of the Pendletons, too, but the same gentle force had, with-

out curb or check-rein, so guided him that while he lived he led proudly with never a suspicion that he was being led. And since the death of Gray's mother and Marjorie's father each that was left had been faithful to the partner gone, and in spite of prediction and gossip, the common neighborhood prophecy had remained unfulfilled.

A mile farther onward, the face of the land on each side changed suddenly and sharply and became park-like. Not a ploughed acre was visible, no tree-top was shattered, no broken boughs hung down. The worm fence disappeared and neat white lines flashed divisions of pastures, it seemed, for miles. A great amphitheatrical red barn sat on every little hill or a great red rectangular tobacco barn. A huge dairy was building of brick. Paddocks and stables were everywhere, macadamized roads ran from the main highway through the fields, and on the highest hill visible stood a great villa —a colossal architectural stranger in the land— and Burnham was driving by a row of neat red cottages, strangers, too, in the land. In the old Stonewall neighborhood that Burnham had left the gradual depopulation around old Hiram left him almost as alone as his pioneer grandfather had been, and the home of the small farmers about him had been filled by the tobacco tenant. From the big villa emanated a similar force with a similar tendency, but old Hiram, compared with old Morton Sanders, was as a slow fire to a lightning-bolt. Sanders was from the East, had unlimited wealth, and loved race-horses. Purchasing a farm for them, the Saxon virus in his Kentucky blood for land had gotten hold of him, and he, too, had started depopulating the country; only where old Hiram bought roods, he bought acres; and where Hiram bagged the small farmer for game, Sanders gunned for the aristocrat as well. It was for Sanders that Colonel Pendleton had gone to the mountains long ago to gobble coal lands. It was to him that the roof over little Jason's head and the earth under his feet had been sold, and the schoolmaster smiled a little bitterly when he turned at last into a gate and drove toward a stately old home in the midst of ancient cedars, for he was thinking of the little mountaineer and of the letter St. Hilda had sent him years ago.

"Jason has come back," she wrote, "'to learn some way o' gittin' his land back.'"

For the school-master's reflections during his long drive had not been wholly impersonal. With his own family there had been the same change, the same passing, the workings of the same force in the same remorseless way, and to him, too, the same doom had come. The home to which he was driving had been his, but it was Morton Sanders's now. His brother lived there as manager of Sanders's flocks, herds, and acres, and in the house of his fathers the school-master now paid his own brother for his board.

XVI

THE boy was curled up on the rear seat of the smoking-car. His face was upturned to the glare of light above him, the train bumped, jerked, and swayed; smoke and dust rolled in at the open window and cinders stung his face, but he slept as peacefully as though he were in one of the huge feather-beds at his grandfather's house—slept until the conductor shook him by the shoulder, when he opened his eyes, grunted, and closed them again. The train stopped, a brakeman yanked him roughly to his feet, put a cheap suit-case into his hand, and pushed him, still dazed, into the chill morning air. The train rumbled on and left him blinking into a lantern held up to his face, but he did not look promising as a hotel guest and the darky porter turned abruptly; and the boy yawned long and deeply, with his arms stretched above his head, dropped on the frosty bars of a baggage-truck and rose again shivering. Cocks were crowing, light was showing in the east, the sea of mist that he well knew was about him, but no mountains loomed above it, and St. Hilda's prize pupil, Jason Hawn, woke sharply at last with a tingling that went from head to foot. Once more he was in the

land of the Blue-grass, his journey was almost
over, and in a few hours he would put his confident feet on a new level and march on upward.
Gradually, as the lad paced the platform, the
mist thinned and the outlines of things came out.
A mysterious dark bulk high in the air showed as
a water-tank, roofs new to mountain eyes jutted
upward, trees softly emerged, a desolate dusty
street opened before him, and the cocks crowed
on lustily all around him and from farm-houses
far away. The crowing made him hungry, and
he went to the light of a little eating-house and
asked the price of the things he saw on the coun-
ter there, but the price was too high. He shook
his head and went out, but his pangs were so
keen that he went back for a cup of coffee and a
hard-boiled egg, and then he heard the coming
thunder of his train. The sun was rising as he
sped on through the breaking mist toward the
Blue-grass town that in pioneer days was known
as the Athens of the West. In a few minutes the
train slackened in mid-air and on a cloud of mist
between jutting cliffs, it seemed, and the startled
lad, looking far down through it, saw a winding
yellow light, and he was rushing through autumn
fields again before he realized that the yellow
light was the Kentucky River surging down from
the hills. Back up the stream surged his memories, making him faint with homesickness, for
it was the last link that bound him to the moun-

tains. But both home and hills were behind him now, and he shook himself sharply and lost himself again in the fields of grass and grain, the grazing stock and the fences, houses, and barns that reeled past his window. Steve Hawn met him at the station with a rattle-trap buggy and stared at him long and hard.

"I'd hardly knowed ye—you've growed like a weed."

"How's the folks?" asked Jason.

"Stirrin'."

Silently they rattled down the street, each side of which was lined with big wagons loaded with tobacco and covered with cotton cloth—there seemed to be hundreds of them.

"Hell's a-comin' about that terbaccer up here," said Steve.

"Hell's a-comin' in the mountains if that robber up here at the capital steals the next election for governor," said Jason, and Steve looked up quickly and with some uneasiness. He himself had heard vaguely that somebody, somewhere, and in some way, had robbed his own party of their rights and would go on robbing at the polls, but this new Jason seemed to know all about it, so Steve nodded wisely.

"Yes, my feller."

Through town they drove, and when they started out into the country they met more wagons of tobacco coming in.

154

"How's the folks in the mountains?"

"About the same as usual," said the boy. "Grandpap's poorly. The war's over just now —folks 'r' busy makin' money. Uncle Arch's still takin' up options. The railroad's comin' up the river"—the lad's face darkened—"an' land's sellin' fer three times as much as you sold me out fer."

Steve's face darkened too, but he was silent.

"Found out yit who killed yo' daddy?"

Jason's answer was short.

"If I had I wouldn't tell you."

"Must be purty good shot now?"

"I hain't shot a pistol off fer four year," said the lad again shortly, and Steve stared.

"Whut devilmint are you in up here now?" asked Jason calmly and with no apparent notice of the start Steve gave.

"Who's been a-tellin' you lies about me?" asked Steve with angry suspicion.

"I hain't heerd a word," said Jason coolly. "I bet you burned that toll-gate the morning I left here. Thar's devilmint goin' on everywhar, an' if there's any around you I know you can't keep out o' it."

Steve laughed with relief.

"You can't git away with devilmint here like you can in the mountains, an' I'm 'tendin' to my own business."

Jason made no comment and Steve went on:

"I've paid fer this hoss an' buggy an' I got things hung up at home an' a leetle money in the bank, an' yo' ma says she wouldn't go back to the mountains fer nothin'."

"How's Mavis?" asked Jason abruptly.

"Reckon you wouldn't know her. She's al'ays runnin' aroun' with that Pendleton boy an' gal, an' she's chuck-full o' new-fangled notions. She's the purtiest gal I ever seed, an'," he added slyly, "looks like that Pendleton boy's plumb crazy 'bout her."

Jason made no answer and showed no sign of interest, much less jealousy, and yet, though he was thinking of the Pendleton girl and wanted to ask some question about her, a little inconsistent rankling started deep within him at the news of Mavis's disloyalty to him. They were approaching the lane that led to Steve's house now, and beyond the big twin houses were visible.

"Yo' Uncle Arch's been here a good deal, an' he's tuk a powerful fancy to Mavis an' he's goin' to send her to the same college school in town whar you're goin'. Marjorie and Gray is a-goin' thar too, I reckon."

Jason's heart beat fast at these words. Gray had the start of him, but he would give the Blue-grass boy a race now in school and without. As they turned into the lane, he could see the woods —could almost see the tree around which he had circled drunk, raging, and shooting his pistol, and his face burned with the memory. And over in the hollow he had met Marjorie on her pony, and he could see the tears in her eyes, hear her voice, and feel the clasp of her hand again. Though neither knew it, a new life had started for him there and then. He had kept his promise, and he wondered if she would remember and be glad.

His mother was on the porch, waiting and watching for him, with one hand shading her eyes. She rushed for the gate, and when he stepped slowly from the buggy she gave a look of wondering surprise and pride, burst into tears, and for the first time in her life threw her arms around him and kissed him, to his great confusion and shame. In the doorway stood a tall, slender girl with a mass of black hair, and she, too, with shining eyes rushed toward him, stopping defiantly short within a few feet of him when she met his cool, clear gaze, and, without even speaking his name, held out her hand. Then with intuitive suspicion she flashed a look at Steve and knew that his tongue had been wagging. She flushed angrily, but with feminine swiftness caught her lost poise and, lifting her head, smiled.

"I wouldn't 'a' known ye," she said.

"An' I wouldn't 'a' known you," said Jason.

The girl said no more, and the father looked at his daughter and the mother at her son, puzzled by the domestic tragedy so common in this land of ours, where the gates of opportunity swing

wide for the passing on of the young. But of
the two, Steve Hawn was the more puzzled and
uneasy, for Jason, like himself, was a product of
the hills and had had less chance than even he to
know the outside world.

The older mountaineer wore store clothes, but
so did Jason. He had gone to meet the boy,
self-assured and with the purpose of patronage
and counsel, and he had met more assurance than
his own and a calm air of superiority that was
troubling to Steve's pride. The mother, always
apologetic on account of the one great act of
injustice she had done her son, felt awe as she
looked, and as her pride grew she became abject,
and the boy accepted the attitude of each as his
just due. But on Mavis the wave of his influence
broke as on a rock. She was as much changed
from the Mavis he had last seen as she was at
that time from the little Mavis of the hills, and
he felt her eyes searching him from head to foot
just as she had done that long-ago time when he
saw her first in the hunting-field. He knew that
now she was comparing him with even higher
standards than she was then, and that now, as
then, he was falling short, and he looked up suddenly and caught her eyes with a grim, confident
little smile that made her shift her gaze con-
fusedly. She moved nervously in her chair and
her cheeks began to burn. And Steve talked on
—volubly for him—while the mother threw in a

timid homesick question to Jason now and then
about something in the mountains, and Mavis
kept still and looked at the boy no more. By
and by the two women went to their work, and
Jason followed Steve about the little place to look
at the cow and a few pigs and at the garden and
up over the hill to the tobacco-patch that Steve
was tending on shares with Colonel Pendleton.
After dinner Mavis disappeared, and the step-
mother reckoned she had gone over to see Marjorie Pendleton—"she was al'ays a-goin' over
thar"—and in the middle of the afternoon the
boy wandered aimlessly forth into the Blue-grass
fields.

Spring green the fields were, and the woods,
but scarcely touched by the blight of autumn,
were gray as usual from the limestone turnpike,
which, when he crossed it, was ankle-deep in dust.
A cloud of yellow butterflies fluttered crazily before him in a sunlight that was hardly less golden,
and when he climbed the fence a rabbit leaped
beneath him and darted into a patch of iron-
weeds. Instinctively he leaped after it, crashing
through the purple crowns, and as suddenly
stopped at the foolishness of pursuit, when he
had left his pistol in his suit-case, and with another sharp memory of the rabbit hunt he had
encountered when he made his first appearance in
that land. Half unconsciously then his thoughts
turned him through the woods and through a

pasture toward the twin homes of the Pendletons, and on the top of the next hill he could see
them on their wooded eminences—could even see
the stile where he had had his last vision of Marjorie, and he dropped in the thick grass, looking
long and hard and wondering.

Around the corner of the yard fence a negro
appeared leading a prancing iron-gray horse, the
front doors opened, a tall girl in a black riding-
habit came swiftly down the walk, and a moment
later the iron-gray was bearing her at a swift
gallop toward the turnpike gate. As she disappeared over a green summit, his heart stood quite
still. Could that tall woman be the little girl
who, with a tear, a tremor of the voice, and a
touch of the hand, had swerved him from the
beaten path of a century? Mavis had grown, he
himself had grown—and, of course, Marjorie, too,
had grown. He began to wonder whether she
would recollect him, would know him when he
met her face to face, would remember the promise
she had asked and he had given, and if she would
be pleased to know that he had kept it. In the
passing years the boy had actually lost sight of
her as flesh and blood, for she had become enshrined among his dreams by night and his dreams
by day; among the visions his soul had seen when
he had sat under the old circuit rider and heard
pictured the glories of the blessed when mortals
should mingle with the shining hosts on high;

and above even St. Hilda, on the very pinnacle of his new-born and ever-growing ambitions, Marjorie sat enthroned and alone. Light was all he remembered of her—the light of her eyes and of her hair—yes, and that one touch of her hand. His heart turned to water at the thought of seeing her again and his legs were trembling when he rose to start back through the fields. Another rabbit sprang from its bed in a tuft of grass, but he scarcely paid any heed to it. When he crossed the creek a muskrat was leisurely swimming for its hole in the other bank, and he did not even pick up a stone to throw at it, but walked on dreaming through the woods. As he was about to emerge from them he heard voices ahead of him, high-pitched and angry, and with the caution of his race he slipped forward and stopped, listening. In a tobacco-patch on the edge of the woods Steve Hawn had stopped work and was leaning on the fence. Seated on it was one of the small farmers of the neighborhood. They were not quarrelling, and the boy could hardly believe his ears.

"I tell you that fellow—they're callin' him the autocrat already—that fellow will have two of his judges to your one at every election booth in the State. He'll steal every precinct and he'll be settin' in the governor's chair as sure as you are standing here. I'm a Democrat, but I've been half a Republican ever since this free-silver fool-

ishness came up, and I'm going to vote against
him. Now, all you mountain people are Republicans, but you might as well all be Democrats.
You haven't got a chance on earth. What are
you goin' to do about it?"

Steve Hawn shook his head helplessly, but
Jason saw his huge hand grip his tobacco knife
and his own blood beat indignantly at his temples. The farmer threw one leg back over the
fence.

"There'll be hell to pay when the day comes,"
he said, and he strode away, while the mountaineer
leaned motionless on the fence with his grip on
the knife unrelaxed.

Noiselessly the boy made his way through the
edge of the woods, out under the brow of a hill,
and went on his restless way up the bank of the
creek toward Steve's home. When he turned
toward the turnpike he found that he had passed
the house a quarter of a mile, so he wheeled
back down the creek, and where the mouth of the
lane opened from the road he dropped in a spot
of sunlight on the crest of a little cliff, his legs
weary but his brain still tirelessly at work. These
people of the Blue-grass were not only robbing
him and his people of their lands, but of their
political birthright as well. The fact that the
farmer was on his side but helped make the boy
know it was truth, and the resentments that
were always burning like a bed of coals deep

within him sprang into flames again. The shadows lengthened swiftly about him and closed over him, and then the air grew chill. Abruptly he rose and stood rigid, for far up the lane, and coming over a little hill, he saw the figure of a man leading a black horse and by his side the figure of a woman—both visible for a moment before they disappeared behind the bushes that lined the lane. When they were visible again Jason saw that they were a boy and girl, and when they once more came into view at a bend of the lane and stopped he saw that the girl, with her face downcast, was Mavis. While they stood the boy suddenly put his arm around her, but she eluded him and fled to the fence, and with a laugh he climbed on his horse and came down the lane. In a burning rage Jason started to slide down the cliff and pull the intruder, whoever he was, from his horse, and then he saw Mavis, going swiftly through the fields, turn and wave her hand. That stopped him still—he could not punish where there was apparently no offence—so with sullen eyes he watched the mouth of the lane give up a tall lad on a black thoroughbred, his hat in his hand and his handsome face still laughing and still turned for another glimpse of the girl. Another handwave came from Mavis at the edge of the woods, and glowering Jason stood in full view unseen and watched Gray Pendleton go thundering past him down the road.

Mavis had not gone to see Marjorie—she had sneaked away to meet Gray; his lips curled contemptuously—Mavis was a sneak, and so was Gray Pendleton. Then a thought struck him—why was Mavis behaving like a brush-girl this way, and why didn't Gray go to see her in her own home, open and above-board, like a man? The curl of the boy's lips settled into a straight, grim line, and once more he turned slowly down the stream that he might approach Steve's house from another direction. Half an hour later, when he climbed the turnpike fence, he heard the gallop of iron-shod feet and he saw bearing down on him an iron-gray horse. It was Marjorie. He knew her from afar; he gripped the rail beneath him with both hands and his heart seemed almost to stop. She was looking him full in the face now, and then, with a nod and a smile she would have given a beggar or a tramp, she swept him by.

XVII

THERE was little about Jason and his school career that John Burnham had not heard from his friend St. Hilda, for she kept sending at intervals reports of him, so that Burnham knew how doggedly the lad had worked in school and out; what a leader he was among his fellows, and how, that he might keep out of the feud, he had never gone to his grandfather's even during vacations, except for a day or two, but had hired himself out to some mountain farmer and had toiled like a slave, always within St. Hilda's reach. She had won Jason's heart from the start, so that he had told her frankly about his father's death, the coming of the geologist, the sale of his home, the flight of his mother and Steve Hawn, his shooting at Babe Honeycutt, and his own flight after them, but at the brink of one confession he always balked. Never could St. Hilda learn just why he had given up the manly prerogatives of pistol, whiskey-jug, and a deadly purpose of revenge, to accept in their place, if need be, the despised duties of women-folks. But his grim and ready willingness for the exchange appealed to St. Hilda so strongly that she had always saved him as much of these duties as she could.

The truth was that the school-master had slyly
made a diplomatic use of their mutual interest
in Jason that was masterly. There had been little
communication between them since the long-ago
days when she had given him her final decision
and gone on her mission to the mountains, until
Jason had come to be an important link between
them. Gradually, after that, St. Hilda had slowly
come to count on the school-master's sympathy
and understanding, and more than once she had
written not only for his advice but for his help
as well. And wisely, through it all, Burnham
had never sounded the personal note, and smilingly he had noted the passing of all suspicion
on her part, the birth of her belief that he was
cured of his love for her and would bother her no
more, and now, in her last letter announcing
Jason's coming to the Blue-grass, there was a distinct personal atmosphere that almost made him
chuckle. St. Hilda even wondered whether he
might not care, during some vacation, to come
down and see with his own eyes the really remark-
able work he knew she was doing down there.
And when he wrote during the summer that he
had been called to the suddenly vacated chair of
geology in the college Jason had been prepared
for, her delight thrilled him, though he had to
wonder how much of it might be due to the fact
that her protégé would thus be near him for help
and counsel.

His face was almost aglow when he drove out through the gate that morning on his way to the duties of his first day. The neighborhood children were already on their way to school, but they were mostly the children of tobacco tenants, and when he passed the school-house he saw a young woman on the porch—two facts that were significant. The neighborhood church was going, the neighborhood school was going, the man-teacher was gone—and he himself was perhaps the last of the line that started in coonskin caps and moccasins. The gentleman farmers who had made the land distinct and distinguished were renting their acres to tobacco tenants on shares and were moving to town to get back their negro servants and to provide their children with proper schooling. And those children of the gentle people, it seemed, were growing more and more indifferent to education and culture, and less and less marked by the gentle manners that were their birthright. And when he thought of the toll-gate war, the threatened political violence almost at hand, and the tobacco troubles which he knew must some day come, he wondered with a sick heart if a general decadence was not going on in the land for which he would have given his life in peace as readily as in war. In the mountains, according to St. Hilda, the people had awakened from a sleep of a hundred years. Lawlessness was on the decrease, the feud was disappearing, railroads were coming in, the hills were beginning to give up the wealth of their timber, iron, and coal. County schools were increasing, and the pathetic eagerness of mountain children to learn and the pathetic hardships they endured to get to school and to stay there made her heart bleed and his ache to help them. And in his own land, what a contrast! Three years before, the wedge of free silver had split the State in twain. Into this breach had sprung that new man with the new political method that threatened disaster to the commonwealth. To his supporters, he was the enemy of corporations, the friend of widows and orphans, the champion of the poor—this man; to his enemies, he was the most malign figure that had ever thrust head above the horizon of Kentucky politics—and so John Burnham regarded him; to both he was the autocrat, cold, exacting, imperious, and his election bill would make him as completely master of the commonwealth as Diaz in Mexico or Menelik in Abyssinia. The dazed people awoke and fought, but the autocrat had passed his bill. It was incredible, but could he enforce it? No one knew, but the midsummer convention for the nomination of governor came, and among the candidates he entered it, the last in public preference. But he carried that convention at the pistol's point, came out the Democratic nominee, and now stood smilingly ready to face the most terrible political storm that had ever broken over Kentucky. The election was less than two months away, the State was seething as though on the trembling crisis of a civil war, and the division that John Burnham expected between friend and friend, brother and brother, and father and son had come. The mountains were on fire and there might even be an invasion from those black hills led by the spirit of the Picts and Scots of old, and aided and abetted by the head, hand, and tongue of the best element of the Blue-grass. The people of the Blue-grass had known little and cared less about these shadowy hillsmen, but it looked to John Burnham as though they might soon be forced to know and care more than would be good for the peace of the State and its threatened good name.

A rattle-trap buggy was crawling up a hill ahead of him, and when he passed it Steve Hawn was flopping the reins, and by him was Mavis with a radiant face and sparkling eyes.

"Where's Jason?" John Burnham called, and the girl's face grew quickly serious.

"Gone on, afoot," laughed Steve loudly. "He started 'bout crack o' day."

The school-master smiled. On the slope of the next hill, two carriages, each drawn by a spanking pair of trotters, swept by him. From one he got a courteous salute from Colonel Pendleton and a happy shout from Gray, and from the other a radiant greeting from Marjorie and her mother. Again John Burnham smiled thoughtfully. For him the hope of the Blue-grass was in the joyous pair ahead of him, the hope of the mountains was in the girl behind and the sturdy youth streaking across the dawn-wet fields, and in the four the hope of his State; and his smile was pleased and hopeful.

Soon on his left were visible the gray lines of the old Transylvania University where Jefferson Davis had gone to college while Abraham Lincoln was splitting rails and studying by candlelight a hundred miles away, and its campus was dotted with swiftly moving figures of boys and girls on their way to the majestic portico on the hill. The streets were filled with eager young faces, and he drove on through them to the red-brick walls of the State University, on the other side of the town, where his labors were to begin. And when, half an hour later, he turned into the campus afoot, he found himself looking among the boys who thronged the walk, the yard, and the entrances of the study halls for the face of Jason Hawn.

Tremblingly the boy had climbed down from the fence after Marjorie galloped by him the day before, had crossed the pike slowly, sunk dully at the foot of an oak in the woods beyond, and sat there, wide-eyed and stunned, until dark. Had he been one of the followers of the star of Bethlehem, and had that star vanished suddenly from the heavens, he could hardly have known such darkness, such despair. For the time Mavis and Gray passed quite out of the world while he was wrestling with that darkness, and it was only when he rose shakily to his feet at last that they came back into it again. Supper was over when he reached the house, but Mavis had kept it for him, and while she waited on him she tried to ask him questions about his school-life in the mountains, to tell him of her own in the Blue-grass— tried to talk about the opening of college next day, but he sat silent and sullen, and so, puzzled and full of resentment, she quietly withdrew. After he was through, he heard her cleaning the dishes and putting them away, and he saw her that night no more. Next morning, without a word to her or to his mother, he went out to the barn where Steve was feeding.

"If you'll bring my things on in the buggy, I reckon I'll just be goin' on."

"Why, we can all three git in the buggy."

Jason shook his head.

"I hain't goin' to be late."

Steve laughed.

"Well, you'll shore be on time if you start now. Why, Mavis says——"

But Jason had started swiftly on, and Steve, puzzled, did not try to stop him. Mavis came out on the porch, and he pointed out the boy's figure going through the dim fields. "Jason's gone on," he said, "afeerd he'll be late. That boy's plum' quar."

Jason was making a bee-line for more than the curve of the pike, for more than the college—he was making it now for everything in his life that was ahead of him, and he meant now to travel it without help or hindrance, unswervingly and alone. With St. Hilda, each day had started for him at dawn, and whether it started that early at the college in town he did not ask himself or anybody else. He would wait now for nothing —nobody. The time had come to start, so he had started on his own new way, stout in body, heart, and soul, and that was all.

Soft mists of flame were shooting up the eastern horizon, soft dew-born mists were rising from little hollows and trailing through the low trees. There had been a withering drought lately, but the merciful rain had come, the parched earth had drunk deep, and now under its mantle of rich green it seemed to be heaving forth one vast long sigh of happy content. The corn was long ready for the knife, green sprouts of winter wheat were feathering their way above the rich brown soil, and the cut upturned tobacco stalks, but dimly seen through the mists, looked like little hunch-backed witches poised on broomsticks, and ready for flight at dawn. Vast deviltry those witches had done, for every cut field, every poor field, recovering from the drastic visit of years before, was rough, weedy, shaggy, unkempt, and worn. The very face of the land showed decadence, and, in the wake of the witches, white top, dockweed, ragweed, cockle burr, and sweet fern had up-leaped like some joyous swarm of criminals un-leashed from the hand of the law, while the beau-tiful pastures and grassy woodlands, their dignity outraged, were stretched here and there between them, helpless, but breathing in the very mists their scorn.

When he reached the white, dusty road, the fires of his ambition kept on kindling with every step, and his pace, even in the cool of the early morning, sent his hat to his hand, and plastered his long lank hair to his temples and the back of his sturdy sunburnt neck. The sun was hardly star-pointing the horizon when he saw the lumi-nous smoke-cloud over the town. He quickened his step, and in his dark eyes those fires leaped into steady flames. The town was wakening from sleep. The driver of a milk-cart pointed a gen-eral direction for him across the roof-tops, but when he got into the wilderness of houses he lost that point of the compass and knew not which way to turn. On a street corner he saw a man in a cap and a long coat with brass buttons on it, a black stick in his hand, and something bulg-ing at his hip, and light dawned for Jason.

"Air you the constable?" he asked, and the policeman grinned kindly.

"I'm one of 'em," he said.

"Well, how do I git to the college I'm goin' to?"

The officer grinned good-naturedly again, and pointed with his stick.

"Follow that street, and hurry up or you'll get a whippin'."

"Thar now," thought Jason, and started into a trot up the hill, and the officer, seeing the boy's suddenly anxious face, called to him to take it easy, but Jason, finding the pavements rather uneven, took to the middle of the street, and without looking back sped on. It was a long run, but Jason never stopped until he saw a man standing at the door of a long, low, brick building with the word "Tobacco" painted in huge letters above its closed doors, and he ran across the street to him.

"Whar's the college?"

The man pointed across the street to an entrance between two gray stone pillars with pyramidal tops, and Jason trotted back, and trotted on through them, and up the smooth curve of the road. Not a soul was in sight, and on the empty steps of the first building he came to Jason dropped, panting.

XVIII

THE campus was thick with grass and full of trees, there were buildings of red brick everywhere, and all were deserted. He began to feel that the constable had made game of him, and he was indignant. Nobody in the mountains would treat a stranger that way; but he had reached his goal, and, no matter when "school took up," he was there.

Still, he couldn't help rising restlessly once, and then with a deep breath he patiently sat down again and waited, looking eagerly around meanwhile. The trees about him were low and young —they looked like maples—and multitudinous little gray birds were flitting and chattering around him, and these he did not know, for the English sparrow has not yet captured the mountains. Above the closed doors of the long brick building opposite the stone-guarded gateway he could see the word "Tobacco" printed in huge letters, and farther away he could see another similar sign, and somehow he began wondering why Steve Hawn had talked so much about the troubles that were coming over tobacco, and seemed to care so little about the election troubles that had put the whole State on the wire edge

of quivering suspense. Half an hour passed and
Jason was getting restless again, when he saw an
old negro shuffling down the stone walk with a
bucket in one hand, a mop in the other, and trailing one leg like a bird with a broken wing.

"Good-mornin', son."

"Do you know whar John Burnham is?"

"Whut's dat—whut's dat?"

"I'm a-lookin' fer John Burnham."

"Look hyeh, chile, is you referrin' to Perfesser
Burnham?"

"I reckon that's him."

"Well, if you is, you better axe fer him jes*
that-a-way—Per*fes*ser *Per*fesser—Burnham. Well,
Perfesser Burnham won't sanctify dis hall wid
his presence fer quite a long while—quite a long
while. May I inquire, son, if yo' purpose is to
attend dis place o' learnin'?"

"I come to go to college."

"Yassuh, yassuh," said the old negro, and with
no insolence whatever he guffawed loudly.

"Well, suh, looks lak you come a long way, an*
you sutinly got hyeh on time—you sho did. Well,
son, you jes' set hyeh as long as you please an*
walk aroun' an' come back an' den ef you set hyeh
long enough agin, you'se a-gwine to see Perfesser
Burnham come right up dese steps."

So Jason took the old man's advice, and strolled
around the grounds. A big pond caught his eye,
and he walked along its grassy bank and under

the thick willows that fringed it. He pulled himself to the top of a high board fence at the upper end of it, peered over at a broad, smooth athletic-field, and he wondered what the two poles that stood at each end with a cross-bar between them could be, and why that tall fence ran all around it. He stared at the big chimney of the power-house, as tall as the trunk of a poplar in a "dead-ening" at home, and covered with vines to the top, and he wondered what on earth that could be. He looked over the gate at the president's house. Through the windows of one building he saw hanging rings and all sorts of strange para-phernalia, and he wondered about them, and, peering through one ground-floor window, he saw three beds piled one on top of the other, each separated from the other by the length of its legs. It would take a step-ladder to get into the top bed—good Lord, did people sleep that way in this college? Suppose the top boy rolled out! And every building was covered with vines, and it was funny that vines grew on houses, and why in the world didn't folks cut 'em off? It was all wonder—nothing but wonder—and he got tired of wondering and went back to his steps and sat patiently down again. It was not long now before windows began to bang up and down in the dormitory near him. Cries and whistles began to emanate from the rooms, and now and then a head would protrude, and its eyes never failed,

it seemed, to catch and linger on the lonely, still
figure clinging to the steps. Soon there was a
rush of feet downstairs, and a crowd of boys
emerged and started briskly for breakfast. Girls
began to appear—short-skirted, with and without hats, with hair up and hair down—more girls
than he had ever seen before—tall and short, fat
and thin, and brunette and blonde. Students
began to stroll through the campus gates, and
now and then a buggy or a carriage would enter
and whisk past him to deposit its occupants in
front of the building opposite from where he sat.
What was going on over there? He wanted to
go over and see, for school might be taking up
over there, and, from being too early, he might
be too late after all; but he might miss John
Burnham, and if he himself were late, why lots
of the boys and girls about him would be late too,
and surely if they knew, which they must, they
would not let that happen. So, all eyes, he sat
on, taking in everything, like the lens of a camera.
Some of the boys wore caps, or little white hats
with the crown pushed in all around, and, though
it wasn't muddy and didn't look as though it were
going to rain, each one of them had his "britches"
turned up, and that puzzled the mountain boy
sorely; but no matter why they did it, he wouldn't
have to turn his up, for they didn't come to the
tops of his shoes. Swiftly he gathered how different he himself was, particularly in clothes,

from all of them. Nowhere did he see a boy
who matched himself as so lonely and set apart,
but with a shake of his head he tossed off his
inner plea for sympathetic companionship, and
the little uneasiness creeping over him—proudly.
There was a little commotion now in the crowd
nearest him, all heads turned one way, and Jason
saw approaching an old gentleman on crutches,
a man with a thin face that was all pure intel-
lect and abnormally keen; that, centuries old in
thought, had yet the unquenchable soul-fire of
youth. He stopped, lifted his hat in response to
the cheers that greeted him, and for a single instant over that thin face played, like the winking
eye of summer lightning, the subtle humor that
the world over is always playing hide-and-seek in
the heart of the Scot. A moment, and Jason
halted a passing boy with his eye.

"Who's that ole feller?" he blurted.

The lad looked shocked, for he could not know
that Jason meant not a particle of disrespect.

"That 'ole feller,'" he mimicked indignantly and
with scathing sarcasm, "is the president of this
university"; and he hurried on while Jason miserably shrivelled closer to the steps. After that he
spoke to nobody, and nobody spoke to him, and
he lifted his eyes only to the gateway through
which he longed for John Burnham to come. But
the smile of the old president haunted him. There
sat a man on heights no more to be scaled by him
than heaven, and yet that puzzling smile for the

blissful ignorance, in the young, of how gladly the old would give up their crowns in exchange for the swift young feet on the threshold—no wonder the boy could not understand. Through that gate dashed presently a pair of proud, high-headed black horses—"star-gazers," as the Kentuckians call them—with a rhythmic beat of high-lifted feet, and the boy's eyes narrowed as the carriage behind them swept by him, for in it were Colonel Pendleton and Gray, with eager face and flashing eyes. There was a welcoming shout when Gray leaped out, and a crowd of students rushed toward him and surrounded him. One of them took off his hat, lifted both hands above his head, and then they all barked out a series of barbaric yells with a long shout of Gray's full name at the end, while the Blue-grass lad stood among them, flushed and embarrassed but not at all displeased. Again Jason's brow knitted with wonder, for he could not know what a young god in that sternly democratic college Gray Pendleton, aristocrat though he was, had made himself, and he shrank deeper still into his loneliness and turned wistful eyes again to the gate. Somebody had halted in front of him, and he looked up to see the same lad of whom he had just asked a question.

"And that *young* feller," said the boy in the same mimicking tone, "is another president—of the sophomore class and the captain of the football team."

Lightning-like and belligerent, Jason sprang to

his feet. "Air you pokin' fun at *me?*" he asked
thickly and clenching his fists.

Genuinely amazed, the other lad stared at him
a moment, smiled, and held out his hand.

"I reckon I was, but you're all right. Shake!"

And within Jason, won by the frank eyes and
winning smile, the tumult died quickly, and he
shook—gravely.

"My name's Burns—Jack Burns."

"Mine's Hawn—Jason Hawn."

The other turned away with a wave of his hand.
"See you again."

"Shore," said Jason, and then his breast heaved
and his heart seemed to stop quite still. Another
pair of proud horses shot between the stone pillars,
and in the carriage behind them was Marjorie.
The boy dropped to his seat, dropped his chin in
both hands as though to keep his face hidden, but
as the sound of her coming loudened he simply could not help lifting his head. Erect, happy,
smiling, the girl was looking straight past him, and
he felt like one of the yellow grains of dust about
her horses' feet. And then within him a high,
shrill little yell rose above the laughter and vocal
hum going on around him—there was John Burnham coming up the walk, the school-master, John
Burnham—and Jason sprang to meet him. Immediately Burnham's searching eyes fell upon him,
and he stopped—smiling, measuring, surprised.
Could this keen-faced, keen-eyed, sinewy, tall lad

be the faithful little chap who had trudged sturdily at his heels so many days in the mountains?

"Well, well, well," he said; "why, I wouldn't have known you. You got here in time, didn't you?"

"I have been waitin' fer you," said Jason. "Miss Hilda told me to come straight to you."

"That's right—how is she?"

"She ain't well—she works too hard."

The school-master shook his head with grave concern.

"I know. You've been lucky, Jason. She is the best woman on earth."

"I'd lay right down here an' die fer her right now," said the lad soberly. So would John Burnham, and he loved the lad for saying that.

"She said you was the best man on earth—but I knowed that," the lad went on simply; "an' she told me to tell you to make me keep out o' fights and study hard and behave."

"All right, Jason," said Burnham with a smile. "Have you matriculated yet?"

Jason was not to be caught napping. His eyes gave out the quick light of humor, but his face was serious.

"I been so busy waitin' fer you that I reckon I must 'a' forgot that."

The school-master laughed.

"Come along."

Through the thick crowd that gave way respectfully to the new professor, Jason followed across the road to the building opposite, and up the steps into a room where he told his name and his age, and the name of his father and mother, and pulled from his pocket a little roll of dirty bills. There was a fee of five dollars for "janitor." Jason did not know what a janitor was, but John Burnham nodded when he looked up inquiringly and Jason asked no question. There was another fee for "breakage," and that was all, but the latter item was too much for Jason.

"S'pose I don't break nothin'," he asked shrewdly, "do I git that back?"

Then registrar and professor laughed.

"You get it back."

Down they went again.

"That's a mighty big word fer such little doin's," the boy said soberly, and the school-master smiled.

"You'll find just that all through college now, Jason, but don't wait to find out what the big word means."

"I won't," said Jason, "next time."

Many eyes now looked on the lad curiously when he followed John Burnham back through the crowd to the steps, where the new professor paused.

"I passed Mavis on the road. I wonder if she has come."

"I don't know," said Jason, and a curious something in his tone made John Burnham look at him quickly—but he said nothing.

"Oh, well," he said presently, "she knows what to do."

A few minutes later the two were alone in the new professor's recitation-room.

"Have you seen Marjorie and Gray?"

The lad hesitated.

"I seed—I saw 'em when they come in."

"Gray finishes my course this year. He's going to be a civil engineer."

"So'm I," said Jason; and the quick shortness of his tone again made John Burnham look keenly at him.

"You know a good deal about geology already—are you going to take my course too?"

"I want to know just what to do with that land o' mine. I ain't forgot what you told me—to go away and git an education—and when I come back what that land 'ud be worth."

"Yes, but——"

The lad's face had paled and his mouth had set.

"I'm goin' to git it back."

Behind them the door had opened, and Gray's spirited, smiling face was thrust in.

"Good morning, professor," he cried, and then, seeing Jason, he came swiftly in with his hand outstretched.

"Why, how are you, Jason? Mavis told me yesterday you were here. I've been looking for you. Glad to see you."

Watching both, John Burnham saw the look of

surprise in Gray's face when the mountain boy's whole frame stiffened into the rigidity of steel, saw the haughty uplifting of the Blue-grass boy's chin, as he wheeled to go, and like Gray, he, too, thought Jason had never forgotten the old feud between them. For a moment he was tempted to caution Jason about the folly of it all, but as suddenly he changed his mind. Outside a bugle blew.

"Go on down, Jason," he said instead, "and follow the crowd—that's chapel—prayer-meeting," he explained.

At the foot of the stairs the boy mingled with the youthful stream pouring through the wide doors of the chapel hall. He turned to the left and was met by the smiling eyes of his new acquaintance, Burns, who waved him good-humoredly away:

"This is the sophomore corner—I reckon you belong in there."

And toward the centre Jason went among the green, the countrified, the uneasy, and the unkempt. The other half of the hall was banked with the faces of young girls—fresh as flowers—and everywhere were youth and eagerness, eagerness and youth. The members of the faculty were climbing the steps to a platform and ranging themselves about the old gentleman with the crutches. John Burnham entered, and the vault above rocked with the same barbaric yells that Jason had heard given Gray Pendleton, for Burn-

ham had been a mighty foot-ball player in his
college days. The old president rose, and the
tumult sank to reverential silence while a silver
tongue sent its beautiful diction on high in a
prayer for the bodies, the minds, and the souls
of the whole buoyant throng in the race for which
they were about to be let loose. And that was
just what the tense uplifted faces suggested to
John Burnham—he felt in them the spirit of the
thoroughbred at the post, the young hound straining at the leash, the falcon unhooded for flight,
when, at the president's nod, he rose to his feet
to speak to the host the welcome of the faculty
within these college walls and the welcome of the
Blue-grass to the strangers from the confines of
the State—particularly to those who had jour-
neyed from their mountain homes. "These young
people from the hills," he said, "for their own
encouragement and for all patience in their own
struggle, must always remember, and the young
men and women of the Blue-grass, for tolerance
and a better understanding, must never forget, in
what darkness and for how long their sturdy kinspeople had lived, how they were just wakening
from a sleep into which, not of their own fault,
they had lapsed but little after the Revolution;
how eagerly they had strained their eyes for the
first glimmer from the outside world that had
come to them, and how earnestly now they were
fighting toward the light. So isolated, so primitive

were they only a short while ago that neighbor
would go to neighbor asking 'Lend us fire,' and
now they were but asking of the outer world,
'Lend us fire.' And he hoped that the young
men and women from those dark fastnesses who
had come there to light their torches would keep
them burning, and take them back home still
sacredly aflame, so that in the hills the old question with its new meaning could never again be
asked in vain.''

Jason's eyes had never wavered from the
speaker's face, nor had Gray's, but, while John
Burnham purposely avoided the eyes of both,
he noted here and there the sudden squaring of
shoulders, and the face of a mountain boy or girl
lift quickly and with open-mouthed interest remain fixed; and far back he saw Mavis, wide-
eyed and deep in some new-born dream, and he
thought he saw Marjorie turn at the end to look
at the mountain girl as though to smile understanding and sympathy. A mental tumult still
held Jason when the crowd about him rose to go,
and he kept his seat. John Burnham had been
talking about Mavis and him, and maybe about
Marjorie and Gray, and he had a vague desire to
see the school-master again. Moreover, a doubt,
at once welcome and disturbing to him, had
coursed through his brain. If secret meetings
in lanes and by-ways were going on between
Mavis and Gray, Gray would hardly have been

so frank in saying he had seen Mavis the previous afternoon, for Gray must know that Jason knew there had been no meeting at Steve Hawn's house. Perhaps Gray had overtaken her in the lane quite by accident, and the boy was bothered and felt rather foolish and ashamed when, seeing John Burnham still busy on the platform, he rose to leave.

On the steps more confusion awaited him. A group of girls was standing to one side of them, and he turned hurriedly the other way. Light footsteps followed him, and a voice called:

"Oh, Jason!"

His blood rushed, and he turned dizzily, for he knew it was Marjorie. In her frank eyes was a merry smile instead of the tear that had fixed them in his memory, but the clasp of her hand was the same.

"Why, I didn't know you yesterday—did I? No wonder. Why, I wouldn't have known you now if I hadn't been looking for you. Mavis told me you'd come. Dear me, what a *big* man you are. Professor Burnham told me all about you, and I've been so proud. Why, I came near writing to you several times. I'm expecting you to lead your class here, and "—she took in with frank admiration his height and the breadth of his shoulders—"Gray will want you, maybe, for the foot-ball team."

The crowds of girls near by were boring him

into the very ground with their eyes. His feet
and his hands had grown to enormous propor-
tions and seemed suddenly to belong to somebody else. He felt like an ant in a grain-hopper,
or as though he were deep under water in a long
dive and must in a moment actually gasp for
breath. And, remembering St. Hilda, he did
manage to get his hat off, but he was speechless.
Marjorie paused, the smile did not leave her
eyes, but it turned serious, and she lowered her
voice a little.

"Did you keep your promise, Jason?"

Then the boy found himself, and as he had said
before, that winter dusk, he said now soberly:

"I give you my hand."

And, as before, taking him literally, Marjorie
again stretched out her hand.

"I'm so glad."

Once more the bugle sent its mellow summons
through the air.

"And you are coming to our house some Saturday night to go coon-hunting—good-by."

Jason turned weakly away, and all the rest of
the day he felt dazed. He did not want to see
Mavis or Gray or Marjorie again, or even John
Burnham. So he started back home afoot, and
all the way he kept to the fields through fear that
some one of them might overtake him on the
road, for he wanted to be alone. And those fields
looked more friendly now than they had looked at

dawn, and his heart grew lighter with every step. Now and then a rabbit leaped from the grass before him, or a squirrel whisked up the rattling bark of a hickory-tree. A sparrow trilled from the swaying top of a purple ironwood, and from grass, and fence-rail, and awing, meadow larks were fluting everywhere, but the song of no wood-thrush reached his waiting ear. Over and over again his brain reviewed every incident of the day, only to end each time with Marjorie's voice, her smile with its new quality of mischief, and the touch of her hand. She had not forgotten—that was the thrill of it all—and she had even asked if he had kept his promise to her. And at that thought his soul darkened, for the day would come when he must ask to be absolved of one part of that promise, as on that day he must be up and on his dead father's business. And he wondered what, when he told her, she would say. It was curious, but the sense of the crime involved was naught, as was the possible effect of it on his college career—it was only what that girl would say. But the day might still be long off, and he had so schooled himself to throwing aside the old deep, sinister purpose that he threw it off now and gave himself up to the bubbling relief that had come to him. That meeting in the lane must have been chance, John Burnham was kind, and Marjorie had not forgotten. He was not alone in the world, nor was he even lonely, for everywhere that day he had found a hand stretched out to help him.

Mavis was sitting on the porch when he walked through the gate, and the moment she saw his face a glad light shone in her own, for it was the old Jason coming back to her:

"Mavie," he said huskily, "I reckon I'm the biggest fool this side o' hell, whar I reckon I ought to be."

Mavis asked no question, made no answer. She merely looked steadily at him for a moment, and then, brushing quickly at her eyes, she rose and turned into the house. The sun gave way to darkness, but it kept on shining in Jason's heart, and when at bedtime he stood again on the porch, his gratitude went up to the very stars. He heard Mavis behind him, but he did not turn, for all he had to say he had said, and the break in his reserve was over.

"I'm glad you come back, Jasie," was all she said, shyly, for she understood, and then she added the little phrase that is not often used in the mountain world:

"Good-night."

From St. Hilda, Jason, too, had learned that phrase, and he spoke it with a gruffness that made the girl smile:

"Good-night, Mavie."

XIX

JASON drew the top bed in a bare-walled, bare-floored room with two other boys, as green and countrified as was he, and he took turns with them making up those beds, carrying water for the one tin basin, and sweeping up the floor with the broom that stood in the corner behind it. But even then the stark simplicity of his life was a luxury. His meals cost him three dollars a week, and that most serious item began to worry him, but not for long. Within two weeks he was meeting a part of that outlay by delivering the morning daily paper of the town. This meant getting up at half past three in the morning, after a sleep of five hours and a half, but if this should begin to wear on him, he would simply go earlier to bed; there was no sign of wear and tear, however, for the boy was as tough as a bolt-proof black gum-tree back in the hills, his capacity for work was prodigious, and the early rising hour but lengthened the range of each day's activities. Indeed Jason missed nothing and nothing missed him. His novitiate passed quickly, and while his fund for "breakage" was almost gone, he had, without knowing it, drawn no little attention to himself. He had wandered innocently into "Heaven"—the seniors' hall—a satanic offence

for a freshman, and he had been stretched over a
chair, "strapped," and thrown out. But at dawn
next morning he was waiting at the entrance and
when four seniors appeared he tackled them all
valiantly. Three held him while the fourth went
for a pair of scissors, for thus far Jason had escaped
the tonsorial betterment that had been inflicted on
most of his classmates. The boy stood still, but in
a relaxed moment of vigilance he tore loose just as
the scissors appeared, and fled for the building opposite. There he turned with his back to the wall.

"When I want my hair cut, I'll git my mammy
to do it or pay fer it myself," he said quietly, but
his face was white. When they rushed on, he
thrust his hand into his shirt and pulled it out with
a mighty oath of helplessness—he had forgotten
his knife. They cut his hair, but it cost them two
bloody noses and one black eye. At the flag-rush
later he did not forget. The sophomores had en-
ticed the freshmen into the gymnasium, stripped
them of their clothes, and carried them away,
whereat the freshmen got into the locker-rooms
of the girls, and a few moments later rushed from
the gymnasium in bloomers to find the sophomores
crowded about the base of the pole, one of them
with an axe in his hand, and Jason at the top with
his hand again in his shirt.

"Chop away!" he was shouting, "but I'll git
some o' ye when this pole comes down." Above
the din rose John Burnham's voice, stern and

angry, calling Jason's name. The student with
the axe had halted at the unmistakable sincerity of
the boy's threat.

"Jason," called Burnham again, for he knew
what the boy meant, and the lad tossed knife and
scabbard over the heads of the crowd to the grass,
and slid down the pole. And in the fight that followed, the mountain boy fought with a calm, half-
smiling ferocity that made the wavering freshmen
instinctively surge behind him as a leader, and the
onlooking foot-ball coach quickly mark him for
his own. Even at the first foot-ball "rally," where
he learned the college yells, Jason had been singled
out, for the mountaineer measures distance by the
carry of his voice and with a "whoop an' a holler"
the boy could cover a mile. Above the din, Jason's clear cry was, so to speak, like a cracker on
the whip of the cheer, and the "yell-master," a
swaying figure of frenzied enthusiasm, caught his
eye in time, nodded approvingly, and saw in him a
possible yell-leader for the freshman class. After
the rally the piano was rolled joyously to the centre
of the gymnasium and a pale-faced lad began to
thump it vigorously, much to Jason's disapproval,
for he could not understand how a boy could, or
would, play anything but a banjo or a fiddle.
Then, with the accompaniment of a snare-drum,
there was a merry, informal dance, at which Jason
and Mavis looked yearningly on. And, as that
night long ago in the mountains, Gray and Mar-

jorie floated like feathers past them, and over
Gray's shoulder the girl's eyes caught Jason's fixed
on her, and Mavis's fixed on Gray; so on the next
round she stopped a moment near them.

"I'm going to teach you to dance, Jason," she
said, as though she were tossing a gauntlet to
somebody, "and Gray can teach Mavis."

"Sure," laughed Gray, and off they whirled
again.

The eyes of the two mountaineers met, and they
might have been back in their childhood again,
standing on the sunny river-bank and waiting for
Gray and Marjorie to pass, for what their tongues
said then their eyes said now:

"I seed you a-lookin' at him."

"'Tain't so—I seed you a-lookin' at her."

And it was true now as it was then, and then as
now both knew it and both flushed. Jason turned
abruptly away, for he knew more of Mavis's secret
than she of his, and it was partly for that reason
that he had not yet opened his lips to her. He had
seen no consciousness in Gray's face, he resented
the fact, somehow, that there was none, and his
lulled suspicions began to stir again within him.
In Marjorie's face he had missed what Mavis had
caught, a fleeting spirit of mischief, which stung
the mountain girl with jealousy and a quick fierce
desire to protect Jason, just as Jason, with the
same motive, was making up his mind again to
keep a close eye on Gray Pendleton. As for Mar-

jorie, she, too, knew more of Mavis's secret than Mavis knew of hers, and of the four, indeed, she was by far the wisest. During the years that Jason was in the hills she had read as on an open page the meaning of the mountain girl's flush at any unexpected appearance of Gray, the dumb adoration for him in her dark eyes, and more than once, riding in the woods, she had come upon Mavis, seated at the foot of an oak, screened by a clump of elder-bushes and patiently waiting, as Marjorie knew, to watch Gray gallop by. She even knew how unconsciously Gray had been drawn by all this toward Mavis, but she had not bothered her head to think how much he was drawn until just before the opening of the college year, for, from the other side of the hill, she, too, had witnessed the meeting in the lane that Jason had seen, and had wondered about it just as much, though she, too, had kept still. That the two boys knew so little, that the two girls knew so much, and that each girl resented the other's interest in her own cousin, was merely a distinction of sex, as was the fact that matters would have to be made very clear before Jason or Gray could see and understand. And for them matters were to become clearer, at least—very soon.

XX

ALREADY the coach had asked Jason to try foot-ball, but the boy had kept away from the field, for the truth was that he had but one suit of clothes and he couldn't afford to have them soiled and torn. Gray suspected this, and told the coach, who explained to Jason that practice clothes would be furnished him, but still the boy did not come until one day when, out of curiosity, he wandered over to the field to see what the game was like. Soon his eyes brightened, his lips parted, and his face grew tense as the players swayed, clenched struggling, fell in a heap, and leaped to their feet again. And everywhere he saw Gray's yellow head darting among them like a sun-ball, and he began to wonder if he could not outrun and out-wrestle his old enemy. He began to fidget in his seat and presently he could stand it no longer, and he ran out into the field and touched the coach on the shoulder.

"Can I git them clothes now?"

The coach looked at his excited face, nodded with a smile, and pointed to the gymnasium, and Jason was off in a run.

The matter was settled in the thrill and struggle of that one practice game, and right away Jason

showed extraordinary aptitude, for he was quick,
fleet, and strong, and the generalship and tactics
of the game fascinated him from the start. And
when he discovered that the training-table meant
a savings-bank for him, he counted his money,
gave up the morning papers without hesitation or
doubt, and started in for the team. Thus he and
Gray were brought violently together on the field,
for within two weeks Jason was on the second
team, but the chasm between them did not close.
Gray treated the mountain boy with a sort of curt
courtesy, and while Jason tackled him, fell upon
him with a savage thrill, and sometimes wanted to
keep on tightening his wiry arms and throttling
him, the mountain boy could discover no personal
feeling whatever against him in return, and he
was mystified. With the ingrained suspicion of
the mountaineer toward an enemy, he supposed
Gray had some cunning purpose. As captain,
Gray had been bound, Jason knew, to put him on
the second team, but as day after day went by
and the magic word that he longed for went un-
said, the boy began to believe that the sinister purpose of Gray's concealment was, without evident
prejudice, to keep him off the college team. The
ball was about to be snapped back on Gray's side,
and Gray had given him one careless, indifferent
glance over the bent backs of the guards, when
Jason came to this conclusion, and his heart began
to pound with rage. There was the shock of

bodies, the ball disappeared from his sight, he saw
Gray's yellow head dart three times, each time a
different way, and then it flashed down the side
line with a clear field for the goal. With a bound
Jason was after him, and he knew that even if
Gray had wings, he would catch him. With a
flying leap he hurled himself on the speeding figure
in front of him, he heard Gray's breath go out in a
quick gasp under the fierce lock of his arms, and,
as they crashed to the ground, Jason for one savage
moment wanted to use his teeth on the back of the
sunburnt neck under him, but he sprang to his
feet, fists clenched and ready for the fight. With
another gasp Gray, too, sprang lightly up.

"Good!" he said heartily.

No mortal fist could have laid Jason quite so
low as that one word. The coach's whistle blew
and Gray added carelessly: "Come around, Hawn,
to the training-table to-night."

No mortal command could have filled him with
so much shame, and Jason stood stock-still and
speechless. Then, fumbling for an instant at his
shirt collar as though he were choking, he walked
swiftly away. As he passed the benches he saw
Mavis and Marjorie, who had been watching the
practice. Apparently Mavis had started out into
the field, and Marjorie, bewildered by her indignant outcry, had risen to follow her; and Jason,
when he met the accusing fire of his cousin's eyes,
knew that she alone, on the field, had understood

it all, that she had started with the impulse of
protecting Gray, and his shame went deeper still.
He did not go to the training-table that night,
and the moonlight found him under the old willows wondering and brooding, as he had been—
long and hard. Gray was too much for him, and
the mountain boy had not been able to solve the
mystery of the Blue-grass boy's power over his
fellows, for the social complexity of things had un-
ravelled very slowly for Jason. He saw that each
county had brought its local patriotism to college
and had its county club. There were too few students from the hills and a sectional club was forming, "The Mountain Club," into which Jason
naturally had gone; but broadly the students were
divided into "frat" men and "non-frat" men,
chiefly along social lines, and there were literary
clubs of which the watchword was merit and
nothing else. In all these sectional cliques from
the Purchase, Pennyroyal, and Peavine, as the
western border of the State, the southern border,
and the eastern border of hills were called; indeed,
in all the sections except the Bear-grass, where
was the largest town and where the greatest wealth
of the State was concentrated, he found a wide-
spread, subconscious, home-nursed resentment
brought to that college against the lordly Blue-
grass. In the social life of the college he found
that resentment rarely if ever voiced, but always tirelessly at work. He was not surprised

then to discover that in the history of the college, Gray Pendleton was the first plainsman, the first aristocrat, who had ever been captain of the team and the president of his class. He began to understand now, for he could feel the tendrils of the boy's magnetic personality enclosing even him, and by and by he could stand it no longer, and he went to Gray.

"I wanted to kill you that day."

Gray smiled.

"I knew it," he said quietly.

"Then why——"

"We were playing foot-ball. Almost anybody can lose his head *entirely*—but *you* didn't. That's why I didn't say anything to you afterward. That's why you'll be captain of the team after I'm gone."

Again Jason choked, and again he turned speechless away, and then and there was born within him an idolatry for Gray that was carefully locked in his own breast, for your mountaineer openly worships, and then but shyly, the Almighty alone. Jason no longer wondered about the attitude of faculty and students of both sexes toward Gray, no longer at Mavis, but at Marjorie he kept on wondering mightily, for she alone seemed the one exception to the general rule. Like everybody else, Jason knew the parental purpose where those two were concerned, and he began to laugh at the daring presumptions of his own past dreams and to worship now only from afar. But he could not know the effect of that parental purpose on that wilful, high-strung young person, the pique that Gray's frank interest in Mavis brought to life within her, and he was not yet far enough along in the classics to suspect that Marjorie might weary of hearing Aristides called the Just. Nor could he know the spirit of coquetry that lurked deep behind her serious eyes, and was for that reason the more dangerously effective.

He only began to notice one morning, after the foot-ball incident, that Marjorie was beginning to notice him; that, worshipped now only on the horizon, his star seemed to be drawing a little nearer. A passing lecturer had told Jason much of himself and his people that morning. The mountain people, said the speaker, still lived like the pioneer forefathers of the rest of the State. Indeed they were "our contemporary ancestors"; so that, sociologically speaking, Jason, young as he was, was the ancestor of all around him. The thought made him grin and, looking up, he caught the mischievous eyes of Marjorie, who later seemed to be waiting for him on the steps:

"Good-morning, grandfather," she said demurely, and went rapidly on her way.

XXI

MEANWHILE that political storm was raging and Jason got at the heart of it through his morning paper and John Burnham. He knew that at home Republicans ran against Republicans for all offices, and now he learned that his own mountains were the Gibraltar of that party, and that the line of its fortifications ran from the Big Sandy, three hundred miles by public roads, to the line of Tennessee. When free silver had shattered the Democratic ranks three years before, the mountaineers had leaped forth and unfurled the Republican flag over the State for the first time since the Civil War. Ballots were falsified—that was the Democratic cry, and that was the Democratic excuse for that election law which had been forced through the Senate, whipped through the lower house with the party lash, and passed over the veto of the Republican governor by the new Democratic leader—the bold, cool, crafty, silent autocrat. From bombastic orators Jason learned that a fair ballot was the bulwark of freedom, that some God-given bill of rights had been smashed, and the very altar of liberty desecrated. And when John Burnham explained how the autocrat's triumvirate could at will appoint and remove

officers of election, canvass returns, and certify
and determine results, he could understand how
the "atrocious measure," as the great editor of the
State called it, "was a ready chariot to the governor's chair." And in the summer convention
the spirit behind the measure had started for that
goal in just that way, like a scythe-bearing chariot
of ancient days, but cutting down friend as well as
foe. Straightway, Democrats long in line for hon-
ors, and gray in the councils of the party, bolted;
the rural press bolted; and Jason heard one bolter
thus cry his fealty and his faithlessness: "As
charged, I do stand ready to vote for a yellow dog,
if he be the regular nominee, but lower than that
you shall not drag me."

The autocrat's retort was courteous.

"You have a brother in the penitentiary."

"No," was the answer, "but your brothers have
a brother who ought to be."

The pulpit thundered. Half a million Kentuckians, "professing Christians and temperance
advocates," repudiated the autocrat's claim to
support. A new convention was the cry, and the
wheel-horse of the party, an ex-Confederate, ex-
governor, and aristocrat, answered that cry. The
leadership of the Democratic bolters he took as a
"sacred duty"—took it with the gentle statement
that the man who tampers with the rights of the
humblest citizen is worse than the assassin, and
should be streaked with a felon's stripes, and

suffered to speak only through barred doors.
From the same tongue, Jason heard with puckered
brow that the honored and honest yeomanry of
the commonwealth, through coalition by judge
and politician, would be hoodwinked by the leger-
demain of ballot-juggling magicians; but he did
understand when he heard this yeomanry called
brave, adventurous self-gods of creation, slow to
anger and patient with wrongs, but when once
stirred, let the man who had done the wrong—
beware! Long ago Jason had heard the Republican chieftain who was to be pitted against such a
foe characterized as "a plain, unknown man, a
hill-billy from the Pennyroyal, and the nominee
because there was no opposition and no hope."
But hope was running high now, and now with the
aristocrat, the autocrat, and the plebeian from
the Pennyroyal—whose slogan was the repeal of
the autocrat's election law—the tricornered fight
was on.

On a hot day in the star county of the star
district, the autocrat, like Cæsar, had a fainting
fit and left the Democrats, explaining for the rest
of the campaign that Republican eyes had seen a
big dirk under his coat; and Jason never rested
until with his own eyes he had seen the man who
had begun to possess his brain like an evil dream.
And he did see him and heard him defend his law
as better than the old one, and declare that never
again could the Democrats steal the State with

mountain votes—heard him confidently leave to
the common people to decide whether imperialism
should replace democracy, trusts destroy the business of man with man, and whether the big railroad of the State was the servant or the master of
the people. He heard a senator from the national
capital, whose fortunes were linked with the autocrat's, declare that leader as the most maligned
figure in American politics, and that he was without a blemish or vice on his private or public life,
but, unlike Pontius Pilate, Jason never thought
to ask himself what was truth, for, in spite of the
mountaineer's Blue-grass allies, the lad had come
to believe that there was a State conspiracy to
rob his own people of their rights. This autocrat
was the head and front of that conspiracy; while
he spoke the boy's hatred grew with every word,
and turned personal, so that at the close of the
speech he moved near the man with a fierce desire
to fly at his throat then and there. The boy even
caught one sweeping look—cool, fearless, insolent,
scorning—the look the man had for his enemies—
and he was left with swimming head and trembling knees. Then the great Nebraskan came,
and Jason heard him tell the people to vote against
him for President if they pleased—but to stand
by Democracy; and in his paper next morning
Jason saw a cartoon of the autocrat driving the
great editor and the Nebraskan on a race-track,
hitched together, but pulling like oxen apart. And

through the whole campaign he heard the one Republican cry ringing like a bell through the State: "Elect the ticket by a majority that *can't* be counted out."

Thus the storm went on, the Republicans crying for a free ballot and a fair count, flaunting on a banner the picture of a man stuffing a ballot-box and two men with shot-guns playfully interrupting the performance, and hammering into the head of the State that no man could be trusted with unlimited power over the suffrage of a free people. Any ex-Confederate who was for the autocrat, any repentant bolter that swung away from the aristocrat, any negro that was against the man from the Pennyroyal, was lifted by the beneficiary to be looked on by the public eye. The autocrat would cut down a Republican majority by contesting votes and throw the matter into the hands of the legislature—that was the Republican prophecy and the Republican fear. Manufacturers, merchants, and ministers pleaded for a fair election. An anti-autocratic grip became prevalent in the hills. The Hawns and Honeycutts sent word that they had buried the feud for a while and would fight like brothers for their rights, and from more than one mountain county came the homely threat that if those rights were denied, there would somewhere be "a mighty shovellin' of dirt." And so to the last minute the fight went on.

The boy's head buzzed and ached with the multifarious interests that filled it, but for all that the autumn was all gold for him and with both hands he gathered it in. Sometimes he would go home with Gray for Sunday. With Colonel Pendleton for master, he was initiated into exercises with dirk and fencing-foil, for not yet was the boxing-glove considered meet, by that still old-fashioned courtier, for the hand of a gentleman. Sometimes he would spend Sunday with John Burnham, and wander with him through the wonders of Morton Sanders' great farm, and he listened to Burnham and the colonel talk politics and tobacco, and the old days, and the destructive changes that were subtly undermining the glories of those old days. In the tri-cornered foot-ball fight for the State championship, he had played one game with Central University and one with old Transylvania, and he had learned the joy of victory in one and in the other the heart-sickening depression of defeat. One never-to-be-forgotten night he had gone coon-hunting with Mavis and Marjorie and Gray—riding slowly through shadowy woods, or recklessly galloping over the blue-grass fields, and again, as many times before, he felt his heart pounding with emotions that seemed almost to make it burst.

For Marjorie, child of sunlight, and Mavis, child of shadows, riding bareheaded together under the brilliant moon, were the twin spirits of the night, and that moon dimmed the eyes of both only as she dimmed the stars. He saw Mavis swerving at every stop and every gallop to Gray's side, and always he found Marjorie somewhere near him. And only John Burnham understood it all, and he wondered and smiled, and with the smile wondered again.

There had been no time for dancing lessons, but the little comedy of sentiment went on just the same. In neither Mavis nor Jason was there the slightest consciousness of any chasm between them and Marjorie and Gray, though at times both felt in the latter pair a vague atmosphere that neither would for a long time be able to define as patronage, and so when Jason received an invitation to the first dance given in the hotel ballroom in town, he went straight to Marjorie and solemnly asked "the pleasure of her company" that night.

For a moment Marjorie was speechless.

"Why, Jason," she gasped, "I—I—you're a freshman, and anyhow——"

For the first time the boy gained an inkling of that chasm, and his eyes turned so fiercely sombre and suspicious that she added in a hurry:

"It's a joke, Jason—that invitation. No freshman can go to one of those dances."

Jason looked perplexed now, and still a little suspicious.

"Who'll keep me from goin'?" he asked quietly.

"The sophomores. They sent you that invitation to get you into trouble. They'll tear your clothes off."

As was the habit of his grandfather Hawn, Jason's tongue went reflectively to the hollow of one cheek, and his eyes dropped to the yellow leaves about their feet, and Marjorie waited with a tingling thrill that some vague thing of importance was going to happen. Jason's face was very calm when he looked up at last, and he held out the card of invitation.

"Will that git—get me in, when I a-get to the door?"

"Of course, but——"

"Then I'll be th-there," said Jason, and he turned away.

Now Marjorie knew that Gray expected to take her to that dance, but he had not yet even mentioned it. Jason had come to her swift and straight; the thrill still tingled within her, and before she knew it she had cried impulsively:

"Jason, if you get to that dance, I'll—I'll dance every square dance with you."

Jason nodded simply and turned away.

The mischief-makers soon learned the boy's purpose, and there was great joy among them, and when Gray finally asked Marjorie to go with him, she demurely told him she was going with Jason. Gray was amazed and indignant, and he pleaded with her not to do anything so foolish.

"Why, it's outrageous. It will be the talk of the town. Your mother won't like it. Maybe they won't do anything to him because you are along, but they might, and think of you being mixed up in such a mess. Anyhow I tell you— you *can't* do it."

Marjorie paled and Gray got a look from her that he had never had before.

"Did I hear you say '*can't*'?" she asked coldly. "Well, I'm not going with him—he won't let me. He's going alone. I'll meet him there."

Gray made a helpless gesture.

"Well, I'll try to get the fellows to let him alone—on your account."

"Don't bother—he can take care of himself."

"Why, Marjorie!"

The girl's coldness was turning to fire.

"Why don't you take Mavis?"

Gray started an impatient refusal, and stopped —Mavis was passing in the grass on the other side of the road, and her face was flaming violently.

"She heard you," said Gray in a low voice.

The heel of one of Marjorie's little boots came sharply down on the gravelled road.

"Yes, and I hope she heard *you*—and don't you ever—ever—ever say *can't* to me again." And she flashed away.

The news went rapidly through the college and, as Gray predicted, became the talk of the young people of the town. Marjorie's mother did object

violently, but Marjorie remained firm—what harm
was there in dancing with Jason Hawn, even if he
was a poor mountaineer and a freshman? She
was not a snob, even if Gray was. Jason himself
was quiet, non-communicative, dignified. He refused to discuss the matter with anybody, ignored
comment and curiosity, and his very silence sent a
wave of uneasiness through some of the sophomores and puzzled them all. Even John Burnham,
who had severely reprimanded and shamed Jason
for the flag incident, gravely advised the boy not
to go, but even to him Jason was respectfully non-
committal, for this was a matter that, as the boy
saw it, involved his *rights*, and the excitement grew
quite feverish when one bit of news leaked out.
At the beginning of the session the old president,
perhaps in view of the political turmoil imminent,
had made a request that one would hardly hear
in the chapel of any other hall of learning in the
broad United States.

"If any student had brought with him to college any weapon or fire-arm, he would please de-
liver it to the commandant, who would return it
to him at the end of the session, or whenever he
should leave college."

Now Jason had deliberated deeply on that request; on the point of personal privilege involved
he differed with the president, and a few days
before the dance one of his room-mates found not
only a knife, but a huge pistol—relics of Jason's

feudal days—protruding from the top bed. This was the bit of news that leaked, and Marjorie paled when she heard it, but her word was given, and she would keep it. There was no sneaking on Jason's part that night, and when a crowd of sophomores gathered at the entrance of his dormitory they found a night-hawk that Jason had hired, waiting at the door, and patiently they waited for Jason.

Down at the hotel ballroom Gray and Marjorie waited, Gray anxious, worried, and angry, and Marjorie with shining eyes and a pale but determined face. And she shot a triumphant glance toward Gray when she saw the figure of the young mountaineer framed at last in the doorway of the ballroom. There Jason stood a moment, uncouth and stock-still. His eyes moved only until he caught sight of Marjorie, and then, with them fixed steadily on her, he solemnly walked through the sudden silence that swiftly spread through the room straight for her. He stood cool, calm, and with a curious dignity before her, and the only sign of his emotion was in a reckless lapse into his mountain speech.

"I've come to tell ye I can't dance with ye. Nobody can keep me from goin' whar I've got a right to go, but I won't stay nowhar I'm not wanted."

And, without waiting for her answer, he turned and stalked solemnly out again.

XXII

THE miracle had happened, and just how nobody could ever say. The boy had appeared
in the door-way and had paused there full in the
light. No revolver was visible—it could hardly
have been concealed in the much-too-small clothes
that he wore—and his eyes flashed no challenge.
But he stood there an instant, with face set and
stern, and then he walked slowly to the old rattle-
trap vehicle, and, unchallenged, drove away, as,
unchallenged, he walked quietly back to his room
again. That defiance alone would have marked
him with no little dignity. It gave John Burnham
a great deal of carefully concealed joy, it dumfounded Gray, and, while Mavis took it as a matter of course, it thrilled Marjorie, saddened her,
and made her a little ashamed. Nor did it end
there. Some change was quickly apparent to Jason in Mavis. She turned brooding and sullen,
and one day when she and Jason met Gray in the
college yard, she averted her eyes when the latter
lifted his cap, and pretended not to see him. Jason saw an uneasy look in Gray's eyes, and when
he turned questioningly to Mavis, her face was
pale with anger. That night he went home with
her to see his mother, and when the two sat on the

porch in the dim starlight after supper, he bluntly asked her what the matter was, and bluntly she told him. Only once before had he ever spoken of Gray to Mavis, and that was about the meeting in the lane, and then she scorned to tell him whether or not the meeting was accidental, and Jason knew thereby that it was. Unfortunately he had not stopped there.

"I saw him try to kiss ye," he said indignantly.

"Have you never tried to kiss a girl?" Mavis had asked quietly, and Jason reddened.

"Yes," he admitted reluctantly.

"And did she always let ye?"

"Well, no—not——"

"Very well, then," Mavis snapped, and she flaunted away.

It was different now, the matter was more serious, and now they were cousins and Hawns. Blood spoke to blood and answered to blood, and when at the end Mavis broke into a fit of shame and tears, a burst of light opened in Jason's brain and his heart raged not only for Mavis, but for himself. Gray had been ashamed to go to that dance with Mavis, and Marjorie had been ashamed to go with him—there was a chasm, and with every word that Mavis spoke the wider that chasm yawned.

"Oh, I know it," she sobbed. "I couldn't believe it at first, but I know it now"—she began to drop back into her old speech—"they come down in the mountains, and grandpap was nice to 'em,

and when we come up here they was nice to us.
But down thar and up here we was just queer and
funny to 'em—an' we're that way yit. They're
good-hearted an' they'd do anything in the world
fer us, but we ain't their kind an' they ain't ourn.
They knowed it and we didn't—but I know it
now."

So that was the reason Marjorie had hesitated
when Jason asked her to go to the dance with him.

"Then why did she go?" he burst out. He had
mentioned no name even, but Mavis had been following his thoughts.

"Any gal 'ud do that fer fun," she answered,
"an' to git even with Gray."

"Why do you reckon——"

"That don't make no difference—she wants to
git even with me, too."

Jason wheeled sharply, but before his lips could
open Mavis had sprung to her feet.

"No, I hain't!" she cried hotly, and rushed into
the house.

Jason sat on under the stars, brooding. There
was no need for another word between them.
Alike they saw the incident and what it meant;
they felt alike, and alike both would act. A few
minutes later his mother came out on the porch.

"Whut's the matter with Mavis?"

"You'll have to ask her, mammy."

With a keen look at the boy, Martha Hawn
went back into the house, and Jason heard Steve's
heavy tread behind him.

"I know whut the matter is," he drawled. "Thar hain't nothin' the matter 'ceptin' that Mavis ain't the only fool in this hyeh fambly."

Jason was furiously silent, and Steve walked chuckling to the railing of the porch and spat over it through his teeth and fingers. Then he looked up at the stars and yawned, and with his mouth still open, went casually on:

"I seed Arch Hawn in town this mornin'. He says folks is a-hand-grippin' down thar in the mountains right an' left. Thar's a truce on betwixt the Hawns an' Honeycutts an' they're gittin' ready fer the election together."

The lad did not turn his head nor did his lips open.

"These fellers up here tried to bust our county up into little pieces once—an' do you know why? Bekase we was so *lawless*." Steve laughed savagely. "They're gittin' wuss'n we air. They say we stole the State fer that bag o' wind, Bryan, when we'd been votin' the same way fer forty years. Now they're goin' to gag us an' tie us up like a yearlin' calf. But folks in the mountains ain't a-goin' to do much bawlin'—they're gittin' ready."

Still Jason refused to answer, but Steve saw that the lad's hands and mouth were clenched.

"They're gittin' *ready*," he repeated, "an' I'll be thar."

XXIII

BUT the sun of election day went down and a breath of relief passed like a south wind over the land. Perhaps it was the universal recognition of the universal danger that prevented an outbreak, but the morning after found both parties charging fraud, claiming victory, and deadlocked like two savage armies in the crisis of actual battle. For a fortnight each went on claiming the victory. In one mountain county the autocrat's local triumvirate was surrounded by five hundred men, while it was making its count; in another there were three thousand determined onlookers; and still another mountain triumvirate was visited by nearly all the male inhabitants of the county who rode in on horseback and waited silently and threateningly in the court-house square.

At the capital the arsenal was under a picked guard and the autocrat was said to be preparing for a resort to arms. A few mountaineers were seen drifting about the streets, and the State offices —"just a-lookin' aroun' to see if their votes was a-goin' to be counted in or not."

At the end of the fortnight the autocrat claimed the fight by one vote, but three days before Thanks-

giving Day two of the State triumvirate declared
for the Republican from the Pennyroyal—and
resigned.

"Great Cæsar!" shouted Colonel Pendleton.
"Can the one that's left appoint his *own* board?"

Being for the autocrat, he not only could but did
—for the autocrat's work was only begun. The
contest was yet to come.

Meanwhile the great game was at hand. The
fight for the championship lay now between the
State University and old Transylvania, and, amid
a forest of waving flags and a frenzied storm from
human throats, was fought out desperately on the
day that the nation sets aside for peace, prayer,
and thanksgiving. Every atom of resentment,
indignation, rebellion, ambition that was stored
up in Jason went into that fight. It seemed to
John Burnham and to Mavis and Marjorie that
their team was made up of just one black head
and one yellow one, for everywhere over the field
and all the time, like a ball of fire and its shadow,
those two heads darted, and, when they came together, they were the last to go down in the crowd
of writhing bodies and the first to leap into view
again—and always with the ball nearer the enemy's goal. Behind that goal each head darted
once, and by just those two goals was the game
won. Gray was the hero he always was; Jason
was the coming idol, and both were borne off the
field on the shoulders of a crowd that was hoarse

with shouting triumph and weeping tears of joy.
And on that triumphal way Jason swerved his eyes
from Marjorie and Mavis swerved hers from Gray.
There was no sleep for Jason that night, but the
next night the fierce tension of mind and muscle
relaxed and he slept long and hard; and Sunday
morning found him out in the warm sunlight of
the autumn fields, seated on a fence rail—alone.

He had left the smoke cloud of the town behind
him and walked aimlessly afield, except to take the
turnpike that led the opposite way from Mavis
and Marjorie and John Burnham and Gray, for he
wanted to be alone.   Now, perched in the crotch
of a stake-and-ridered fence, he was calmly, search-
ingly, unsparingly taking stock with himself.

In the first place the training-table was no more,
and he must go back to delivering morning papers.
With foot-ball, with diversions in college and in the
country, he had lost much time and he must make
that up.   The political turmoil had kept his mind
from his books and for a while Marjorie had taken
it away from them altogether.   He had come to
college none too well prepared, and already John
Burnham had given him one kindly warning; but
so supreme was his self-confidence that he had
smiled at the geologist and to himself.   Now he
frowningly wondered if he had not lost his head
and made a fool of himself; and a host of worries
and suspicions attacked him so sharply and suddenly that, before he knew what he was doing, he

had leaped panic-stricken from the fence and at a
half-trot was striking back across the fields in a
bee-line for his room and his books. And night
and day thereafter he stuck to them.

Meanwhile the struggle was going on at the
capital, and by the light of every dawn the boy
drank in every detail of it from the morning paper that was literally his daily bread. Two weeks
after the big game, the man from the Pennyroyal
was installed as governor. The picked guard at
the arsenal was reinforced. The contesting autocrat was said to have stored arms in the penitentiary, a gray, high-walled fortress within a stone's
throw of the governor's mansion, for the Democratic warden thereof was his loyal henchman.
The first rumor of the coming of the mountaineers
spread, and the capital began to fill with the ward
heelers and bad men of the autocrat.

A week passed, there was no filing of a protest, a
pall of suspense hung over the land like a black
cloud, and under it there was no more restless
spirit than Jason, who had retreated into his own
soul as though it were a fortress of his hills. No
more was he seen at any social gathering—not
even at the gymnasium, for the delivery of his
morning papers gave him all the exercise that he
needed and more. His hard work and short hours
of sleep began to tell on him. Sometimes the
printed page of his book would swim before his
eyes and his brain go panic-stricken. He grew

pale, thin, haggard, and worn, and Marjorie saw
him only when he was silently, swiftly striding from
dormitory to class-room and back again—grim,
reticent, and non-approachable. When Christmas
approached he would not promise to go to Gray's
nor to John Burnham's, and he rarely went now
even to his mother. In Mavis Hawn, Gray found
the same mystifying change, for when the morbidly
sensitive spirit of the mountaineer is wounded,
healing is slow and cure difficult. One day, however, each pair met. Passing the mouth of the
lane, Gray saw Mavis walking slowly along it
homeward and he rode after her. She turned
when she heard his horse behind her, her chin
lifted, and her dark sullen eyes looked into his
with a stark, direct simplicity that left him with
his lips half open—confused and speechless. And
gently, at last:

"What's the matter, Mavis?"

Still she looked, unquestioning, uncompromis-
ing, and turned without answer and went slowly
on home while the boy sat his horse and looked
after her until she climbed the porch of her cottage
and, without once turning her head, disappeared
within. But Jason at his meeting with Marjorie
broke his grim reticence in spite of himself. She
had come upon him at sunset under the snowy
willows by the edge of the ice-locked pond. He
had let the floodgates down and she had been
shaken and terrified by the torrent that rushed

from him. The girl shrank from his bitter denun-
ciation of himself. He had been a fool. The mid-
year examinations would be a tragedy for him, and
he must go to the "kitchen" or leave college with
pride broken and in just disgrace. Fate had
trapped him like a rat. A grewsome oath had
been put on him as a child and from it he could
never escape. He had been robbed of his birthright by his own mother and the people of the
Blue-grass, and Marjorie's people were now robbing
his of their national birthrights as well. The boy
did not say her people, but she knew that was what
he meant, and she looked so hurt that Jason spoke
quickly his gratitude for all the kindness that had
been shown him. And when he started with his
gratitude to her, his memories got the better of
him and he stopped for a moment with hungry
eyes, but seeing her consternation over what might
be coming next, he had ended with a bitter smile
at the further bitter proof she was giving him.

"But I understand—now," he said sternly to
himself and sadly to her, and he turned away without seeing the quiver of her mouth and the starting
of her tears.

Going to his mother's that afternoon, Jason
found Mavis standing by the fence, hardly less pale
than the snow under her feet, and looking into the
sunset. She started when she heard the crunch
of his feet, and from the look of her face he knew
that she thought he might be some one else.

He saw that she had been crying, and as quickly she knew that the boy was in a like agony of mind. There was only one swift look—a mutual recognition of a mutual betrayal—but no word passed then nor when they walked together back to the house, for race and relationship made no word possible. Within the house Jason noticed his mother's eyes fixed anxiously on him, and when Mavis was clearing up in the kitchen after supper, she subtly shifted her solicitude to the girl in order to draw some confession from her son.

"Mavis wants to go back to the mountains."

The ruse worked, for Jason looked up quickly and then into the fire while the mother waited.

"Sometimes I want to go back myself," he said wearily; "it's gittin' too much for me here."

Martha Hawn looked at her husband stretched on the bed in a drunken sleep and began to cry softly.

"It's al'ays been too much fer me," she sobbed. "I've al'ays wanted to go back."

For the first time Jason began to think how lonely her life must be, and, perhaps as the result of his own suffering, his heart suddenly began to ache for her.

"Don't worry, mammy—I'll take ye back some day."

Mavis came back from the kitchen. Again she had been crying. Again the same keen look passed between them and with only that look

Jason climbed the stairs to her room. As his eyes wandered about the familiar touches the hand of civilization had added to the bare little chamber it once was, he saw on the dresser of varnished pine one touch of that hand that he had never noticed before—the picture of Gray Pendleton. Evidently Mavis had forgotten to put it away, and Jason looked at it curiously a moment—the frank face, strong mouth, and winning smile—but he never noticed that it was placed where she could see it when she kneeled at her bedside, and never guessed that it was the last earthly thing her eyes rested on before darkness closed about her, and that the girl took its image upward with her even in her prayers.

XXIV

THE red dawn of the twentieth century was stealing over the frost-white fields, and in the alien house of his fathers John Burnham was watching it through his bedroom window. There had been little sleep for him that New Year's night, and even now, when he went back to bed, sleep would not come.

The first contest in the life of the State was going on at the little capital. That capital was now an armed camp. The law-makers there themselves were armed, divided, and men of each party were marked by men of the other for the first shot when the crisis should come. There was a Democratic conspiracy to defraud—a Republican conspiracy to resist by force to the death. Even in the placing of the ballots in the box for the drawing of the contest board, fraud was openly charged, and even then pistols almost leaped from their holsters. Republicans whose seats were contested would be unseated and the autocrat's triumph would thus be sure—that was the plan wrought out by his inflexible will and iron hand. The governor from the Pennyroyal swore he would leave his post only on a stretcher. Disfranchisement was on the very eve of taking place, liberty was at stake, and Kentuckians unless aroused to action would be a free people no longer. The Republican cry was that the autocrat had created his election triumvirate, had stolen his nomination, tried to steal his election, and was now trying to steal the governorship. There was even a meeting in the big town of the State to determine openly whether there should be resistance to him by force. Two men from the mountains had met in the lobby of the Capitol Hotel and a few moments later, under the drifting powder smoke, two men lay wounded and three lay dead. The quarrel was personal, it was said, but the dial-hand of the times was left pointing with sinister prophecy at tragedy yet to come. And in the dark of the first moon of that century the shadowy hillsmen were getting ready to swoop down. And it was the dawn of the twentieth century of the Christian era that Burnham watched, the dawn of the one hundred and twenty-fifth year of the nation's life—of the one hundred and seventh year of statehood for Kentucky. And thinking of the onward sweep of the world, of the nation, North, East, West, and South, the backward staggering of his own loved State tugged sorely at his heart.

In chapel next morning John Burnham made another little talk—chiefly to the young men of the Blue-grass among whom this tragedy was taking place. No inheritance in American life was better than theirs, he told them—no better ideals in the relations of family, State, and nation. But the State was sick now with many ills and it was coming to trial now before the judgment of the watching world. If it stood the crucial fire, it would be the part of all the youth before him to maintain and even better the manhood that should come through unscathed. And if it failed, God forbid, it would be for them to heal, to mend, to upbuild, and, undaunted, push on and upward again. And as at the opening of the session he saw again, lifted to him with peculiar intenseness, the faces of Marjorie and Gray Pendleton, and of Mavis and Jason Hawn—only now Gray looked deeply serious and Jason sullen and defiant. And at Mavis, Marjorie did not turn this time to smile. Nor was there any furtive look from any one of the four to any other, when the students rose, though each pair of cousins drifted together on the way out, and in pairs went on their separate ways.

The truth was that Marjorie and Gray were none too happy over the recent turn of affairs. Both were too fine, too generous, to hurt the feelings of others except with pain to themselves. They knew Mavis and Jason were hurt but, hardly realizing that between the four the frank democracy of childhood was gone, they hardly knew how and how deeply. Both were mystified, greatly disturbed, drawn more than ever by the proud withdrawal of the mountain boy and girl, and both were anxious to make amends. More than once Gray came near riding over to Steve Hawn's and trying once more to understand and if possible to explain and restore good feeling, but the memory of his rebuff from Mavis and the unapproachable quality in Jason made him hesitate. Naturally with Marjorie this state of mind was worse, because of the brink of Jason's confession for which she knew she was much to blame, and because of the closer past between them. Once only she saw him striding the fields, and though she pulled in her horse to watch him, Jason did not know; and once he came to her when he did not know that she knew. It was the night before the mid-year examinations and Marjorie, in spite of that fact, had gone to a dance and, because of it, was spending the night in town with a friend. The two girls had got home a little before three in the morning, and Marjorie had put out her light and gone to bed but, being sleepless, had risen and sat dreaming before the fire. The extraordinary whiteness of the moonlight had drawn her to the window when she rose again, and she stood there like a tall lily, looking silent sympathy to the sufferers in the bitter cold outside. She put one bare arm on the sill of the closed window and looked down at the snow-crystals hardly less brilliant under the moon than they would be under the first sun-rays next morning, looked through the snow-laden branches of the trees, over the

white house-tops, and out to the still white fields—
the white world within her answering the white
world without as in a dream. She was thinking
of Jason, as she had been thinking for days, for
she could not get the boy out of her mind. All
night at the dance she had been thinking of him,
and when between the stone pillars of the gateway
a figure appeared without overcoat, hands in pockets and a bundle of something under one arm, the
hand on the window-sill dropped till it clutched
her heart at the strangeness of it, for her watching
eyes saw plain in the moonlight the drawn white
face of Jason Hawn. He tossed something on the
porch and her tears came when she realized what
it meant. Then he drew a letter out of his
pocket, hesitated, turned, turned again, tossed it
too upon the porch, and wearily crunched out
through the gate. The girl whirled for her dress-
ing-gown and slippers, and slipped downstairs to
the door, for her instinct told her the letter was
for her, and a few minutes later she was reading
it by the light of the fire.

"I know where you are," the boy had written.
"Don't worry, but I want to tell you that I take
back that promise I made in the road that day."

John Burnham's examination was first for Jason
that morning, and when the boy came into the
recitation-room the school-master was shocked by
the tumult in his face. He saw the lad bend list-

lessly over his papers and look helplessly up and around—worn, brain-fagged, and half wild—saw him rise suddenly and hurriedly, and nodded him an excuse before he could ask for it, thinking the boy had suddenly gone ill. When he did not come back Burnham got uneasy, and after an hour he called another member of the faculty to take his place and hurried out. As he went down the corridor a figure detached itself from a group of girls and flew after him. He felt his arm caught tightly and he turned to find Marjorie, white, with trembling lips, but struggling to be calm:

"Where is Jason?" Burnham recovered quickly.

"Why, I don't believe he is very well," he said with gentle carelessness. "I'm going over now to see him. I'll be back in a minute." Wondering and more than ever uneasy, Burnham went on, while the girl unconsciously followed him to the door, looking after him and almost on the point of wringing her hands. In the boy's room Burnham found an old dress-suit case packed and placed on the study table. On it was a pencil-scribbled note to one of his room-mates:

"I'll send for this later," it read, and that was all.

Jason was gone.

XXV

THE little capital sits at the feet of hills on the edge of the Blue-grass, for the Kentucky River that sweeps past it has brought down those hills from the majestic highlands of the Cumberland. The great railroad of the State had to bore through rock to reach the place and clangs impudently through it along the main street. For many years other sections of the State fought to wrest this fountain-head of law and government from its moorings and transplant it to the heart of the Blue-grass, or to the big town on the Ohio, because, as one claimant said:

"You had to climb a mountain, swim a river, or go through a hole to get to it."

This geographical witticism cost the claimant his eternal political life, and the capital clung to its water, its wooded heaps of earth, and its hole in the gray wall. Not only hills did the river bring down but birds, trees, and even mountain mists, and from out the black mouth of that hole in the wall and into those morning mists stole one day a long train and stopped before the six great gray pillars of the historic old State-house. Out of this train climbed a thousand men, with a thousand guns, and the mists might have been the breath of the universal whisper:

"The mountaineers are here!"

Of their coming Jason had known for some time from Arch Hawn, and just when they were to come he had learned from Steve. The boy had not enough carfare even for the short ride of less than thirty miles to the capital, so he rode as far as his money would carry him and an hour before noon found him striding along on foot, his revolver bulging at his hip, his dogged eyes on the frozen turnpike. It was all over for him, he thought with the passionate finality of youth—his college career with its ambitions and dreams. He was sorry to disappoint Saint Hilda and John Burnham, but his pride was broken and he was going back now to the people and the life that he never should have left. He would find his friends and kinsmen down there at the capital, and he would play his part first in whatever they meant to do. Babe Honeycutt would be there, and about Babe he had not forgotten his mother's caution. He had taken his promise back from Marjorie merely to be free to act in a double emergency, but Babe would be safe until he himself was sure. Then he would tell his mother what he meant to do, or after it was done, and as to what she would then say the boy had hardly a passing wonder, so thin yet was the coating with which civilization had veneered him. And yet the boy almost smiled to himself to think how submerged that childhood oath was now in the big new hatred that had grown within him for the man who was threatening the political life of his people and his State—had grown steadily since the morning before he had taken the train in the mountains for college in the Blue-grass. On the way he had stayed all night in a little mountain town in the foot-hills. He had got up at dawn, but already, to escape the hot rays of an August sun, mountaineers were coming in on horseback from miles and miles around to hear the opening blast of the trumpet that was to herald forth their wrongs. Under the trees and along the fences they picketed their horses, thousands of them, and they played simple games patiently, or patiently sat in the shade of pine and cedar waiting, while now and then a band made havoc with the lazy summer air. And there, that morning, Jason had learned from a red-headed orator that "a vicious body of deformed Democrats and degenerate Americans" had passed a law at the capital that would rob the mountaineers of the rights that had been bought with the blood of their forefathers in 1776, 1812, 1849, and 1865. Every ear caught the emphasis on "rob" and "rights," the patient eye of the throng grew instantly alert and keen and began to burn with a sinister fire, while the ear of it heard further how, through that law, their ancient Democratic enemies would throw *their*

votes out of the ballot-box or count them as they
pleased—even for *themselves*. If there were three
Democrats in a mountain county—and the
speaker had heard that in one county there was
only one—that county could under that law run
every State and national election to suit itself.
Would the men of the mountains stand that?—
No! *He* knew them—that orator did. *He* knew
that if the spirit of liberty, that at Jamestown and
Plymouth Rock started blazing its way over a
continent, lived unchanged anywhere, it dwelt,
however unenlightened and unenlightening, in a
heart that for an enemy was black with hate, red
with revenge, though for the stranger, white and
kind; that in an eagle's isolation had kept strung
hard and fast to God, country, home; that ticking
clock-like for a century without hurry or pause
was beginning to quicken at last to the march-
rhythm of the world—the heart of the Southern
hills. Now the prophecy from the flaming tongue
of that red-headed orator was coming to pass, and
the heart of the Kentucky hills was making answer.

It was just before noon when the boy reached
the hill overlooking the capital. He saw the
gleam of the river that came down from the
mountains, and the home-thrill of it warmed him
from head to foot. Past the cemetery he went,
with a glimpse of the statue of Daniel Boone rising
above the lesser dead. A little farther down was
the castle-like arsenal guarded by soldiers, and he

looked at them curiously, for they were the first he had ever seen. Below him was the gray, gloomy bulk of the penitentiary, which was the State building that he used to hear most of in the mountains. About the railway station he saw men slouching whom he knew to belong to his people, but no guns were now in sight, for the mountaineers had checked them at the adjutant-general's office, and each wore a tag for safe-keeping in his button-hole. Around the Greek portico of the capitol building he saw more soldiers lounging, and near a big fountain in the State-house yard was a Gatling-gun which looked too little to do much harm. Everywhere were the stern, determined faces of mountain men, walking the streets staring at things, shuffling in and out of the buildings; and, through the iron pickets of the yard fence, Jason saw one group cooking around a camp-fire. A newspaper man was setting his camera for them and the boy saw a big bearded fellow reach under his blanket. The photographer grasped his instrument and came flying through the iron gate, crying humorously, "Excuse *me!*"

And then Jason ran into Steve Hawn, who looked at him with mild wonder and, without a question, drawled simply:

"I kind o' thought you'd be along."

"Is grandpap here?" asked the boy, and Steve shook his head.

"He was too po'ly—but thar's more Hawns and

236

Honeycutts in town than you kin shake a stick at, an' they're walkin' round hyeh jes like brothers. Hello, hyeh's one now!"

Jason turned to see big Babe Honeycutt, who, seeing him, paled a little, smiled sheepishly, and, without speaking, moved uneasily away. Whereat Steve laughed.

"Looks like Babe is kind o' skeered o' you fer *some* reason— Hello, they're comin'!"

A group had gathered on the brick flagging between the frozen fountain and the Greek portico of the old capitol, and every slouching figure was moving toward it. Among them Jason saw Hawns and Honeycutts—saw even his old enemy, "little Aaron" Honeycutt, and he was not even surprised, for in a foot-ball game with one college on the edge of the Blue-grass, he had met a pair of envious, hostile eyes from the side-lines and he knew then that little Aaron, too, had gone away to school. From the habit of long hostility now, Jason swerved to the other edge of the crowd. From the streets, the boarding-houses, the ancient Capitol Hotel, gray, too, as a prison, from the State buildings in the yard, mountaineers were surging forth and massing before the capitol steps and around the big fountain. Already the Democrats had grown hoarse with protest and epithet. It was an outrage for the Republicans to bring down this "mountain army of intimidationists" —and only God knew what they meant to do or might do. The autocrat might justly and legally unseat a few Republicans, to be sure, but one open belief was that these "unkempt feudsmen and outlaws" would rush the legislative halls, shoot down enough Democrats to turn the Republican minority, no matter how small, into a majority big enough to enforce the ballot-proven will of the people. Wild, pale, horrified faces began to appear in the windows of the houses that bordered the square and in the buildings within the yard— perhaps they were going to do it now. Every soldier stiffened where he stood and caught his gun tightly, and once more the militia colonel looked yearningly at the Gatling-gun as helpless as a fire-cracker in the midst of the crowd, and then imploringly to the adjutant-general, who once again smiled and shook his head. If sinister in purpose, that mountain army was certainly well drilled and under the dominant spirit of some amazing leadership, for no sound, no gesture, no movement came from it. And then Jason saw a pale, dark young man, the secretary of state, himself a mountain man, rise above the heads of the crowd and begin to speak.

"You are not here as revolutionists, criminals, or conspirators, because you are loyal to government and law."

The words were big and puzzling to the untutored ears that heard them, but a grim, enigmatical smile was soon playing over many a rugged face.

238

"You are here under your God-given bill of rights to right your wrongs through petitions to the legislators in whose hands you placed your liberties and your laws. And to show how non-partisan this meeting is, I nominate as chairman a distinguished Democrat and ex-Confederate soldier."

And thereupon, before Jason's startled eyes, rose none other than Colonel Pendleton, who silently swept the crowd with his eyes.

"I see from the faces before me that the legislators behind me shall not overturn the will of the people," he said quietly but sonorously, and then, like an invocation to the Deity, the dark young mountaineer slowly read from the paper in his hand how they were all peaceably assembled for the common good and the good of the State to avert the peril hovering over its property, peace, safety, and happiness. How they prayed for calmness, prudence, wisdom; begged that the legislators should not suffer themselves to be led into the temptation of partisan pride or party predilection; besought them to remember that their own just powers were loaned to them by the people at the polls, and that they must decide the people's will and not their own political preference; implored them not to hazard the subversion of that supreme law of the land; and finally begged them to receive, and neither despise nor spurn, their earnest petition, remonstrance, but preserve and

239

promote the safety and welfare and, above all, the honor of the commonwealth committed to their keeping.

There was no applause, no murmur even of approval—stern faces had only grown sterner, hard eyes harder, and that was all. Again the mountain secretary of state rose, started to speak, and stopped, looking over the upturned faces and toward the street behind them; and something in his look made every man who saw it turn his head. A whisper started on the outer edge of the crowd and ran backward, and men began to tiptoe and crane their necks. A tall figure was entering the iron gateway—and that whisper ran like a wind through the mass, the whisper of a hated name. The autocrat was coming. The mountaineers blocked his royal way to the speaker's chair behind them, but he came straight on. His cold, strong, crafty face was suddenly and fearlessly uplifted when he saw the hostile crowd, and a half-scornful smile came to his straight thin lips. A man behind him put a detaining hand on his shoulder, but he shook it off impatiently. Almost imperceptibly men swerved this way and that until there was an open way through them to the State-house steps, and through that human lane, nearly every man of which was at that moment longing to take his life, the autocrat strode, meeting every pair of eyes with a sneer of cold defiance. Behind him the lane closed; the crowd gasped at the daring of the man and slowly melted away. The mountain secretary followed him into the Senate with the resolutions he had just read, and the autocrat, still with that icy smile, received and passed them—into oblivion.

That night the mountain army disappeared as quickly as it had come, on a special train through that hole in the wall and with a farewell salute of gun and pistol into the drum-tight air of the little capital. But a guard of two hundred stayed, quartered in boarding-houses and the executive buildings, and hung about the capitol with their arms handy, or loitered about the contest-board meetings where the great "steal" was feared. So those meetings adjourned to the city hall where the room was smaller, admission more limited, and which was, as the Republicans claimed, a Democratic arsenal. Next day the Republicans asked for three days more for testimony and were given three hours by the autocrat. The real fight was now on, every soul knew it, and the crisis was at hand.

And next morning it came, when the same bold figure was taking the same way to the capitol. A rifle cracked, a little puff of smoke floated from a window of a State building, and on the brick flagging the autocrat sank into a heap.

The legislature was at the moment in session. The minority in the House was on edge for the next move. The secretary was droning on and beating time, for the autocrat was late that morning, but he was on his way. Cool, wary, steeled to act relentlessly at the crucial moment, his hand was within reach of the prize, and the play of that master-hand was on the eve of a master-stroke. Two men hurried into the almost deserted square, the autocrat and his body-guard, a man known in the annals of the State for his ready use of knife or pistol. The rifle spoke and the autocrat bent double, groaned harshly, clutched his right side, and fell to his knees. Men picked him up, the building emptied, and all hurried after the throng gathering around the wounded man. There was the jostling of bodies, rushing of feet, the crowding of cursing men to the common centre of excitement. A negro pushed against a white man. The white man pulled his pistol, shot him dead, and hardly a look was turned that way. The doors of the old hotel closed on the wounded man, his friends went wild, and chaos followed. It was a mountain trick, they cried, and a mountaineer had turned it. The lawless hillsmen had come down and brought their cowardly custom of ambush with them. The mountain secretary of state was speeding away from the capitol at the moment the shot was fired, and that was a favorite trick of alibi in the hills. That shot had come from his window. Within ten minutes the terrified governor had ringed every State building with bayonets and had telegraphed for more

militia. Nobody, not even the sheriff, could enter
to search for the assassin: what else could this
mean but that there was a conspiracy—that the
governor himself knew of the plot to kill and was
protecting the slayer? About the State-house,
even after the soldiers had taken possession, stood
rough-looking men, a wing of the army of intimi-
dation. A mob was forming at the hotel, and
when a company of soldiers was assembled to meet
it, a dozen old mountaineers, looking in the light
of the camp-fires like the aged paintings of pioneers on the State-house walls, fell silently and
solemnly in line with Winchesters and shot-guns.
The autocrat's bitterest enemies, though unregret-
ting the deed, were outraged at the way it was
done, and the rush of sympathy in his wake could
hardly fail to achieve his purpose now. That
night even, the Democratic members tried to decide the contest in the autocrat's favor. That
night the governor adjourned the legislature to a
mountain town, and next morning the legislators
found their chambers closed. They tried to meet
at hotel, city hall, court-house; and solons and
soldiers raced through the streets and never could
the solons win. But at nightfall they gathered
secretly and declared the autocrat governor of the
commonwealth. And the wild rumor was that
the wounded man had passed before his name was
sealed by the legislative hand, and that the feet
of a dead man had been put into a living one's

shoes. That night the news flashed that one mountaineer as assassin and a mountain boy as accomplice had been captured and were on the way to jail. And the assassin was Steve and the boy none other than Jason Hawn.

XXVI

ONE officer pushed Jason up the steps of the car with one hand clutched in the collar of the boy's coat. Steve Hawn followed, handcuffed, and as the second officer put his foot on the first step, Steve flashed around and brought both of his huge manacled fists down on the man's head, knocking him senseless to the ground.

"Git, Jason!" he yelled, but the boy had already got. Feeling the clutch on his coat collar loosen suddenly, he had torn away and, without looking back even to see what the crashing blow was that he heard, leaped from the moving train into the darkness on the other side of the train. One shot that went wild followed him, but by the time Steve was subdued by the blow of a pistol butt and the train was stopped, Jason was dashing through a gloomy woodland with a speed that he had never equalled on a foot-ball field. On top of a hill he stopped for a moment panting and turned to listen. There were no sounds of pursuit, the roar of the train had started again, and he saw the lights of it twinkling on toward the capital. He knew they would have bloodhounds on his trail as soon as possible; that every railway-station agent would have a description of him and be on the lookout

for him within a few hours; and that his mother's
house would be closely watched that night: so,
gathering his breath, he started in the long, steady
stride of his foot-ball training across the fields and,
a fugitive from justice, fled for the hills. The
night was crisp, the moon was not risen, and the
frozen earth was slippery, but he did not dare to
take to the turnpike until he saw the lights of
farm-houses begin to disappear, and then he
climbed the fence into the road and sped swiftly
on. Now and then he would have to leap out of
the road again and crouch close behind the fence
when he heard the rattle of some coming vehicle,
but nothing overtook him, and when at last he
had the dark silent fields and the white line of the
turnpike all to himself he slowed into a swift walk.
Before midnight he saw the lights of his college
town ahead of him and again he took to the fields
to circle about it and strike the road again on the
other side where it led on toward the mountains.
But always his eyes were turned leftward toward
those town lights that he was leaving perhaps forever and on beyond them to his mother's home.
He could see her still seated before the fire and
staring into it, newly worn and aged, and tearless;
and he knew Mavis lay sleepless and racked with
fear in her little room. By this time they all must
have heard, and he wondered what John Burnham
was thinking, and Gray, and then with a stab at
his heart he thought of Marjorie. He wondered

if she had got his good-by note—the taking back of his promise to her. Well, it was all over now. The lights fell behind him, the moon rose, and under it he saw again the white line of the road. He was tired, but he put his weary feet on the frozen surface and kept them moving steadily on. At the first cock-crow, he passed the house where he had stayed all night when he first rode to the Blue-grass on his old mare. A little later lights began once more to twinkle from awakening farm-houses. The moon paled and a whiter light began to steal over the icy fields. Here was the place where he and the old mare had seen for the first time a rail-road train. Hunger began to gnaw within him when he saw the smoke rising from a negro cabin down a little lane, and he left the road and moved toward it. At the bars which let into a little barn-yard an old negro was milking a cow, and when, at the boy's low cry of "Hello!" he rose to his feet, a ruse came to Jason quickly.

"Seen any chestnut hoss comin' along here?"

The old man shook his head.

"I jist got up, son."

"Well, he got away from me an' I reckon he's gone back toward home. I started before break-fast—can I get a bite here?"

It looked suspicious—a white man asking a negro for food, and Jason had learned enough in the Blue-grass to guess the reason for the old dar-ky's hesitation, for he added quickly:

247

"I don't want to walk all the way back to that white house where I was goin' to get something to eat."

A few minutes later the boy was devouring corn-bread and bacon so ravenously that again he saw suspicion in the old darky's eyes, and for that reason when he struck the turnpike again he turned once more into the fields. The foot-hills were in sight now, and from the top of a little wooded eminence he saw the beginning of the dirt road and he almost shouted his gladness aloud. An hour later he was on top of the hill whence he and his old mare had looked first over the land of the Blue-grass, and there he turned to look once more. The sun was up now and each frozen weed, belated corn-stalk, and blade of grass caught its light, shattered it into glittering bits, and knit them into a veil of bewildering beauty for the face of the yet sleeping earth. The lad turned again to the white breasts of his beloved hills. The nation's army could never catch him when he was once among them—and now Jason smiled.

XXVII

BACK at the little capital, the Pennyroyal governor sat pat behind thick walls and the muskets of a thousand men. The militia, too, remained loyal, and the stacking up of ammunition in the adjutant-general's office went merrily on. The dead autocrat was reverently borne between two solid walls of living people to the little cemetery on the high hill overlooking the river and with tribute of tongue and pen was laid to rest, but beneath him the struggle kept on. Mutual offers of compromise were mutually refused and the dual government went on. The State-house was barred to the legislators. To test his authority the governor issued a pardon—the Democratic warden of the penitentiary refused to recognize it. A company of soldiers came from his own Pennyroyal home and the wing of the mountain army still hovered nigh. Meanwhile companies of militia were drafted for service under the banner of the dead autocrat. The governor ate and slept in the State-house—never did he leave it. Once more a Democratic mob formed before the square and the Gatling-gun dispersed it. The President at Washington declined to interfere.

249

Then started the arrests. It was declared that
the fatal shot came from the window of the office
of the pale, dark young secretary of state, and
that young mountaineer was taken—with a pardon
from the governor in his pocket; his brother, a captain of the State guard, the ex-secretary of state,
also a mountain man, and still another mountaineer were indicted as accessories before the fact
and those indictments charged complicity to the
Pennyroyal governor himself. And three other
men who were found in the executive building were
indicted for murder along with Steve and Jason
Hawn. Indeed, the Democrats were busy un-
earthing, as they claimed, a gigantic Republican
conspiracy. No less than one hundred thousand
dollars was offered as a reward for the conviction
of the murderers, and the Republican cry was that
with such a sum it was possible to convict even
the innocent. In turn, Liberty Leagues were even
formed throughout the State to protect the innocent, and lives and property were pledged to that
end, but the ex-secretary of state fled for refuge
across the Ohio, and the governor over there refused to give him up.

The Democrats held forth at the Capitol Hotel
—the Republicans at the executive building. The
governor sent arms from the State arsenal to his
mountain capital. Two speakers were always on
hand in the Senate, and war talk once again became rife. There was a heavy guard of soldiers at

every point in the Capitol Square, there were sentries at the governor's mansion, and the rumor was that the militia would try to arrest the lieutenant-governor who now was successor to the autocrat. So, to guard him, special police were sworn in— police around the hotel, police in the lobby, police patrolling the streets day and night; a system of signals was formed to report suspicious movements of troops, and more men were stationed at convenient windows and in dark alleyways, armed with pistols, but with rifles and shot-guns close at hand, while the police station was full of arms and ammunition. To the courts it was at last agreed that the whole matter should go, and there was panting peace for a while.

A curious pall overhung the college the morning of Jason's flight for the hills. The awful news spread from lip to lip, hushing shouts and quelling laughter. The stream of students moved into the chapel with little noise—a larger stream than usual, for the feeling was that there would be comment from the old president. A common seriousness touched the face of every teacher on the platform and deepened the seriousness of the young faces that looked expectantly upward. In the centre of the freshman corner one seat only was vacant, and that to John Burnham suggested the emptiness of even more than death. Among the girls one chair, too, yawned significantly, for Mavis was not there and the two places might have been side by side, so close was the mute link between them. But no word of Jason reached any curious ear, and only a deeper feeling in the old president's voice when it was lifted, and a deeper earnestness in his prayer that especial guidance might now be granted the State in the crisis it was passing through, showed that the thought of all hearts was working alike in his. At noon the news of Jason's escape and flight spread like fire through town and college—then news that bloodhounds were on his trail, that the trail led to the hills, and that a quick capture was certain. Before night the name of the boy was on the lips of the State and for a day at least on the lips of the nation.

The night before, John Burnham had gone down to the capital to see Jason. All that day he had been hardly able to keep his mind on book or student, all day he had kept recalling how often the boy had asked him about this or that personage in history who had sought to win liberty for his people by slaying with his own hand some tyrant. He knew what part politics, the awful disregard of human life, and the revengeful spirit of the mountains had played in the death of the autocrat, but he knew also that if there was in that mountain army that had gone to the capital the fearful, mistaken, higher spirit of the fanatic it was in the breast of Jason Hawn. He believed, however, that in the boy the spirit was all there was, and that the deed must have been done by some hand

that had stolen the cloak of that spirit to conceal a
malicious purpose. Coming out of his class-room,
he had seen Gray, whose face showed that he was
working with the same bewildering, incredible
problem. Outside Marjorie had halted him and
tremblingly told him of Jason's long-given promise and how he had taken it back; and so as he
drove to the country that afternoon his faith in
Jason was miserably shaken and a sickening fear
for the boy possessed him. He was hardly aware
he had reached his own gate, so lost in thought
was he all the way, until his horse of its own accord
stopped in front of it, and then he urged it on with
a sudden purpose to go to Jason's mother. On
top of the hill he stopped again, for Marjorie's
carriage was turning into the lane that led to
Martha Hawn's house. His kindly purpose had
been forestalled and with intense relief he turned
back on his heart-sick way homeward.

With Marjorie, too, it had been a sudden
thought to go to Jason's mother, but as she drew
near the gate she grew apprehensive. She had
not been within the house often and then only for a
moment to wait for Mavis. She had always been
half-fearful and ill at ease with the sombre-faced
woman who always searched her with big dark
eyes whose listlessness seemed but to veil mysteries
and hidden fires. As she was getting out of her
carriage she saw Martha Hawn's pale face at the
window. She expected the door to be opened, as

she climbed the steps, but it was not, and when she timidly knocked there was no bid to enter. She was even about to turn away bewildered and indignant when the door did open and a forbidding figure stood before her

"Mavis has gone down to see her pappy."

"Yes, I know—but I thought I'd come——"

She halted helplessly. She did not know that knocking was an unessential formality in the hills; she did not realize that it was her first friendly call on Martha Hawn; and curiously enough the mountain woman became at that moment the quicker of the two.

"Come right in and set down," she said with a sudden change of manner. "Rest yo' hat thar on the bed, won't you?"

The girl entered, her rosy face rising from her furs, and she seemed to flood the poor little room with warmth and light and make it poor indeed. She sat down and felt the deep black eyes burning at her not unkindly now and with none of her own embarrassment, for she had expected to find a woman bowed with grief and she found her unshaken, stolid, calm. For the first time she noticed that Jason had got his eyes and his brow from his mother, and now her voice was an echo of his.

"They've got dogs atter my boy," she said simply.

That was all she said, but it started the girl's

tears, for there was not even resentment in the voice—only the resignation that meant a life-long comradeship with sorrow. Marjorie had tried to speak, but tears began to choke her and she turned her face to hide them. She had come to comfort, but now she felt a hand patting her on the shoulder.

"Why, honey, you mustn't take on that-a-way. Jason wouldn't want nobody to worry 'bout him— not fer a minute. They'll never ketch him—never in this world. An' bless yo' dear heart, honey, this ain't nothin'. Ever'thing 'll come out all right. Why, I been used to killin' an' fightin' an' trouble all my life. Jason hain't done nothin' he didn't think was right—I know that—an' if hit was right I'm glad he done hit. I ain't so shore 'bout Steve, but the Lord's been good to Steve fer holdin' off his avengin' hand even this long. Hit'll all come out right—don't you worry."

Half an hour later the girl on her way home found Colonel Pendleton at his gate on horseback, apparently waiting for some one, and, looking back through the carriage window, Marjorie saw Gray galloping along behind her. She did not stop to speak with the colonel, and a look of uneasy wonder crossed his face as she drove by.

"What's the matter with Marjorie?" he asked when Gray drew nigh. The boy shook his head worriedly.

"She's been to the Hawns," he said, and the

colonel looked grave. Twenty minutes later Mrs. Pendleton sat in her library, also looking grave. Marjorie had told her where she had been and why she had gone, and the mother, startled by the girl's wildness and distress, had barely opened her lips in remonstrance when Marjorie, in a whirlwind of tears and defiance, fled to her room.

XXVIII

ON through the snowy mountains Jason went, keeping fearlessly now to the open road, and telling the same story to the same question that was always looked, even when not asked, by every soul with whom he passed a word: he had gone to the capital when the mountain people went down, he had been left behind, and, having no money, was obliged to make his way back home on foot. Always he was plied with questions, but news of the death of the autocrat had not yet penetrated that far. Always he was gladly given food and lodging, and sometimes his host or some horseman, overtaking him, would take him up behind and save him many a weary mile. Boldly he went until one morning he stood on the icy, glittering crest of Pine Mountain and looked down a white wooded ravine to the frozen Cumberland locked motionless in the valley below. He could see the mouth of Hawn Branch and the mouth of Honeycutt Creek—could see the spur, the neck of which once separated Mavis's home from his—and with a joyful throb and a quickly following pang he plunged down the ravine. Ahead of him was the house of a Honeycutt and he had no fear, but as he swiftly approached it along the river road, he saw two men, strangers, appear on the porch and instinctively he scudded noiselessly behind a great clump of evergreen rhododendron and lay flat to the frozen earth. A moment later they rode by him at a walk and talking in low, earnest tones.

"He's sure to come back here," said one, "and it won't be long before some Honeycutt will give him away. This peace business ain't skin-deep and a five-dollar bill will do the trick for us and I'll find the right man in twenty-four hours."

The other man grunted an assent and the two rode on. Already they were after Jason; they had guessed where he would go, and the boy knew that what he had heard from these men was true. When he rose now he kept out of the road and skirted his way along the white flanks of the hills. Passing high up the spur above Hawn Branch, he could see his grandfather's house. A horse was hitched to the fence and a man was walking toward the porch and the lad wondered if that stranger, too, could be on his trail. On upward he went until just below him he could see the old circuit rider's cabin under a snow-laden pine, and all up and down the Hawn Creek were signs of activity from the outside world. Already he had watched engineers mapping out the line of railway up the river. He had seen the coming of the railroad darkies who lived in shacks like cave-men, who were little above brutes and driven like slaves by rough men in blue woollen shirts and high-laced

boots. And now he saw that old Morton Sanders'
engineers had mapped out a line up the creek of
his fathers; that the darkies had graded it and
their wretched shacks were sagging drunkenly
here and there from the hill-sides. Around the
ravine the boy curved toward the neck of the
dividing spur and half-unconsciously toward the
little creek where he had uncovered his big vein of
coal, and there where with hand, foot, and pick he
had toiled so long was a black tunnel boring into
the very spot, with supporting columns of wood
and a great pile of coal at its gaping mouth. The
robbery was under way and the boy looked on with
fierce eyes at the three begrimed and coal-black-
ened darkies hugging a little fire near by. Cautiously he backed away and slipped on down to a
point where he could see his mother's old home and
Steve Hawn's, and there he almost groaned. One
was desolate, deserted, the door swinging from one
hinge, the chimney fallen, every paling of the
fence gone and the roof of the little barn caved in.
Smoke was coming from Steve Hawn's chimney,
and in the porch were two or three slatternly negro
women. The boy knew the low, sinister meaning
of their presence on public works; and these blacks
ate, slept, and plied their trade in the home of
Mavis Hawn! All the old rebellion and rage of
his early years came back to him and boiled the
more fiercely that his mother's home could never
be hers, nor Mavis's hers—for a twofold reason

now—again. It was nearing noon and the boy's
hunger was a keen pain. Rapidly he went down
the crest of the spur until his grandfather's house
was visible beneath him. The horse at the front
fence was gone, but as he slipped toward the rear
of the house he looked into the stable to make
sure that the horse was not there. And then a
moment later he reached the back porch and noiselessly opened the door—so noiselessly that the
old man sitting in front of the fire did not hear.

"Grandpap," he called tremulously.

The old man started and turned his great
shaggy head. He said nothing, but it seemed to
the boy that from under his bushy brows a flash
of lightning was searching him from head to foot.

"Well," he rumbled scathingly, "you've been
a-playin' hell, hain't ye? I mought 'a' knowed
whut would happen with Honeycutts a-leadin'
that gang. I tol' 'em to go up thar an' fight open
—man to man. They don't know nothin' but
way-layin'. A thousand of 'em shootin' one pore
man in the back! Whut 've I been tryin' to
l'arn ye since you was a baby? God knows I
wanted him killed. Why," thundered the old
man savagely, "didn't *you* kill him face to face?"

The boy's chin had gone up proudly while the
old man talked and now there was a lightning-
flash in his own eyes.

"I tried to git him face to face fer three days.
I knowed he had a gun. I was aimin' to give him

a chance fer his life. But seemed like thar wasn't no other——"

"Stop!" thundered the old man again, "don't you say a word."

There was a loud "Hello" at the gate.

"Thar they air now," said the old man with a break in his voice, and as he rose from his chair he said sternly: "An' stay right where you air."

Through the window the boy saw the two horsemen who had passed him in the road that morning. His eyes grew wild and he began to tremble violently, but he stood still. The old man went to the door.

"Hyeh he is, men," he shouted; "come in hyeh an' git him."

Then he turned to the boy.

"You air goin' back thar an' stand yore trial like a man."

The boy leaped wildly for the door, but the old man caught him and with one hand held him as though he were a child, and thus the two astonished detectives from the Blue-grass found them, and they gaped at the mystery, for they knew the kinship of the two. One pulled from his pocket a pair of handcuffs, and old Jason glared at him with contempt.

"Don't you put them things on this boy—he's my grandson. An', anyhow, ef you two full-grown men can't handle a boy without 'em I'll go 'long with you myself."

Shamed, the man put the irons back in his pocket, and the other one started to speak but stopped. The old man turned hospitably toward his unwelcome guests.

"I reckon all o' ye want a bite to eat afore ye start. Mammy!"

The door to the kitchen opened and the aged grandmother halted there, peering through brass-rimmed spectacles at her husband and the two men, and catching sight last of little Jason standing in the corner—trapped, white-faced, silent. Instantly she caught the meaning of the scene, and with a little cry she tottered over to the boy and putting both her hands on his breast began to pat him gently. Then, still helplessly patting him with one hand, she turned to her husband.

"You hain't goin' to give the boy up, Jason?" she asked plaintively, and the old man swerved his face aside and nodded.

"Git up somethin' to eat, mammy," he said with rough gentleness, and without another look or word she turned with her apron at her eyes to the kitchen door. The old man glared out the window, the boy sank on a chair at the corner of the fireplace, and in the face of one of the men there was sympathy. The other, shifty of eyes and crafty of face, spoke harshly.

"How much o' this reward do you want?"

Old Jason wheeled and the other man cried sternly:

"You hain't goin' to give the boy up, Jason?"

"Shut up, you fool!"

"You lop-yeared rattlesnake!" began old Jason, and with a contemptuous gesture dismissed him. "How much is that reward?"

The other man hesitated, and then with the thought that the fact would soon be world-known answered promptly:

"For the capture and conviction of the murderer —one hundred thousand dollars."

The old man gasped at the amazing sum; his face worked suddenly with convulsive rage and calmed in a sudden way that made the watching boy know that something was going to happen. Quietly old Jason walked over to the fire and stood with his back to it. He pulled out his pipe, filled it, and turned again to the mantel-piece as though to reach for a match, but instead whipped two big revolvers from it and wheeled.

"Hands up, men!" he said quietly. For a moment the two were paralyzed, but the thick-set man, whose instincts were quicker, obeyed slowly. The other one started to laugh.

"Up!" called the old man sternly, levelling one pistol, and the laugh stopped, the man's face paled, and his hands flew high.

"Git their guns fer a minute, Jasie, an' put em' up hyeh on the mantel. A hundred thousand dollars is a *leetle* too much."

The kitchen door opened and again the old woman peered through her spectacles within.

"I knowed you wouldn't do it, pap," she said. "Dinner's ready—come on in now, men, an' git a bite to eat."

The thin man's shifty eyes roved to his companion, who had almost begun to smile and who muttered to himself as he rose:

"Well, by God!"

In utter silence the meal went through, except that the old man, with his pistols crossed in his lap, kept urging his guests to the full of their appetites.   Jason ate like a wolf.

"Git a poke, mammy," said old Jason when the boy dropped knife and fork, "an' fill it full o' victuals."

And still with a smile the thick-set man watched her gather food from the table, put it in a paper sack, and hand it to the boy.

"Now git, Jasie—these men air goin' to stay hyeh with me fer' bout an hour, an' then they can go atter ye ef they think they can ketch ye."

With no word at all even of good-by, little Jason noiselessly disappeared.   A few minutes later, sitting in front of the fire with his pistols still in his lap, old Jason Hawn explained:

"Fer a mule, a Winchester, and a hundred dollars I can git most any man in this country killed. Fer a thousand I reckon I could git hit proved that I had stole a side o' bacon or a hoss.   Fer a hundred thousand I could git hit proved that the

President of these United States killed that feller—
an' human natur' is about the same, I reckon,
ever'whar. You don't git no grandson o' mine
when thar's a bunch o' greenbacks like that tied
to the rope that's a-pinin' to hang him."

An hour later he told his guests that they could
be on their way, though he'd be mighty glad to
have 'em stay all night—and they went, both
chagrined, the thin one raging within but obedient
and respectful without, while the other, chuckling
at his companion's discomfiture and no little at
his own, watched with a smile the old fellow's
method of speeding his parting guests.

"Git on yo' hosses, men," he suggested, and
when the two stepped from the porch he replaced
his own guns on the mantel and followed them
with both of their guns in one hand and a Winchester in the other. While they were mounting
he walked to the corner of the yard, laid both
their pistols on the fence, walked back to the
porch, and stood there with his Winchester in the
hollow of his arm.

"Ride by thar, men, and git yo' guns; an' I
reckon," he suggested casually but convincingly,
"when you pick 'em up you better not *even look
back—nary one o' ye.*"

"Can you beat it?" murmured the quiet man,
while the other snarled helplessly.

"An' when you git down to town you can tell
the sheriff. He's a Honeycutt, an' he won't come

atter me, but I'll go down thar to him an' pay my leetle fine."

Again the man said:

"Well, *by* God!"

And as the two rode on, the old fellow's voice followed them:

"Come ag'in, men—I wish ye both well."

Two nights later St. Hilda, reading by her fire, heard a tap on her window-pane, and, looking up, saw Jason's pale face outside. She ran to the door, and the boy stumbled wearily toward the threshold and stopped with a look of fear and piteous appeal. She stretched out her arms to him, and, broken at last, the boy sank at her feet, and, with his head in her lap, sobbed out of his heart the truth.

XXIX

ST. HILDA herself took Jason back to the Blue-grass, took him to the gray frowning prison at the capital, and with streaming eyes watched the iron gates close between them. Then she went home, sent for John Burnham, and within an hour both started working for the boy's freedom, for Jason must keep on with his studies, and, with Steve Hawn in jail, must help his mother. Through Gray's influence Colonel Pendleton, and through Marjorie's, Mrs. Pendleton as well, offered to go sponsors for the boy's appearance at his trial. The man from the Pennyroyal who sat in the governor's chair, and even the successor to the autocrat who was trying to pre-empt that seat, gave letters to help, and before any prison pallor could touch the boy's sun-tanned face he was out in the open air once more on bail. And when old Jason Hawn in the mountains heard what had happened, he laughed.

"Well, I reckon if he's indicted only fer *helpin'* Steve, he ain't in much danger, fer they can't git him onless they git Steve, an' if thar *is* one man no money can ketch—that man is slick Steve Hawn. An' lemme tell ye: if the right feller was from the mountains an' only mountain folks knows it, they hain't *nuver* goin' to find him out. Mebbe I was a leetle hasty—mebbe I was."

After one talk with John Burnham, the old president suggested that Jason drop down into the "kitchen" and go on with his books, but against this plan Jason shook his head. He was going to raise Steve Hawn's tobacco crop on shares with Colonel Pendleton, he would study at home, and John Burnham saw, moreover, that the boy shrank from the ordeal of college associations and any further hurt to his pride.

The pores of the earth were beginning to open now to the warm breath of spring. Already Martha Hawn and Mavis had burnt brush on the soil to kill the grass, and Jason ploughed the soil and harrowed it with minute care, and sowed the seed broadcast by hand. Within two weeks lettuce-like leaves were peeping through the ground, and Jason and Mavis stretched canvas over the beds to hold in the heat of day and hold off the frost of night. Three weeks later came the first ploughing; then there was ploughing and ploughing and ploughing again, and weeding and weeding and weeding again. Just before ripening, the blooms came—blooms that were for all the word like the blooms of purple rhododendron back in the hills, and then the task of suckering began. Sometimes Mavis would help and the mother started in to work like a man, but the boy had absorbed from his environment its higher ideal of woman and, all he could, he kept

both of them out of the tobacco field. This made
it all the harder for him and there was no let-up to
his toil. Just the same, Jason put in every spare
moment on his books, and in Mavis's little room,
which had been turned over to him, his lamp
burned far into every night. When he struck a
knotty point or problem, he would walk over to
John Burnham's for help, or the school-master, as
he went to and fro from his college duties, would
find the boy on a fence by the roadside waiting
with his question for him. All the summer Jason
toiled. When there was no hard labor, always he
had to fight the tobacco worms with spray, and
hand, and boot-heel, until the rich dark-green of
the leaves took on a furry, velvety sheen—until at
ripening they turned to a bright gold and were
ready for the chisel-bladed, double-edged knife
with which the plants are cut close to the ground.
Then they must be hung on upright tobacco sticks,
stalks upward, to wilt under the August sun, and
then on to be housed in Colonel Pendleton's great
barns to dry within their slitted walls. Several
times during the summer Arch Hawn came by
and looked at the boy's work with keen, approving
eye and in turn won a falling-off in Jason's old
prejudice against him; for Arch had built a church
in the county-seat in the mountains, had helped
the county schools, was making ready to help
the mountain people fight unjust claims to their
lands, and, himself charged with helping to bring

the mountain army down to the capital, stood
boldly ready to surrender to the call of the law
—he even meant to help Steve Hawn in his
trouble, for Steve, after an examining trial, had
been remanded back to prison without bail: and
he was going to help Jason in his trial, which
would closely follow Steve's.

All summer, too, Gray and Marjorie were riding or driving past the tobacco field, and Jason
and Mavis, when they saw either or both coming,
would move to the end of the field that was far-
thest from the turnpike and, turning their backs,
would pretend not to see. Sometimes the two
mountaineers would be caught where avoidance
was impossible, and then Marjorie and Gray would
call out cheerily and with a smile—to get in return
from the children of the soil a grave, silent nod of
the head and a grave, answering glance of the eye
—for neither knew the part the Blue-grass boy and
girl had played in the getting of Jason's freedom,
until one late afternoon of the closing summer
days, for John Burnham had been asked to keep
the matter a secret. But Steve Hawn had learned
from his lawyer and had told his wife Martha
when she came to visit him in prison; and that
late afternoon she was in the tobacco field when
Mavis and Jason moved to the other end and
turned their backs as Marjorie rode by on her way
home and Gray an hour later galloped past the
other way.

"I reckon," she said quietly to Jason, "ef you knowed whut that boy an' gal has been a-doin' fer ye, you wouldn't be a-actin' that-a-way."

And then she explained and started for home. Both stood still—silent and dumfounded—and only Mavis spoke at last.

"*Both* of us beholden to *both* of 'em."

Jason made no answer, but bent to his work. When Mavis, too, started for home he stayed behind without explanation, and when she was out of sight he climbed the fence at the edge of the woods, and sat there looking toward the sunset fading behind Marjorie's home.

XXX

THE tobacco was dry now, for the autumn was at hand. It must come to case yet, then it must be stripped, the grades picked out, and left then in bulk for sale. With all this Jason had nothing to do. He had done good work on his books during the spring and autumn, such good work that, with the old president's gladly given permission, he was allowed a special examination which admitted him with but one or two "conditions" into his own sophomore class. Then was there the extraordinary spectacle of a college boy —quiet, serious, toiling—making the slow way toward the humanities under charge of murder and awaiting trial for his life. And that course Jason Hawn followed with a dignity, reticence, and self-effacement that won the steadily increasing respect of every student and teacher within the college walls. A belief in his innocence became wide-spread, and that coming trial began to be regarded in time as a trial of the good name of the college itself. A change of venue had been obtained and the trial was to be held in the college town. It came in mid-December. Jason, neatly dressed, sat beside his lawyer, and his mother, in black, and Mavis sat quite near him. In the first row among the spectators were Gray and Marjorie and Colonel Pendleton. Behind them was John Burnham, and about him and behind him were several other professors, while the room was crowded with students. The boy was pale when he went to the witness-chair, and the court-room was as still as a wooded ravine in the hills when he began to tell his story, which apparently no other soul than his own lawyer had ever heard; indeed it was soon apparent that even he had never heard it all.

"I went down there to kill him," the boy said calmly, though his eyes were two deep points of fire—so calmly, indeed, that as one man the audience gasped audibly—"an' I reckon all of ye know why. My grandpap al'ays told me the meanest thing a man could do was to shoot another man in the back. I tried for three days to git face to face with him. I knowed he had a gun all the time, an' I meant to give him a fair chance fer his life. That mornin' I heard through the walls of the boardin'-house I was in—an' I didn't know who was doin' the talkin'—that the man was goin' to be waylaid right then an' I run over to that ex-ec-u-tive building to reach Steve Hawn an' keep *him* anyways from doin' the shootin'. I heard the shots soon as I got inside the door, and purty soon I met Steve runnin' down the stairs. 'I didn't do it!' Steve says, 'but any feller from the mountains better git away from *here*.' We

run out through the yard an' got into Steve's
buggy an' travelled the road till we was ketched—
an' that's all I know."

And that was all. No other fact, no other admission, no other statement could the rigid, bitter
cross-examination bring from the lad's lips than
just those words; and those words alone the jury
carried to their room. Nor were they long gone.
Back they came, and again the court-room was
as the holding in of one painful breath, and then
tears started in the eyes of the woman in black,
the mountain girl by her side, and in Marjorie's,
and the court-room broke into stifled cheer, for
the words all heard were:

"Not guilty."

At the gate of the college a crowd of students, led
by Gray Pendleton, awaited Jason. The boy was
borne aloft on their shoulders through the yard
amid the cheers of boys and girls—was borne on
into the gymnasium, and before the lad could quite
realize what was going on he heard himself cheered
as captain of the foot-ball team for the next year,
and was once more borne out, around and aloft
again—while John Burnham with a full heart, and
Mavis and Marjorie with wet eyes, looked smilingly on. A week later Arch Hawn persuaded the
boy to allow him to lend him money to complete
his course and a week later still it was Christmas
again. Christmas night there was a glad gather-

ing at Colonel Pendleton's. Even St. Hilda was there, and she and John Burnham, and Colonel Pendleton and Mrs. Pendleton, Gray and Mavis, and Marjorie and Jason, danced the Virginia reel together, and all the stars were stars of Bethlehem to Mavis and Jason Hawn as they crunched across the frozen fields at dawn for home.

XXXI

THE pale, dark young secretary of state had fled from the capital in a soldier's uniform and had been captured with a pardon in his pocket from the Pennyroyal governor, which the authorities refused to honor. The mountain ex-secretary of state had fled across the Ohio, to live there an exile. The governor from the Pennyroyal had carried his case to the supreme court of the land, had lost, and he, too, amid the condemnation of friends and foes, had crossed the same yellow river to the protection of the same Northern State. With his flight the troubles at the capital had passed the acute crisis and settled down into a long, wearisome struggle to convict the assassins of the autocrat. During the year the young secretary of state had been once condemned to death, once to life imprisonment, and was now risking the noose again on a third trial. Jason Hawn's testimony at his own trial, it was thought, would help Steve Hawn. Indeed, another mountaineer, Hiram Honeycutt, an uncle to little Aaron, was, it seemed, in greater danger than Steve, but the suspect in most peril was an auditor's clerk from the Blue-grass; so it looked as though old Jason's prophecy—that the real murderer, if a mountaineer, would never be convicted—might yet come true. The autocrat was living on in the hearts of his followers as a martyr to the cause of the people, and a granite shaft was to rise in the little cemetery on the river bluff to commemorate his deeds and his name. His death had gratified the blood-lust of his foes, his young Democratic successor would amend that "infamous election law" and was plainly striving for a just administration, and so bitterness began swiftly to abate, tolerance grew rapidly, and the State went earnestly on trying to cure its political ills. And yet even while John Burnham and his like were congratulating themselves that cool heads and strong hands had averted civil war, checked further violence, and left all questions to the law and the courts, the economic poison that tobacco had been spreading through the land began to shake the commonwealth with a new fever: for not liberty but daily bread was the farmer's question now.

The Big Trust had cut out competitive buyers, cut down prices to the cost of production, and put up the price of the tobacco bag and the plug. So that the farmer must smoke and chew his own tobacco, or sell it at a loss and buy it back again at whatever price the trust chose to charge him. Already along the southern border of the State the farmers had organized for mutual protection and the members had agreed to plant only half the

usual acreage. When the non-members planted
more than ever, masked men descended upon
them at night and put the raiser to the whip and
his barn to the torch. It seemed as though the passions of men, aroused by the political troubles and
getting no vent in action, welcomed this new outlet,
and already the night-riding of ku-klux and toll-
gate days was having a new and easy birth. And
these sinister forces were sweeping slowly toward
the Blue-grass. Thus the injection of this new
problem brought a swift subsidence of politics in
the popular mind. It caused a swift withdrawal
of the political background from the lives of the
Pendletons and dwarfed its importance for the
time in the lives of the Hawns, for again the following spring Colonel Pendleton, in the teeth of
the coming storm, raised tobacco, and so, for his
mother, did Jason Hawn.

In the mountains, meanwhile, the trend, contra-
riwise, was upward—all upward. Railroads were
building, mines were opening, great trees were
falling for timber. Even the Hawns and Honeycutts were too busy for an actual renewal of
the feud, though the casual traveller was amazed
to discover slowly how bitter the enmity still was.
But the feud in no way checked the growth going
on in all ways, nor was that growth all material.
More schools than St. Hilda's had come into
the hills from the outside and were doing hardly
less effective work. County schools, too, were in-

creasing in number and in strength. More and more mountain boys and girls were each year going away to college, bringing back the fruits of their work and planting the seeds of them at home. The log cabin was rapidly disappearing, the frame cottages were being built with more neatness and taste, and garish colors were becoming things of the past. Indeed, a quick uplift through all the mountains was perceptible to any observant eye that had known and knew now the hills. To the law-makers at the capital and to the men of law and business in the Blue-grass, that change was plain when they came into conflict with the lawyers and bankers and merchants of the highlands, for they found this new hillsman shrewd, resourceful, quick-witted, tenacious, and strong, and John Burnham began to wonder if the vigorous type of Kentuckian that seemed passing in the Blue-grass might not be coming to a new birth in the hills. He smiled grimly that following spring when he heard that a company of mountain militia from a county that was notorious for a desperate feud had been sent down to keep order in the tobacco lowlands; he kept on smiling every time he heard that a mountaineer had sold his coal lands and moved down to buy some blue-grass farm, and wondering how far this peaceful dispossessment might go in time; and whether a fusion of these social extremes of civilization might not be in the end for the best good of the State. And he knew that the basis of his every speculation about the fortunes of the State rested on the intertwining hand of fate in the lives of Marjorie and Gray Pendleton and Mavis and Jason Hawn.

XXXII

IN June, Gray Pendleton closed his college career as he had gone through it—like a meteor—and Jason went for the summer to the mountains, while Mavis stayed with his mother, for again Steve Hawn had been tried and convicted and returned to jail to await a new trial. In the mountains Jason got employment at some mines below the county-seat, and there he watched the incoming of the real "furriners," Italians, "Hunks," and Slavs, and the uprising of a mining town. He worked, too, in every capacity that was open to him, and he kept his keen eyes and keen mind busy that he might know as much as possible of the great machine that old Morton Sanders would build and set to work on his mother's land. And more than ever that summer he warmed to his uncle Arch Hawn for the fight that Arch was making to protect native titles to mountain lands —a fight that would help the achievement of the purpose that, though faltering at last, was still deep in the boy's heart.

In the autumn, when he went back to college, Gray had set off to some Northern college for a post-graduate course in engineering and Marjorie had gone to some fashionable school in the great city of the nation for the finishing touches of hats and gowns, painting and music, and for a wider knowledge of her own social world. That autumn the tobacco trouble was already pointing to a crisis for Colonel Pendleton. The whip and lash and the destruction of seed-beds had been ineffective, and as the trust had got control of the trade, the raisers must now get control of the raw leaf in the field and in the barn. That autumn Jason himself drifted into a mass-meeting of growers in the court-house one day on his way home from college. An orator from the Far West with a shock of black hair and gloomy black brows and eyes urged a general and permanent alliance of the tillers of the soil. An old white-bearded man with cane and spectacles and a heavy goatee working under a chew of tobacco tremulously pleaded for a pooling of the crops. The answer was that all would not pool, and the question was how to get all in. A great-shouldered, red-faced man and a bull-necked fellow with gray, fearless eyes, both from the southern part of the State, openly urged the incendiary methods that they were practising at home—the tearing up of tobacco-beds, burning of barns, and the whipping of growers who refused to go into the pool. And then Colonel Pendleton rose, his face as white as his snowy shirt, and bowed courteously to the chairman.

"These gentlemen, I think, are beside themselves," he said quietly, "and I must ask your permission to withdraw."

Jason followed him out to the court-house door and watched him, erect as a soldier, march down the street, and he knew the trouble that was in store for the old gentleman, for already he had heard similar incendiary talk from the small farmers around his mother's home.

The following June Marjorie and Gray Pendleton brought back finishing touches of dress, manner, and atmosphere to the dazzled envy of the less fortunate, in spite of the fact that both bore their new claims to distinction with a modesty that would have kept a stranger from knowing that they had ever been away from home. Jason and Mavis were still at the old university when the two arrived. To the mountaineers all four had once seemed almost on the same level, such had once been the comradeship between them, but now the old chasm seemed to yawn wider than ever between them, and there was no time for it to close, if closing were possible, for again Jason went back to the hills—this time to Morton Sanders' opening mines—and, this time, Mavis went with him to teach Hawns and Honeycutts in a summer school on the outskirts of the little mining town. Again for Jason the summer was one of unflagging work and learning—learning all he could, all the time. He had discovered that to get his land back through the law, he must prove that Arch Hawn

or Colonel Pendleton not only must have known
about the big seam of coal, not only must have
concealed the fact of their knowledge from his
mother and Steve Hawn, but, in addition, must
have told one or both, with the purpose of fraud,
that the land was worth no more than was visible
to the eye in timber and seams of coal that were
known to all.   That Colonel Pendleton could have
been guilty of such underhandedness was absurd.
Moreover, Jason's mother said that no such statement had been made to her by either, though Steve
had sworn readily that Arch had said just that
thing to him.   But Jason began to believe that
Steve had lied, and Arch Hawn laughed when he
heard of Jason's investigations.

"Son, if you want that land back, or, ruther,
the money it's worth, you git right down to work,
learn the business, and *dig* it back in another way."

And that was what Jason, half unconsciously,
was doing.   And yet, with all the ambition that
was in him, his interest in the work, his love for
the hills, his sense of duty to his people and his
wish to help them, the boy was sorely depressed
that summer, for the talons with which the fate
of birth and environment clutched him seemed to
be tightening now again.

The trials of Steve Hawn and of Hiram Honeycutt for the death of the autocrat were bringing back the old friction.   Charges and counter-
charges of perjury among witnesses had freshened

the old enmity between the Hawns and the Honeycutts. Jason himself had once to go back to the Blue-grass as witness, and when he returned he learned that the charge whispered against him, particularly by little Aaron, was that he had sworn falsely for Steve Hawn and falsely against Hiram Honeycutt. Again Babe Honeycutt had come back from the West and had quietly slipped out of the mountains again, and Jason was led to believe it was on his account. So once more the old oath began to weigh heavily upon him, for everybody seemed to take it as much for granted that he would some day fulfil that oath as that, after the dark of the moon, that moon would rise again. Moreover, fate was inexorably pushing him and little Aaron into the same channels that their fathers had followed and putting on each the duty and responsibility of leadership. And Jason, though shirking nothing, turned sick and faint of heart and was glad when the summer neared its close.

Through all his vacation he and Mavis had seen but little of each other, though Mavis lived with the old circuit rider and Jason in a little shack on the spur above her, for the boy was on the night shift and through most of the day was asleep. Moreover, both were rather morose and brooding, each felt the deep trouble of the other, and to it each paid the mutual respect of silence. How much Mavis knew, Jason little guessed, though he was always vaguely uneasy under the constant search of her dark eyes, and often he would turn toward her expecting her to speak. But not until the autumn was at hand and they were both making ready to go back to the Blue-grass did she break her silence. The news had just reached them that Steve Hawn had come clear at last and was at home—and Mavis heard it with little elation and no comment. Next day she announced calmly that she was not going back with Jason, but would stay in the hills and go on with her school. Jason stared questioningly, but she would not explain—she only became more brooding and silent than ever, and only when they parted one drowsy day in September was the thought within her betrayed:

"I reckon maybe you won't come back again."

Jason was startled. She knew then—knew his discontent, his new longing to break the fetters of the hills, knew even that in his dreams Marjorie's face was still shining like a star. "Course I'm comin' back," he said, with a little return of his old boyish roughness, but his eyes fell before hers as he turned hurriedly away. He was rolling away from the hills, and his mind had gone back to her seated with folded hands and unseeing eyes in the old circuit rider's porch, dreaming, thinking— thinking, dreaming—before he began fully to understand. He remembered his mother telling him how unhappy Mavis had been the summer the two were alone in the Blue-grass, and how she had kept away from Marjorie and Gray and all to herself.

He recalled Mavis telling him bitterly how she had once overheard some girl student speak of her as the daughter of a jail-bird. He began to see that she had stayed in the Blue-grass that summer on his mother's account and on her account would have gone back with him again. He knew that there was no disloyalty to her father in her decision, for he knew that she would stick to him, jail-bird or whatever he was, till the end of time. But now neither her father nor Jason's mother needed her. Through eyes that had gained a new vision in the Blue-grass Mavis had long ago come to see herself as she was seen there; and now to escape wounds that any malicious tongue could inflict she would stay where the sins of fathers rested less heavily on the innocent. There was, to be sure, good reason for Jason to feel as Mavis felt—he had been a jail-bird himself—but not to act like her—no. And then as he rolled along he began to wonder what part Gray might be playing in her mind and heart. The vision of her seated in the porch thinking—thinking—would not leave him, and a pang of undefined remorse for leaving her behind started within him. She, too, had outgrown his and her people as he had—perhaps she was as rebellious against her fate as he was against his own, but, unlike him, utterly helpless. And suddenly the boy's remorse merged into a sympathetic terror for the loneliness that was hers.

XXXIII

DOWN in the Blue-grass a handsome saddle-horse was hitched at the stile in front of Colonel Pendleton's house and the front door was open to the pale gold of the early sun. Upstairs Gray was packing for his last year away from home, after which he too would go to Morton Sanders' mines, on the land Jason's mother once had owned. Below him his father sat at his desk with two columns of figures before him, of assets and liabilities, and his face was gray and his form seemed to have shrunk when he rose from his chair; but he straightened up when he heard his boy's feet coming down the stairway, forced a smile to his lips, and called to him cheerily. Together they walked down to the stile.

"I'm going to drive into town this morning, dad," said Gray. "Can I do anything for you?"

"No, son—nothing—except come back safe."

In the distance a tree crashed to the earth as the colonel was climbing his horse, and a low groan came from his lips, but again he quickly recovered himself at the boy's apprehensive cry.

"Nothing, son. I reckon I'm getting too fat to climb a horse—good-by."

He turned and rode away, erect as a youth of twenty, and the lad looked after him puzzled and alarmed. One glance his father had turned toward the beautiful woodland that had at last been turned over to axe and saw for the planting of tobacco, and it was almost the last tree of that woodland that had just fallen. When the first struck the earth two months before, the lad now recalled hearing his father mutter:

"This is the meanest act of my life."

Suddenly now the boy knew that the act was done for him—and his eyes filled as he looked after the retreating horseman upon whose shoulders so much secret trouble weighed. And when the elder man passed through the gate and started down the pike, those broad shoulders began to droop, and the lad saw him ride out of sight with his chin close to his breast. The boy started back to his packing, but with a folded coat in his hand dropped in a chair by the open window, looking out on the quick undoing in that woodland of the Master's slow upbuilding for centuries, and he began to recall how often during the past summer he had caught his father brooding alone, or figuring at his desk, or had heard him pacing the floor of his bedroom late at night; how frequently he had made trips into town to see his lawyer, how often the lad had seen in his mail, lately, envelopes stamped with the name of his bank; and, above all, how often the old family doctor had driven out from town, and though there was never a complaint, how failing had been his father's health, and how he had aged. And suddenly Gray sprang to his feet, ordered his buggy and started for town.

Along the edge of the bleeding stumps of noble trees the colonel rode slowly, his thoughts falling and rising between his boy in the room above and his columns of figures in the room below. The sacrilege of destruction had started in his mind years before from love of the one, but the actual deed had started under pressure of the other, and now it looked as though each motive would be thwarted, for the tobacco war was on in earnest now, and again the poor old commonwealth was rent as by a forked tongue of lightning. And, like the State, the colonel too was pitifully divided against himself.

Already many Blue-grass farmers had pooled their crops against the great tobacco trust—already they had decided that no tobacco at all should be raised that coming year just when the colonel was deepest in debt and could count only on his tobacco for relief. And so the great-hearted gentleman must now go against his neighbor, or go to destruction himself and carry with him his beloved son. Toward noon he reined in on a little knoll above the deserted house of the old general, the patriarchal head of the family—who had passed not many years before—the rambling old house, stuccoed with aged brown and still in the faithful

clasp of ancient vines. The old landmark had
passed to Morton Sanders, and on and about it the
ruthless hand of progress was at work. The atmosphere of careless, magnificent luxury was gone.
The servants' quarters, the big hen-house, the old
stables with gables and sunken roofs, the staggering fences, the old blacksmith-shop, the wheelless
windmill—all were rebuilt or torn away. Only the
arched gate-way under which only thoroughbreds
could pass was left untouched, for Sanders loved
horses and the humor of that gate-way, and the
old spring-house with its green dripping walls. No
longer even were the forest trees in the big yard
ragged and storm-torn, but trimmed carefully,
their wounds dressed, and sturdy with a fresh lease
on life; only the mournful cedars were unchanged
and still harping with every passing wind the same
requiem for the glory that was gone. With another groan the old colonel turned his horse toward
home—the home that but for the slain woodlands
would soon pass in that same way to house a
Sanders tenant or an overseer.

When he reached his front door he heard his
boy whistling like a happy lark in his room at the
head of the stairway. The sounds pierced him
for one swift instant and then his generous heart
was glad for the careless joy of youth, and instead
of going into his office he slowly climbed the stairs.
When he reached the door of the boy's room, he
saw two empty trunks, the clothes that had been

in them tossed in a whirlwind over bed and chair
and floor, and Gray hanging out of the window and
shouting to a servant:

"Come up here, Tom, and help put my things
back—I'm not going away."

A joyous whoop from below answered:

"Yassuh, yassuh; my Gord, but I *is* glad. Why,
de colonel——"

Just then the boy heard a slight noise behind
him and he turned to see his father's arms
stretched wide for him.

Gray remained firm. He would not waste another year. He had a good start; he would go to
the mines and begin work, and he could come home
when he pleased, if only over Sunday. So, as
Mavis had watched Jason leave to be with Marjorie in the Blue-grass, so Marjorie now watched
Gray leave to be with Mavis in the hills. And
between them John Burnham was again left
wondering.

XXXIV

AT sunset Gray Pendleton pushed his tired horse across the Cumberland River and up into the county-seat of the Hawns and Honeycutts. From the head of the main street two battered signs caught his eye—Hawn Hotel and Honeycutt Inn—the one on the right-hand side close at hand, and the other far down on the left, and each on the corner of the street. Both had double balconies, both were ramshackle and unpainted, and near each was a general store, run now by a subleader of each faction—Hiram Honeycutt and Shade Hawn—for old Jason and old Aaron, except in councils of war and business, had retired into the more or less peaceful haven of home and old age. Naturally the boy drew up and stopped before Hawn Hotel, from the porch of which keen eyes scrutinized him with curiosity and suspicion, and before he had finished his supper of doughy biscuits, greasy bacon, and newly killed fried chicken, the town knew but little less about his business there than he himself. That night he asked many questions of Shade Hawn, the proprietor, and all were answered freely, except where they bore on the feud of half a century, and then Gray encoun-

tered a silence that was puzzling but significant and
deterrent. Next morning everybody who spoke
to him called him by name, and as he rode up the
river there was the look of recognition in every
face he saw, for the news of him had gone ahead
the night before. At the mouth of Hawn Creek,
in a bend of the river, he came upon a school-
house under a beech-tree on the side of a little hill;
through the open door he saw, amidst the bent
heads of the pupils, the figure of a young woman
seated at a desk, and had he looked back when he
turned up the creek he would have seen her at the
window, gazing covertly after him with one hand
against her heart. For Mavis Hawn, too, had
heard that Gray was come to the hills. All morning she had been watching the open door-way, and
yet when she saw him pass she went pale and had
to throw her head up sharply to get her breath.
Her hands trembled, she rose and went to the
window, and she did not realize what she was doing
until she turned to meet the surprised and curious
eyes of one of the larger girls, who, too, could see
the passing stranger, and then the young school-
mistress flushed violently and turned to her seat.
The girl was a Honeycutt, and more than once that
long, restless afternoon Mavis met the same eyes
searching her own and already looking mischief.
Slowly the long afternoon passed, school was dismissed, and Mavis, with the circuit rider's old dog
on guard at her heels, started slowly up the creek

with her eyes fixed on every bend of the road she turned and on the crest of every little hill she climbed, watching for Gray to come back. Once a horse that looked like the one he rode and glimpsed through the bushes far ahead made her heart beat violently and stopped her, poised for a leap into the bushes, but it was only little Aaron Honeycutt, who lifted his hat, flushed, and spoke gravely; and Mavis reached the old circuit rider's gate, slipped around to the back porch and sat down, still in a tumult that she could not calm. It was not long before she heard a clear shout of "hello" at the gate, and she clenched her chair with both hands, for the voice was Gray's. She heard the old woman go to the door, heard her speak her surprise and hearty welcome—heard Gray's approaching steps.

"Is Mavis here?" Gray asked.

"She ain't got back from school."

"Was that her school down there at the mouth of the creek?"

"Shore."

"Well, I wish I had known that."

Calmly and steadily then Mavis rose, and a moment later Gray saw her in the door and his own heart leaped at the rich, grave beauty of her. Gravely she shook hands, gravely looked full into his eyes, without a question sat down with quiet hands folded in her lap, and it was the boy who was embarrassed and talked. He would live with the superintendent on the spur just above and he would be a near neighbor. His father was not well. Marjorie was not going away again, but would stay at home that winter. Mavis's step-mother was well, and he had not seen Jason before he left—they must have passed each other on the way. Since Mavis's father was now at home, Jason would stay at the college, as he lost so much time going to and fro. Gray was glad to get to work, he already loved the mountains; but there had been so many changes he hardly remembered the creek—how was Mavis's grandfather, old Mr. Hawn? Mavis raised her eyes, but she was so long answering that the old woman broke in:

"He's mighty peart fer sech a' old man, but he's a-breakin' fast an' he ain't long fer this wuld." She spoke with the frank satisfaction that, among country folks, the old take in ushering their contemporaries through the portals, and Gray could hardly help smiling. He rose to leave presently, and the old woman pressed him to stay for supper; but Mavis's manner somehow forbade, and the boy climbed back up the spur, wondering, ill at ease, and almost shaken by the new beauty the girl seemed to have taken on in the hills. For there she was at home. She had the peace and serenity of them: the pink-flecked laurel was in her cheeks, the white of the rhododendron was at the base of her full round throat, and in her eyes were the sleepy shadows of deep ravines. It might not be so lonely for him after all in his exile, and the vision of the girl haunted Gray when he went to bed that night and made him murmur and stir restlessly in his sleep.

XXXV

ONCE more, on his way for his last year at college, Jason Hawn had stepped into the chill morning air at the railway junction, on the edge of the Blue-grass. Again a faint light was showing in the east, and cocks were crowing from a low sea of mist that lay motionless over the land, but this time the darky porter reached without hesitation for his bag and led him to the porch of the hotel, where he sat waiting for breakfast. Once more at sunrise he sped through the breaking mist and high over the yellow Kentucky River, but there was no pang of homesickness when he looked down upon it now. Again fields of grass and grain, grazing horses and cattle, fences, houses, barns reeled past his window, and once more Steve Hawn met him at the station in the same old rattletrap buggy, and again stared at him long and hard.

"Ain't much like the leetle feller I met here three year ago—air ye?"

Steve was unshaven and his stubbly, thick, black beard emphasized the sickly touch of prison pallor that was still on his face. His eyes had a new, wild, furtive look, and his mouth was cruel and bitter. Again each side of the street was lined

298

with big wagons loaded with tobacco and covered with cotton cloth. Steve pointed to them.

"Rickolect whut I tol' you about hell a-comin' about that terbaccer?"

Jason nodded.

"Well, hit's come." His tone was ominous, personal, and disturbed the boy.

"Look here, Steve," he said earnestly, "haven't you had enough now? Ain't you goin' to settle down and behave yourself?"

The man's face took on the snarl of a vicious dog.

"No, by God!—I hain't. The trouble's on me right now. Colonel Pendleton hain't treated me right—he cheated me out——"

Steve got no further; the boy turned squarely in the buggy and his eyes blazed.

"That's a lie. I don't know anything about it, but I know it's a lie."

Steve, too, turned furious, but he had gone too far, and had counted too much on kinship, so he controlled himself, and with vicious cunning whipped about.

"Well," he said in an injured tone, "I mought be mistaken. We'll see—we'll see."

Jason had not asked about his mother, and he did not ask now, for Steve's manner worried him and made him apprehensive. He answered the man's questions about the mountains shortly, and with diabolical keenness Steve began to probe old wounds.

"I reckon," he said sympathetically, "you hain't found no way yit o' gittin' yo' land back?"

"No."

"Ner who shot yo' pap?"

"No."

"Well, I hear as how Colonel Pendleton owns a lot in that company that's diggin' out yo' coal. Mebbe you might git it back from him."

Jason made no answer, for his heart was sinking with every thought of his mother and the further trouble Steve seemed bound to make. Martha Hawn was standing in her porch with one hand above her eyes when they drove into the mouth of the lane. She came down to the gate, and Jason put his arms around her and kissed her; and when he saw the tears start in her eyes he kissed her again while Steve stared, surprised and uncomprehending. Again that afternoon Jason wandered aimlessly into the blue-grass fields, and again his feet led him to the knoll whence he could see the twin houses of the Pendletons bathed in the yellow sunlight, and their own proud atmosphere of untroubled calm. And again, even, he saw Marjorie galloping across the fields, and while he knew the distressful anxiety in one of the households, he little guessed the incipient storm that imperious young woman was at that moment carrying within her own breast from the other. For Marjorie missed Gray; she was lonely and she was bored; she had heard that Jason had been home several days;

she was irritated that he had not been to see her,
nor had sent her any message, and just now what
she was going to do, she did not exactly know or
care.   Half an hour later he saw her again, coming
back at a gallop along the turnpike, and seeing
him, she pulled in and waved her whip.   Jason
took off his hat, waved it in answer, and kept
on, whereat imperious Marjorie wheeled her horse
through a gate into the next field and thundered
across it and up the slope toward him.   Jason
stood hat in hand—embarrassed, irresolute, pale.
When she pulled in, he walked forward to take her
outstretched gloved hand, and when he looked up
into her spirited face and challenging eyes, a great
calm came suddenly over him, and from it emerged
his own dominant spirit which the girl instantly
felt.   She had meant to tease, badger, upbraid,
domineer over him, but the volley of reproachful
questions that were on her petulant red lips
dwindled lamely to one:

"How's Mavis, Jason?"

"She's well as common."

"You didn't see Gray?"

"No."

"I got a letter from him yesterday.   He's living
right above Mavis.   He says she is more beautiful
than ever, and he's already crazy about his life
down there—and the mountains."

"I'm mighty glad."

She turned to go, and the boy walked down the

hill to open the gate for her—and sidewise Marjorie scrutinized him. Jason had grown taller, darker, his hair was longer, his clothes were worn and rather shabby, the atmosphere of the hills still invested him, and he was more like the Jason she had first seen, so that the memories of childhood were awakened in the girl and she softened toward him. When she passed through the gate and turned her horse toward him again, the boy folded his arms over the gate, and his sunburnt hands showed to Marjorie's eyes the ravages of hard work.

"Why haven't you been over to see me, Jason?" she asked gently.

"I just got back this mornin'."

"Why, Gray wrote you left home several days ago."

"I did—but I stopped on the way to visit some kinfolks."

"Oh. Well, aren't you coming? I'm lonesome, and I guess you will be too—without Mavis."

"I won't have time to get lonesome."

The girl smiled.

"That's ungracious—but I want you to take the time."

The boy looked at her; since his trial he had hardly spoken to her, and had rarely seen her. Somehow he had come to regard his presence at Colonel Pendleton's the following Christmas night as but a generous impulse on their part that was to end then and there. He had kept away from Marjorie thereafter, and if he was not to keep away now, he must make matters very clear.

"Maybe your mother won't like it," he said gravely. "I'm a jail-bird."

"Don't, Jason," she said, shocked by his frankness; "you couldn't help that. I want you to come."

Jason was reddening with embarrassment now, but he had to get out what had been so long on his mind.

"I'm comin' once anyhow. I know what she did for me and I'm comin' to thank her for doin' it."

Marjorie was surprised and again she smiled.

"Well, she won't like that, Jason," she said, and the boy, not misunderstanding, smiled too.

"I'm comin'."

Marjorie turned her horse.

"I hope I'll be at home."

Her mood had turned to coquetry again. Jason had meant to tell her that he knew she herself had been behind her mother's kindness toward him, but a sudden delicacy forbade, and to her change of mood he answered:

"You will be—when I come."

This was a new deftness for Jason, and a little flush of pleasure came to the girl's cheeks and a little seriousness to her eyes.

"Well, you *are* mighty nice, Jason—good-by."

"Good-by," said the boy soberly.

At her own gate the girl turned to look back, but

Jason was striding across the fields. She turned again on the slope of the hill but Jason was still striding on. She watched him until he had disappeared, but he did not turn to look and her heart felt a little hurt. She was very quiet that night, so quiet that she caught a concerned look in her mother's eyes, and when she had gone to her room her mother came in and found her in a stream of moonlight at her window. And when Mrs. Pendleton silently kissed her, she broke into tears.

"I'm lonely, mother," she sobbed; "I'm so lonely."

A week later Jason sat on the porch one night after supper and his mother came to the doorway.

"I forgot to tell ye, Jason, that Marjorie Pendleton rid over here the day you got here an' axed if you'd come home."

"I saw her down the pike that day," said Jason, not showing the surprise he felt. Steve Hawn, coming around the corner of the house, heard them both and on his face was a malicious grin.

"Down the pike," he repeated. "I seed ye both a-talkin', up thar at the edge of the woods. She looked back at ye twice, but you wouldn't take no notice. Now that Gray ain't hyeh I reckon you mought——"

The boy's protest, hoarse and inarticulate, stopped Steve, who dropped his bantering tone and turned serious.

"Now looky here, Jason, yo' uncle Arch has

tol' me about Gray and Mavis already up thar in the mountains, an' I see what's comin' down here fer you. You an' Gray ought to have more sense —gittin' into such trouble——"

"Trouble!" cried the boy.

"Yes, I know," Steve answered. "Hit is funny fer me to be talkin' about trouble. I was born to it, as the circuit rider says, as the sparks fly upward. Thar ain't no hope fer me, but you——"

The boy rose impatiently but curiously shaken by such words and so strange a tone from his step-father. He was still shaken when he climbed to Mavis's room and was looking out of her window, and that turned his thoughts to her and to Gray in the hills. What was the trouble that Steve had already heard about Mavis and Gray, and what the trouble at which Steve had hinted—for him? Once before Steve had dropped a bit of news, also gathered from Arch Hawn, that during the truce in the mountains little Aaron Honeycutt had developed a wild passion for Mavis, but at that absurdity Jason had only laughed. Still the customs of the Blue-grass and the hills were widely divergent, and if Gray, only out of loneliness, were much with Mavis, only one interpretation was possible to the Hawns and Honeycutts, just as only one interpretation had been possible for Steve with reference to Marjorie and himself, and Steve's interpretation he contemptuously dismissed. His grandfather might make trouble for Gray, or Gray

305

and little Aaron might clash. He would like to
warn Gray, and yet even with that wish in his
mind a little flame of jealousy was already licking
at his heart, though already that heart was thumping at the bid of Marjorie. Impatiently he began
to wonder at the perverse waywardness of his own
soul, and without undressing he sat at the window
—restless, sleepless, and helpless against his war-
ring self—sat until the shadows of the night began
to sweep after the light of the sinking moon. When
he rose finally, he thought he saw a dim figure
moving around the corner of the barn. He rubbed
his eyes to make sure, and then picking up his
pistol he slipped down the stairs and out the side
door, taking care not to awaken his mother and
Steve. When he peered forth from the corner of
the house, Steve's chestnut gelding was outside
the barn and somebody was saddling him. Some
negro doubtless was stealing him out for a ride, as
was not unusual in that land, and that negro Jason
meant to scare half to death. Noiselessly the boy
reached the hen-house, and when he peered around
that he saw to his bewilderment that the thief was
Steve. Once more Steve went into the barn, and
this time when he come out he began to fumble
about his forehead with both hands, and a moment
later Jason saw him move toward the gate, masked
and armed. A long shrill whistle came from the
turnpike and he heard Steve start into a gallop
down the lane.

XXXVI

IT was three days before Steve Hawn returned, ill-humored, reddened by drink, and worn. As ever, Martha Hawn asked no questions and Jason betrayed no curiosity, no suspicion, though he was not surprised to learn that in a neighboring county the night riders had been at their lawless work, and he had no doubt that Steve was among them. Jason would be able to help but little that autumn in the tobacco field, for it was his last year in college and he meant to work hard at his books, but he knew that the dispute between his step-father and Colonel Pendleton was still unsettled—that Steve was bitter and had a secret relentless purpose to get even. He did not dare give Colonel Pendleton a warning, for it was difficult, and he knew the fiery old gentleman would receive such an intervention with a gracious smile and dismiss it with haughty contempt; so Jason decided merely to keep a close watch on Steve.

On the opening day of college, as on the opening day three years before, Jason walked through the fields to town, but he did not start at dawn. The dew-born mists were gone and the land lay, with no mystery to the eye or the mind, under a brilliant sun—the fields of stately corn, the yellow tents of wheat gone from the golden stretches of stubble, and green trees rising from the dull golden sheen of the stripped blue-grass pastures. The cut, up-turned tobacco no longer looked like hunchbacked witches on broom-sticks and ready for flight, for the leaves, waxen, oily, inert, hung limp and listless from the sticks that pointed like needles to the north to keep the stalks inclined as much as possible from the sun. Even they had taken on the Midas touch of gold, for all green and gold that world of blue-grass was—all green and gold, except for the shaggy unkempt fields where the king of weeds had tented the year before and turned them over to his camp followers—ragweed, dockweed, white-top, and cockle-burr. But the resentment against such an agricultural outrage that the boy had caught from John Burnham was no longer so deep, for that tobacco had kept his mother and himself alive and the father of his best friend must look to it now to save himself from destruction. All the way Jason, walking leisurely, confidently, proudly, and with the fires of his ambition no less keen, thought of the green mountain boy who had torn across those fields at sunrise, that when "school took up" he might not be late—thought of him with much humor and with no little sympathy. When he saw the smoke cloud over the town he took to the white turnpike and quickened his pace. Again the campus of the rival old Transylvania was dotted with students moving to and

fro.   Again the same policeman stood on the same
corner, but now he shook hands with Jason and
called him by name.   When he passed between the
two gray stone pillars with pyramidal tops and
swung along the driveway between the maple-trees
and chattering sparrows, there were the same boys
with caps pushed back and trousers turned up, the
same girls with hair up and hair down, but what
a difference now for him!   Even while he looked
around there was a shout from a crowd around
John Burnham's doorway; several darted from
that crowd toward him and the crowd followed.   A
dozen of them were trying to catch his hand at
once, and the welcome he had seen Gray Pendleton
once get he got now for himself, for again a pair
of hands went high, a series of barbaric yells were
barked out, and the air was rent with the name of
Jason Hawn.   Among them Jason stood flushed,
shy, grateful.   A moment later he saw John Burnham in the doorway—looking no less pleased and
waiting for him.   Even the old president paused
on his crutches for a handshake and a word of welcome.   The boy found himself wishing that Marjorie—and Mavis—were there, and, as he walked
up the steps, from out behind John Burnham Marjorie stepped—proud for him and radiant.

And so, through that autumn, the rectangular,
diametric little comedy went on between Marjorie
and Jason in the Blue-grass and between Gray and
Mavis in the hills.   No Saturday passed that Ja-

son did not spend at his mother's home or with
John Burnham, and to the mother and Steve and to
Burnham his motive was plain—for most of the boy's
time was spent with Marjorie Pendleton. Somehow Marjorie seemed always driving to town or
coming home when Jason was on his way home
or going to town, and somehow he was always
afoot and Marjorie was always giving him a kindly
lift one or the other way. Moreover, horses were
plentiful as barn-yard fowls on Morton Sanders'
farm, and the manager, John Burnham's brother,
who had taken a great fancy to Jason, gave him a
mount whenever the boy pleased. And so John
Burnham saw the pair galloping the turnpikes or
through the fields, or at dusk going slowly toward
Marjorie's home. Besides, Marjorie organized
many hunting parties that autumn, and the moon
and the stars looking down saw the two never
apart for long. About the intimacy Mrs. Pendleton and the colonel thought little. Colonel Pendleton liked the boy, Mrs. Pendleton wanted Marjorie at home, and she was glad for her to have
companionship. Moreover, to both, Marjorie was
still a child, anything serious would be absurd, and
anyway Marjorie was meant for Gray.

In the mountains Gray's interest in his life
was growing every day. He liked to watch things
planned and grow into execution. His day began
with the screech of a whistle at midnight. Every
morning he saw the sun rise and the mists unroll

and the drenched flanks of the mountains glisten and drip under the sunlight. During the afternoon he woke up in time to stroll down the creek, meet Mavis after school and walk back to the circuit rider's house with her. After supper every night he would go down the spur and sit under the honeysuckles with her on the porch. The third time he came the old man and woman quietly withdrew and were seen no more, and this happened thereafter all the time. Meanwhile in the Blue-grass and the hills the forked tongues of gossip began to play, reaching last, as usual, those who were most concerned, but, as usual, reaching them, too, in time. In the Blue-grass it was criticism of Colonel and Mrs. Pendleton, their indifference, carelessness, blindness, a gaping question of their sanity at the risk of even a suspicion that such a mating might be possible—the proud daughter of a proud family with a nobody from the hills, unknown except that he belonged to a fierce family whose history could be written in human blood; who himself had been in jail on the charge of murder; whose mother could not write her own name; whose step-father was a common tobacco tenant no less illiterate, and with a brain that was a hotbed of lawless mischief, and who held the life of a man as cheap as the life of a steer fattening for the butcher's knife. But in all the gossip there was no sinister suggestion or even thought save in the primitive inference of this same Steve Hawn.

In the mountains, too, the gossip was for a while innocent. To the simple democratic mountain way of thinking, there was nothing strange in the intimacy of Mavis and Gray. There Gray was no better than any mountain boy. He was in love with Mavis, he was courting her, and if he won her he would marry her, and that simply was all— particularly in the mind of old grandfather Hawn. Likewise, too, was there for a while nothing sinister in the talk, for at first Mavis held to the mountain custom, and would not walk in the woods with Gray unless one of the school-children was along— nothing sinister except to little Aaron Honeycutt, whose code had been a little poisoned by his two years' stay outside the hills.

Once more about each pair the elements of social tragedy began to concentrate, intensify, and become active. The new development in the hills made business competition keen between Shade Hawn and Hiram Honeycutt, who each ran a hotel and store in the county-seat. As old Jason Hawn and old Aaron Honeycutt had retired from the leadership, and little Jason and little Aaron had been out of the hills, leadership naturally was assumed by these two business rivals, who revived the old hostility between the factions, but gave vent to it in a secret, underhanded way that disgusted not only old Jason but even old Aaron as well. For now and then a hired Hawn would drop a Honeycutt from the bushes and a hired Honeycutt would drop a Hawn. There was, said old Jason with an oath of contempt, no manhood left in the feud. No principal went gunning for a principal—no hired assassin for another of his kind.

"Nobody ain't shootin' the *right* feller," said the old man. "Looks like hit's a question of which hired feller gits fust the man who hired the other feller."

And when this observation reached old Aaron he agreed heartily.

"Fer once in his life," he said, "old Jason Hawn kind o' by accident is a-hittin' the truth." And each old man bet in his secret heart, if little Aaron and little Jason were only at home together, things would go on in quite a different way.

In the lowlands the tobacco pool had been formed and, when persuasion and argument failed, was starting violent measures to force into the pool raisers who would not go in willingly. In the western and southern parts of the State the night riders had been more than ever active. Tobacco beds had been destroyed, barns had been burned, and men had been threatened, whipped, and shot. Colonel Pendleton found himself gradually getting estranged from some of his best friends. He quarrelled with old Morton Sanders, and in time he retired to his farm, as though it were the pole of the earth. His land was his own to do with as he pleased. No man, no power but the Almighty and the law, could tell him what he *must* do. The tobacco pool was using the very methods of the trust it was seeking to destroy. Under those circumstances he considered his duty to himself paramount to his duty to his neighbor, and his duty to himself he would do; and so the old gentleman lived proudly in his loneliness and refused to know fear, though the night riders were getting busy now in the counties adjacent to the Blue-grass, and were threatening raids into the colonel's own county—the proudest in the State. Other "independents" hardly less lonely, hardly less hated, had electrified their barbed-wire fences, and had hired guards—fighting men from the mountains—to watch their barns and houses, but such an example the colonel would not follow, though John Burnham pleaded with him, and even Jason dared at last to give him a covert warning, with no hint, however, that the warning was against his own step-father Steve. It was the duty of the law to protect him, the colonel further argued; the county judge had sworn that the law would do its best; and only when the law could not protect him would the colonel protect himself.

And so the winter months passed until one morning a wood-thrush hidden in green depths sent up a song of spring to Gray's ears in the hills, and in the Blue-grass a meadow-lark wheeling in the sun-light showered down the same song upon the heart of Jason Hawn.

Almost every Saturday Mavis would go down

to stay till Monday with her grandfather Hawn. Gray would drift down there to see her—and always, while Mavis was helping her grandmother in the kitchen, Gray and old Jason would sit together on the porch. Gray never tired of the old man's shrewd humor, quaint philosophy, his hunting tales and stories of the feud, and old Jason liked Gray and trusted him more the more he saw of him. And Gray was a little startled when it soon became evident that the old man took it for granted that in his intimacy with Mavis was one meaning and only one.

"I al'ays thought Mavis would marry Jason," he said one night, "but, Lordy Mighty, I'm nigh on to eighty an' I don't know no more about gals than when I was eighteen. A feller stands more chance with some of 'em stayin' away, an' agin if he stays away from some of 'em he don't stand no chance at all. An' agin I rickollect that if I hadn't 'a' got mad an' left grandma in thar jist at one time an' hadn't 'a' come back jist at the right time another time, I'd 'a' lost her—shore. Looks like you're cuttin' Jason out mighty fast now—but which kind of a gal Mavis in thar is, I don't know no more'n if I'd never seed her."

Gray flushed and said nothing, and a little later the old man went frankly on:

"I'm gittin' purty old now an' I hain't goin' to last much longer, I reckon. An' I want you to know if you an' Mavis hitch up fer a life-trot

315

tergether I aim to divide this farm betwixt her an' Jason, an' you an' Mavis can have the half up thar closest to the mines, so you can be close to yo' work."

The boy was saved any answer, for the old man expected and waited for none, so simple was the whole matter to him, but Gray, winding up the creek homeward in the moonlight that night, did some pretty serious thinking. No such interpretation could have been put on the intimacy between him and Mavis at home, for there companionship, coquetry, sentiment, devotion even, were possible without serious parental concern. Young people in the Blue-grass handled their own heart affairs, and so they did for that matter in the hills, but Gray could not realize that primitive conditions forbade attention without intention: for life was simple, mating was early because life was so simple, and Nature's way with humanity was as with her creatures of the fields and air except for the eye of God and the hand of the law. A license, a few words from the circuit rider, a cleared hill-side, a one-room log cabin, a side of bacon, and a bag of meal—and, from old Jason's point of view, Gray and Mavis could enter the happy portals, create life for others, and go on hand in hand to the grave. So that where complexity would block Jason in the Blue-grass, simplicity would halt Gray in the hills. To be sure, the strangeness, the wildness, the activity of the life had fascinated Gray. He loved to ride the mountains and trails—even to slosh along the river road with the rain beating on him, dry and warm under a poncho. Often he would be caught out in the hills and have to stay all night in a cabin; and thus he learned the way of life away from the mines and the river bottoms. So far that poor life had only been pathetic and picturesque, but now when he thought of it as a part of his own life, of the people becoming through Mavis his people, he shuddered and stopped in the moonlit road—aghast. Still, the code of his father was his, all women were sacred, and with all there would be but one duty for him, if circumstances, as they bade fair to now, made that one duty plain. And if his father should go under, if Morton Sanders took over his home and the boy must make his own way and live his life where he was—why not? Gray sat in the porch of the house on the spur, long asking himself that question. He was asking it when he finally went to bed, and he went with it, unanswered, to sleep.

XXXVII

THE news reached Colonel Pendleton late one afternoon while he was sitting on his porch— pipe in mouth and with a forbidden mint julep within easy reach. He had felt the reticence of Gray's letters, he knew that the boy was keeping back some important secret from him as long as he could, and now, in answer to his own kind, frank letter Gray had, without excuse or apology, told the truth, and what he had not told the colonel fathomed with ease. He had hardly made up his mind to go at once to Gray, or send for him, when a negro boy galloped up to the stile and brought him a note from Marjorie's mother to come to her at once—and the colonel scented further trouble in the air.

There had been a turmoil that afternoon at Mrs. Pendleton's. Marjorie had come home a little while before with Jason Hawn and, sitting in the hallway, Mrs. Pendleton had seen Jason on the stile, with his hat in one hand and his bridle reins in the other, and Marjorie halting suddenly on her way to the house and wheeling impetuously back toward him. To the mother's amazement and dismay she saw that they were quarrelling—quarrelling as only lovers can. The girl's face was flushed with anger, and her red lips were winging out low, swift, bitter words. The boy stood straight, white, courteous, and unanswering. He lifted his chin a little when she finished, and unanswering turned to his horse and rode away. The mother saw her daughter's face pale quickly. She saw tears as Marjorie came up the walk, and when she rose in alarm and stood waiting in the doorway, the girl fled past her and rushed weeping upstairs.

Mrs. Pendleton was waiting in the porch when the colonel rode to the stile, and the distress in her face was so plain even that far away, that the colonel hurried up the walk, and there was no greeting between the two:

"It's Marjorie, Robert," she said simply, and the old gentleman, who had seen Jason come out of the yard gate and gallop toward John Burnham's, guessed what the matter was, and he took the slim white hands that were clenched together and patted them gently:

"There—there! Don't worry, don't worry!"

He led her into the house, and at the top of the steps stood Marjorie in white, her hair down and tears streaming down her face:

"Come here, Marjorie," called Colonel Pendleton, and she obeyed like a child, talking wildly as she came:

"I know what you're going to say, Uncle Bob—

I know it all. I'm tired of all this talk about family, Uncle Bob, I'm tired of it."

She had stopped a few steps above, clinging with one trembling hand to the balcony, as though to have her say quite out before she went helplessly into the arms that were stretched out toward her:

"Dead people are dead, Uncle Bob, and only live people really count. People have to be alive to help you and make you happy. I want to be happy, Uncle Bob—I want to be happy. I know all about the Pendletons, Uncle Bob. They were Cavaliers—I know all that—and they used to ride about sticking lances into peasants who couldn't afford a suit of armor, but they can't do anything for me now, and they mustn't interfere with me now. Anyhow, the Sudduths were plain people and I'm not a bit ashamed of it, mother. Great-grandfather Hiram lived in a log cabin. Grandfather Hiram ate with his knife. I've *seen* him do it, and he kept on doing it when he knew better just out of habit or stubbornness, but Jason's people ate with their knives because they didn't *have* anything but *two*-pronged forks—I heard John Burnham say that. And Jason's family is as good as the Sudduths, and maybe as the Pendletons, and he wouldn't know it because his grandfathers were out of the world and were too busy, fighting Indians and killing bears and things for food. They didn't have *time* to keep their family trees trimmed, and they didn't *care* anything about the

320

old trees anyhow, and I don't either. John Burnham has told me——"

"Marjorie!" said the colonel gently, for she was
getting hysterical. He held out his arms to her,
and with another burst of weeping she went into
them.

Half an hour later, when she was calm, the
colonel got her to ride over home with him, and
what she had not told her mother Marjorie on the
way told him—in a halting voice and with her
face turned aside.

"There's something funny and deep about him,
Uncle Bob, and I never could reach it. It piqued
me and made me angry. I knew he cared for me,
but I could never make him tell it."

The colonel was shaking his old head wisely and
comprehendingly.

"I don't know why, but I flew into a rage with
him this afternoon about nothing, and he never
answered me a word, but stood there listening—
why, Uncle Bob, he stood there like—like a—a
gentleman—till I got through, and then he turned
away—he never did say anything, and I was so
sorry and ashamed that I nearly died. I don't
know what to do now—and he won't come back,
Uncle Bob—I know he won't."

Her voice broke again, and the colonel silenced
her by putting one hand comfortingly on her
knee and by keeping still himself. His shoulders
drooped a little as they walked from the stile to-

ward the house, and Marjorie ran her arm through his:

"Why, you're a little tired, aren't you, Uncle Bob?" she said tenderly, and he did not answer except to pat her hand, against which she suddenly felt his heart throb. He almost stumbled going up the steps, and deadly pale he sank with a muffled groan into a chair. With a cry the girl darted for a glass of water, but when she came back, terrified, he was smiling:

"I'm all right—don't worry. I thought that sun to-day was going to be too much for me."

But still Marjorie watched him anxiously, and when the color came back to his face she went behind him and wrapped her arms about his neck and put her mouth to his ear:

"I'm just a plain little fool, Uncle Bob, and, as Gray says, I talk through my aigrette. Now, don't you and mother worry—don't worry the least little bit," and she tightened her arms and kissed him several times on his forehead and cheek. "I must go now—and if you don't take better care of yourself I'm going to come over here and take care of you myself."

She was in front of him now and looking down fondly; and a wistfulness that was almost child-like had come into the colonel's face:

"I wish you could, little Marjorie—I wish you would."

He watched her gallop away—turning to wave

her whip to him as she went over the slope, her tears gone and once more radiant and gay—and the sadness of the coming twilight slowly overspread the colonel's face. It was the one hope of his life that she would one day come over to take care of him—and Gray. On into the twilight he sat still and thoughtful. It looked serious for her and Gray. Back his mind flashed to that night of the dance in the mountains, when the four were children, and his wonder then as to what might take place if that mountain boy and girl should have the chance in the world that had already come to them. He began to wonder how much of her real feeling Marjorie might have concealed— how much Gray in his letters was keeping back of his. Such a union was preposterous. He realized too late now the danger to youth of simple proximity—he knew the exquisite sensitiveness of Gray in any matter that meant consideration for others and for his own honor, the generous warmhearted impulsiveness of Marjorie, and the appeal that any romantic element in the situation would make to them both. Perhaps he ought to go to the mountains. There was much he might say to Gray, but what to Jason, or to Marjorie, with that life-absorbing motive of his own—and his affairs at such a crisis? The colonel shook his head helplessly. He was very tired, and wished he could put the matter off till morning when he was rested and his head was clear, but the questions had sunk talons into his heart and brain that would not be unloosed, and the colonel rose wearily and went within.

Marjorie looked serious after she told her mother that night that she feared her uncle was not well, for Mrs. Pendleton became very grave:

"Your Uncle Robert is very far from well. I'm afraid sometimes he is sicker than any of us know."

"Mother!"

"And he is in great trouble, Marjorie."

The girl hesitated:

"Money trouble, mother?" she asked at last. "Why, you—we—why don't——"

The mother interrupted with a shake of her head:

"He would go bankrupt first."

"Mother?"

The older woman looked up with apprehension, so suddenly charged with an incredible something was the girl's tone:

"Why don't you marry Uncle Robert?"

The mother clutched at her heart with both hands, for an actual spasm caught her there. Every trace of color shot from her face, and with a rush came back—fire. She rose, gave her daughter one look that was almost terror, and quickly left the room.

Marjorie sat aghast. She had caught with careless hand the veil of some mystery—what long-hidden shrine was there behind it, what sacred deeps long still had she stirred?

XXXVIII

JASON HAWN rode rapidly to one of Morton Sanders' great stables, put his horse away himself, and, avoiding the chance of meeting John Burnham, slipped down the slope to the creek, crossed on a water gap, and struck across the sunset fields for home. He had felt no anger at Marjorie's mysterious outbreak—only bewilderment; and only bewilderment he felt now.

But as he strode along with his eyes on the ground, things began to clear a little. The fact was that, as he had become more enthralled by the girl's witcheries, the more helpless and stupid he had become. Marjorie's nimble wit had played about his that afternoon like a humming-bird around a sullen sunflower. He hardly knew that every word, every glance, every gesture was a challenge, and when she began stinging into him sharp little arrows of taunt and sarcasm he was helpless as the bull's-hide target at which the two sometimes practised archery. Even now when the poisoned points began to fester, he could stir himself to no anger—he only felt dazed and hurt and sore. Nobody was in sight when he reached his mother's home and he sat down on the porch in the twilight wretched and miserable. Around the corner of the house presently he heard his mother and Steve coming, and around there they stopped for some reason for a moment.

"I seed Babe Honeycutt yestiddy," Steve was saying. "He says thar's a lot o' talk goin' on about Mavis an' Gray Pendleton. The Honeycutts air doin' most o' the talkin' an' looks like the ole trouble's comin' up again. Old Jason is tearin' mad an' swears Gray'll have to git out o' them mountains——"

Jason heard them start moving and he rose and went quickly within that they might know he had overheard. After supper he was again on the porch brooding about Mavis and Gray when his mother came out. He knew that she wanted to say something, and he waited.

"Jason," she said finally, "you don't believe Colonel Pendleton cheated Steve—do you?"

"No," said the lad sharply. "Colonel Pendleton never cheated anybody in his life—except himself."

"That's all I wanted to know," she sighed, but Jason knew that was not all she wanted to say.

"Jason, I heerd two fellers in the lane to-day talkin' about tearin' up Colonel Pendleton's tobacco beds."

The boy was startled, but he did not show it.

"Nothin' but talk, I reckon."

"Well, if I was in his place I'd git some guards."

Marjorie sat at her window a long time that

327

night before she went to sleep. Her mother had
come in, had held her tightly to her breast, and
had gone out with only a whispered good-night.
And while the girl was wondering once more at the
strange effect of her naïve question, she recalled
suddenly the yearning look of her uncle that afternoon when she had mentioned Gray's name.
Could there be some thwarted hope in the lives of
Gray's father and her mother that both were now
trying to realize in the lives of her and Gray? Her
mother had never spoken her wish, nor doubtless
Gray's father to him—nor was it necessary, for as
children they had decided the question themselves,
as had Mavis and Jason Hawn, and had talked
about it with the same frankness, though with each
pair alike the matter had not been mentioned for
a long time. Then her mind leaped, and after it
leaped her heart—if her Uncle Robert would not
let her mother help him, why, she too could never
help Gray, unless—why, of course, if Gray were in
trouble she would marry him and give him everything she had. The thought made her glow, and
she began to wish Gray would come home. He
had been a long time in those hills, his father was
sick and worried—and what was he doing down
there anyhow? He had mentioned Mavis often
in his first letters, and now he wrote rarely, and he
never spoke of her at all. She began to get resentful and indignant, not only at him but at Mavis,
and she went to bed wishing more than ever that

Gray would come home. And yet playing around in her brain was her last vision of that mountain boy standing before her, white and silent—"like a gentleman"—and that vision would not pass even in her dreams.

Through Colonel Pendleton's bed-room window an hour later two pistol shots rang sharply, and through that window the colonel saw a man leap the fence around his tobacco beds and streak for the woods. From the shadow of a tree at his yard fence another flame burst, and by its light he saw a crouching figure. He called out sharply, the figure rose and came toward him, and in the moonlight the colonel saw uplifted to him, apologetic and half shamed, the face of Jason Hawn.

"No harm, colonel," he called. "Somebody was tearing up your tobacco beds and I just scared him off. I didn't try to hit him."

The colonel was dazed, but he spoke at last gently.

"Well, well, I can't let you lose your sleep this way, Jason; I'll get some guards now."

"If you won't let me," said the boy quickly, "you ought to send for Gray."

The old gentleman looked thoughtful.

"Of course, perhaps I ought—why, I will."

"He won't come again to-night," said Jason. "I shot close enough to scare him, I reckon. Good-night, colonel."

"Thank you, my boy—good-night."

XXXIX

IT was court day at the county-seat. A Honey-cutt had shot down a Hawn in the open street, had escaped, and a Hawn posse was after him. The incident was really a far effect of the recent news that Jason Hawn was soon coming back home —and coming back to live. Straightway the professional sneaks and scandal-mongers of both factions got busy to such purpose that the Honeycutts were ready to believe that the sole purpose of Jason's return was to revive the feud and incidentally square a personal account with little Aaron. Old Jason Hawn had started home that afternoon almost apoplectic with rage, for word had been brought him that little Aaron had openly said that it was high time that Jason Hawn came home to look after his cousin and Gray Pendleton went home to take care of his. It was a double insult, and to the old man's mind subtly charged with a low meaning. Old as he was, he had tried to find little Aaron, but the boy had left town.

Gray and Mavis were seated on the old man's porch when he came in sight of his house, for it was Saturday, and Mavis started the moment she saw her grandfather's face, and rose to meet him.

"What's the matter, grandpap?" The old

man waved her back. "Git back inter the house," he commanded shortly. "No—stay whar you air. When do you two aim to git married?" Had a bolt of lightning flashed through the narrow sunlit space between him and them, the pair could not have been more startled, blinded. Mavis flushed angrily, paled, and wheeled into the house. Gray rose in physical response to the physical threat in the old man's tone and fearlessly met the eyes that were glaring at him.

"I don't know what you mean, Mr. Hawn," he said respectfully. "I——"

"The hell you don't," broke in the old man furiously. "I'll give ye jes two minutes to hit the road and git a license. I'll give ye an hour an' a half to git back. An' if you don't come back I'll make Jason foller you to the mouth o' the pit o' hell an' bring ye back alive or dead." Again the boy tried to speak, but the old man would not listen.

"Git!" he cried, and, as the boy still made no move, old Jason hurried on trembling legs into the house. Gray heard him cursing and searching inside, and at the corner of the house appeared Mavis with both of the old man's pistols and his Winchester.

"Go on, Gray," she said, and her face was still red with shame. "You'll only make him worse, an' he'll kill you sure."

Gray shook his head: "No!"

"Please, Gray," she pleaded; "for God's sake—for my sake."

That the boy could not withstand. He started for the gate with his hat in hand—his head high, and, as he slowly passed through the gate and turned, the old man reappeared, looked fiercely after him, and sank into a chair sick with rage and trembling. As Mavis walked toward him with his weapons he glared at her, but she passed him by as though she did not see him, and put the Winchester and pistols in their accustomed places. She came out with her bonnet in her hand, and already her calmness and her silence had each had its effect—old Jason was still trembling, but from his eyes the rage was gone.

"I'm goin' home, grandpap," she said quietly, "an' if it wasn't for grandma I wouldn't come back. You've been bullyin' an' rough-ridin' over men-folks and women-folks all your life, but you can't do it no more with *me*. An' you're not goin' to meddle in *my* business any more. You know I'm a good girl—why didn't you go after the folks who've been talkin' instead o' pitchin' into Gray? You know he'd die before he'd harm a hair o' my head or allow you or anybody else to say anything against my good name. An' I tell you to your face"—her tone fiercened suddenly—"if you hadn't 'a' been an old man an' my grandfather, he'd 'a' killed you right here. An' I'm goin' to tell you something more. He ain't responsible

for this talk—*I* am. He didn't know it was goin'
on—*I* did. I'm not goin' to marry him to please
you an' the miserable tattletales you've been listenin' to. I reckon *I* ain't good enough—but I
know my kinfolks ain't fit to be his—even by
marriage. My daddy ain't, an' *you* ain't, an'
there ain't but one o' the whole o' our tribe who
is—an' that's little Jason Hawn. Now you let
him alone an' you let me alone."

She put her bonnet on, flashed to the gate, and
disappeared in the dusk down the road. The old
man's shaggy head had dropped forward on his
chest, he had shrunk down in his chair bewildered,
and he sat there a helpless, unanswering heap.
When the moon rose, Mavis was seated on the
porch with her chin in both hands. The old circuit
rider and his wife had gone to bed. A whippoorwill was crying with plaintive persistence far up a
ravine, and the night was deep and still about her,
save for the droning of insect life from the gloomy
woods. Straight above her stars glowed thickly,
and in a gap of the hills beyond the river, where the
sun had gone down, the evening star still hung like
a great jewel on the velvety violet curtain of the
night, and upon that her eyes were fixed. On the
spur above, her keen ears caught the soft thud
of a foot against a stone, and her heart answered.
She heard a quick leap across the branch, the sound
of a familiar stride along the road, and saw the
quick coming of a familiar figure along the edge of

333

the moonlight, but she sat where she was and as she was until Gray, with hat in hand, stood before her, and then only did she lift to him eyes that were dark as the night but shining like that sinking star in the little gap. The boy went down on one knee before her, and gently pulled both of her hands away from her face with both his own, and held them tightly.

"Mavis," he said, "I want you to marry me—won't you, Mavis?"

The girl showed no surprise, said nothing—she only disengaged her hands, took his face into them, and looked with unwavering silence deep into his eyes, looked until he saw that the truth was known in hers, and then he dropped his face into her lap and she put her hands on his head and bent over him, so that her heart beat with the throbbing at his temples. For a moment she held him as though she were shielding him from every threatening danger, and then she lifted his face again.

"No, Gray—it won't do—hush, now." She paused a moment to get self-control, and then she went on rapidly, as though what she had to say had been long prepared and repeated to herself many times:

"I knew you were coming to-night. I know why you were so late. I know why you came. Hush, now—I know all that, too. Why, Gray, ever since I saw you the first time—you remember?

334

—why, it seems to me that ever since then, even,
I've been thinkin' o' this very hour. All the time
I was goin' to school when I first went to the Blue-
grass, when I was walkin' in the fields and workin'
around the house and always lookin' to the road
to see you passin' by—I was thinkin', thinkin' all
the time. It seems to me every night of my life I
went to sleep thinkin'—I was alone so much and
I was so lonely. It was all mighty puzzlin' to
me, but that time you didn't take me to that
dance—hush now—I began to understand. I told
Jason an' he only got mad. He didn't understand,
for he was wilful and he was a man, and men
don't somehow seem to see and take things like
women—they just want to go ahead and make
them the way they want them. But I understood
right then. And then when I come here the
thinkin' started all over again differently when I
was goin' back and forwards from school and
walkin' around in the woods and listenin' to the
wood-thrushes, and sittin' here in the porch at
night alone and lyin' up in the loft there lookin'
out of the little window. And when I heard you
were comin' here I got to thinkin' differently, because I got to hopin' differently and wonderin' if
some miracle mightn't yet happen in this world
once more. But I watched you here, and the
more I watched you, the more I began to go back
and think as I used to think. Your people ain't
mine, Gray, nor mine yours, and they won't be—

not in our lifetime. I've seen you shrinkin' when you've been with me in the houses of some of my own kin—shrinkin' at the table at grandpap's and here, at the way folks eat an' live—shrinkin' at oaths and loud voices and rough talk and liquor-drinkin' and all this talk about killin' people, as though they were nothin' but hogs—shrinkin' at everybody but me. If we stayed here, the time would come when you'd be shrinkin' from me— don't now! But you ain't goin' to stay here, Gray. I've heard Uncle Arch say you'd never make a business man. You're too trustin', you've been a farmer and a gentleman for too many gen-erations. You're goin' back home—you've got to —some day—I know that, and then the time would come when you'd be ashamed of me if I went with you. It's the same way with Jason and Marjorie. Jason will have to come back here—how do you suppose Marjorie would feel here, bein' a woman, if you feel the way you do, bein' a man? Why, the time would come when she'd be ashamed o' him—only worse. It won't do, Gray." She turned his face toward the gap in the hills.

"You see that star there? Well, that's your star, Gray. I named it for you, and every night I've been lookin' out at it from my window in the loft. And that's what you've been to me and what Marjorie's been to Jason—just a star—a dream. We're not really real to each other—you an' me— and Marjorie and Jason ain't. Only Jason and I

are *real* to each other and only you and Marjorie.
Jason and I have been worshippin' stars, and
they've looked down mighty kindly on us, so that
they came mighty nigh foolin' us and themselves.
I read a book the other day that said ideals were
stars and were good to point the way, but that
people needed lamps to follow that way. It won't
do, Gray. You are goin' back home to carry a
lamp for Marjorie, and maybe Jason'll come back
to these hills to carry a lantern for me."

Throughout the long speech the boy's eyes had
never wavered from hers. After one or two ef-
forts to protest he had listened quite intensely, mar-
velling at the startling revelation of such depths of
mind and heart—the startling penetration to the
truth, for he knew it was the truth. And when
she rose he stayed where he was, clinging to her
hand, and kissing it reverently. He was speechless
even when, obeying the impulse of her hand, he
rose in front of her and she smiled gently.

"You don't have to say one word, Gray—I understand, bless your dear, dear heart, I understand. Good-by, now." She stretched out her
hand, but his trembling lips and the wounded
helplessness in his eyes were too much for her, and
she put her arms around him, drew his head to
her breast, and a tear followed her kiss to his forehead. At the door she paused a moment.

"And until he comes," she half-whispered, "I
reckon I'll keep my lamp burning." Then she
was gone.

Slowly the boy climbed back to the little house on the spur, and to the porch, on which he sank wearily. While he and Marjorie and Jason were blundering into a hopeless snarl of all their lives, this mountain girl, alone with the hills and the night and the stars, had alone found the truth— and she had pointed the way. The camp lights twinkled below. The moon swam in majestic splendor above. The evening star still hung above the little western gap in the hills. It was his star; it was sinking fast: and she would keep her lamp burning. When he climbed to his room, the cry of the whippoorwill in the ravine came to him through his window—futile, persistent, like a human wail for happiness. The boy went to his knees at his bedside that night, and the prayer that went on high from the depths of his heart was that God would bring the wish of her heart to Mavis Hawn.

XL

GRAY PENDLETON was coming home. Like Jason, he, too, waited at the little junction for dawn, and swept along the red edge of it, over the yellow Kentucky River and through the blue-grass fields. Drawn up at the station was his father's carriage and in it sat Marjorie, with a radiant smile of welcome which gave way to sudden tears when they clasped hands—tears that she did not try to conceal. Uncle Robert was in bed, she said, and Gray did not perceive any significance in the tone with which she added, that her mother hardly ever left him. She did not know what the matter was, but he was very pale, and he seemed to be growing weaker. The doctor was cheery and hopeful, but her mother, she emphasized, was most alarmed, and again Gray did not notice the girl's peculiar tone. Nor did the colonel seem to be worried by the threats of the night riders. It was Jason Hawn who was worried and had persuaded the colonel to send for Gray. The girl halted when she spoke Jason's name, and the boy looked up to find her face scarlet and her eyes swerve suddenly from his to the passing fields. But as quickly they swerved back to find Gray's face aflame with the thought of Mavis. For a

moment both looked straight ahead in silence, and
in that silence Marjorie became aware that Gray
had not asked about Jason, and Gray that Marjorie had not mentioned Mavis's name.   But now
both made the omission good—and Gray spoke
first.

Mavis was well.   She was still teaching school.
She had lived a life of pathetic loneliness, but she
had developed in an amazing way through that
very fact, and she had grown very beautiful.   She
had startled him by her insight into—he halted
—into everything—and how was Jason getting
along?   The girl had been listening, covertly
watching, and had grown quite calm.   Jason, too,
was well, but he looked worried and overworked.
His examinations were going on now.   He had
written his graduating speech but had not shown
it to her, though he had said he would.   Her
mother and Uncle Robert had grown very fond of
him and admired him greatly, but lately she had
not seen him, he was so busy.   Again there was a
long silence between them, but when they reached
the hill whence both their homes were visible Marjorie began as though she must get out something
that was on her mind before they reached Colonel
Pendleton's gate.

"Gray," she said hesitantly and so seriously
that the boy turned to her, "did it ever cross your
mind that there was ever any secret between
Uncle Robert and mother?"

The boy's startled look was answer enough and she went on telling him of the question she had asked her mother.

"Sometimes," she finished, "I think that your father and my mother must have loved each other first and that something kept them from marrying. I know that they must have talked it over lately, for there seems to be a curious understanding between them now, and the sweetest peace has come to both of them."

She paused, and Gray, paralyzed with wonder, still made no answer. They had passed through the gate now and in a moment more would be at Gray's home. Around each barn Gray saw an armed guard; there was another at the yard gate, and there were two more on the steps of the big portico.

"Maybe," the girl went on naïvely, almost as though she were talking to herself, "that's why they've both always been so anxious to have us—" Again she stopped—scarlet.

XLI

JASON HAWN'S last examination was over, and he stepped into the first June sunlight and drew it into his lungs with deep relief. Looking upward from the pavement below, the old president saw his confident face.

"It seems you are not at all uneasy," he said, and his keen old eyes smiled humorously.

Jason reddened a little.

"No, sir—I'm not."

"Nor am I," said the old gentleman, "nor will you forget that this little end is only the big beginning."

"Thank you, sir."

"You are going back home? You will be needed there."

"Yes, sir."

"Good!"

It was the longest talk Jason had ever had with the man he all but worshipped, and while it was going on the old scholar was painfully climbing the steps—so that the last word was flung back with the sharp, soldier-like quality of a command given by an officer who turned his back with perfect trust that it would be obeyed, and in answer to that trust the boy's body straightened and his very

soul leaped. He went to his room in the seniors'
hall that was called "Heaven" by the lower
classmen and dropped into a chair by the open
window. He looked around at his books, and he
already felt the pang of parting from old friends.
But, after all, it was a little end, and the big beginning was at that moment at hand—a beginning that the old president did not suspect. Gray
Pendleton had come home to trouble, and while
his friend is in trouble, the mountaineer's trouble
does not end. Jason sprang from his chair, went
to his boarding-house for a hasty lunch, and
started for the court-house. There he had himself
sworn in as a deputy sheriff, and busy with
thoughts of the threats of the night riders that
had reached him through his mother, he saw from
the court-house steps a crowd gathering down the
street on each side of the main street, and soon
down it came a militia company with a Gatling-gun
in its midst. The tobacco warehouses of the town
were threatened and the county judge was waking
up. On he hurried to his mother's home—his
every speculation busy with Steve Hawn. Steve
was not the man who had tried to destroy Colonel
Pendleton's tobacco beds, for his mother had as-
sured him that her husband was at home that night
and asleep. He began to wonder if his mother
were protecting Steve and at the same time trying
to prevent all the mischief she could, for lately
Steve had been quiet and secretive, and had talked

much about changing his ways, that he no longer had any resentment against Colonel Pendleton, and wanted now to live a better life. His talk might have fooled Jason but for the fact that he shrewdly noted the little effect it all had on his mother. Entering the mouth the lane, Jason saw Steve going from the yard gate to the house, and his brows wrinkled angrily—Steve was staggering. He came to the door and glared at Jason.

"Whut you doin' out hyeh?"

"I'm goin' to see Gray through his troubles," said Jason quietly.

"I kind o' thought you had troubles enough o' yo' own," sneered the man.

Jason did not answer. His mother was seated within with her back to the door, and when she turned Jason saw that she had been weeping, and, catching sight of a red welt on her temple, he walked over to her.

"How'd that happen, mammy?"

She hesitated and Jason whirled with such fury that his mother caught him with both arms, and Steve lost no time reaching for his gun.

"I jammed it agin the kitchen door, Jasie."

He looked at her, knew that she was lying, and when he turned to go, halted at the door.

"If you ever *touch* my mother again," he said with terrifying quiet, "I'll kill you as sure as there is a God in heaven to forgive me."

Across the midsummer fields Jason went swiftly.

On his right, half of a magnificent woodland was being laid low—on his left, another was all gone—and with Colonel Pendleton both, he knew, had been heart-breaking deeds of necessity, for his first duty, that gentleman claimed, was to his family and to his creditors, and nobody could rob him of his right to do what he pleased, much less what he ought, with his own land. And so the colonel still stood out against friend and neighbor, and open and secret foes. His tobacco beds had been raided, one of his barns had been burned, his cattle had been poisoned, and, sick as he was, threats were yet coming in that the night riders would burn his house and take his life. Across the turnpike were the fields and untouched woodlands of Marjorie, and it looked as though the hand of Providence had blessed one side of the road and withered the other with a curse. On top of the orchard fence, to the western side of the house, Jason sat a while. The curse was descending on Gray's innocent head and he had had the weakness and the folly to lift his eyes to the blessing across the way. As Mavis had pointed out the way to Gray, so Marjorie, without knowing it, had pointed the way for him. When long ago he had been helpless before her by the snow-fringed willows at the edge of the pond in the old college yard, she had been frightened and had shrunk away. When he gained his self-control, she had lost hers, and in her loneliness had come trailing toward him almost like

a broken-winged young bird looking for mother
help—and he had not misunderstood, though his
heart ached for her suffering as it ached for her.
And Marjorie had been quite right—he had never
come back after that one quarrel, and he would
never come. The old colonel had gone to him, but
he had hardly more than opened his lips when he
had both hands on the boy's shoulders with broken
words of sympathy and then had turned away—so
quickly had he seen that Jason fully understood the
situation and had disposed of it firmly, proudly,
and finally—for himself. The mountains were for
Jason—there were his duty and the work of his life.
Under June apples turning golden, and amid the
buzzing of bees, the boy went across the orchard,
and at the fence he paused again. Marjorie and
her mother were coming out of the house with
Gray, and Jason watched them walk to the stile.
Gray was tanned, and even his blonde head had
been turned copper by the mountain sun, while
the girl looked like a great golden-hearted lily.
But it was Gray's face as he looked at her that
caught the boy's eyes and held them fast, for the
face was tense, eager, and worshipping.

He saw Marjorie and her mother drive away,
saw Gray wave to them and turn back to the
house, and then he was so shocked at the quick
change to haggard worry that draped his friend
like a cloak from head to foot that he could hardly
call to him. And so Jason waited till Gray had

346

passed within, and then he leaped the fence and made for the portico. Gray himself answered his ring and with a flashing smile hurried forward when he saw Jason in the doorway. The two clasped hands and for one swift instant searched each other's eyes with questions too deep and delicate to be put into words—each wondering how much the other might know, each silent if the other did not know. For Gray had learned from his father about Steve Hawn, and Jason's suspicions of Steve he had kept to himself.

"My father would like to have you as our guest, Jason, while I am here," Gray said with some embarrassment, "but he doesn't feel like letting you take the risk."

Jason threw back the lapel of his coat that covered his badge as deputy.

"That's what I'm here for," he said with a smile, "but I think I'd better stay at home. I'll be on hand when the trouble comes."

Gray, too, smiled.

"You don't have to tell me that."

"How is the colonel?"

"He's pretty bad. He wants to see you."

Jason lowered his voice when they entered the hallway. "The soldiers have reached town to-day. If there's anything going to be done, it will probably be done to-night."

"I know."

"We won't tell the colonel."

347

"No."

Then Gray led the way to the sick-room and softly opened the door. In a great canopied bed lay Colonel Pendleton with his face turned toward the window, through which came the sun and air, the odors and bird-songs of spring-time, and when that face turned, Jason was shocked by its waste and whiteness and by the thinness of the hand that was weakly thrust out to him. But the fire of the brilliant eyes burned as ever; there was with him, prone in bed, still the same demeanor of stately courtesy; and Jason felt his heart melt and then fill as always with admiration for the man, the gentleman, who unconsciously had played such a part in the moulding of his own life, and as always with the recognition of the unbridgable chasm between them—between even him and Gray. The bitter resentment he had first felt against this chasm was gone now, for now he understood and accepted. As men the three were equal, but father and son had three generations the start of him. He could see in them what he lacked himself, and what they were without thought he could only consciously try to be—and he would keep on trying. The sick man turned his face again to the window and the morning air. When he turned again he was smiling faintly and his voice was friendly and affectionate:

"Jason, I know why you are here. I'm not going to thank you, but I—Gray"—he paused ever

so little, and Jason sadly knew what it meant—
"will never forget it. I want you two boys to be
friends as long as you live. I'm sorry, but it looks
as though you would both have to give up yourselves to business—particularly sorry about Gray,
for that is my fault. For the good of our State I
wish you both were going to sit side by side at
Frankfort, in Congress, and the Senate, and fight
it out"—he smiled whimsically—"some day for
the nomination for the Presidency. The poor old
commonwealth is in a bad way, and it needs just
such boys as you two are. The war started us
downhill, but we might have done better—I know
I might. The earth was too rich—it made life too
easy. The horse, the bottle of whiskey, and the
plug of tobacco were all too easily the best—
and the pistol always too ready. We've been car-
tooned through the world with a fearsome, half-
contemptuous slap on the back. Our living has
been made out of luxuries. Agriculturally, socially, politically, we have gone wrong, and but for
the American sense of humor the State would be
in a just, nation-wide contempt. The Ku-Klux,
the burning of toll-gates, the Goebel troubles, and
the night rider are all links in the same chain of lawlessness, and but for the first the others might not
have been. But we are, in spite of all this, a law-
abiding people, and the old manhood of the State
is still here. Don't forget that—*the old manhood
is here.*"

Jason had sat eager-eyed and listening hard. Bewildered Gray felt his tears welling, for never had he heard in all his life his father talk this way. Again Colonel Pendleton turned his face to the window and went on as though to the world outside.

"I wouldn't let anybody out there say this about us, nor would you, and maybe if I thought I was going to live many years longer I might not be saying it now, for some Kentuckian might yet make me eat my words."

At this the eyes of the two boys crossed and both smiled faintly, for though the sick man had been a generous liver, his palate could never have known the taste of one of his own words.

"I don't know—but our ambition is either dying or sinking to a lower plane, and what a pity, for the capacity is still here to keep the old giants still alive if the young men could only see, feel, and try. And if I were as young as one of you two boys, I'd try to find and make the *appeal*."

He turned his brilliant eyes to Jason and looked for a moment silently.

"The death-knell of me and mine has been sounded unless boys like Gray here keep us alive after death, but the light of your hills is only dawn· ning. It's a case of the least shall be first, for your pauper counties are going to be the richest in the State. The Easterners are buying up our farms as they would buy a yacht or a motor-car, the tobacco tenants are getting their mites of land here and there, and even you mountaineers, when you sell your coal lands, are taking up Blue-grass acres. Don't let the Easterner swallow you, too. Go home, and, while you are getting rich, enrich your citizenship, and you and Gray help land-locked, primitive old Kentucky take her place among the modern sisterhood that is making the nation. To use a phrase of your own—get busy, boys, get busy after I am gone."

And then Colonel Pendleton laughed.

"I am hardly the one to say all this, or rather I am just the one because I am a—failure."

"Father."

The word came like a sob from Gray.

"Oh, yes, I am—but I have never lied except for others, and I have not been afraid."

Again his face went toward the window.

"Even now," he added in a solemn whisper that was all to himself, "I believe, and am not afraid."

Presently he lifted himself on one elbow and with Gray's assistance got to a sitting posture. Then he pulled a paper from beneath his pillow.

"I want to tell you something, Jason. That was all true, every word you said the first time Gray and I saw you at your grandfather's house, and I want you to know now that your land was bought over my protest and without my knowledge. My own interest in the general purchase was in the form of stock, and here it is."

Jason's heart began to beat violently.

"Whatever happens to me, this farm will have to be sold, but there will be something left for Gray. This stock is in Gray's name, and it is worth now just about what would have been a fair price for your land five years after it was bought. It is Gray's, and I am going to give it to him." He handed the paper to bewildered Gray, who looked at it dazedly, went with it to the window, and stood there looking out—his father watching him closely.

"You might win in a suit, Jason, I know, but I also know that you could never collect even damages."

At these words Gray wheeled.

"Then this belongs to you, Jason."

The father smiled and nodded approval and assent.

That night there was a fusillade of shots, and Jason and Gray rushed out with a Winchester in hand to see one barn in flames and a tall figure with a firebrand sneaking toward the other. Both fired and the man dropped, rose to his feet, limped back to the edge of the woods, and they let him disappear. But all the night, fighting the fire and on guard against another attack, Jason was possessed with apprehension and fear—that limping figure looked like Steve Hawn. So at the first streak of dawn he started for his mother's home, and when that early he saw her from afar standing on the porch and apparently looking for him, he went toward her on a run. She looked wild-eyed, white, and sleepless, but she showed no signs of tears.

"Where's Steve, mammy?" called Jason in a panting whisper, and when she nodded back through the open door his throat eased and he gulped his relief.

"Is he all right?"

She looked at him queerly, tried to speak, and began to tremble so violently that he stepped quickly past her and stopped on the threshold—shuddering. A human shape lay hidden under a brilliantly colored quilt on his mother's bed, and the rigidity of death had moulded its every outline.

"I reckon you've done it at last, Jasie," said a dead, mechanical voice behind him.

"Good God, mammy—it must have been Gray or me."

"One of you, shore. He said he saw you shoot at the same time, and only one of you hit him. I hope hit was you."

Jason turned—horrified, but she was calm and steady now.

"Hit was fitten fer you to be the one. Babe never killed yo' daddy, Jasie—hit was Steve."

XLII

GRAY PENDLETON, hearing from a house-
servant of the death of Steve Hawn, hurried
over to offer his help and sympathy, and Martha
Hawn, too quick for Jason's protest, let loose the
fact that the responsibility for that death lay between the two. To her simple faith it was Jason's
aim that the intervening hand of God had directed,
but she did not know what the law of this land
might do to her boy, and perhaps her motive was
to shield him if possible. While she spoke, one of
her hands was hanging loosely at her side and the
other was clenched tightly at her breast.

"What have you got there, mammy?" said
Jason gently. She hesitated, and at last held out
her hand—in the palm lay a misshapen bullet.

"Steve give me this—hit was the one that got
him, he said. He said mebbe you boys could tell
whichever one's gun hit come from."

Both looked at the piece of battered, blood-
stained lead with fascinated horror until Gray,
with a queer little smile, took it from her hand, for
he knew, what Jason did not, that the night before
they had used guns of a different calibre, and now
his heart and brain worked swiftly and to a better
purpose than he meant, or would ever know.

"Come on, Jason, you and I will settle the question right now."

And, followed by mystified Jason, he turned from the porch and started across the yard. Standing in the porch, the mother saw the two youths stop at the fence, saw Gray raise his right hand high, and then the piece of lead whizzed through the air and dropped with hardly more than the splash of a raindrop in the centre of the pond. The mother understood and she gulped hard. For a moment the two talked and she saw them clasp hands. Then Gray turned toward home and Jason came slowly back to the house. The boy said nothing, the stony calm of the mother's face was unchanged—their eyes met and that was all.

An hour later, John Burnham came over, told Jason to stay with his mother, and went forthwith to town. Within a few hours all was quickly, quietly done, and that night Jason started with his mother and the body of Mavis's father back to the hills. The railroad had almost reached the county-seat now, and at the end of it old Jason Hawn and Mavis were waiting in the misty dawn with two saddled horses and a spring wagon. The four met with a handshake, a grave "how-dye," and no further speech. And thus old Jason and Martha Hawn jolted silently ahead, and little Jason and Mavis followed silently behind. Once or twice Jason turned to look at her. She was in black, and the whiteness of her face, unstained with tears, lent depth and darkness to her eyes, but the eyes were never turned toward him.

When they entered town there were Hawns in front of one store and one hotel on one side of the street. There were Honeycutts in front of one store and one hotel on the other side, and Jason saw the lowering face of little Aaron, and towering in one group the huge frame of Babe Honeycutt. Silently the Hawns fell in behind on horseback, and on foot, and gravely the Honeycutts watched the procession move through the town and up the winding road.

The pink-flecked cups of the laurel were dropping to the ground, the woods were starred with great white clusters of rhododendron, wood-thrushes, unseen, poured golden rills of music from every cool ravine, air and sunlight were heavy with the richness of June, and every odor was a whisper, every sound a voice, and every shaking leaf a friendly little beckoning hand—all giving him welcome home. The boy began to choke with memories, but Mavis still gave no sign. Once she turned her head when they passed her little log school-house where was a little group of her pupils who had not known they were to have a holiday that day, and whose faces turned awe-stricken when they saw the reason, and sympathetic when Mavis gave them a kindly little smile. Up the creek there and over the sloping green plain of the tree-tops hung a cloud

of smoke from the mines. A few moments more
and they emerged from an arched opening of trees.
The lightning-rod of old Jason's house gleamed
high ahead, and on the sunny crest of a bare little
knoll above it were visible the tiny homes built
over the dead in the graveyard of the Hawns.
And up there, above the murmuring sweep of the
river, and with many of his kin who had died in a
similar way, they laid "slick Steve" Hawn. The
old circuit rider preached a short funeral sermon,
while Mavis and her mother stood together, the
woman dry-eyed, much to the wonder of the clan,
the girl weeping silently at last, and Jason behind
them—solemn, watchful, and with his secret working painfully in his heart. He had forbade his
mother to tell Mavis, and perhaps he would never
tell her himself; for it might be best for her never
to know that her father had raised the little mound
under which his father slept but a few yards away,
and that in turn his hands, perhaps, were lowering
Steve Hawn into his grave.

From the graveyard all went to old Jason's
house, for the old man insisted that Martha Hawn
must make her home with him until young Jason
came back to the mountains for good. Until then
Mavis, too, would stay there with Jason's mother,
and with deep relief the boy saw that the two
women seemed drawn to each other closer than
ever now. In the early afternoon old Jason limped
ahead of him to the barn to show his stock, and

for the first time Jason noticed how feeble his grandfather was and how he had aged during his last sick spell. His magnificent old shoulders had drooped, his walk was shuffling, and even the leonine spirit of his bushy brows and deep-set eyes seemed to have lost something of its old fire. But that old fire blazed anew when the old man told him about the threats and insults of little Aaron Honeycutt, and the story of Mavis and Gray.

"Mavis in thar," he rumbled, "stood up fer him agin me—agin *me*. She 'lowed thar wasn't a Hawn fitten to be kinfolks o' his even by marriage, less'n 'twas you."

"*Me?*"

"An' she told me—*me*—to mind my own business. Is that boy Gray comin' back hyeh?"

"Yes, sir, if his father gets well, and maybe he'll come anyhow."

"Well, that gal in thar is plum' foolish about him, but I'm goin' to let you take keer o' all that now."

Jason answered nothing, for the memory of Gray's worshipping face, when he went down the walk with Marjorie at Gray's own home, came suddenly back to him, and the fact that Mavis was yet in love with Gray began to lie with sudden heaviness on his mind and not lightly on his heart.

"An' as fer little Aaron Honeycutt——"

Over the barn-yard gate loomed just then the huge shoulders of Babe Honeycutt coming from

358

the house where he had gone to see his sister
Martha. Jason heard the shuffling of big feet and
he turned to see Babe coming toward him fearlessly, his good-natured face in a wide smile and
his hand outstretched. Old Jason peered through
his spectacles with some surprise, and then grunted
with much satisfaction when they shook hands.

"Well, Jason, I'm glad you air beginnin' to
show some signs o' good sense. This feud business has got to stop—an' now that you two air
shakin' hands, hit all lays betwixt you and little
Aaron."

Babe colored and hesitated.

"That's jus' whut I wanted to say to Jason
hyeh. Aaron's drinkin' a good deal now. I hears
as how he's a-threatenin' some, but ef Jason kind
o' keeps outen his way an' they git together when
he's sober, hit'll be easy."

"Yes," said old Jason, grimly, "but I reckon
you Honeycutts had better keep Aaron outen his
way a leetle, too."

"I'm a-doin' all I can," said Babe earnestly, and
he slouched away.

"Got yo' gun, Jason?"

"No."

"Well, you kin have mine till you git away
again. I want all this feud business stopped, but
I hain't goin' to have you shot down like a turkey
at Christmas by a fool boy who won't hardly know
whut he's doin'."

Jason started for the house, but the old man stayed at the stable to give directions to a neighbor who had come to feed his stock. It sickened the boy to think that he must perhaps be drawn into the feud again, but he would not be foolish enough not to take all precaution against young Aaron. At the yard fence he stopped, seeing Mavis under an apple-tree with one hand clutching a low bough and her tense face lifted to the west. He could see that the hand was clenched tightly, for even the naked forearm was taut as a bowstring. The sun was going down in the little gap, above it already one pale star was swung, and upon it her eyes seemed to be fixed. She heard his step and he knew it, for he saw her face flush, but without looking around she turned into the house. That night she seemed to avoid the chance that he might speak to her alone, and the boy found himself watching her covertly and closely, for he recalled what Gray had said about her. Indeed, some change had taken place that was subtle and extraordinary. He saw his mother deferring to her—leaning on her unconsciously. And old Jason, to the boy's amazement, was less imperious when she was around, moderated his sweeping judgments, looked to her from under his heavy brows, apparently for approval or to see that at least he gave no offence—deferred to her more than to any man or woman within the boy's memory. And Jason himself felt the emanation from her of some new power that was beginning to chain his thoughts to her. All that night Mavis was on his mind, and when he woke next morning it was Mavis, Mavis still. She was clear-eyed, calm, reserved when she told him good-by, and once only she smiled. Old Jason had brought out one of his huge pistols, but Mavis took it from his unresisting hands and Jason rode away unarmed. It was just as well, for as his train started, a horse and a wild youth came plunging down the river-bank, splashed across, and with a yell charged up to the station. Through the car window Jason saw that it was little Aaron, flushed of face and with a pistol in his hand, looking for him. A sudden storm of old instincts burst suddenly within him, and had he been armed he would have swung from the train and settled accounts then and there. As it was, he sat still and was borne away shaken with rage from head to foot.

XLIII

COMMENCEMENT DAY was over. Jason
Hawn had made his last speech in college, and
his theme was "Kentucky." In all seriousness
and innocence he had lashed the commonwealth
for lawlessness from mountain-top to river-brim,
and his own hills he had flayed mercilessly. In all
seriousness and innocence, when he was packing
his bag three hours later in "Heaven," he placed
his big pistol on top of his clothes so that when the
lid was raised, the butt of it would be within an
inch of his right hand. On his way home he might
meet little Aaron on the train, and he did not pro-
pose to be at Aaron's mercy again.

While the band played, ushers with canes
wrapped with red, white, and blue ribbons had
carried him up notes of congratulation, and among
them was a card from Marjorie and a bouquet from
her own garden. John Burnham's eyes sought his
with pride and affection. The old president, hand-
ing him his diploma, said words that covered him
with happy confusion and brought a cheer from
his fellow-students. When he descended from the
platform, Gray grasped his hand, and Marjorie
with lips and eyes gave him ingenuous congratula-

tions, as though the things that were between them had never been.

An hour later he drove with John Burnham through soldiers in the streets and past the Gatling-gun out into the country, and was deposited at the mouth of the lane. For the last time he went to the little cottage that had been his mother's home and walked slowly around garden and barn, taking farewell of everything except memories that he could never lose. Across the fields he went once more to Colonel Pendleton's, and there he found Gray radiant, for his father was better, and the doctor, who was just leaving, said that he might yet get well. And there was little danger now from the night riders, for the county judge had arranged a system of signals by bonfires through all the country around the town. He had watchers on top of the court-house, soldiers always ready, and motor-cars waiting below to take them to any place of disturbance if a bonfire blazed. So Gray said it was not good-by for them for long, for when his father was well enough he was coming back to the hills. Again the old colonel wished Jason well and patted him on the arm affectionately when they shook hands, and then Jason started for the twin house on the hill across the turnpike to tell Marjorie and her mother good-by.

An hour later Gray found Marjorie seated on a grape-vine bench under honeysuckles in her mother's old-fashioned garden, among flowers and bees. Jason had just told her good-by. For the last time he had felt the clasp of her hand, had seen the tears in her eyes, and now he was going for the last time through the fragrant fields—his face set finally for the hills.

"Father is better, the county judge has waked up, and there is no more danger from the night riders, and so I am going back to the mountains now myself."

"Jason has just gone."

"I know."

"Back to Mavis?"

."I don't know."

Marjorie smiled with faint mischief and grew serious.

"I wonder if you have had the same experience, Gray, that I've had with Mavis and Jason. There was never a time that I did not feel in both a mysterious something that always baffled me—a barrier that I couldn't pass, and knew I never could pass. I've felt it with Mavis, even when we were together in my own room late at night, talking our hearts to each other."

"I know—I've felt the same thing in Jason always."

"What is it?"

"I've heard John Burnham say it's a reserve, a reticence that all primitive people have, especially mountaineers; a sort of Indian-like stoicism, but

364

less than the Indian's because the influences that produce it—isolation, loneliness, companionship with primitive wilds—have been a shorter while at work."

"That's what attracted me," said Marjorie frankly, "and I couldn't help always trying to break it down—but I never did. Was—was that what attracted you?" she asked naïvely.

"I don't know—but I felt it."

"And did you try to break it down?"

"No; it broke me down."

"Ah!" Marjorie looked very thoughtful for a moment. They were getting perilously near the old theme now, and Gray was getting grim and Marjorie petulant.

And then suddenly:

"Gray, did you ever ask Mavis to marry you?"

Gray reddened furiously and turned his face away.

"Yes," he said firmly. When he looked around again a hostile right shoulder was pointing at him, and over the other shoulder the girl was gazing at —he knew not what.

"Marjorie, you oughtn't to have asked me that. I can't explain very well. I—" He stumbled and stopped, for the girl had turned astonished eyes upon him.

"Explain what?" she asked with demure wonder. "It's all right. I came near asking Jason to marry me."

"Marjorie!" exploded Gray.

"Well!"

A negro boy burst down the path, panting:

"Miss Marjorie, yo' mother says you an' Mr. Gray got to come right away."

Both sprang to their feet, Gray white and Marjorie's mischievous face all quick remorse and tenderness. Together they went swiftly up the walk and out to the stile where Gray's horse and buggy were hitched, and without a word Marjorie, bareheaded as she was, climbed into the buggy and they silently sped through the fields.

Mrs. Pendleton met them at the door, her face white and her hands clenched tightly in front of her. Speechless with distress, she motioned them toward the door of the sick-room, and when the old colonel saw them coming together, his tired eyes showed such a leap of happiness that Gray, knowing that he misunderstood, had not the heart to undeceive him, and he looked helplessly to Marjorie. But that extraordinary young woman's own eyes answered the glad light in the colonel's, and taking bewildered Gray by the hand she dropped with him on one knee by the bedside.

"Yes, Uncle Bob," Gray heard her say tenderly, "Gray's not going back to the mountains. He's going to stay here with us, for you and I need him."

The old man laid a hand on the bright head of each, his eyes lighting with the happiness of his life's wish fulfilled, and chokingly he murmured:

"My children—Gray—Marjorie." And then his eyes rose above them to the woman who had glided in.

"Mary—look here."

She nodded, smiling tenderly, and Gray felt Marjorie rising to her feet.

"Call us, mother," she whispered.

Both saw her kneel, and then they were alone in the big hallway, and Gray, still dazed, was looking into Marjorie's eyes.

"Marjorie—Marjorie—do you——"

Her answer was a rush into his outstretched arms, and, locked fast, they stood heart to heart until the door opened behind them. Again hand in hand they kneeled side by side with the mother. The colonel's eyes dimmed slowly with the coming darkness, the smiling, pallid lips moved, and both leaned close to hear.

"Gray — Marjorie — Mary." His last glance turned from them to her, rested there, and then came the last whisper:

"Our children."

XLIV

JASON did not meet young Aaron on the train, though as he neared the county-seat he kept a close watch, whenever the train stopped at a station, on both doors of his car, with his bag on the seat in front of him unbuckled and unlocked. At the last station was one Honeycutt lounging about, but plainly evasive of him. There was a little group of Hawns about the Hawn store and hotel, and more Honeycutts and Hawns on the other side of the street farther down, but little Aaron did not appear. It seemed, as he learned a few minutes later, that both factions were in town for the meeting between Aaron and him, and later still he learned that young Honeycutt loped into town after Jason had started up the river and was much badgered about his late arrival. At the forks of the road Jason turned toward the mines, for he had been casually told by Arch Hawn that he would find his mother up that way. The old circuit rider's wife threw her arms around the boy when he came to her porch, and she smiled significantly when she told him that his mother had walked over the spur that morning to take a look at her old home, and that Mavis had gone with her.

Jason slowly climbed the spur. To his surprise he saw a spiral of smoke ascending on the other side, just where he once used to see it, but he did not hurry, for it might be coming from a miner's cabin that had been built near the old place. On top of the spur, however, he stopped—quite stunned. That smoke was coming out of his mother's old chimney. There was a fence around the yard, which was clear of weeds. The barn was rebuilt, there was a cow browsing near it, and near her were three or four busily rooting pigs. And stringing beans on the porch were his mother—and Mavis Hawn. Jason shouted his bewilderment, and the two women lifted their eyes. A high, shrill, glad answer came from his mother, who rose to meet him, but Mavis sat where she was with idle hands.

"Mammy!" cried Jason, for there was a rich color in the pallid face he had last seen, she looked years younger, and she was smiling. It was all the doing of Arch Hawn—a generous impulse or an act of justice long deferred.

"Why, Jason!" said his mother. "Arch is a-goin' to gimme back the farm fer my use as long as I live."

And Mavis had left the old circuit rider and come to live with her. The girl looked quiet, placid, content—only, for a moment, she sank the deep lights of her eyes deep into his and the scrutiny seemed to bring her peace, for she drew

a long breath and at him her eyes smiled. There
was more when later Mavis had strolled down
toward the barn to leave the two alone.

"Is Mavis goin' to live with you all the time?"

"Hit looks like hit—she brought over ever'thing
she has."

The mother smiled suddenly, looked to see that
the girl was out of sight, and then led the way into
the house and up into the attic, where she reached
behind the rafters.

"Look hyeh," she said, and she pulled into sight
the fishing-pole and the old bow and arrow that
Jason had given Mavis years and years ago.

"She fotched 'em over when I wasn't hyeh an'
hid 'em."

Slyly the mother watched her son's face, and
though Jason said nothing, she got her reward
when she saw him color faintly. She was too wise
to say anything more herself, nor did she show any
consciousness when the three were together in the
porch, nor make any move to leave them alone.
The two women went to their work again, and
while Mavis asked nothing, the mother plied Jason
with questions about Colonel and Mrs. Pendleton
and Marjorie and Gray, and had him tell about his
graduating speech and Commencement Day. The
girl listened eagerly, though all the time her eyes
were fixed on her busy fingers, and when Jason
told that Gray would most likely come back to the
hills, now that his father would get well, she did

not even lift her eyes and the calm of her face changed not at all.

A little later Jason started back over to the mines. From the corner of the yard he saw the path he used to follow when he was digging for his big seam of coal. He passed his trysting-place with Mavis on top of the spur, walled in now, as then, with laurel and rhododendron. Again he felt the same pang of sympathy when he saw her own cabin on the other side, tenanted now by negro miners. Together their feet had beat every road, foot-path, trail, the rocky bed of every little creek that interlaced in the great green cup of the hills about him. So that all that day he walked with memories and Mavis Hawn; all that day it was good to think that his mother's home was hers, that he would find her there when his day's work was done, and that she would be lonesome no more. And it was a comfort when he went down the spur before sunset to see her in the porch, to get her smile of welcome that for all her calm sense of power seemed shy, to see her moving around the house, helping his mother in the kitchen, and, after the old way, waiting on him at the table. Jason slept in the loft of his childhood that night, and again he pulled out the old bow and arrow, handling them gently and looking at them long. From his bed he could look through the same little window out on the night. The trees were full-leafed and as still as though sculptured from the hill of broken shadows and flecks of moonlight that had paled on their way through thin mists just rising. High from the tree-trunks came the high vibrant whir of toads, the calls of katydids were echoing through forest aisles, and from the ground crickets chirped modestly upward. The peace and freshness and wildness of it all! Ah, God, it was good to be home again!

XLV

NEXT day Jason carried over to Mavis and his mother the news of the death of Colonel Pendleton, and while Mavis was shocked she asked no question about Gray. The next day a letter arrived from Gray saying he would not come back to the hills—and again Mavis was silent. A week later Jason was made assistant superintendent in Gray's place by the president of Morton Sanders' coal company, and this Jason knew was Gray's doing. He had refused to accept the stock Gray had offered him, and Gray was thus doing his best for him in another way. Moreover, Jason was to be quartered in Gray's place at the superintendent's little cottage, far up the ravine in which the boy had unearthed the great seam of coal, a cottage that had been built under Gray's personal supervision and with a free rein, for it must have a visitor's room for any officer or stockholder who might come that way, a sitting-room with a wood fireplace, and Colonel Pendleton had meant, moreover, that his son should have all the comfort possible. Jason dropped on the little veranda under a canopy of moon-flowers, exultant but quite overcome. How glad and proud his mother would be —and Mavis. While he sat there Arch Hawn rode by, his face lighted up with a humorous knowing smile.

"How about it?" he shouted.

"D'you have anything to do with this?"

"Oh, just a leetle."

"Well, you won't be sorry."

"Course not. What'd I tell ye, son? You go in now an' *dig* it out. And say, Jason—" He pulled his horse in and spoke seriously: "Keep away from town till little Aaron gets over his spree. You don't know it, but that boy is a fine feller when he's sober. Don't you shoot first now. So long."

The next day Jason ran upon Babe Honeycutt shambling up the creek. Babe was fearless and cordial, and Jason had easily guessed why.

"Babe, my mammy told you something."

The giant hesitated, started to lie, but nodded assent.

"You haven't told anybody else?"

"Nary a livin' soul."

"Well, don't."

Babe shuffled on, stopped, called Jason, and came back close enough to whisper:

"I had all I could do yestiddy to keep little Aaron from comin' up hyeh to the mines to look for ye."

Then he shuffled away. Jason began to get angry now. He had no intention of shooting first or shooting at all except to save his own life, but

374

he went straightway over the spur to get his pistol. Mavis saw him buckling it on, he explained why, and the girl sadly nodded assent.

Jason flung himself into his work now with prodigious energy. He never went to the county-seat, was never seen on the river road on the Honeycutt side of the ancient dead-line, and the tale-bearers on each side proceeded to get busy again. The Hawns heard that Jason had fled from little Aaron the morning Jason had gone back for his Commencement in the Blue-grass. The Honeycutts heard that Aaron had been afraid to meet Jason when he returned to the county-seat. Old Jason and old Aaron were each cautioning his grandson to put an end to the folly, and each was warning his business representative in town with commercial annihilation if he should be discovered trying to bring on the feud again. On the first county-court day Jason had to go to court, and the meeting came. The town was full with members of both factions, armed and ready for trouble. Jason had ridden ahead of his grandfather that morning and little Aaron had ridden ahead of his. Jason reached town first, and there was a stir in the Honeycutt hotel and store. Half an hour later there was a stir among the Hawns, for little Aaron rode by. A few minutes later Aaron came toward the Hawn store, in the middle of the street, swaggering. Jason happened at that moment to be crossing the same street, and a Hawn shouted warning.

Jason looked up and saw Aaron coming. He stopped, turned, and waited until Aaron reached for his gun. Then his own flashed, and the two reports sounded as one. One black lock was clipped from Jason's right temple and a little patch flew from the left shoulder of Aaron's coat. To Jason's surprise Aaron lowered his weapon and began working at it savagely with both hands, and while Jason waited, Aaron looked up.

"Shoot ahead," he said sullenly; "it's a new gun and it won't work."

But no shot came and Aaron looked up again, mystified and glaring, but Jason was smiling and walking toward him.

"Aaron, there are two or three trifling fellows on our side who hate you and are afraid of you. You know that, don't you?"

"Yes."

"Well, the same thing is true about me of two or three men on your side, isn't it?"

"Yes."

"They've been carrying tales from one side to the other. I've never said anything against you."

Aaron, genuinely disbelieving, stared questioningly for a moment—and believed.

"I've never said anything against you, either."

"I believe you. Well, do you see any reason why we should be shooting each other down to oblige a few cowards?"

"No, by God, I don't."

"Well, I don't want to die and I don't believe

376

you do. There are a lot of things I want to do and a lot that you want to do. We want to help our own people and our own mountains all we can, and the best thing we can do for them and for ourselves is to stop this feud."

"It's the God's truth," said Aaron solemnly, but looking still a little incredulous.

"You and I can do it."

"You bet we can!"

"Let's do it. Shake hands."

And thus, while the amazed factions looked on, the two modern young mountaineers, eye to eye and hand gripping hand, pledged death to the long warfare between their clans and a deathless friendship between themselves. And a little later a group of lounging Hawns and Honeycutts in the porches of the two ancient hostile hotels saw the two riding out of town side by side, unarmed, and on their way to bring old Aaron and old Jason together and make peace between them.

The coincidence was curious, but old Aaron, who had started for town, met old Jason coming out of a ravine only a mile from town, for old Jason, with a sudden twitch of memory, had turned to go up a hollow where lived a Hawn he wanted to see and was coming back to the main road again. Both were dim-sighted, both wore spectacles, both of their old nags were going at a walk, making no noise in the deep sand, and only when both horses stopped did either ancient peer forward and see the other.

"Well, by God," quavered both in the same voice. And each then forgot his mission of peace, and began to climb, grunting, from his horse, each hitching it to the fence.

"This is the fust time in five year, Jason Hawn, you an' me come together, an' you know whut I swore I'd do," cackled old Aaron

Old Jason's voice was still deep.

"Well, you've got yo' chance now, you old bag o' bones! Them two boys o' ours air all right but thar hain't no manhood left in this hyeh war o' ours. Hit's just a question of which hired feller gits the man who hired the other feller. We'll fight the ole way. You hain't got a knife—now?"

"Damn yo' hide!" cried old Aaron. "Do you reckon I need hit agin you?" He reached in his pocket and tossed a curved-bladed weapon into the bushes.

"Well," mumbled old Jason, "I can whoop you, fist an' skull, right now, just as I allers have done."

Both were stumbling back into the road now.

"You air just as big a liar as ever, Jase, an' I'm goin' to prove it."

And then the two tottering old giants squared off, their big, knotted, heavily veined fists revolving around each other in the old-fashioned country way. Old Jason first struck the air, was wheeled around by the force of his own blow, and got old Aaron's fist in the middle of the back. Again the Hawn struck blindly as he turned, and

378

from old Aaron's grunt he knew he had got him in the stomach. Then he felt a fist in his own stomach, and old Aaron cackled triumphantly when he heard the same tell-tale grunt.

"Oh, yes, dad-blast ye! Come on agin, son."

They clinched, and as they broke away a blind sweep from old Jason knocked Aaron's brass-rimmed spectacles from his nose.

They fell far apart, and when old Jason advanced again, peering forward, he saw his enemy silently pawing the air with his back toward him, and he kicked him.

"Here I am, you ole idgit!"

"Stop!" shouted old Aaron, "I've lost my specs."

"Whar?"

"I don't know," and as he dropped to his knees old Jason bent too to help him find his missing eyes. Then they went at it again—and the same cry came presently from old Jason.

"Stop, I've lost mine!"

And both being out of breath sat heavily down in the sand, old Jason feeling blindly with his hands and old Aaron peering about him as far as he could see. And thus young Jason and young Aaron found them, and were utterly mystified until the old men rose creakily and got ready for battle again—when both spurred forward with a shout of joy, and threw themselves from their horses.

"Go for him, grandpap!" shouted each, and the two old men turned.

"Uncle Aaron," shouted Jason, "I bet you can lick him!"

"He can't do it, Uncle Jason!" shouted Aaron.

Each old man peered at his own grandson, dumfounded. Neither was armed, both were helpless with laughter, and each was urging on the oldest enemy of his clan against his own grandfather. The face of each old man angered, and then both began to grin sheepishly; for both were too keenwitted not to know immediately that what both really wished for had come to pass.

"Aaron," said old Jason, "the boys have ketched us. I reckon we better call this thing a draw."

"All right," piped old Aaron, "we're a couple o' ole fools anyhow."

So they shook hands. Each grandson helped the other's grandfather laughingly on his horse. and the four rode back toward town. And thus old Jason and old Aaron, side by side in front, and young Jason and young Aaron, side by side behind, appeared to the astonished eyes of Hawns and Honeycutts on the main street of the countyseat. Before the Honeycutt store they stopped, and old Aaron called his henchman into the middle of the street and spoke vigorous words that all the Honeycutts could hear. Then they rode to the Hawn store, and old Jason called his henchman out and spoke like words that all the Hawns could hear. And each old man ended his discourse with a profane dictum that sounded like the vicious snap of a black-snake whip.

"By God, hit's *got* to stop."

Then turned the four again and rode homeward, and for the first time in their lives old Aaron and young Aaron darkened the door of old Jason's house, and in there the jug went round the four of them, and between the best of the old order and the best of the new, final peace was cemented at last.

Jason reached the mines a little before dusk, and the old circuit rider lifted his eyes heavenward that his long prayer had been answered at last and the old woman rocked silently back and forth—her old eyes dimmed with tears.

Then Jason hurried over the hill and took to his mother a peace she had not known even in her childhood, and a joy that she never dreamed would be hers while she lived—that her boy was safe from blood-oaths, a life of watchful terror, and constant fear of violent death. In Mavis's eyes was deep content when the moon rose on the three that night. Jason stayed a while after his mother was gone within, and, as they sat silently together, he suddenly took one of her hands in both his own and kissed it, and then he was gone. She watched him, and when his form was lost in the shadows of the trees she lifted that hand to her own lips.

XLVI

WINTER came and passed swiftly. Throughout it Jason was on the night shift, and day for him was turned into night. Throughout it Mavis taught her school, and she reached home just about the time Jason was going to work, for school hours are long in the hills. Meanwhile, the railroad crept through the county-seat up the river, and the branch line up the Hawn creek to the mines was ready for it. And just before the junction was made, there was an event up that creek in which Mavis shared proudly, for the work in great part was Jason's own. Throughout the winter, coke-ovens had sprung up like great bee-hives along each side of the creek, and the battery of them was ready for firing. Into each, shavings and kindlings were first thrust and then big sticks of wood. Jason tied packing to the end of a pole, saturated it with kerosene, lighted it, and handed it to Mavis. Along the batteries men with similar poles waited for her. The end of the pole was a woolly ball of oily flames, writhing like little snakes when she thrust it into the first oven, and they leaped greedily at the waiting feast and started a tiny gluttonous roar within. With a yell

a grinning darky flourished another mass of little
flames at the next oven, and down the line the
balls of fire flashed in the dusk and disappeared, and
Mavis and Jason and his mother stood back and
waited. Along came eager men throwing wood
and coal into the hungry maws above them. Little black clouds began to belch from them and
from the earth packed around, and over them
arose white clouds of steam. The swirling smoke
swooped down the sides of the batteries and drove
the watching three farther back. Flames burst
angrily from the oven doors and leaped like yellow
lightning up through the belching smoke. Behind
them was the odor of the woods, fresh and damp
and cool, and the sound of the little creek in its
noisy way over rocks and stray fallen timbers.
Down from the mines came mules with their
drivers, their harness rattling as they trotted past,
and from the houses poured women and children
to see the first flaming signs of a great industry.
And good cheer was in the air like wine, for times
were good, and work and promise of work a-plenty.
Exultant Jason felt a hand on his shoulder, and
turned to find the big superintendent smiling at
him.

"You go on the day shift after this," he said.
"Go to bed now."

The boy's eyes glistened, for he had been working for forty-eight hours, and with Mavis and his
mother he walked up the hill. At the cottage he

went inside and came out with a paper in his hand which he handed to Mavis without a word. Then he went back and with his clothes on fell across his bed.

Mavis walked down the spur with her step-mother home. She knew what the paper contained for two days before was the date fixed for the wedding-day of Marjorie and Gray Pendleton, and Gray had written Jason and Marjorie had written her, begging them both to come. By the light of a lamp she read the account, fulsome and feminine, aloud: the line of carriages and motor-cars sweeping from the pike gate between two rows of softly glowing, gently swinging Japanese lanterns, up to the noble old Southern home gleaming like a fairy palace on the top of a little hill; the gay gathering of the gentlefolk of the State; the aisle made through them by two silken white ribbons and leading to the rose-canopied altar; the coming down that aisle of the radiant bride with her flowers, and her bridesmaids with theirs; the eager waiting of the young bridegroom, the bending of two proud, sunny heads close together, and the God-sealed union of their hearts and lives. And then the silent coming of a great gleaming motor-car, the showers of rice, the showering chorus of gay good wishes and good-bys, and then they shot away in the night for some mysterious bourne of the honeymoon. And behind them the dance went on till dawn. The paper dropped in Mavis's lap, and Martha Hawn sighed and rose to get ready for bed.

"My, but some folks is lucky!"

On the porch Mavis waited up awhile, with no envy in her heart. The moon was soaring over the crest of the Cumberland, and somewhere, doubtless, Marjorie and Gray, too, had their eyes lifted toward it. She looked toward the little gap in the western hills where Gray's star had gone down.

"I'm so glad they're happy," she whispered.

The moon darkened just then, and beyond and over the dark spur flashed a new light in the sky, that ran up the mounting clouds like climbing roses of flame. The girl smiled happily. Under it tired Jason was asleep, but the light up there was the work of his hands below, and it hung in the heavens like a pillar of fire.

XLVII

SITTING on the porch next morning, Mavis and Martha Hawn saw Jason come striding down the spur.

"I'm taking a holiday to-day," he said, and there was a light in his eyes and a quizzical smile on his face that puzzled Mavis, but the mother was quick to understand. It was Saturday, a holiday, too, for Mavis, and a long one, for her school had just closed that her children might work in the fields. Without a word, but still smiling to himself, Jason went out on the back porch, got a hoe, and disappeared behind the garden fence. He came back presently with a tin can in his hands and held it out to Mavis.

"Let's go fishing," he said.

While Mavis hesitated the mother, with an inward chuckle, went within and emerged with the bow and arrow and an old fishing-pole.

"Mebbe you'll need 'em," she said dryly.

Mavis turned scarlet and Jason, pretending bewilderment, laughed happily.

"That's just what we do need," he said, with no further surprise, no question as to how those old relics of their childhood happened to be there. His

mother's diplomacy was crude, but he was grateful
for it, and he smiled at her understandingly.

So, like two children again, they set off, as long
ago, over the spur, down the branch, across the
road below the mines, and down into the deep
bowl, filled to the brim with bush and tree, and to
where the same deep pool lay in deep shadows
asleep—Jason striding ahead and Mavis his obedient shadow once more—only this time Jason would
look back every now and then and smile. Nor did
he drop her pole on the ground and turn ungallantly to his bow and arrow, but unwound the line,
baited her hook, cast it, and handed her the pole.
As of yore, he strung his bow, which was a ridicu-
lous plaything in his hands now, and he peered as
of yore into every sunlit depth, but he turned every
little while to look at the quiet figure on the bank,
not squatted with childish abandon, but seated as a
maiden should be, with her skirts drawn decorously
around her pretty ankles. And all the while she
felt him looking, and her face turned into lovely
rose, though her shining eyes never left the pool
that mirrored her below. Only her squeal was the
same when, as of yore, she flopped a glistening
chub on the bank, and another and another. Nor
did he tell her she was "skeerin' the big uns" and
set her to work like a little slave, but unhooked
each fish and put on another worm. And only was
Jason little Jason once more when at last he saw
the waving outlines of an unwary bass in the

depths below. Again Mavis saw him crouch, saw
again the arrow drawn to his actually paling cheek,
heard again the rushing hiss through the air and
the burning hiss into the water, and saw a bass
leap from the convulsed surface. Only this time
there was no headless arrow left afloat, for, with a
boyish yell, Jason dragged his squirming captive
in. This time Jason gathered the twigs and built
the fire and helped to clean the fish. And when all
was ready, who should step forth with a loud laugh
of triumph from the bushes but the same giant—
Babe Honeycutt!

"I seed you two comin' down hyeh," he shouted.
"Hit reminded me o' ole times. I been settin'
thar in the bushes an' the smell o' them fish might'
nigh drove me crazy. An' this time, by the
jumpin' Jehosiphat, I'm a-goin' to have my share."

Babe did take his share, and over his pipe grew
reminiscent.

"I'm mighty glad you didn't git me that day,
Jason," he said, with another laugh, "an' I reckon
you air too now that——"

He stopped in confusion, for Jason had darted
him a warning glance. So confused was he, indeed,
that he began to feel suddenly very much in the
way, and he rose quickly, and with a knowing look
from one to the other melted with a loud laugh into
the bushes again

"Now, wasn't that curious?" said Jason, and
Mavis nodded silently.

All the time they had been drifting along the backward current of memories, and perhaps it was that current that bore them unconsciously along when they rose, for unconsciously Jason went on toward the river, until once more they stood on the little knoll whence they had first seen Gray and Marjorie ride through the arched opening of the trees. Hitherto, speech had been as sparse between them as it had been that long-ago day, but here they looked suddenly into each other's eyes, and each knew the other's thought.

"Are you sorry, Mavis?"

She flushed a little.

"Not now"; and then shyly, "are you?"

"Not now," repeated Jason.

Back they went again, lapsing once more into silence, until they came again to the point where they had started to part that day, and Mavis's fear had led him to take her down the dark ravine to her home. The spirals of smoke were even rising on either side of the spur from Jason's cottage and his mother's home, and both high above were melting into each other and into the drowsy haze that veiled the face of the mountain. Jason turned quickly, and the subdued fire in his eyes made the girl's face burn and her eyes droop.

"Mavis," he said huskily, "do you remember what I said that day right here?"

And then suddenly the woman became the brave.

"Yes, Jasie," she said, meeting his eyes un-

flinchingly now and with a throb of desire to end
his doubt and suffering quickly:

"And I remember what we both *did*—once."

She looked down toward the old circuit rider's
house at the forks of the road, and Jason's hand and
lip trembled and his face was transfigured with un-
believable happiness.

"Why, Mavis—I thought you—Gray—Mavis,
will you, will you?"

"Poor Jasie," she said, and almost as a mother
to a child who had long suffered she gently put
both arms around his neck, and, as his arms crushed
her to him, lifted her mouth to meet his.

Two hours it took Jason to go to town and back,
galloping all the way. And then at sunset they
walked together through the old circuit rider's gate
and to the porch, and stood before the old man
hand in hand.

"Me an' Mavis hyeh want to git married," said
Jason, with a jesting smile, and the old man's memory was as quick as his humor.

"Have ye got a license?" he asked, with a
serious pursing of his lips. "You got to have a
license, an' hit costs two dollars an' you got to be
a man."

Jason smilingly pulled a paper from his pocket,
and Mavis interrupted:

"He's *my* man."

"Well, he will be in a minute—come in hyeh."

The old circuit rider's wife met them at the door and hugged them both, and when they came out on the porch again, there was Jason's mother hurrying down the spur and calling to them with a half-tearful laugh of triumph.

"I knowed it—oh, I knowed it."

The news spread swiftly. Within half an hour the big superintendent was tumbling his things from the cottage into the road, for his own family was coming, he explained to Jason's mother, and he needed a larger house anyway. And so Babe Honeycutt swung twice down the spur on the other side and up again with Mavis's worldly goods on his great shoulders, while inside the cottage Martha Hawn and the old circuit rider's wife were as joyously busy as bees. On his last trip Mavis and Jason followed, and on top of the spur Babe stopped, cocked his ear, and listened. Coming on a slow breeze up the ravine from the river far below was the long mellow blast of a horn.

"'I God," laughed Babe triumphantly, "ole Jason's already heerd it."

And, indeed, within half an hour word came that the old man must have the infair at his house that night, and already to all who could hear he had blown welcome on the wind.

So, at dusk, when Jason, on the circuit rider's old nag, rode through camp with Mavis on a pillion behind in laughing acceptance of the old pioneer custom, women and children waved at them from doorways and the miners swung their hats and cheered them as they passed. There was an old-fashioned gathering at the old Hawn home that night. Old Aaron and young Aaron and many Honeycutts were there; the house was thronged, fiddles played old tunes for nimble feet, and Hawns and Honeycutts ate and drank and made merry until the morning sun fanned its flames above the sombre hills.

But before midnight Jason and Mavis fared forth pillion-fashion again. Only, Jason too rode sidewise every now and then that he might clasp her with one arm and kiss her again and again under the smiling old moon. Through the lights and noise of the mighty industry that he would direct, they passed and climbed on.

Soon only lights showed that their grimy little working world was below. Soon they stood on the porch of their own little home. To them there the mighty on-sweeping hills sent back their own peace, God-guarded and never to be menaced by the hand of man. And there, clasped in each other's arms, their spirits rushed together, and with the spiral of smoke from their own hearth-stones, went upward.

Mavis on a pillion behind in laughing acceptance of the old pioneer
custom

XLVIII

GENTLY that following midsummer the old president's crutch thumped the sidewalk leading to the college. Between the pillars of the gateway he paused, lifted his undimmed keen blue eyes, and more gently still the crutch thumped on the gravelled road as he passed slowly on under the trees. When he faced the first deserted building, he stopped quite still. The campus was deserted and the buildings were as silent as tombs. That loneliness he had known many, many years; but there was a poignant sorrow in it now that was never there before, for only that morning he had turned over the reins of power into a pair of younger hands. The young men and young women would come again, but now they would be his no longer. There would be the same eager faces, dancing eyes, swift coming and going, but not for him. The same cries of greeting, the tramp of many feet, shouts from the playgrounds—but not for his ears. The same struggle for supremacy in the class-room—but not for his favor and his rewarding hand. That hand had all but upraised each building, brick by brick and stone by stone. He had started alone, he had fought alone, and in

spite of his Scotch shrewdness, business sagacity,
indomitable pluck and patience, and a nation-
wide fame for scholarship, the fight had been hard
and long. He had won, but the work was yet
unfinished, and it was his no longer. For a little
while he stood there, and John Burnham, coming
from his class-room with a little bag of books, saw
the still figure on crutches and paused noiselessly
on the steps. He saw the old scholar's sensitive
mouth quiver and his thin face wrenched with pain,
and he guessed the tragedy of farewell that was
taking place. He saw the old president turn suddenly, limp toward the willow-trees, and Burnham knew that he could not bear at that moment
to pass between those empty beloved halls. And
Burnham watched him move under the willows
along the edge of the quiet pond, watched him
slowly climbing a little hill on the other side of the
campus, and then saw him wearily pass through his
own gate—home. He wished that the old scholar
could know how much better he had builded than
he knew; could know what an exchange and
clearing-house that group of homely buildings was
for the human wealth of the State. And he
wondered if in the old thoroughbred's heart was
the comfort that his spirit would live on and on to
help mould the lives of generations unborn, who
might perhaps never hear his name.

There was a youthful glad light in John Burnham's face when he turned his back on the de-

serted college, for he, too, was on his way at last
to the hills—and St. Hilda. As he swept through
the Blue-grass he almost smiled upon the passing
fields. The betterment of the tobacco troubles
was sure to come, and only that summer the
farmer was beginning to realize that in the end
the seed of his blue-grass would bring him a better
return than the leaf of his troublesome weed-king.
There were groaning harvests that summer and
herds of sheep and hogs and fat cattle. There was
plenty of wheat and rye and oats and barley and
corn yet coming out of the earth, and, as woodland
after woodland reeled past his window, he realized
that the trees were not yet all gone. Perhaps after
all his beloved Kentucky would come back to her
own, and there was peace in his grateful heart.

Two nights later, sitting on the porch of her
little log cabin, he told St. Hilda about Gray and
Marjorie, as she told him about Mavis and Jason
Hawn. Gray and Jason had gone back, each to
his own, having learned at last what Mavis and
Marjorie, without learning, already knew—that
duty is to others rather than self, to life rather than
love. But John Burnham now knew that in the
dreams of each girl another image would live always; just as always Jason would see another's
eyes misty with tears for him and feel the comforting clutch of a little hand, while in Gray's heart
a wood-thrush would sing forever.

And, looking far ahead, both could see strong

young men hurrying up from the laggard Blue-grass into the lagging hills and strong young men hurrying down from them, and could hear the heart of the hills beating as one with the heart of the Blue-grass, and both beating as one with the heart of the world.

THE END